THESE
MILLIONS
OF YEARS

THESE
MILLIONS
OF YEARS

BRUCE MCALPINE

Matador
Unit E2 Airfield Business Park,
Harrison Road, Market Harborough,
Leicestershire. LE16 7UL
Tel: 0116 2792299
Email: books@troubador.co.uk
Web: www.troubador.co.uk/matador
Twitter: @matadorbooks

ISBN 978 1803130 576

British Library Cataloguing in Publication Data.
A catalogue record for this book is available from the British Library.

Printed and bound in Great Britain by 4edge Limited
Typeset in 12pt Adobe Jenson Pro by Troubador Publishing Ltd, Leicester, UK

Matador is an imprint of Troubador Publishing Ltd

If I should die in any town of the downstream,
the south, the west or the orient in these millions
of years, let me be brought back so that I may
be buried in Akhetaten.

Pharaoh Akhenaten
1363-1336 BC

The Egyptian Pharaoh Akhenaten is the ancient world's most mysterious figure. By the time he came to the throne in 1351 BC, Egypt had been a civilised nation state for almost two thousand years.

Shortly after his coronation, the young Pharaoh moved the age-old capital from Thebes, near modern Luxor, to a virgin site at el-Amarna. There he outlawed the pantheon of ancient gods and established the world's first monotheistic religion, worshiping only the sun – the 'Aten'. He changed his name from the traditional form of Amenhotep to Akhenaten – 'Beloved of the Aten' – banished the priesthood and became the god's sole representative on earth. It was a religious and political revolution unlike anything the ancient world had ever seen.

During his unstable seventeen-year reign, Egypt disintegrated both economically and socially as Akhenaten became increasingly eccentric and isolated from his court. He died in 1336 BC, possibly murdered, and was succeeded by his 12 year-old son, Tutankhamun, whose relatively minor tomb was discovered by Howard Carter in the Valley of the Kings in 1922.

After Akhenaten's death there was a fierce return to orthodoxy. The dead king was branded as a heretic, his name was proscribed, his statues, palaces, inscriptions and temples were all destroyed and his final burial place remains unknown.

LUXOR TEMPLE, EGYPT JANUARY TWENTY-SECOND, 1989

By the time he arrives a crowd has gathered at the gates. The *corniche* road has been blocked, so he stops the taxi and walks the last hundred yards.

It is a perfect winter morning. On the far bank of the Nile the mountains have shaken off the early mist and stand clear and dragon-backed against the cloudless sky. Later, as the heat comes on, the sky will turn a milky white, but for now it is a dense enamelled blue.

Mohammed al-Fakhry elbows his way impatiently through the crowd. As he approaches the temple entrance, the crush grows denser. In an attempt to quell the mounting chaos, the police have thrown a makeshift barrier across the road. A handful of enterprising *caleche* drivers have obviously bribed their way through. They are calling out to the passers-by while their horses clatter their hooves on the tarmac and toss their heads, making the brass on their heavy harnesses glitter in the early sunlight. Directly in front of the gate groups of bewildered tourists are huddled together while their guides argue loudly with the white-uniformed policemen blocking the entrance.

When Al-Fakhry finally arrives the guards salute and wave him through. News travels fast here and a local journalist, obviously ahead of the pack, leans over the wooden railing and calls out; but Al-Fakhry raises a dismissive hand and strides on into the deserted temple enclosure. There will be time for statements later, for photographs, even for television interviews. Perhaps the President himself might come – if it is really as important as Rassoul had indicated on the telephone.

He passes between the two colossal statues of Ramesses II, his head barely at the level of their ankle bones and enters the first courtyard. The place is deserted; even the guards have gone to watch. In this confined space the uproar fades away, replaced by an eerie silence. As he hurries along the Processional Way the huge sandstone columns tower up on either side against the unbroken blue of the sky. Gradually the passage opens out to reveal the vast Solar Court built by the Pharaoh Amenhotep III fourteen centuries before the birth of Christ.

At first everything seems reassuringly familiar – the broad, dusty space laid bare by the slanting morning sun, the graceful columns carved in the shape of closed papyrus flowers, throwing dense purple shadows into the colonnade. The usual early morning calm. Then, in the far right corner of the court, he sees something strange. A small group of men, dressed in *galabiyas*, are standing with their heads bowed, apparently staring at the ground. A soldier with a rifle slung across his back stands behind them, smoking a cigarette. In the stillness the smoke wreathes up white against the backdrop of shadow. Behind the soldier, two long-handled shovels protrude from a mound of earth.

As al-Fakhry makes his way across the court a bizarre sight greets him. Between the legs of the silent onlookers a man's white turbaned head is lurching out of the earth. This is followed by his hunched shoulders, then his back, arched with effort and streaked black by the sweat on his *galabiya*. Gradually the figure emerges, pushing a battered wooden wheelbarrow piled high with sand. The barrow shudders as it bumps off the makeshift ramp and spills part of its load. As they become aware of al-Fakhry's presence, the figures part with a murmur of excitement. Al-Fakhry can feel his heart thud against his ribs as he reaches the lip of the opening and stares down in astonishment.

Twelve feet below him an alabaster statue of a kneeling man lies on its back, half-buried in sand. Beside it another sculpture has been swathed in protective foam-rubber and secured with ropes. Half-way down the pit wall a pair of black stone legs protrudes from the earth, as if a body has been rammed in by some giant hand. Amongst the chaos four figures crouch, their turbaned heads bent over something on the ground between them.

"Abdul!"

Abdul Rassoul looks up. As his eyes focus on the figure above, his round, weather-beaten face splits into a broad smile. "Welcome! Welcome, sir! And *mabrouk!* Congratulations!" He spreads his arms. "By tomorrow night you will be famous. We will *all* be famous. Even the Americans will watch us on television. *In'sh Allah!*"

The three workmen beside him straighten and stare upwards. They are clutching heavy wooden-handled hoes. Rassoul holds a large brush like a fly-whisk in his right hand. Between them, at the centre of the pit, is a low, rectangular mound. Al-Fakhry stays staring down, struggling to find words to match the strangeness of the situation. Finally he says simply, "You have done well. You will all be rewarded."

The workmen smile and nudge one another meaningfully.

"And we are not finished!" exclaims Rassoul, indicating the long mound with a wave of his brush. "We are lucky, still above the water table. The sand is as dry as the desert. Shall we continue?"

Al-Fakhry nods. Rassoul turns and begins to flick the brush rhythmically backwards and forwards. The dry sand flows away easily. And slowly the object becomes visible. At first there is a high pedestal in dark red stone, inscribed all around with hieroglyphs. Then come delicate, long-toed feet encased in sandals; hard-edged shins and massive block-square knees; a ridged kilt elaborately knotted at the waist; a bare, powerful torso. And finally, unmistakably, the unblemished features of the Pharaoh Amenhotep III, Egypt's great Sun King. Al-Fakhry gasps and steps back. It's like watching a body being reborn from the earth after three and a half thousand years.

He turns and walks unsteadily away, trying to regain his composure. That one look has told him that the statue is a masterpiece, one of the greatest discoveries, surely enough to make him celebrated in the annals of archaeology for all time. But something else is tugging insistently at his mind. As if drawn by a magnet, he can feel his brain being pulled back to the scene he has witnessed just ten days before, as he had stood right here in the shade of the colonnade. At the time it had seemed just an absurdity, an irritating tourists' pantomime: the white-robed figures moving in their strange ritual, the raised hands, the sudden cry.....

But now?

With the blood beating in his head, he leans back against one of the sandstone columns and gazes up at the sky.

ONE

It is after seven when Finn Connors finally parks the car in the narrow Chelsea street. The rain has eased and the heavy bruise of cloud is beginning to break. In front of the broad-fronted, mellow brick house, which is both his home and his art gallery, a drain has blocked. A lake of mottled brown has swamped the pavement and encircled the base of the nearest plane tree. He skirts this by pulling himself along the iron railings, then jumps the last three feet to the safety of the stone steps. Here he pauses and arches his long back. He has been up since four to catch the first flight to Geneva, where he has wasted five hours in the customs free-port, inspecting room after room of overpriced forgeries recently shipped in from Beirut. And now, as he pushes open the heavy oak door, he can feel the tiredness penetrate him like the sudden workings of a drug.

In the panelled hall the lights are off. For a moment he stands there, soaking in the familiar calm – the muted colours of the antique Persian rug on the polished floor, the faint hint of beeswax in the air, the vase of Arum lilies on the long oak table whose surface glows in the dim light. Above all, the silence.

At the far end of the hall double doors stand open, revealing an artist's studio, almost the size of a tennis court. Its high ceiling is panelled with pitched roof-lights through which the weak evening sun is beginning to slide. The room is sparsely furnished: the walls are whitewashed, seagrass matting covers the floor. In the centre two high-backed chairs face a linen-covered sofa across a low table. At the far end of the room stands a Roman statue of a nude athlete, caught in the act of crowning himself with a laurel wreath. Even in the half-light the marble seems to glow as if lit from within. For a moment he smiles, remembering the strange accident of its discovery.

It had been Giuseppe Albertini whose call had woken him early that morning. Something had been dug up in the construction of the new ring road east of Rome. A truck had been hastily commandeered and the object discretely spirited away before any interfering officials from the Antiquities Service could be notified. When Finn arrived that evening he found something so heavily encrusted that even the pose of the statue had scarcely been recognisable. An *ad hoc* committee consisting of Giuseppe, the excavator operator, the truck driver and a dubious middleman with a piratical patch over one eye had somehow come up with an asking price of fifty thousand dollars. It was an absurd sum for an object that was barely more than a lump of rock. Finn had crouched and with his thumb carefully rubbed at the thick layer of iron-hard incrustation. Suddenly a fragment had splintered away and he was staring down at a tiny patch of glittering white marble. Carefully smearing the place over he had turned and unhesitatingly agreed to the deal. Even at the time, with the adrenalin pumping in his veins, he had been ominously aware that the rest of the sculpture might turn out to be uncleanable and he would be left with a misshapen and worthless piece of marble. By any normal standards it had been an insanely reckless gamble.

But three months later he had visited the workshop of his gifted restorer, Sandro Crivelli, in his disused garage in a run-down part of Battersea. He had entered the bleak room and there at the far end, surrounded by Sandro's debris, had stood the statue. Freed from its carapace of dirt, every muscle and sinew now clearly visible, the limbs perfectly proportioned, it rose from the chaos of the room like a body miraculously reborn from the earth. For a moment Finn had felt light-headed, as if the room had been drained of oxygen and a huge wave of adrenalin swept through him. Then his dealer's brain clicked in. Sandro's months of painstaking labour, soaking and scraping the marble with scalpels and brushes, then leaching out the stains with chemical poultices had quite simply added a zero to the price.

He reaches out and eases down the battery of metal switches beside the door. The room bursts into pools of amber light. On the wall to his left an ancient Assyrian relief shows a man in a high crown spearing an advancing lion from his horse-drawn chariot. To his right, on a low pedestal, is a life-sized statue of a man, squatting with his knees hunched under his chin, carved in black granite. The body is so completely swathed in a cloak that only the delicate face, the tips of the toes and the open right hand, held out in supplication, are visible. In the flat space where the cloak appears stretched between the sharp vertical shinbones a long inscription of Egyptian hieroglyphs has been beautifully incised – an owl turned full-face towards the viewer, a bending man holds a stick, a coiling snake, a series of small jars.....

Although his knowledge of hieroglyphs is rudimentary, he knows this inscription by heart:

I, the royal Vizier Amenmose, High Priest of Amun, beloved of the Great King, Nebkheperure Tutankhamun, Steward of the King's estates, Overseer of the Treasury, General of the Lord of the Two Lands say:

I have been a true and faithful servant of the great God Amun, King of Eternity. I have purified His temples and anointed His statues. I have been a refuge for the wretched, a float for the drowning, a ladder for him who is in the abyss.

I, closest in favour to the King, have obeyed His Majesty's bidding and He has rewarded me. I alone of all the nobles have performed that deed, most cherished, most secret, known only to the King's heart, that His spirit might go forth and reside amongst the Immortals for all eternity.

I, Amenmose, stand now in the Great Court of Truth, clear of speech, pure of heart, living in truth, justified.

The arched eyebrows, slanting almond-shaped eyes and slim aquiline nose give the face an almost feminine delicacy. The gently curved lips are drawn back in a half-smile. There's a strange, moving intimacy to Amenmose's proud boast of being closest in favour to the Pharaoh; and Finn loves the thought that this figure, carved three and a half thousand years ago, somewhere in the Nile valley where crocodiles and hippopotami still roamed, now sits in his Chelsea house, staring out trustingly into eternity. And he loves too the mystery of that unnamed deed that had ensured the immortality of Amenmose's master, the Pharaoh Tutankhamun. The opaque phrase has puzzled Egyptologists ever since the statue's discovery. There have been many theories, but no solution.

Lower down, between the finely jointed toes, are three additional lines of hieroglyphs:

*O pilgrims of the Two Lands, place offerings, a thousand
of bread, beer, beef and fowl, a thousand of all things good
and pure in the palm of my hand and I, Amenmose,
Guardian of the Gates, will deliver your request to the
gods.*

It's an old joke of Chloe's to leave incoming cheques in the
open palm. But today the hand is empty – as it has been for
the last three months – and the joke is starting to wear thin.
Despite his undeniable record as a dealer, he is now more than
two million pounds in debt and the bank is beginning to press.

He leaves the studio, passes through his spacious office and
into the adjoining kitchen where he throws open the fridge
and removes a tray of ice and a large crystal tumbler. That's the
trouble with the art business, as a high-end dealer, when you
make just one big sale, the sensation is euphoric. Overnight
your debts are erased and you are a millionaire again, back
cruising the market like a predatory shark. But when things
stick – and they can stick unpredictably for months on end –
you are suddenly at the mercy of the system, a cornered beast
with the predators closing in.

He pours himself a large scotch and adds a dash of water,
then goes back to his office, gathers the pile of letters Chloe
has left open on his desk and sinks back on the sofa opposite
the French windows. To outsiders the whole international
art world seems to float on a wave of enviable luxury, flying
first class, dining at the best restaurants, staying at the best
hotels, drinking – *of course* – only the very best champagne.
And how the dealers love to foster that exotic myth! It gives
them glamour and status. But just below the surface swirls a
huge, treacherous current of debt that can suck you down at
any moment if the financial tide turns.

The setting sun brings a flash of colour to the garden, making the bank of daffodils flame against the high brick wall. Slowly he begins leafing through the pile of post. There's the usual bunch of invoices – none of which he can pay at this moment – and a few newspaper cuttings of the art market from his press agency. Little else of interest. Close to the bottom is a cutting heavily bordered in red that Chloe has taken from this morning's *Times*. He pulls it out and scans it briefly. The Italian government is demanding the return of eighteen ancient objects now in the Metropolitan Museum in New York, which they claim to have been illicitly excavated and illegally exported. His eyes run to the bottom and an air bubble of anxiety inflates in his stomach: the Supreme Court in Rome has indicted the Director of the museum *in absentia* on criminal charges of smuggling and dishonestly handling stolen goods. He lets out a sharp puff of breath, tosses the cutting aside and takes a long pull of the scotch.

Ten years before, when he had first entered this strange world of antiquities, things had been very different. Back then it had been a fascinating, rogue branch of the art market, peopled by a motley crowd of furtive gentlemen dealers, a few eccentric collectors and fringed about by the bands of scavenging *tomboroli* – tough groups of local grave robbers, who had carved out territories for themselves all around the Mediterranean. It was an addictively exciting time, a kind of giant treasure hunt. Spectacular antiquities were being unearthed almost daily. Prices were absurdly low. No one had much bothered about export licences. The market had pulsed with excitement.

But then gradually things began to change. Wealthy speculators, sensing an undervalued asset, entered the market. As prices spiralled, the Mediterranean countries, which for decades had remained indifferent to the secretive export of their antiquities, suddenly began to impose draconian penalties. As a result, the supply of objects dwindled. But prices – obeying the laws of the market – spiralled still higher. And the once sleepy antiquities world became a high-priced, cut-throat emporium, financed by Swiss bankers and threatened by international law suits.

At the very bottom of the pile of letters are Chloe's usual typed notes:

– Edward Drummond from the bank telephoned yet again. I told him you were salmon fishing in Iceland(!) and couldn't be reached until next week. Thought you might need some breathing space – but he's getting quite insistent.

– We had a visit from a rather mysterious but charming Mr Alexander Lascaris. Apparently he's a documentary film-maker. He was vague about what he actually wanted – just said he'd heard of you – but I think he may have something to sell. Perhaps you should call him? His card is on your desk. He also said that Channel Four is showing a repeat of one of his films about ancient Egypt at eight this evening – just in case you're interested?

– Two ladies called, asking for your whereabouts. (The 'list' is on your desk). They both hinted that their husbands are away this week. Your private life is getting almost as complicated to organise as your finances…

– Hope the trip to Geneva was successful? I'll be in at the usual time tomorrow.

Finn drops the sheet of paper on the sofa beside him and lets out a puff of breath. Alexander Lascaris? The name means nothing. He's probably just some bore or weirdo trying to sell a piece of worthless junk, which he believes is worth a fortune. Where once he might have felt a surge of curiosity at the prospect of what his visitor might have to offer, today there's just a jaded sense of *deja-vu*.

He takes another pull of the scotch, stretches and glances at his watch – just after eight. He crosses to the cupboard under the oak bookshelves and opens the doors to reveal the television set. Then he sinks back onto the sofa and presses the Channel Four button on the remote control. Looming out of the dark screen comes a clichéd shot of an enormous scarlet sun edging above the silhouette of the Pyramids. The view is carefully angled to conceal the vast, unromantic sprawl of modern Cairo and its fourteen million hopelessly overcrowded and under-housed inhabitants. Quasi-oriental music warbles as the title slowly materialises like dripping ectoplasm – *The Secret Life of Ancient Egypt*. The scene shifts to a group of pale-faced Europeans, absurdly dressed in white *galabeyas*. They are standing huddled in front of the Sphinx on the Giza plateau, looking like displaced extras from the set of Lawrence of Arabia. He gives an ironic smile, but pushes the red *Record* button, just in case there's something worth saving for his archive. Then he leans back and crosses his legs. After a day of sitting in aeroplanes and looking at rooms full of forgeries in the Geneva Freeport, he's happy to settle for another scotch and an hour's banal entertainment.

*

It is three o'clock when Finn wakes. He feels strangely anxious and disorientated. He lies for a while, wondering what has jolted him so suddenly across the borders of sleep

8

into hyper-wakefulness. Outside, London seems unnaturally quiet. Suddenly, as he lies there, out of nowhere, something detonates in his brain. Within seconds he is out of bed and running down the stairs two at a time, pulling on his towelling bathrobe as he goes. Without putting on the lights he hurries through the dark studio and goes directly to his office. He grabs the remote control from the table and presses the *Rewind* button.

The minutes flick back on the indigo screen ... Fifty-five ... fifty ... forty-five ...*Play*. Up comes a strongly lit shot of the famous zodiac ceiling at Denderah, the narrator intoning, "The very origins of astrology are to be found here in ..." No. *Forward*. This time there's a scene of an absurd New Age ritual in a temple court. White-robed figures circle with their hands linked. A faint hum of chanting echoes in the background, *Raa ..... maa ...* Then a breathless voice-over: "*Today the modern astrologer David Mountjoy recreates the ancient temple rituals ...*"

And suddenly he can feel the hairs on the back of his neck literally begin to rise as another scene superimposes itself on his brain. He turns down the sound and watches the screen carefully now, focusing not on the figures, but on the background. He recognises the south-west corner of Luxor's Great Solar Court. Directly behind the central point of the group a papyrus capital of one of the huge columns is half broken away. The camera pans. He counts: the broken column is three in from the corner on the south side. A tall Egyptian guard in a sky blue *galabiya* and sand-coloured turban stands in the colonnade beneath it, watching the circling figures. The shot tracks now, slightly shaky, the camera hand-held. Another view materialises, this time from a slightly different angle. Again he counts: the central point of the group is now exactly in line with the fifth column on the west side. He presses the *Pause* button. The scene of the circling figures flickers and freezes. Three columns in on the south side, five on the west ...

He reaches out, runs his hand along the bottom shelf of the tall oak bookcase and pulls out a coffee-table sized book – *Ancient Egypt, The Great Discoveries* by Nicholas Reeves. He flicks through until he finds a full-page illustration. He lays it open on the desk – a shot looking down into a deep excavation pit. At the bottom, four Egyptian workmen are staring upwards, their faces alive with excitement. Scattered all around are statues, one swathed in foam rubber, another still half buried. And, at the very centre, on its back, lies the now famous sculpture of the Pharaoh Amenhotep III, hands clenched to his sides, the left leg striding boldly forward. It is one of those photographs, like Howard Carter at the entrance to Tutankhamun's tomb, that instantly announces its place in history. His glance shifts to the text on the opposite page:

The Luxor Statue Cache

> *One of the most dramatic finds of the Twentieth Century was the discovery just beneath the Great Solar Court of Luxor Temple of a group of twenty-two statues of outstanding quality, including the celebrated figure of Amenhotep III, probably the most beautiful Egyptian sculpture ever found. The cache was discovered by chance during routine maintenance on 22 January 1989 .....*

He flips over the page to an elevated panoramic view of the court, with the excavation pit in the centre of the frame. For a moment the room seems to sway around him. He doesn't need to count. Inside his brain an invisible marksman is already lining up the cross-wires. Three columns to the south, five to the west and – like a time warp – the same tall figure in the blue *galabiya*. The pit is exactly where the ritual had taken place. *Exactly.* As if the two events have been precisely superimposed. He runs his hands through his hair. He can feel the adrenalin pumping through his system. It couldn't be, could it? *Surely?*

He grabs the remote control and fast-forwards, snapping his fingers as if to defuse his excitement. *Play.* The credits come looming out of the screen – technicians, acknowledgements, thanks. Blank. Then: *Written, Produced and Directed by Alexander Lascaris.* He lets the shot fade. Up comes the final frame: *Copyright, Papyrus Films 1990.* Nineteen-ninety? Of course, the *following* year! The spiritualist weirdoes in their white robes must have chosen that particular spot for the ritual – where the deep excavation pit had now been filled in – precisely because they *already knew* about the discovery. Probably they had some insane idea of summoning up the spirit of the long-dead Pharaoh Amenhotep from the earth! He snorts at the absurdity. It is, after all, just a bogus piece of New Age chicanery. Nothing more.

Nothing more? asks an ironic voice in his head. He sits down and slowly runs a hand across the stubble on his jaw. How long does it actually take to make a film? To assemble the pieces? To edit and present it? Could it conceivably – *just conceivably* – be the other way around? First the ritual, *then* the discovery? Both in the same place….. And suddenly, as if all the oxygen has been drained from the room, he feels giddy. He reaches for his laptop and taps into *Google*. Then: *Alexander Lascaris, documentary film maker.*

He notices that his hand is shaking.

TWO

"Of course the film's an old one....." Alexander Lascaris' voice drifts from the kitchen. The enunciation is archaically precise, like a BBC announcer from the fifties. It's as if, despite the fluency, he still isn't quite sure of the language. "It was a devil to get finished, I can tell you. Masses of editing. We shot far too much film, of course. Glad you liked it though. I get a lot of crank calls from oddballs who think they're reincarnated Pharaohs and all that stuff. But frankly I prefer my feedback from people like yourself who really know about Egypt." There's a pause for the opening and shutting of cupboards, then the clatter of beans in the grinder.

"The coffee takes time, I'm afraid," calls out Lascaris above the noise. "I just can't get used to the instant stuff. Too many years in the Middle East and Central America spoils you for that. Feel free to look at any of the antiquities. Do pick them up if you like. Though I'm afraid they won't be quite of your standard."

My standard? thinks Finn. So Mr Lascaris has obviously been doing some discreet checking of his own. After all, it isn't hard to gather information in the art market, particularly if you have the investigative skills of a documentary film-maker. For a start, all art dealers love to gossip, primarily about themselves and then, usually with malicious relish, about the competition. And if so, what would the inquisitive

Mr Alexander Lascaris have discovered as he trawled his way around the London art world? *Ah yes, Finn Connors…a self-invented ex-Dubliner – he doesn't really have the right background for this business, you know… very successful, of course, though his methods are a bit suspect… good taste* (said grudgingly)*… charming when he wants to be… a serial womaniser… somewhat arrogant… a gambler with a ruthless streak… definitely going to overreach himself one of these days … Oh, and yes* – this last in a meaningful whisper – *it seems he hasn't been paying his bills recently…* That one would be spreading like wildfire.

While the coffee machine wheezes and clatters in the background, Finn's meticulous dealer's eye starts to inventory his surroundings. The wall to his left is covered by wooden shelves, crammed with books and magazines. To his right, a similar construction bristles with small sculptures and artefacts. In front of the French windows that open onto the small garden stands a long, polished oak table. Rich Moroccan fabrics spread across the comfortable sofas and chairs. In the far corner, two large metal trunks with heavy brass fitments are stacked on top of each other. It's an eccentric environment, bohemian but definitely elegant.

Alexander Lascaris' website had shown a steady stream of documentaries about the ancient world, produced over the last decade. The range was impressive: from Aztec Peru to Shang Dynasty China. But the focus – at least to judge from the titles – was firmly on the New Age so-called 'mysteries' of ancient civilisations. The credits included *The Magic Stones of Zimbabwe; The Hidden Code of the Inca Pyramids; The Oracle Bones of Ancient China* and – inevitably, thought Finn – *The Curse of Tutankhamun Explained.*

Two addresses were listed – one in La Valetta, Malta, the other here in Islington. The Islington number produced, after just two rings, the almost accentless voice of Alexander Lascaris. He was delighted by Finn's lavish praise of his documentary and returned the compliment about the gallery, and his secretary had been *so* charming. He would, of course, be most happy to meet and discuss the film. Finn put down the receiver and smiled, knowing that the hook had been smoothly taken.

But as soon as the freshly painted door to the small terraced house had opened, his expectation of a dishevelled New Age figure with a straggly beard and shapeless sweater and a general air of incompetence was swiftly confounded. For there stood a short, compact figure, no more than five feet six, with a dark-complexion and a Latin, almost Levantine, alertness in his features. Something about the ease of the stance reminded Finn of a cat. Alexander Lascaris was curiously kitted out in pale blue dungarees, a bright check shirt, and scuffed white trainers. The top of his bald head was polished to a mahogany brown and lower down there circled a crescent of black ringlets which gave him the air of a renegade monk. A small piratical gold earring pierced his right lobe. But it was the eyes that seized Finn's attention – a deep chestnut brown, alive and intelligent, with a look of detached, sardonic humour. How on earth did such a man come to be obsessed by things as cranky as astrology, ancient curses and the foretelling of the future from the entrails of dead animals?

Still puzzled, Finn crosses the room and begins to inspect the shelves. Closer to he can see just *how many* objects there are. They cram every shelf and spill across the mantelpiece. The cultural range is vast – Benin bronze heads, terracotta Buddhas, Scandinavian flint axe-heads, a jade Olmec mask, Indian sandstone Bodhisattvas, stone weights from Sumeria and something – presumably meso-American – that appears

14

to be a large, stylised stone penis. But the main focus is clearly on ancient Egypt. There are tiny blue faience amulets, ceramic scarab beetles, alabaster headrests, stone statuettes of gods and goddesses, flakes of papyrus, a gruesomely alive mummified hand..... It's a Victorian gentleman's collection, the magpie assemblage of an obsessively curious traveller.

"I call it my shoe-string collection ....." Lascaris emerges from the kitchen carrying a lacquered tray with a coffee pot and cups, which he positions carefully on the carved Persian door that serves as a low table. Then he sits down on one of the long linen sofas and gestures for Finn to do the same. "Referring, of course, to the budget on which it was bought, not the subject matter," he adds with a smile of what appears to be genuine warmth.

Finn is used to puzzling people out. It is one of the skills that has made him so successful in the art world, seeing behind the crafted facades, unravelling the silent subtexts. But something about Alexander Lascaris feels disturbingly opaque. Whatever his eccentric ideas on archaeology, the man certainly has both taste and charm. But, of course, in those countries where Lascaris makes his films – shadowy, dangerous places like Guatemala and Egypt, Yemen and Nepal – charm is the very least he would need to navigate his way past the hordes of corrupt and greedy officials blocking his path, holding out their hands for bribes.....

Lascaris glances up from pouring the coffee and gives Finn a faintly quizzical look, as if to inform him that he has been aware of the close inspection. Then he says casually, "As a matter of fact, I picked something up when I was last in Egypt a few weeks ago. It seems quite nice. Perhaps you'd care to take a look?"

Without waiting for a reply, he rises, crosses to a table beside one of the bookcases and returns with a small black cardboard box, fastened by two broad rubber bands. Inwardly Finn smiles – so Chloe's assessment had been correct: Mr Lascaris has something to sell. The deliberate air of mystery has simply been a prelude to this moment, a hook to pull him in. Or so Mr Lascaris thinks.

Lascaris sits down, snaps aside the bands and gently eases off the tight lid. Inside is a crush of tissue paper. Finn watches the careful movement of the long, delicate fingers as Lascaris folds back the paper. Then he reaches inside, scoops something into his palm and stretches out his arm towards Finn. Finn can sense the pulse of suppressed energy in the other man, the typically anxious excitement of the would-be vendor. He leans forward and takes the tiny object in his right hand.

At first he's just aware of the feathery lightness of it, the coldness in the centre of his palm. Then his eyes focus and his art dealer's brain clicks in: *Egyptian. Undoubtedly genuine. Beautiful. Of the very, very highest quality.* And in that instant all his recent ennui with the antiquities market evaporates in a burst of adrenalin.

In his open hand lies a small, flat, almost heart-shaped box, made of egg-shell thin faience. It's of a type he has seen before, familiar but extremely rare: a shallow container for holding cosmetic powders. The flat lid, which is made in the form of a lotus flower, can be opened by swivelling it around an ivory pin, which pierces both sections. The pin has blackened and split, but is miraculously still in place. The state of preservation is extraordinary.

Finn bends closer. The lotus unfurls with exquisite grace and precision. The turquoise background is traced with lines of brilliant cobalt blue. Such superb workmanship can surely only be the product of the Eighteenth Dynasty, the high point of Egyptian art, around 1,500 B.C. Instinctively his brain begins to ratchet up the price.

"You can take a look inside," says Lascaris. "The pin is delicate, but it won't break."

Very carefully Finn swivels the lid aside. He can feel the excitement gather inside him like a pulse. Acutely aware of Lascaris's silent watching, he tries to keep his hands steady. Normally, the insides of such boxes are divided into three compartments for the three important Egyptian cosmetic powders – kohl, henna and malachite – but here the flat space is unbroken. And there, exactly in the centre, is something that makes Finn's breathing stop.

Traced in brilliant blue against the pale background is a royal cartouche, the oval loop that could only be used to contain the sacred name of the Pharaoh. And, within the loop, are minute, precise hieroglyphs. He recognises them instantly – the name of the heretical Pharaoh Akhenaten, the Pharaoh whose monuments had been destroyed by his successors, his images defaced and his tomb and its contents never found, presumably smashed and scattered beyond recognition. Surely such an object could only come from the royal burial itself. But *how?*

Finn leans back in his chair and stares at Lascaris. Struggling to keep his voice steady, he asks, "Where did you get this?"

Lascaris spreads his hands slightly, almost a gesture of apology. "I have friends."

"Egyptian friends?"

Lascaris gives a brief nod. Finn steadies his elbow for a moment against the edge of the sofa. Then he stretches out his arm and hands back the box. "It's quite a nice antiquity," he says casually, his dealer's experience coming to his aid. "Almost certainly genuine. And in rather good condition."

A long silence follows. Is Lascaris waiting for him to ask the price? Finn remembers the advice of an old Cairo dealer: *Never feed the pigeons too early. Wait and they will always come to you.* And besides, there seems to be something more here than just the possibility of buying. Something that Finn doesn't quite understand.

Lascaris is busy replacing the cosmetic box in its container. He carefully refolds the tissue paper and snaps the rubber bands back in place. While all this is going on, Finn's brain is scrambling to catch up with the situation. Does Lascaris know whose cartouche the little box contains? Can he read the hieroglyphs? Does he have *any idea* of its significance? Or its true value? And, for a moment, a sickening feeling of uncertainty washes over Finn. He has come with the aim of effortlessly extracting some information about David Mountjoy and his rituals from an unwary Alexander Lascaris. Yet, in the space of less than twenty minutes, the other man has somehow seized the initiative and thrown him completely off balance. And, in any case, what the hell is he doing here at all, having crossed half of London to talk to someone who makes cut-price films about weird voodoo rituals? After all, he doesn't even believe in astrology and magic and reanimated Egyptian rites. In short, his presence here makes no sense at all. And suddenly, as if his brain has just jumped a gear, he senses the strange, somnambulistic quality to this visit, almost as if he has been *conveyed* to this place, rather than brought by his own rational thought.

Lascaris calmly lays the box aside and coughs, as if to break the spell that has settled over the room. "Which part of the film was it that caught your interest, Mr Connors? You said on the 'phone there was one section in particular."

Finn starts for a moment, suddenly aware of those subtle, almost feral eyes studying him. Then he feels a ripple of relief.

He is back on his original agenda. "It was the sequence about the astrologer and his rituals …" He trots out the prepared response.

"David Mountjoy?"

Finn nods. "Right. I have a special interest in ancient Egyptian customs that have survived into the present. I was wondering if you knew anything more about the ritual you filmed. Or whether you knew the astrologer personally?"

Lascaris sets down his cup and raises his eyes enquiringly. Finn stays steady under the gaze. "I've met Mountjoy a few times," he says slowly. "And, of course, I've been aware of his progress, as it were, for quite some time. He leads these tours to Egypt twice a year, so our paths have crossed on a number of occasions while I've been filming."

"What do you make of him?"

"Mountjoy? He's pleasant enough." A slight hesitation. "He's certainly unusual."

"In what way?"

Lascaris gives a casual shrug. "Something odd about the eyes, I suppose. It's as if he's always looking into some private territory of his own."

Again Finn studies him, searching for clues. Does Lascaris actually believe in astrology? What does he *really* think of Mountjoy? Crank or guru? It's hard to credit that a man of such obvious intelligence would be taken in by a New Age charlatan. He decides on a new tack.

"Was there anything unusual about the ritual you showed in the film?"

Lascaris puts his head back and to one side, as if weighing his answer. "Oh, it was unusual alright ….."

Despite his sudden bristling attention, Finn manages to keep his face impassive. "How?"

"Well, normally those performance, are quite brief," goes on Lascaris. "But this was a special one, apparently known as the Rite of the Solar Return. It took over an hour. I filmed the whole thing; then cut it down for the programme, of course."

"*An hour?* In the middle of the Luxor Temple? Do the Egyptians allow that?"

Lascaris shrugs. "I imagine it's frowned on, but somehow Mountjoy seems to get away with it. As I said, he's unusual …" He pauses. "Anyhow, that particular ritual of The Solar Return is apparently only performed when a member of the tour group has their birthday. Mountjoy tries to coincide it exactly with the time of their birth. He claims it's a precise recreation of an ancient temple ritual. Apparently it represents a sort of symbolic death and resurrection. All the participants have to dress in white *tarbooshes* and *galabiyas* – as you saw in the film. As it happened, that one was Mountjoy's own birthday. His fortieth. So it was unusually spectacular."

"And Mountjoy decides where these rituals take place?"

Lascaris pauses for a moment. "Yes. I've seen him do it several times. It's a very strange performance. He seems to go into a sort of hypnotic trance. Then he wanders and weaves like a cat looking for a resting place until he finds what is apparently the right spot." Lascaris shrugs. "Don't ask me how it works."

"What was it like to be there," asks Finn casually, taking care to keep is voice neutral, "on that particular day?"

Lascaris sits back, crosses his legs and folds his arms, as if about to tell a story. "It was … somehow … impressive." For once the perfect English seems to falter. "I remember it was a beautifully clear January morning, just after the temple had opened. I was almost the only other person there, apart from the guards – and my film crew, of course. I watched from the colonnade. It was an eerie scene, I can tell you – the white-robed figures moving through those elaborate patterns in the deserted court, while one of them sat playing a flute." He pauses and closes his eyes for a moment. Is this deliberate theatre? wonders Finn. But Lascaris seems genuinely lost in the memory. "At the end they formed themselves into two circles, hands linked, moving in opposite directions, with Mountjoy in the centre. Then they began to revolve faster and faster, and I remember there was a strange feeling of energy somehow being kindled. It had something almost shamanistic about it. Then, quite unexpectedly, Mountjoy began to shake. He shook like an epileptic. He staggered, spun round and collapsed as if he'd had a heart attack. For a moment I was actually afraid he might be dead. But then it became clear that it was part of the ritual, because the group gathered round him, just picked him up and lifted him above their heads. It was an extraordinary sight – they held him out as if they were offering him up to the sun. Then they let out an ear-splitting cry."

"It sounds suitably dramatic."

Lascaris cocks an eyebrow as if to counter Finn's obvious irony. "Oh, it was dramatic allright."

For a while there is silence. At length Finn asks as casually as he can, "When exactly was this particular ritual?"

For a long while Lascaris doesn't answer. Then he puffs out his cheeks, rises slowly, as if having come to some kind of decision and crosses to one of the bookshelves. He reaches high up and extracts a small black notebook, one of several stacked together. He begins leafing through. "My shooting schedule," he explains as his fingers sift through the pages, then stop. "Ah, here we are. Luxor Temple Great Court. Mountjoy Solar Return ritual. 8.25 a.m. January 12th. Total shooting duration: 62 minutes." The eyes flick up.

Finn meets the gaze. "What year was that?"

There is a long pause. "Nineteen eighty-nine."

For a moment Finn feels slightly faint, as if all his blood had been pumped into his head. *Nineteen-eighty-nine? The same year as the great discovery.* The same year – *but ten days before.*

Lascaris comes and sits down opposite him, perching on the edge of the sofa. He folds his hands together and stares at Finn. "Congratulations, Mr Connors."

Years of dissembling as a dealer come to Finn's aid. He stretches out his arms in a display of indifference and laces his fingers behind his head. "On what precisely?"

"On coming to the right conclusion."

"And that is?"

"I think," says Lascaris slowly. "That both you and I know the answer to that."

Finn stays silent.

"No one as professionally interested in Egyptology as yourself," goes on Lascaris, "could be unaware that on the morning of the twenty-second of January nineteen-eighty-nine, totally without warning, the ground in the south-west corner of Great Solar Court of the Luxor Temple suddenly gave way to reveal twenty-three intact statues, including the now famous sculpture of the Pharaoh Amenhotep III. They had been lying buried there, unsuspected, undiscovered, through three and a half thousand years of war and invasion and upheaval and even excavation. Not to mention hordes of tourists. And then they just spontaneously reveal themselves ten days *to the minute* after Mountjoy's Rite of the Solar Return." He pauses. "And in exactly the spot where the ritual had taken place. So ....." Lascaris spreads his hands, leaving the sentence uncompleted.

"How can you be so sure it was the same time and place?"

"I was there," says Lascaris simply. "I saw both events."

"From what I've heard it was purely a chance find. Some engineers were underpinning one of the nearby columns. They must have disturbed the structure of the soil and it just caved in." He shrugs. "Pure coincidence surely?"

"*Pure coincidence?*" Lascaris fingers the tiny gold ring in the lobe of his right ear and gives an ironic lift of his eyebrows. "Yes, *of course*. That's precisely what I tried to tell myself as well. At least, at first. Although I didn't truly believe it even then." He gives Finn an appraising look. "Just as I suspect you do not truly believe it now. Otherwise you wouldn't be here, Mr Connors." Finn shifts uncomfortably under the scrutiny. "Do you remember the surprise discovery of the tomb of Ramesses VI in the Valley of the Kings three years ago?"

"Yes, of course."

"Mountjoy's ritual had been performed right there, just six weeks before, exactly above the concealed entrance to the tomb. And the sudden unearthing of the huge hoard of mummies in the Fayum oasis …..?" The eyes are unwavering. "There too." He pauses to allow the effect of his words to sink in. "Obviously I became curious. Who wouldn't under the circumstances? So I started making some discreet enquiries. As a film-maker I have very good contacts in Egypt. What I found confirmed everything I had felt when I first saw that hole open up in the ground in the Luxor Temple."

Finn tries to keep his voice steady. "And that was?"

"That everywhere a member of David Mountjoy's tour has their birthday and Mountjoy performs his Rite of the Solar Return, sooner or later, almost without fail, in that precise spot, an archaeological discovery is made. Usually a spectacular discovery. Sometimes very spectacular. And thus far no one seems to have made the connection." He pauses. "Except you and I apparently"

Finn lets out a derisive puff of breath. "Except *you*, I think you mean. Frankly I find the whole thing a little hard to believe. For a start Mountjoy himself would realise."

Lascaris shrugs. "It would seem that Mr Mountjoy isn't interested in such things. He's a mystic, not a dealer or an archaeologist. He does his ritual. He moves on. Months later a discovery is made. He probably doesn't even hear about it. Often it takes the Egyptians years to announce such finds – and then perhaps only in some obscure archaeological journal. So there's really no reason why Mountjoy would realise." He shrugs. "Anyhow, he appears not to. And as for the rest of the world," he makes a dismissive gesture, "archaeologists are not the kind of people to correlate their discoveries with the antics of an apparently deranged crank like Mountjoy."

Finn rises and walks slowly across to the long oak table by the window. He runs his hand over its polished surface, as if needing to be reassured by its solidity. *This is crazy,* he thinks. *Completely crazy. Why am I even bothering to listen? But,* whispers another voice softly in his head, *Isn't this precisely why you came?*

He stands for a moment, aware for the first time of the distant growl of the traffic in the City Road. He feels light-headed. He turns back to face Lascaris. "Frankly, I simply can't imagine ….."

He stops. Lascaris has reached into his pocket and pulled out a folded sheet of green paper. He holds it out. "I have here," he says quietly, "the programme for David Mountjoy's next tour to Egypt".

Reluctantly Finn takes it. The front page is headed by a drawing of the sun disk flanked by two elaborately feathered, outstretched wings. Above them rear two cobra's heads. He runs his eye down the page. *Eternal Egypt – An Esoteric Exploration of the Ancient Egyptian Temple Landscape... led by David Mounjoy, World Renowned Astrologer, Tarot Reader, Psychic and Expert on the Mysteries of Ancient Egypt.... A unique opportunity to reawaken your own inner gods and goddesses....*

The pretentious New Age language is absurd. Finn turns the page to a detailed day-by-day itinerary. And suddenly he grunts, as if he has been winded.

"What is it?"

"The dates. My birthday falls right in the middle of it."

Lascaris observes him dispassionately. "I think," he says slowly, "that you and I had better talk."

THREE

Rain drips from the tiled porch. Nadia Rusedska huddles deeper into her coat and pulls up the collar. She checks her watch. Two minutes to twelve. A faint sickness is swirling in her stomach, that familiar mixture of excitement and anxiety, like standing outside the principle's study waiting to be reprimanded. Even after all these years there still seems to be some chemical lying dormant in her blood that he always manages to activate.

From her very first day at the Institute of Fine Arts in New York she had felt a deep need to be special to him. The one time she had failed is still etched in her memory. She had been briefly in love – or, at least, in lust – with a beautiful blonde basketball player, who had kept her happily in bed for the best part of the week. When Dortmann handed back her hopelessly inadequate essay with the simple words, "This is not what I expect from you," a hot cloud of shame had enveloped her. Even now, years later, the thought of it can make her face flush crimson and prickle her spine with heat.

In the year since he has retired from the Institute, moved to England and settled here in the Oxfordshire countryside to complete his long overdue *magnum opus*, she has never once been down to visit him. She knows he hates distractions while he is writing and his reputation for being difficult with visitors is legendary. Taking his time has always felt like using up a precious commodity.

On the far side of the gravel drive the leaves on an enormous lime tree are so laden with water that the branches look as if they might collapse at any minute. At its base a blackbird is digging hungrily into the freshly mown grass. She checks her watch again. Twelve o'clock precisely. She pulls the collar of her gabardine raincoat higher and puts her finger to the porcelain button in its polished brass surround. Deep inside the house a bell chimes.

Professor Bernard Dortmann has been standing for the last few minutes at the open French windows of his study, listening to the patter of rain on the leaves of the azalea bushes. Between the banks of lavender the flagstone path leading to the orchard glistens in the dull light. In the distance, the edges of Swan's Wood are still hazed white with hawthorns. He sniffs the air. He likes rain. Even now it reminds him of his native Germany, of the thick woods and rolling hills of Prussia. He likes its softness and its quiet. Likes its decisiveness. The sky is a soft shell grey and the rain looks set to continue till evening. He clasps his hands behind his back and turns to the room. At seventy-two he still stands straight, despite the pain in his spine. His hair, swept back from his high forehead, is full and dark. Only the short beard that covers the point of his chin is threaded with grey. And his mind is as alert as ever. On good days he might be taken for ten years younger.

His eyes sweep the room, checking. Books, pipes, pencils, photographs. Everything exactly as he has left it. Mrs Baines has seen to that. He has been gone for two weeks, lecturing in Berlin and Freiburg, Hildesheim and Munich, Hanover and

Stuttgart, the major German centres of Egyptology. And now he needs to get back to his writing. But not today. He turns and moves towards his desk. His visitor will be here at any moment. She had made the appointment just as he had been leaving to catch the flight. She will arrive punctually – everyone knows better than to be late for Professor Dortmann.

Just as he is about to sit, the doorbell chimes. He walks down the long flagged corridor, crosses the hall and opens the heavy oak door. She looks like a waif, standing there, bundled in her raincoat, her face childishly expectant. Single drops of rain bead her unprotected auburn hair. He allows himself a brief smile of welcome, then holds out his hand and ushers her inside.

Nadia perches on the edge of the leather armchair. She knows she has to come straight to the point; he has little patience with small-talk. "I've come to ask your opinion about something."

Dortmann nods slightly. He has turned his chair around and sits facing her, his hands folded in his lap.

"The day before I telephoned you I had a visit from a man called Alexander Lascaris." The Professor frowns, as if searching his memory, then shakes his head. "He's from Malta. A documentary film maker apparently. He specialises in films about the ancient world. I'd never heard of him either. But he seemed to know a surprising amount about *me*. He knew I'd studied under you in New York and then worked at Yale. He even knew how long I'd been at the museum in Edinburgh. And he tried to flatter me by suggesting ….." She looks down at the carpet for a moment. "By suggesting that I had a good reputation and that I was known to be more open-minded about the antiquities market than most Egyptologists. Anyway ….."

She unclasps her hands and reaches for the soft leather briefcase propped against the side of her chair. She uncrosses her long legs, smooths out her skirt and balances the case on her lap. "He showed me something that I found quite extraordinary. He wouldn't leave it with me and wouldn't even let me photograph it. He was very secretive. But ….." She unzips the case and extracts three sheets of white paper. She runs her thumb across the corners to check they are all there. "Immediately after he left I made sketches from memory."

She passes the sheets across. Dortmann leans forward and takes them, then reaches behind him and grasps a pair of gold-rimmed spectacles from the corner of the desk. He positions them carefully on the bridge of his nose and looks down.

"To scale?"

"As best I could from memory."

Dortmann smiles thinly. "So all those tedious line-drawing exercises at the Institute were not entirely in vain." He hunches over the top sheet, frowning in concentration. Nadia's fingers play nervously along the edge of her skirt. "I'm not sure I got all the details of the lotus quite right. I only had it in my hands for about two minutes."

Dortmann continues to study the drawing in silence. The hollow chattering of a woodpecker reverberates in the distance. "Aha! There's an old friend," he says quietly to himself. Then, "It's made of faience?"

"Yes."

He sits back with the papers on his knees. The chair creaks. "It's a cosmetic box, of course. You will have recognised that. Nearly all of these date from the Twenty-sixth Dynasty, around 600 BC. A few are known to be later."

"Yes. The most famous one is in the Louvre. It was excavated at Tanis."

Dortmann nods approvingly.

"But ...." she goes on. "The thing is...I don't think this one *is* from Dynasty Twenty-six." She catches his frown of disapproval and presses on quickly. "What you can't see from the drawing is the colour. It was an extraordinary glossy turquoise, picked out with cobalt blue. Then the faience is incredibly thin, like egg-shell. In general the workmanship was exquisite. I've never seen anything quite like it. I think it's far too fine to be from Dynasty Twenty-six, which was, after all, an era of decline. And ....." She hesitates, twisting the attaché case.

"And?"

"Look at the next sheet."

Dortmann shuffles the papers. There is a long moment of silence. His eyes flicker at her over the top of his gilt spectacles. Then down again. He runs a hand over his clipped, greying beard. Then he rises and crosses to the crowded wooden bookshelves that line the left side of the room. He selects a thin volume, leafs briefly through it, then lays it open on the desk. Still standing, he places the sheet of paper carefully down beside it. Nadia can feel her heart thud wildly against her ribs.

"It's unquestionably the cartouche of Akhenaten, the so-called heretic Pharaoh," he murmurs quietly. "And the late form of the name. So it must come from the end of his reign." He reaches out his left hand, takes hold of his pipe and begins to scrape tobacco into the bowl with his middle finger from the open leather pouch beside it. "Akhenaten indeed...." He turns, his eyebrows raised in enquiry. "You're quite sure it's genuine?"

"Absolutely certain. No one could fake anything *that* good."

He sinks into his chair, tamps the tobacco flat with the side of the match box. "Perhaps the inscription has been added recently by some enterprising forger?" He strikes a match and looks at her quizically from over the dancing yellow flame. "Such things do happen, you know. And Akhenaten's cartouche would quadruple its value on the market."

"I'm sure not. I examined the hieroglyphs very carefully under a magnifying glass. The feint crackly patina that covers the surface of the rest of the box also runs identically *over* the inscription. So the hieroglyphs must have been done at the same time." She pauses to catch her breath. "Also the blue of the inscription matches *exactly* the details of the lotus painted on the lid. So they must be contemporary too. And ....." She tries to steady the fluttering excitement in her voice. "And it was that particular shade that we call 'Amarna blue', that's so specific to the reign of Akhenaten. Surely no one can fake that? The technique was lost in antiquity."

Dortmann studies the sheets of paper again, shuffling them between his hands. His lips pucker around the stem of his pipe, sending a slow trail of grey-blue smoke towards the open French window. Then he sits back. Nadia heaves a small inward sigh of relief, as if she has just come through a cross-examination.

"So ...." He regards her over the rim of his glasses. "It would appear that we have here – at least according to one of my most able students ...." He allows himself a small smile "..... a unique cosmetic box of the highest artistic quality, purporting to belong to the infamous Pharaoh Akhenaten, suddenly appearing in England out of apparently nowhere, produced by a man none of us has ever heard of. Correct?" She nods. Dortmann hooks his fingers around the bowl of the pipe and rubs the stem up and down his cheek. "You realise that, on the face of it – assuming we accept that the object is genuine, which it certainly appears to be – that can mean only one thing?"

"That it must come from Akhenaten's tomb?" She tries to control the tremble in her voice.

Dortmann nods. "Yes. But the real questions are: Which tomb? Where? And when?"

Nadia frowns. "I don't understand."

"Well, it may not be quite as simple as one might think. Let's just look at the facts for a moment." He draws once more on the pipe, then settles back in his chair and folds his hands. "As you know, Akhenaten, who reigned for just fifteen years from 1351 to 1336 BC, was a revolutionary Pharaoh, quite unlike all his predecessors. The watchword of the Egyptian state had always been stability. Change was regarded as evil, anathema. But he was quite different, possibly insane. He overthrew all the old gods, abandoned the religious and political centres of his ancestors, and then established a monotheistic religion at a new capital on virgin soil at el-Amarna. It was intended to be an ideal city of light and beauty. Of course, things didn't work out that way. It was a gigantic upheaval, unlike anything the ancient world had ever seen. Monotheism was a concept that simply didn't exist then – and it certainly wasn't popular, particularly with the traditional ruling classes and the priesthood." Nadia leans back and crosses her legs. She recognises the smooth tone of his delivery from the lecture hall at the Institute. Much of what he is saying is already familiar to her, but she doesn't want to interrupt his flow now and besides, his knowledge of this period of Egyptian history is unrivalled. "His original tomb, you will doubtless recall," goes on Dortmann steadily, "was a huge series of chambers cut into the rock in a narrow ravine that runs into the cliffs behind the ancient city that he had created at el-Amarna. It was discovered by the French in the 1890s."

"But it had been looted?"

He nods, "Yes. As usual. Or at least it had been *cleared*. Which isn't necessarily quite the same thing. You see, the excavators found the tomb largely empty. That is true. There was, however, enough remaining evidence to decipher the royal names of both Akhenaten and his wife, the famously beautiful Queen Nefertiti. So it was clear that *at some point* Akhenaten had been buried there. But it's not at all clear that that was his final resting place."

There is a soft knock on the door. A grey-haired woman in her sixties appears. She has bright blue eyes and red cheeks that look as if they may have been polished. She is wearing a long floral dress. She smiles at Nadia.

"It's all done then, Professor ....." She pauses. "Unless you'd like me to stay and serve lunch .....?"

"Thank you, no. That will not be necessary." He turns to Nadia. "You will stay for lunch, won't you?"

She hesitates, suddenly confused. Then quickly she says, "Yes, I'd love to."

"It's all in the Aga then," says the woman. "So I'll be getting along. Unless there's anything else you need?"

"No. Everything is in excellent order, as always. Thank you very much, Mrs Baines."

"I'll see you tomorrow then, Professor." She nods to Dortmann, smiles again at Nadia and closes the door silently behind her.

"Mrs Baines makes what some of my students would call 'a mean moussaka.'"

Nadia smiles. "That's really very kind." Inexplicably she can feel herself begin to blush. She looks down to gather her composure. Then she says, "So you think that Akhenaten's whole burial may have been moved somewhere else in antiquity?"

Dortmann nods. Then he glances at his watch. "I'm mindful of not wanting to turn Mrs Baines' moussaka into a ritual cremation." He rises. "It will only take a few minutes."

"Can't I help you?"

"That is most kind. But no." At the door he pauses. "Did your Mr Lascaris offer the cosmetic box to you for sale?"

Nadia turns in her chair. "No… that is ….. well ….." She spreads her hands. "That was the really funny part. It was all very unclear. He *said* he had come to ask my opinion; but I sensed he already knew exactly what the object was. And although he didn't actually offer it, he still had that kind of anxious expression that dealers always have when they're trying to sell you something. There was something very odd about it all."

"And what did you do?"

She shrugs. "I suppose I sort of pre-empted him. There was something about him that made me uneasy, as if he might be a snooping undercover journalist looking for a scoop about smuggled antiquities – '*Museum curator buys looted treasures*' – that sort of thing. So I gave him my frostiest, academic blue-stocking speech that the museum never considered anything for purchase unless it has an impeccable provenance stretching back at least a hundred years." Her voice assumes the cut-glass accent of an English boarding-school.

Dortmann smiles. "That was probably wise. Lunch will be ready in about five minutes. Please feel free to look at any of the books." He gestures towards the cases and closes the door silently behind him.

Suddenly she feels absurdly spoilt. She smiles and cradles her arms across her chest. Then she rises and allows her gaze to circle the room. How intimate it feels to be left alone in his study! She sniffs the masculine smell of leather and pipe tobacco. Opposite her French windows give out on to the damp lawn and the orchard beyond. The walls are lined with Napoleonic prints of Egypt in gilt frames. In the centre of the room stands his massive mahogany desk with deep drawers. Books and racks of pipes and a heavy earthenware ashtray are arranged in orderly fashion across its leather top.

She turns to the bookshelves, which cover the entire long wall opposite the chimney. They stretch from floor to ceiling. A wooden ladder is propped against one end. It's clearly an extensive Egyptological library. She recognises several rare out-of-print excavation folios, and a prized set of The Journal of Egyptian Archaeology complete all the way back to 1914. Her glance shifts to the low table beside the desk. It carries a small stack of books, a tobacco tin, matches and – seemingly the only really personal and non-masculine object in the room – a black-and-white photograph in a dark wooden frame.

Curious, she bends and picks it up. It shows the head and shoulders of a girl in her twenties wearing an open-necked check shirt. In the background are what look like fir trees. Long dark hair is swept back from the broad forehead, perhaps caught in a pony-tail. The face is attractive but strong-featured, almost masculine, the eyes widely spaced. The jaw and mouth look determined, wilful. Daughter? Ex-wife? Even, conceivably, mother? There's no way of assessing the age of the print. She turns the frame over in the hope of some identification. Nothing.

How little the world seems to know about Professor Bernard Dortmann. Academically he is a public figure; yet no one knows with certainty about his past. 'It's rumoured that …. he's supposed to have …' escaped from Nazi Germany, fought in the United States army, married and divorced, a child killed in a tragic accident. At least one other child. Other wives? Mistresses? It is all speculation. And certainly nothing about his manner invites questions.

And what a strange mixture he is! Part disciplined scholar, part old-style gentleman, part rigid Prussian officer. And definitely part maverick. She has seen him take on the archaeological establishment with relish. Most other Egyptologists believe that all archaeological discoveries should be scientifically excavated and retained by the countries where they have been found. Dortmann, with his decades of experience in Egypt, knows that, in practice, this usually leads to endless delays, corruption and frequently the disappearance of the objects altogether. He believes in collecting, both by museums and individuals. And he is not afraid to speak his mind on the topic. In the last three decades he has advised most of the major museums and collectors around the world. His colleagues admire his rigorous scholarship and unrivalled knowledge of Egyptology. But they also envy his easy connections to the rich and famous, and disapprove of his cavalier behaviour with regard to collecting. To them he's like a dangerous rogue elephant.

He has aged since she last saw him. Despite his cast-iron self-discipline, she can sense that he is beginning a losing struggle to keep his ramrod straight back from bowing. She has seen him wince as he rose from his chair. And it feels like more than just a physical change. There is still the same formal old-fashioned courtesy, the same civilised worldliness – such a relief after the stuffy, self-satisfied parochialism of Edinburgh. But there's something more now. A loneliness perhaps? Even a vulnerability? Is it just her imagination, or does he seem to soften in her presence? She smiles to herself, then glances in the mirror above the mantelpiece. She tosses her head and flicks her hair back behind her ears.

To the left of the fireplace a door has been left half ajar. Curious, she eases it open and flicks on the light switch. Inside is a small, windowless room, a kind of large walk-in cupboard. It is piled high with carefully labelled cardboard boxes. She knows what this is; he had shown it to her once in the annexe to his office at the Institute in New York – an archive of Egyptian sculpture unrivalled anywhere in the world, the product of decades of photographing, measuring, researching in museum basements and private collections from Leningrad to Sydney, from Cairo to Buenos Aries. Each box contains literally hundreds of black and white photographs and small yellow index cards, crammed with notes and measurements. It is a whole lifetime's work. But she knows too that this *magnum opus* that would crown his life's labour – The Corpus of Ancient Egyptian Sculpture, a work that would stretch into several volumes – has scarcely even been started. And at seventy-two time is running out. Instinctively she places a hand over her heart.

Over the course of forty years, literally thousands of students have passed through his care. When you studied under Bernard Dortmann you didn't just become an Egyptologist, you became a 'Dortmann Student'. Many of them now hold high-ranking museum posts and even professorships around the globe. They are instantly recognisable, even decades after graduation, by their intellectual rigour, their encyclopedic knowledge of Egyptology and – she has sometimes heard it said – by their arrogance. But amongst this distinguished group she senses – despite his reserve – that she is somehow special to him. Her academic credentials are now impeccable and her rise has been meteoric from her desolate childhood in Gdansk to doctoral student at the University of Yale and on to the full curatorship in Edinburgh.....

She hears footsteps echoing down the flagstones of the passage. Quickly she shuts the door, snaps off the light and steps back into the room.

The dining-room overlooks the orchard at the back of the house. The rain has stopped now and the grass is thickly strewn with white blossom. The polished oak table has been formally laid with silver, white napkins and crystal glasses. Dortmann serves the food from a hot-plate on the sideboard, then fills their glasses with red wine from a decanter. He stands behind Nadia and pulls out her chair for her.

Over the meal he asks her about Edinburgh, about her work, her apartment and friends. Even – to her surprise – whether she has a boy-friend there. Embarrassed she looks down at her plate and shakes her head. She doesn't elaborate on how unattractive she finds her male colleagues at the museum and indeed pretty much all the Scotsmen she has met there. Nor how much this sexual desert is starting to trouble her. Down here, with him, it's a different world. Here she feels like the treasured daughter returning home for the university vacation. At one point Dortmann allows himself a broad smile and a chuckle as she describes the archaic dustiness of the museum and its administrative incompetence, like something out of a Dickens novel. Slowly, as the meal progresses, she can feel the formality within him begin to uncoil.

It is only after he has cleared away the cheese plates and served coffee that she feels able to return to their original topic. She carefully drops a cube of brown sugar into her cup, then looks up at him. "So what do *you* think happened to the burial of Akhenaten?"

Dortmann rubs a hand over his bearded chin and sits back. "Well, as you know, the newly-built city of Amarna was abandoned shortly after Akhenaten's death. His successor, Tutankhamun, moved the capital back to the traditional site of Thebes near modern Luxor. That meant that Akhenaten's original tomb at Amarna would have been left unguarded – the treasury was nearly empty and they simply didn't have the resources to leave a whole platoon of soldiers at a deserted site – and no royal tomb would remain unlooted for long unless it was carefully watched. The pickings were just too big. So, if you didn't want the tomb to be plundered, the only solution would have been to move the entire burial to somewhere safer."

"Like the Valley of the Kings?"

Dortmann nods. "Exactly. Or, at least, move it temporarily."

"But surely, since Tutankhamun, who succeeded him, destroyed all Akhenaten's monuments and images and tried to erase his memory anyway, why didn't they just leave his burial to be looted? Why go to all the effort and expense to make him safe?"

Dortmann sips his coffee, then sets down the cup. "It's a good question, but I don't think it's quite that simple. Politically, Tutankhamun was on very shaky ground when he came to the throne. He wasn't much more than a boy, and in the chaotic aftermath of Akhenaten's reign the Empire was in turmoil and close to collapse. He and his advisers had to move very carefully in order not to let the situation tip over the edge into outright rebellion or possible anarchy. So even if Tutankhamun thought Akhenaten was a heretic, he couldn't really stand by and openly allow the tomb of a former Pharaoh to be robbed and desecrated." He smiles thinly. "It wouldn't really set a very good precedent for the tombs of future Pharaohs, including himself, would it? So obviously it would have made political sense for him to protect the tombs of *all* his ancestors, even including crazy, heretical Akhenaten's."

"So what *did* happen to Akhenaten's tomb then?"

"Well ….." Dortmann frowns thoughtfully and realigns the small silver coffee-spoon so that it is precisely at right angles to the handle of his cup. He gives a small shrug. "It's a mystery. In 1907 a maverick millionaire American by the name of Theodore Davis discovered a tomb in the Valley of the Kings, which archaeologists now refer to, somewhat unromantically, as tomb Fifty-Five. It clearly hadn't been looted, because the door seals were still intact. It contained a rather grand coffin, obviously made for a Pharaoh, but the name of the occupant had been deliberately chiselled out and, very bizarrely, there were almost no significant grave goods, such as one would expect with a coffin of that scale. He pauses. "In short, it looked like the hasty *re*-burial of an unidentified Pharaoh who must have fallen out of favour."

"Akhenaten?"

Dortmann spreads his hands. "Possibly. Certainly a large number of scholars have thought that over the years. But I disagree with them – for a whole host of reasons. For what it's worth, I personally believe it's the mummy of Smenkhara, Akhenaten's obscure, short-lived, possibly homosexual co-regent."

Nadia eyes him carefully. "So you think that Akhenaten's *real* tomb has yet to be found?"

Dortmann nods slowly.

"And if it were found ….?"

He lets out a small puff of breath. "If it were found *looted* – and even if all the treasures were already gone – as is most likely," he pauses, "it would, of course, still be a discovery of major archaeological importance."

"And if it were found *unlooted* …?"

Dortmann sets down his cup and looks at her. His eyes

are smiling quizzically. "That ......," he says, "as you well know, Nadia, would be the Holy Grail of Egyptology."

Their eyes meet. There is a moment of silence before Nadia presses on. "So if an object, obviously from Akhenaten's tomb, suddenly appears on the antiquities market, it can surely only mean one thing…"

Dortmann holds up his hand as if to forestall her excitement. "That someone has clandestinely discovered his tomb?" He shakes his head. "Sadly, not necessarily. There are at least two possible explanations, and the more likely one is, I'm afraid, rather more prosaic. We tend to think that a Pharaoh's burial goods are either tightly locked up with him in his undiscovered tomb, or else long ago looted, smashed to pieces, the gold and silver melted down. But history isn't quite so neat. Strange things can happen in the course of four thousand years. What may have occurred – and this is not uncommon – is that, in the removal to the new burial place, some enterprising workman or priest spirited away one or two precious objects for himself and carefully hid them underground. But, for whatever reason – maybe war, or even his own death – he was never able to return to retrieve them." He pauses and holds out the silver coffee pot to Nadia. She shakes her head. "So it is just possible that someone has recently found just such a small secret hoard from the tomb. But that doesn't necessarily mean that they have found the actual tomb itself."

"But mightn't such a hoard be buried close to the undiscovered tomb – which would at least give an indication of its whereabouts?" She can hear the slight tremble in her voice.

Dortmann looks at her for a long time in silence. "It might," he says slowly. "It just might."

They are standing on the flagstones of the whitewashed hallway. A mahogany rack in the corner is crammed with walking sticks. Above hangs an array of hats – a tweed deerstalker, a soft white Panama with a black band, a peaked khaki cap. The faint aroma of pipe tobacco mingles with the smell of floor polish. They face each other uncertainly. Then Dortmann picks up her raincoat and holds it open for her. She slides her arms in, turns up the collar, and flicks out her hair.

"I'm going to Egypt at the end of next month," he says. She turns in surprise. "I shall probably stay several weeks. I still have a lot of work to do, photographing and re-measuring and so on, to get the Corpus ready for publication. I have a number of, shall we say, unconventional contacts there. Would you like me to keep my ears open for anything about your Mr Lascaris and his mysterious find?"

Her eyes widen, her face lights up with excitement. "That would be fantastic! And …." She hesitates.

He raises his eyebrows, waits for her to continue.

"And it's possible I may be in Egypt myself then. I've been given a one-term sabbatical. We get one every three years. I've got funding from the Arts Council to complete my research on the Tombs of the Nobles at Thebes …." Her voice falters. "Obviously I wouldn't want …."

Dortmann moves past her and opens the front door. The rain has stopped. The clouds are beginning to break.

"Send me your arrival details," he says. "I'll collect you at the airport."

FOUR

.

"Lost your luggage?"

The conveyor belt wheezes and shudders to a halt. At the sound of his voice Lara turns. He is standing just behind her, smiling confidently, one hand on his hip. He is dressed in khaki chinos and a blue denim shirt, a worn canvas bag slung casually over his left shoulder. She had seen him when she boarded the plane in London, sitting in the almost empty First Class section. She noticed the name tag on the bag on the seat beside him – Finn Connors. Presumably Irish and, from the look of him, probably full of self-satisfied blarney. He clearly wasn't a businessman, at least not in any conventional sense; there was something far too relaxed and bohemian about him. He had deliberately caught her eye as she passed down the aisle, and she had equally ostentatiously looked away. But still, she has to admit he's hard to ignore – tall, fair-haired and slim, with intense blue eyes and an expensive-looking suntan. Obviously dangerous, but still she can't help being intrigued. And besides, right now she needs help.

She spreads her hands in desperation. "Yes. You too?"

"Uh-huh. Okay, let's see what we can find."

He glances round the echoing baggage hall, which is rapidly emptying. An old man in a striped *galabiya* is sweeping rubbish into a corner. He gathers it into a pile, leans his brush against the wall and walks slowly away to light a cigarette.

"It's worth hunting around," he says. "Sometimes they just seem to come off somewhere else for no good reason. Sometimes, of course, they just get stolen. I never check-in anything valuable when I come here. It's safer to carry it." He pats the canvas bag on his shoulder. She notices the smooth worn shine of the broad strap, like an army officer's belt and the expensive solidity of the brass buckles. Although she doesn't entirely trust him, there's a pleasant reassurance in his apparent imperturbability.

"You sound like a veteran."

"Right. A tired and pissed-off veteran at the moment. I like flying Egyptair because it is just so Egyptian, but comfort is not one of their strengths."

"Even in First Class?" she asks ironically.

He ignores her and jerks his head sideways. "Come on, let's sniff around. What does yours look like?"

"A khaki canvas hold-all with brown leather handles." She follows him in the direction of a frosted glass partition with a narrow opening in its centre. Beside it stands a soldier in army fatigues. A cigarette clings to his lower lip, a black sub-machine gun is cradled casually in the crook of his right arm. Lara glances at it nervously. Something about it's hardness and brutality feels shocking. That, and the fact that the soldier looks far too young and unpredictable to be in charge of it. Her companion ignores the soldier and walks purposefully through the doorway. Lara follows him. The soldier glances at them but doesn't move.

"Why didn't he stop you?"

"He would have if we'd hesitated," he calls over his shoulder. "Rule number one in Egypt: always look as if you know exactly what you're doing, even when you don't. Or *especially* when you don't. That way you don't get hassled. The place is full of soldiers and they all look scary, but in reality they're much more nervous than you are. Bluff is the essential weapon here."

They emerge into a smaller room with a concrete floor and a low gap in the wall that opens out onto the airport tarmac. Through the opening, they can see a trolley, piled with suitcases, standing in the harsh sunlight. Beyond it, the view is liquefying in the afternoon heat. Beside the opening, a man is squatting on his haunches smoking. Against the opposite wall, a small mountain of bags had been carelessly piled together. Some are half open, clothes pathetically hanging out.

Lara stares in astonishment. "Who on earth owns all these?"

"People like you and me." He walks up to the pile and casually kicks the bottom ones aside.

Lara lets out a cry. "There it is!" She points to the abandoned baggage cart on the tarmac outside.

He walks over to the crouching man and gestures at the trolley. The man looks up, but doesn't move. Then she sees him reach into the pocket of his chinos, pull out two notes and hold them out.

A minute later he is coming towards her, a suitcase in each hand. He smiles at her. "Job done. Now let's see if we can find you a taxi."

As they step through the last swing doors, the world around them seems to explode. *"Hey Mister! Hey Madame! You want special taxi, tour Cairo? See Pyramids? Good price! Good price!"* Figures with dark corrugated faces, swathed in grey robes and white turbans are pulling insistently at their sleeves. A swarm of porters in sand-coloured boiler suits crowd round them, trying to grab their bags. Small boys chase in and out amongst the crowd, offering plastic models of the pyramids. The place smells of diesel fumes, tobacco smoke, garbage and strange spices. For a moment Lara's head begins to spin.

Outside the terminal the heat hits her like a wall. Her companion holds tight to their bags and stares straight ahead. Apparently immune to the chaos, he walks calmly towards a line of dusty black taxis. Lara follows, her anxiety at being taken over by this stranger temporarily outweighed by the relief of his protection. Everything here seems so much louder, faster, stranger, more intense than she had expected.

He hands both bags to the driver and turns to her. "I think it would be a good idea if we share a taxi into town. If you've never been in Cairo before, it might feel safer. And, looking the way you do, you're going to attract a lot of attention around here. What hotel are you staying at?"

"The Omar Khayam," she says, ignoring the all too obvious compliment.

He raises his eyebrows and his face broadens into a slow smile. "It must be my lucky day," he says and opens the car door for her. And, despite her wariness, she smiles back and feels a small knot of tension ease inside her.

On the drive into Cairo the car judders in and out of pot-holes. At moments the driver behaves like a man possessed, shooting red lights and accelerating through the gaps between cars, his hand gripping the horn. Then, without warning, he lapses into a kind of drugged torpor, creeping along blindly at fifteen miles an hour. Lara glances at her companion. He is leaning back looking out of the window, apparently unconcerned. She notices his strangely beautiful, classical profile – the forehead gliding straight through into his nose, the clear line of his jaw and the obviously sensual mouth. It's as if he has just stepped off the Parthenon frieze. Why don't I feel more nervous, she wonders, being driven to a hotel in a strange city with a man I've only met ten minutes ago? Perhaps it's just the relief of not having to fend for herself in the first overwhelming shock of Cairo. And, to be honest, it's hard to be anxious with him. The male predatoriness feels only skin-deep, as if you're not really supposed to take it too seriously. And there's an uncomplicated ease about him that just invites you to relax.

On either side of the highway the desert is sprouting brutal high-rise apartment blocks. Most seem only half finished; those that are finished look about to collapse. A concrete flyover spirals above them, then stops vertiginously in mid-air, weeds sprouting from its jagged end. In the deep pools of shade beneath, a Bedouin encampment has been set up, the tents of bright cloth huddled together in a makeshift village.

"It looks like an unfinished building site."

He laughs. "The *whole* of Cairo looks like an unfinished building site! You'll get used to it."

"Where are we?"

"Heliopolis. It's a suburb of Cairo. Ten years ago it was virgin desert with just a handful of up-market villas. Now, as you see, it's a brand new slum rapidly nearing completion."

"You seem very well informed. How many times have you been here?"

He shrugs. "No idea. I just know this is the fourth time they've lost my luggage. Or, at least, nearly lost it."

"Business?"

"No. I just like it here." He pushes a hand through his thick blonde hair and smiles at her, a smile obviously intended to forestall further questions.

Undeterred, she asks, "What do you do?"

"You mean work?"

"Yes."

He looks out of the window. "I'm a banker."

"*Really?*"

He turns and raises his eyebrows in a sardonic look of enquiry.

She laughs. "Sorry, I'm just insatiably curious by nature."

That's okay. I feel duly flattered by the attention."

"It's just that you …" She breaks off, pointing out of the open window. "My God! *Look!* Look at that!"

They are passing the old colonial structure of the Cairo railway station. The once carefully fretted woodwork is rotted and peeling. And there in front of it, marooned in the centre of a traffic island, stands a gigantic, red stone statue of a man dressed in a pleated kilt. He is striding aggressively forward, his arms held tight to his sides, an elaborate crown on his head.

Lara holds her hand to her open mouth. "My God! It's gigantic! It must be taller than a London house!"

Her companion laughs. "Welcome to Egypt! It completely destroys our puny European sense of scale, doesn't it? It makes us look like cultural pygmies."

The taxi shudders to a halt, snarled in the traffic, belching fumes. Lara leans across, cranes her neck and stares up at the massive granite shins towering above them.

"It's Ramesses II. It was carved from a single block of granite by people who didn't even have steel tools. Then they rolled it on logs down to the Nile and ferried it on barges five hundred miles up river from Aswan, where it was quarried. It's more than three thousand years old and weighs about a hundred tons." He chuckles. "But if you think that's big, you've got a few surprises in store."

Gradually the taxi begins to inch forward.

"What are you going to do while you're here?"

"Oh," she chafes the palms of her hands together. "I've signed up for some slightly strange tour."

"Slightly strange?"

"It's a sort of semi-mystical New Age kind of thing. It's organised by some English astrologer."

A strange look passes across his face. Then he turns away and, for a while, he is silent, gazing at the passing city. "Me too," he says at length. His tone is vague.

"*What?*"

"Me too. I think I'm on the same tour."

"Are you joking?"

He faces her. "No," he says flatly.

"But what on earth are *you* doing on a tour like that?"

He shrugs. "Perhaps you don't know me quite as well as you obviously think you do. Maybe I just thought it would be different." He points out of the window beside her. "Look, there's the University of Cairo." She glances briefly at the high brick wall with palm trees towering behind it. "Anyhow," he counters. "Why are *you* doing the tour if you find it so strange?"

"That, I have to say, is a good question." She rakes her fingers through her short honey-blonde hair. Perhaps he's right. Perhaps she has simply misjudged him. Still, he certainly doesn't *look* like her idea of a banker.

He gives her a slightly lopsided smile. "Since it seems we're going to be together for the next two and a half weeks, maybe we should introduce ourselves. I'm Finn Connors."

"I know. You advertise it on your bag. And I'm Lara Rostock, by the way." Then she hesitates, suddenly aware that, for the first time since her wedding day, she has instinctively used her maiden name.

"Rostock?"

"My great-grandfather was Russian. But I'm more prosaic – born in Wales." She stretches out her arm with mock formality and they shake hands just as the driver hits the horn and swerves perilously close a donkey-cart crossing in front of them.

"Christ!" She grabs the back of the seat in front.

He laughs. "And I suppose you think I'm trying to pick you up."

She glances at him out of the corners of her eyes and smiles slightly. "Maybe."

"*Maybe?* Well, you're right. I am. And I don't think I'm making a very good job of it."

She turns to face him. "No. You're not. It's absolutely terrible!"

And suddenly they both burst out laughing.

FIVE

Mohammed al-Fakhry is seated at his metal-topped desk on the eighth floor of the Ministry of Culture in Cairo's Gamalea district. It's a shabby concrete structure, built only five years ago, but already showing signs of terminal decay. Plaster is falling in lumps from the ceiling, half the windows are jammed, the walls are exhibiting cracks wide enough for a man to be able to insert his hand and the plumbing is hopelessly erratic. Whack! He drops the plastic fly-swatter back on the desk with glum satisfaction. That makes eighteen this morning. Eighteen and three cockroaches. And it's still only ten-thirty.

The electric fan on top of the filing cabinet in the far corner of his cramped office slowly swings its attention in his direction, ruffling the stack of untouched papers on his desk and isolating for a moment the beads of sweat coursing down the back of his neck. Outside the sun is bouncing off the Cairo pavements, placing an invisible lid over the city and choking the air with dust and fumes. Thirty-eight degrees and rising! It seems to get worse every year. But perhaps that's just his age. As Director of Antiquities for the Luxor region and a Grade Two civil servant, he is entitled to a permanent office in Cairo. And air conditioning. The unit had arrived the previous year and sat in its crate outside his room for three months. When

51

the last of the summer heat had finally passed an engineer arrived and installed it projecting through a jagged hole cut in the window. For two days he had sat in near arctic splendour, the envy of his lesser colleagues down the passage. A fitting status, he had proudly told his wife, Rashida, for the man who had overseen the great discovery of the statues in the Luxor Temple. But on the third day there had been a terrifying grating of machinery and the air-conditioner had shuddered to a halt. The official answer to his complaint to the ministry was that they were awaiting the delivery of spare parts from Detroit. Al-Fakhry knew that the machine would never work again.

He picks up the fly-swatter. An enormous cockroach is making its way purposefully across his desk. There is a soft knock on the half-open door and a small boy, wearing a stained *galabiya*, enters carrying a round copper tray on which sits a cup of karkade. The cup is badly chipped and probably only cursorily washed, but he loves this pale amber tea brewed from the leaves of dried hibiscus. Beside the cup sits a thin pile of faxes. The boy sets these down on al-Fakhry's desk and disappears.

Al-Fakhry begins leafing through the faxes. Reports, reports, reports. There's never anything new. And never anything he can change. Another piece of masonry has fallen from a high level in the colonnaded court at Karnak, nearly killing a tourist. The Archaeological Service is three years overdue with that work, and still shows no sign of finishing. More lights have blown in the newly erected museum in Luxor and replacements can only be acquired in the United States. A guard has accepted a bribe from a tourist and allowed him to remove a painted fragment from a tomb that was being reconstructed in the Valley of the Nobles .....

Suddenly al-Fakhry's fingers stop their steady progress through the stack of papers. He shuffles to the edge of his creaking wooden seat and stares at a five-line fax from the Ministry of the Interior.

David Mountjoy, the British tour leader, will arrive tomorrow, 4th August in Cairo on the 17.25 flight from Copenhagen with eighteen tourists to meet with other tourists travelling from London. They will proceed to Luxor by coach, arrivmg on August 7th. He is again to be permitted to perform his rituals in the temple precincts.

Husayn al-Shaikh, Deputy Director, Ministry of the Interior.

Al-Fakhry runs his index finger around the moist inside of his collar, then glances at the date. The fax is already a day old. He feels a nervous sense of foreboding, exactly like the day he had picked up the first clue that Rashida was cuckolding him, an angry, nauseous feeling of impotence. And now here he is *yet again* having to take orders from that serpent al-Shaikh! A man with eyes so cold he can make your blood freeze with one look, always contemptuously overriding and countermanding him.

It had all looked harmless enough in the beginning. Just a few rituals, al-Shaikh had told him, to promote tourism, casually hinting at the alternative if he refused – no job and no pension. How long would Rashida stay with him then? The whole thing was a disgrace, allowing the temples to be used in that way. Deputy Director of the Ministry of the Interior indeed! He knows exactly what that title means. The prisons and cemeteries of Egypt are full of people put there by al-Shaikh and his friends at the so-called Ministry of the Interior.

And every time the crazy Englishman comes there is some sort of trouble. The worst had been the year he had overseen the great discovery in the Luxor Temple. One early morning, ten days after the ground had opened up to reveal the statues, a time when he was still being celebrated, he had made his usual inspection of the temple. And right there, in the dark Holy of Holies, with a shaft of light falling like a torch beam through the circular hole in the stone roof, he had stumbled across Kamel, the most reliable of the temple guards. And the sight has never left him. He was dressed as usual in his freshly washed dark blue galabiya. Only now he was lying on his back on the sandy floor, the ground beside him drenched with blood, his face contorted in a look of horror. Flies were already crawling busily up and down the deep gash actross his throat, as if poor Kamel had been a piece of meat on a butcher's block. Even now he feels sick to think of it.

And then al-Shaikh had arrived on the next flight, dressed in his smart suit. He had surveyed the body without a word while he calmly smoked a cigarette. And then – *nothing*! Poor old Kamel had been carted away in a sack as if he was a bundle of straw – and no questions asked. No investigation! What in the name of Allah did that mean?

He screws up the fax and throws it in the metal bin. He can feel cold lines of sweat making their way down his back.

SIX

Lara is late, of course. She has spent far too long wandering in the hotel gardens, fascinated by the exotic riot of vegetation and the strange names on the small metal plaques – Casuarinas and Frangipani, Bougainvillea and beautiful purple flowered saplings bizarrely called Camel's Foot Tree.

From the other side of the door comes the hum of excited voices. For a moment she hesitates. Normally she enjoys new situations and meeting new people, but this morning there's a strange swell of anxiety in her stomach. Ever since that terrible, bruising fight with Tim ten days ago her inner equilibrium seems to have been overturned so that she feels painfully raw and vulnerable. It's as if her senses are jammed in high alert now and everything around her enters her more deeply.

She sucks in a deep breath, pushes open the door and is confronted by a sea of faces arranged in an oval. Only two empty chairs remain. She crosses the room self-consciously, aware of the curious glances following her and settles into her seat. Slowly she allows her surroundings to come into focus. Corporate meeting rooms must be the same the world over. The place is windowless, with beige hessian walls, a rust brown carpet liberally decorated with coffee stains, a half dead potted plant on a metal stand in one corner and aluminium air-conditioning grills emitting their faint electric hum. She could equally well be in a municipal conference centre in Birmingham, except for the curious aroma of cumin and other exotic spices that seems to pervade the whole hotel.

At the far end of the ring of chairs, directly opposite the door, a small man sits behind a low table with his head bowed. A thick tangle of chestnut hair melds into his luxuriant beard. He is wearing a strange loose, lime green smock and a pair of baggy turquoise Indian trousers. Inside the open leather sandals his feet look unnaturally white, as if he has been shut up in a cave for decades. His delicate bony hands are slowly shuffling a deck of outsized playing cards with brightly coloured backs.

David Mountjoy? She stares in shocked disbelief. Is this really the man to whom she has entrusted herself for the next two and a half weeks? To his right sits a startlingly pretty girl with wide-awake china-blue eyes and a frizz of white-blonde hair that encircles her face like a halo. She is shifting in her seat like an excited child as she smiles and waves across the room with a mechanical movement like a clockwork toy. Her obviously unfettered breasts strain against the deep scoop of her white tee shirt. Tight pale blue trousers cling to her hips. Clearly the sex bomb of the group, thinks Lara.

Most of the rest are women, aged anywhere between twenty-five and sixty-five. Flowered kaftans, broad yoga trousers and beaded necklaces are everywhere. It's like a time-warped photograph of Woodstock from the sixties. In front of the door a tiny, bird-like woman with a mane of loose henna-red hair leans her head sideways on to the shoulder of a massive lumberjack of a man with a curling blond beard. He looks like a Viking warrior. His enormous barrel chest seems ready to burst the scarlet tee shirt and split apart its black Gothic letters – *Visit Jutland*. Between his booted feet rests a large, professional-looking video camera. He is swivelling a thick gold ring on his left hand as he glances nervously around.

Directly across the room sits Finn Connors, the guy from the airport. He had tried to take her for dinner the previous evening, but she refused. She knew exactly where that was headed. His arms are folded across his blue denim shirt, his long khaki-clad legs stretched out in front of him as he leans back casually in his chair and regards the blonde girl with such undisguised carnal interest that Lara almost bursts out laughing. As if distracted by Lara's attention, he turns and smiles at her, then arches an ironic eyebrow. Lara smiles back.

David Mountjoy stops shuffling the cards and holds them out ostentatiously in front of him. The room begins to stutter into silence. The air-conditioning hums overhead. Suddenly the door clicks open and a dark-haired man puts his head into the room. For a moment he frowns. Then he closes the door, crosses the room rapidly and settles into the empty chair beside Lara.

Edward Cavanagh realizes that he has sat down next to the girl he had seen crossing the hotel lobby before breakfast. Dressed in tight khaki trousers and a man's pale blue shirt, her slim figure and delicate elfin features had immediately caught his attention. He had admired her short thatch of honey-coloured hair, her widely spaced grey-green eyes and the almost too broad mouth and had wondered – actually, if he's honest, he had hoped – if she might be one of the group. She walked quickly, gracefully even, but with a kind of adolescent diffidence, as if she didn't quite fully inhabit her body. He knows they have never met, but still there is something strangely familiar about her.

As the room gradually quietens, Edward settles back in his chair. Group therapy had been a major part of his long training and still he hates these tight, exposing huddles. He hates the way – despite all the countless hours of private therapy – that they can still reawaken memories of those first bleak days at boarding school, the feelings suddenly erupting through the surface of his adult life as if the intervening thirty years have never happened. For a moment he wonders if being late has nothing to do with losing his room key. Perhaps it was part of a deep unconscious ambivalence about being here at all. As a psychoanalyst he is given to this kind of obsessive introspection.

David Mountjoy coughs ostentatiously, taps the edge of the cards against the low wooden table in front of him, and lays them face down. The room falls into an expectant silence. Then he looks up. Where his face is visible, his skin looks strangely unlined. His pale blue eyes sparkle behind the thick wire-rimmed glasses. The corners of his mouth twitch in an impish grin. The moist lips look unnaturally pink amongst the thick tangle of beard. He allows the silence to lengthen as he runs his eyes slowly around the circle, pausing for a moment to look intensely into each face.

"Aaah," he breathes. "As a Leo this is the moment I love! I am the very centre of attention."

There is a ripple of laughter. One or two people shift in their chairs. Mountjoy spreads his hands in a messianic gesture of greeting. "Welcome! Welcome to each and every one of you at the start of our twenty-day mystical exploration of the Temple Landscape of Ancient Egypt. During our time here we will be seeing many wonderful things ….. yes, *wonderful things!*" he repeats in a hushed voice. "This will be more than just an *outer* voyage, a mere 'trip down the Nile'…" He etches the inverted commas in the air with his long, delicate fingers. "For what I promise every single one of you is that it will also be an *inner* voyage of self-discovery, a life-changing rite of passage. Though our outer, physical eyes will all see the same things, our inward vision will reflect where each of us is on our own spiritual journey in this incarnation."

Across the circle, Lara watches Finn stretch out his long legs, fold his arms and stare up at the ceiling.

"We will not, as modern tourists do, run from place to place like headless chickens." Pause for laughter. "Nor will we constantly dazzle each other with the pop of our flashbulbs." More laughter. "Instead we will try to move at a pace that enables us to align ourselves with the energies and the wisdom of ancient Egypt."

He stops, checking the faces of rapt attention. His inspection falters at Finn, then moved on.

"For that reason I have structured the tour with only two centres – here in Cairo, and in the south at Luxor, ancient Thebes, one of the great spiritual centres of Egyptian civilisation. From these two bases we will fan out to make our excursions. Some days we will have busy programmes, but others I have deliberately left free. This is not just to allow you to improve your suntans beside the swimming pool." He slides an ostentatious sideways glance towards the blonde girl, who responds with a demure flutter of eyelashes. There is general laughter, one or two comments in Swedish, then more laughter. Mountjoy frowns. Obediently the room falls silent.

He certainly knows how to play an audience, thinks Edward, observing Mountjoy's easy command of the room.

"..... The purpose of these quiet times is to enable you to think. To *meditate*. To allow your spirits to breathe in and align themselves with what is truly the eternal wisdom of this ancient land. And everywhere we go, at the start of each day, and in those places of highest spiritual energy, we will perform rituals to honour the gods and invoke their power within us."

Involuntarily, Edward's eyebrows shoot up. His glance locks with the man's opposite, who gives him an ironic smile, as if to say, "What the hell do you make of all this?"

"….. Some of you may be wondering," goes on Mountjoy in a booming voice, "*Why now?* Why does he choose high summer, instead of a pleasantly cool time like April or October? In short, has David Mountjoy *finally lost the plot?*" Pause for laughter. He raises his right hand. "Not yet. Not yet." He smiles. "The reason I have chosen this moment, despite the heat, is that during these days the Sun in Leo will be in aspect with transiting Uranus, and Pluto is just now entering its own sign of Scorpio. This is a most unusual and powerful combination." His eyes run slowly round the room. "This means that here, in this mystical ancient land, where the psyche is not yet deadened by modern so-called civilisation, strange things may start to happen to you – things that we would usually call '*abnormal*'. Here you will learn that the Invisible World rules the visible, in ways that you can scarcely now imagine. Deeply buried layers of your psyches will start to emerge. You may have disturbing dreams and thoughts, even hallucinations. Some of you will experience apparently impossible 'coincidences', meetings with people you had forgotten or not expected. But these are not coincidences at all. They are *synchronicities* – meaningful encounters orchestrated by your fate for a specific purpose. Hidden aspects of yourselves that you had never known – or never wanted to know – will begin to show themselves. For some there may even be out-of-body experiences."

The room has grown very quiet.

"All this may feel disorientating, sometimes even frightening. But remember, these are all ways that the planets remind us of their constant presence and power in our lives. For at such strange and disturbing moments we become intensely aware of the hidden web of fate that underlies our everyday existence. Such events are signs that your fate is being quickened; that you are being asked to accept those parts of yourself that you have tried to push away, to accept the life that is still unlived in you. In short, to look life – your *real* life – in the face." He pauses. "It is indeed a great privilege to be here in this magical country under this special planetary constellation. It offers all of you a chance for a new beginning."

There is a long silence. Mountjoy clears his throat. "Now, in order to help you centre yourselves and raise your awareness of your own inner state at the all-important start of this exciting voyage, I have arranged a small ritual of initiation."

He leans forward and picks up the thin pack of brightly coloured cards from the table in front of him. They are so large that the spread of his hands can barely hold them. He begins shuffling slowly. Edward is aware of how the level of tension in the room has risen, as if Mountjoy has been slowly, but quite deliberately, ratcheting it up.

"This is the set of the major Arcana of the Tarot pack," goes on Mountjoy. "It is particularly appropriate, since the Tarot has its origins in ancient Egypt, several thousand years ago." He glances up from his shuffling. "Some of you will be familiar with the Tarot, others may not. No matter. The Tarot is not an issue of brute facts and acquired knowledge, but rather of our ability to access our own inner, innate wisdom, to respond to the symbols that will align us with our fate."

He squares the cards in his hands, sets them down on the table, then cuts them twice, moving to the right. He regathers them and rises.

"I shall place the cards face down in the centre of the circle of our field of energy. And I invite each of you, in your own time, to come and select one." He pauses. "Your card will mark

61

where you are on your inner journey. *And* what awaits you. Remember ….." His voice suddenly drops. The circle leans imperceptibly forward to catch the words. "Remember, *you* will choose your card. But ….." He allows the silence to hang in the room. "*The card also chooses you.*"

He rises and spreads the brightly coloured pack in a rough circle in the centre of the floor with the flat of his hand. Then he returns to his seat. The air-conditioning whirrs. Beyond the closed door a trolley clatters past, followed by some muttered words in Arabic.

The blonde girl is first off her chair. She bounces bare-footed into the centre of the circle. For a moment she plays with indecision, toes turned inwards, a finger to her lips, acting the excited child. Then she selects a card and skips back to her place. She looks down and her eyes widen in theatrical wonder. She purses her mouth in a silent 'Oooh!' and clutches the card to the front of her straining tee-shirt.

The rest of the group follows one by one. To Lara's surprise, Finn is amongst the first. He settles back in his chair and looks down at the card. Immediately his eyebrows shoot up in surprise.

Lara's own card shows a naked woman standing on one foot within a blue circle studded with stars. Her voluptuous body is arched ecstatically back. Above her a chequered snake is emerging from the centre of an enormous golden eye and coiling itself sensuously around her hips. Her right foot rests precariously on its open jaws. At each corner a golden-headed monster is breathing blue flame from mouth and nostrils. Underneath is written in Gothic script, 'The Universe'. Whatever it means, she likes its sinuous shape and bright colours. It feels strangely erotic – and somehow challenging, as if it might really reflect the 'unlived life' that Mountjoy has just invoked.

The dark man to her left is the last to rise. Lara studies him with curiosity. He is probably in his early forties. In profile his face is angular, almost hawk-like, with a strong chin and a slightly beaked nose. A thick shock of black hair is streaked white above the temples. There is an air of containment and quiet authority about him. And perhaps too the sense of a man who has suffered; his face is already etched with lines. As he reaches to pick one of the two remaining cards from the floor, she notices what long, beautiful hands he has. He returns to his seat, flips over the card and lets out a slight grunt. Lara glances over his shoulder. He angles the card in her direction. "Not exactly upbeat," he whispers. It shows a man suspended upside-down from a gibbet, a rope looped around one ankle. Beneath is inscribed, 'The Hanged Man'. Despite his casual irony, Lara senses that he is unnerved.

"Sooo…" David Mountjoy rubs the palms of his hands together. "This is your first encounter with the outer manifestation of your inner spiritual state. *And your destiny.* A destiny that will start to show itself over the next three weeks – whether you wish it or not. Keep the card with you at all times. As our journey of exploration unfolds, so will the card gradually give up to you more and more of its inner wisdom." He pauses. "That is if you are prepared to make the effort to attend." Lara looked up from her card. The last sentence carries a steely undertone of authority, something that reminds her uncomfortably of school. The room goes very quiet. "So, before we close," goes on Mountjoy in his usual voice, "I would invite each of you to share with us their name, their chosen tarot card, and a few brief words of feeling about the card."

He turns to the blonde girl on his right. She smiles broadly, then her face composes itself into childlike solemnity. She intones slowly in a sing-song Scandinavian voice, "My name is Birgit ….."

Most of the group speak briefly, but a few seemed seized by an urge to give details of their life, their current emotional state, why they have decided to come on the tour. Occasionally Mountjoy adds comments about the card. His casual references show that almost all the group are already well known to him – and to each other – from previous gatherings. It feels like some kind of class reunion. He also seems to be intimately acquainted with their astrological charts; his sentences are scattered with phrases like, 'the placement of your natal Moon in Gemini', or 'your dark Scorpio energy'.

The introductions proceed anti-clockwise. There is a brief silence when the progress round the circle reaches Finn. He pulls himself up in his chair and looks around. "I'm Finn Connors." He pauses. "And my card doesn't look too encouraging." He holds up the card and rotates it slowly round the room, smiling ironically. It shows a mediaeval tower being struck by lightning. The masonry is toppling, small figures are being hurtled out of the narrow windows like flaming projectiles. Inexplicably Lara feels a cold shock run down her spine.

"Ah!" says Mountjoy. "The Tower! How fascinating!" The smoothness of his tone suggests a certain satisfaction, as if he has already picked Finn out as the potential trouble-maker in the group. Finn stares at him impassively. "When we choose this card," Mountjoy disengages his eyes from Finn's and addresses the room in general, "it indicates that our old life is crumbling – that is our fate – and that a new life is struggling to be born. In short it is a clarion call to wake up." He pauses. "To wake up internally and spiritually. Or else ....."

He leaves the sentence hanging ominously. The two men's eyes lock. Then Finn raises one eyebrow and simply says, "Thank you." He turns to the tousled-haired woman on his right. "Your turn, I think."

"Thank you all," says Mountjoy when the circuit has been completed, "for sharing your thoughts and feelings with us." He gestures towards the single card lying in the centre of the floor. "Only one card remains." He rises and strides purposefully towards it. Then, without looking at it, he holds it up and revolves slowly, smiling. There is a faint swell of laughter and a few muttered comments. "*The Fool!*" he proclaims. "This is the joker in the pack. This is the Trickster. The guide. The one who shows the way! He is the Hermetic figure, the only one who can lead you down into the Underworld – and back up again."

He returns to his chair, lays the card on the table face up and folds his hands. "And now, after all these excitements, I would like us to sit together for a few moments in silent meditation, to mark the beginning of our great journey together through this ancient mystical land."

The room falls silent. Five minutes later David Mountjoy taps the small brass bell on the table in front of him and the room lumbers back into life.

"You will find the programme for each day in the folder under your seat, together with all kinds of practical information. Tomorrow we will leave from the hotel at five to enable us to be first into the great pyramid of Cheops. You will also find a folder with a number of articles I have written on the esoteric aspects of ancient Egypt, together with an explanation of each of the Tarot cards." He claps his hands to quell a sudden outbreak of excited chattering that has erupted in one corner of the room. "Please study this carefully. The Tarot section will be very helpful in unravelling the secret meaning of your own card."

Mountjoy rises and is immediately surrounded by a small circle of women vying for his attention. Raising one hand imperiously he cuts a swathe through them in the direction of Lara and Edward.

"Welcome to Egypt! How nice to meet you both!" He shakes each of them by the hand, looks with bright curiosity into their eyes. Lara is startled. Mountjoy seems to be regarding the two of them as a couple. She searches for some way to explain.

"You are the only two whose astrological charts I haven't yet gone through in detail," says Mountjoy briskly. "Together with Mr Connors, of course. It would be most important for your understanding of your experience over the next three weeks. We have time at leisure here this afternoon. Shall we say two, four and six o'clock respectively?"

He rubs his hands, turns and is gone, without speaking to Finn. He is quickly engulfed in the knot of women waiting behind him.

"I *so* wanted to get the Hierophant card," cries a plaintiff voice. "But instead I got The Chariot!"

Finn crosses the room, shakes Edward's hand warmly and introduces himself. He smiles at Lara. "Hi." She nods back.

Edward glances at her enquiringly. "You two know each other?"

Lara smiles. "He tried to pick me up in a taxi yesterday."

"And failed miserably," says Finn with a theatrically glum face. Then they both laugh.

Edward's gaze flickers between them, trying to gauge their relationship. There seems to be such an easy, teasing complicity that it's hard to believe they have only just met.

"Are you two the only other ones who haven't been astrologised yet?" asks Finn.

Edward nods. "It seems so."

"Me too. But he has already booked me for later today. He obviously didn't want me to escape. So it looks like we've all

66

got a real treat in store." Lara frowns at him, unsure whether he is being ironic. But Finn just smiles and places a hand on each of their shoulders. "I'm happy to have the two of you with me," he says. "Let's see what the web of fate holds for us then!"

"Two, four and six o'clock! Room 424!" booms Mountjoy over his shoulder as he sweeps out of the door, a stream of people in his wake. Finn glances around. The room is almost empty now. The bearded giant, who has introduced himself as Kai, is standing alone in one corner, filming the potted plant.

"It seems," said Finn quietly, "that Spielberg has hot competition." Then he crosses the room, claps Kai on the shoulder and shakes his hand as if they are old friends.

SEVEN

Beyond the high brick wall, thick with pink and yellow bougainvillea, the Cairo traffic hoots and groans.

Edward Cavanagh is lying on an old-fashioned wicker chaise longue in the furthest corner of the hotel garden. Above him towering date palms slat the afternoon sunlight and rib the sky. He is feeling totally disorientated. Trained for years as a psychoanalyst, used to dealing with trauma and the dark workings of the unconscious, how could he suddenly be so shaken by such an unlikely character as David Mountjoy? Yet the fact is that, within the space of their two hour meeting, as Mountjoy had slowly guided him through the placement of the planets at the moment of his birth, he had suddenly seen an unexpected web of meaning underpinning his life that felt far more convincing and satisfying than the elaborate psychological framework he has constructed for himself over a decade of careful study; a system that defies his normal logic and stretches out far beyond his own limited ways of thinking. And in the process he has felt suddenly broken open and strangely vulnerable, as if he has let go of some raft that he has been clinging to all his life.

As he lies now, listening to the distant blare of the traffic, there's a soft creak beside him. He opens his eyes. Lara is sitting on the edge of the chaise longue opposite. She gives a shy smile. "I didn't mean to disturb you," she says. "I just wanted to see how it went with Mountjoy. Curious, I suppose"

There's an awkward silence as he stares at her, trying to refocus his mind. After a while she splays her hands on the cushions and begins to lever herself up. "I'm sorry. I really didn't mean to ....."

"No!" He sits up and swings his legs round to face her. He shakes his head. "Please don't go. I'm sorry. To tell the truth, I think it's left me a bit spaced out. That's all."

"If you'd rather ....."

"No, really. I just need to get my head together."

She sinks back and lets him sit for a while in silence. Then she smiles and says, "It seems to have had quite an impact!"

He nods ruefully. "Whatever skepticism I might have had when I went in evaporated within the first two minutes!"

"What happened?"

"Well ....." He pushes both hands back through his thick mane of hair and shakes his head as if to clear it. "It was a shock, I must say. I'm not sure what I was expecting but, when he looked at my chart, Mountjoy immediately saw things he couldn't possibly have known – my mother's early death, for example. He didn't ask me. He just told me, as if he already knew. But it wasn't just the factual things. He seemed to understand the relationship between my parents – between the three of us better ......" He breaks off for a moment, frowning. "Frankly, far better than *I've* ever been able to! No normal person could have done that. Not even if they'd known me all my life." He pauses. "It was the strangest experience. It was like … well, being somehow broken open and seen right down to the core of my soul."

She stares at him, suddenly aware of the emotional seriousness in this quiet, distant man. She frowns. "What do you do?"

"You mean work?"

"Yes."

"I'm a psychoanalyst."

"Ah, yes." She nods, as if confirming something to herself.

He raises his eyebrows in enquiry.

"I had wondered. I've watched you in the group. It's something about the way you listen to people. It's different. What sort of psychoanalyst?"

"I'm trained as a Jungian, but I suppose my method of working is eclectic."

She cocks her head to one side. "Isn't that exhausting – listening to other people's problems all day long?"

He smiles. "That's the question everyone asks...." But then he hesitates. There are stock answers to this question, of course, but none of them feels quite adequate at this moment. How can he really convey that strange mixture of distance and closeness that he feels with these semi-strangers whose lives he knows so intimately? How explain his ability to walk away from them trying to tell himself that he is untouched by all their grief and neediness? Only, of course, he isn't. On some days, he can feel like a leaking jar, worn so thin by exposure to the rawness of their emotions that almost anyone can poke their fingers through and painfully intrude...

She sits staring at him, waiting for his response

"Well, there's not only the dark side to psychotherapy," he says at last, "any more than there is to the rest of life. There's not just the pain and depression. There's also satisfaction and joy when it works and people's lives get better."

Joy? Somehow the word seems odd coming from him, as if he might be a stranger to it. She starts to say something, then changes her mind. Instead she says, "So what was it about Mountjoy that impressed you so much?"

He leans back and loops his hands around one knee, frowning slightly. Then, to her surprise, he suddenly sits forward again, his eyes alight. "It was extraordinary. It was like stepping into a completely different world, where there's another kind of logic from the one we normally use, somehow another dimension of meaning. We always unconsciously divide the world into two – either one thing or another, one better or worse than the other, but never both equally valid at the same time. So that way something always gets judged or excluded. But this was a totally non-judgmental, non-hierarchical way of looking at the world. It felt more like a generous, breathing organism that allows everything just to be there in its own right. Not black or white, good or bad, better or worse, but a kind of rich polytheism….." The words are tumbling out of him now, his hands weaving patterns in the air. "That probably makes it all sound rather vague and abstract. But it isn't at all, because the whole system is precisely regulated by the movement of the planets, so it has a wonderful, effortless elegance about it, a bit like a spider's web…."

He breaks off, suddenly aware of her intense regard. He makes a vague, dismissive gesture. "Sorry. A very big speech on a totally arcane subject. I can do that sometimes, just running off at the mouth when I'm excited by something."

She can feel the irony coming to guard him. But she doesn't want to lose that sudden, totally unexpected crackle of energy. "Not at all. It sounds beautiful." She stares at him, her fists under her chin. "So do you really think that astrology can uncover things our normal ways of thinking can't? Is that what you're saying?"

"Yes," he says slowly. "In the right hands, I do believe that now." Then he smiles. "Perhaps slightly to my own surprise.

Let's face it, at first sight David Mountjoy isn't exactly the person you'd expect to bring you a startling revelation!"

She laughs. "I know. He does look a little unprepossessing, doesn't he? A bit like an underworld troll. But still, there's something very unusual about him. The eyes maybe? I don't know … It's just a feeling, as if he might have x-ray vision or something odd."

Edward nods. "Well, he certainly had it with me! I suspect that all his showmanship is really just a form of play-acting. He seems to do it for the audience and somehow dismiss it at the same time, as if he's a pantomime villain deliberately hamming it up. But you're right, it feels as if behind all that there's something else... I don't know – a kind of gravitas. Like he knows something more ....." He shrugs. "But, of course, that's what most patients think about their psychoanalysts. And believe me, they're usually totally wrong!"

She laughs, then shifts forward to the edge of the chaise longue. "So what did he tell you about yourself?"

She can sense his withdrawal almost physically. It's as if he has instinctively pulled down a shutter between them. Instantly she regrets her probing question.

"Oh, there was such a lot. Almost too much to take in really ....." His voice trails away and she has a sudden strange flash of memory, so quick and intense that later she will wonder if she has dreamt it: opening the cottage door to find her father gone, the house empty .....

"And how was it for you?" he asks.

She hesitates, fully aware that he is deliberately turning the tables, scrambling back to safer ground. And she isn't at all sure she wants to allow him to do that. Then she glances up and sees a genuine kindness in his eyes and she relents.

"I have to agree with you. It was certainly impressive. Though I'm not sure I can quite match the eloquence of your description." He smiles and spreads his hands as if to excuse himself. "All the technical stuff – the conjunctions and trines and sextiles and whatever – didn't mean much to me. But what he actually said, what he saw, made so much sense for where I am right now ....."

There's a long pause, not uncomfortable, just an easy silence. Then he says, "Am I allowed to ask where it is that you are right now?"

She shrugs. "At a kind of cross-roads, I suppose. According to Mountjoy, I'm just starting something called my Saturn Return. Apparently it usually only happens twice in your life and often creates huge reassessment and upheaval. Mountjoy called it a 'breaking down and rebirthing' for me." She scratches the inverted commas in the air. Then she adds, almost to herself, "I used to be a graphic designer and a painter. I was quite successful. And I realised today that it's exactly three years since I last touched a paint brush."

There's a weight of sadness in her voice and a long silence falls between them. She registers how he leaves her space and she likes that. Most other men would have been just uninterested and talked about something else, probably themselves. Or pressed on her with their busy questions.

He leans forward slightly. "Can I ask what the cross-roads looks like?"

She laughs. "My God, when you ask a question like that, then I can tell you're a psychotherapist!" But he doesn't laugh. Instead he stays looking at her with that same unwavering attention. There's an almost magnetic quality to his listening, she thinks, as if he makes your words, your thoughts almost, somehow more important. And a strange thought strikes her

then – How little real attention I've ever received in my life ....
But still, it doesn't feel quite safe to give herself away entirely.
She shrugs slightly. "Oh, the usual stuff. Marriage and so on
....." Instinctively her right hand slides down and touches the
white groove where her wedding ring has been. She is aware
of his eyes following the movement.

"But I imagine it's not very usual for you," he says gently.

She looks down and shakes her head. And suddenly she
can feel the tears well up. She tries to hold them back. How
could he have opened her up like this in the space of just a
few minutes? But she knows it's hopeless. She covers her face
with her hands and begins to sob, all the pain of the last weeks
suddenly pouring over as she cries uncontrollably.

After a while her sobbing eases and she becomes aware of
his presence again. How strange that he hasn't tried to comfort
her, like any other man would. She wipes her eyes with the
back of her hand like a child and looks up at him. He is still
sitting there with that same intense regard in his face. She has
the odd, illogical sensation that he has actually been *listening*
to her tears. What a weird idea, she thinks.

"Sorry," she says.

"For what?"

She shrugs.

"Many South American Indian tribes used to believe that
you honoured the gods in five ways." She frowns at him in
incomprehension as he begins to tick them off on his fingers.
Where on earth is this leading? "Laughing, dancing, singing,
making love..... And crying." He smiles slightly. "And it seems
to me that you just honoured the gods wonderfully. So I can't
imagine why you would want to apologise."

She laughs. It's as if he's a magician, effortlessly spinning
her mood through a hundred and eighty degrees, unexpectedly

pulling the rabbit out of the hat for her. Very softly he touches the back of her hand. "Would you prefer it if I left you alone now?"

She nods, then watches him until he disappears behind the cypress hedge that screens off the hotel. She lies back and stares up at the sky. It's a dense enamel blue, unlike any colour she has ever seen in Europe. What an extraordinary conversation! Perhaps he's an extraterrestrial, she thinks, and laughs out loud at her silliness, aware of the strange lightness that seems to be buoying her up now, as if she has just shed some kind of invisible burden.

But she' s aware too of the things she hasn't told him, holding them tightly to herself: how Mountjoy had talked about her Lunar Return now in the Twelfth House. For some reason the phrase had embedded itself in her brain, with its suggestions of goddesses and archaic rituals – how it offered her a chance to "reclaim your femininity". At first she had bridled at the suggestion. After all, hasn't she always been pursued by men? But gradually, as Mountjoy talked on, she began to understand that no man had ever really seen and respected her as beautiful. Not her father as she had first blossomed. Certainly not Tim. Not any of her few lovers. Lusted after her, wanted her, needed her to take care of their lives, paraded her as a trophy. Oh, yes, all of those. But what Mountjoy seemed to be talking about was something quite different – a deep belief in herself as feminine, truly beautiful in some kind of archaic sense. Something deeper than she has been aware of before. And the realization of that absence has opened up a well of sadness inside her. She has a sudden image of a huge empty cistern, with just a few drops slowly beginning to pool now on its cracked concrete floor.

So why didn't she tell Edward everything? After all, he had felt so incredibly safe, so understanding. But she remembers too his glance as she had crossed the hotel lobby that first morning, before they had even known that they would meet. That look had been so intense, so different from anything she had ever experienced, that she had felt unnerved by it.

*

Finn Connors is also feeling rattled by his two hour session with David Mountjoy. But, unlike Edward, he doesn't want to talk about it. Least of all with himself. He's angry that Mountjoy can affect him like that. And he resents it that this self-satisfied little leprechaun, with his pretentious conjuring tricks and his phony messianic language seems somehow to have outplayed him

It had all started well enough. He had smiled inwardly as Mountjoy had brought up his 'chart' on the computer screen and turned it towards him – a circle like a bicycle wheel with spokes, surrounded by all kinds of weird, arcane symbols. It had reminded Finn of those B movies he had loved to watch as a teenager about witchcraft and devil worship and Vincent Price in a black cape and exotic dentures, masquerading as a vampire. But then things had started to go wrong.

Mountjoy had gazed at the chart for a long while, his face curiously blank. Then he had turned back and, for an uncomfortably long time, had stared at Finn in silence. Finn stared back, not wanting to be phased, but aware for the first time that there was more than just sparkle in those pale blue eyes; a kind of strange opaqueness too, as if the astrologer was both present and utterly remote at the same time. He remembered Lascaris – *something odd about the eyes* – and suddenly he had a feeling of uncertainty, as if he was a man waiting anxiously while the doctor studied his x-rays. And that feeling wasn't helped by the creeping knowledge that, in these last days, ever since that flickering image of the white-robed figures had frozen itself on his television screen, he has felt strangely unnerved, as if the world isn't quite as he has imagined it, not quite in his control.

Then Mountjoy had started, almost humorously, to outline the familiar – Finn had at least that much knowledge of astrology – characteristics of a Leo: "Extrovert, gregarious, a bit of a showman. Leo likes to be the centre of attention, doesn't he?" Mountjoy smiled. "In case you haven't noticed, I'm one too." But then the smile had faded as he dabbed his finger on the top left corner of the chart. "Only right here, exactly on your Sun – 'conjunct', as we would say – you have two other planets." The thin finger slid over the paper. "This one here is Pluto. So in your case things are going to be quite a lot more complex and difficult. We'll come to that later."

Pluto, Finn knew from classical mythology, was the god of the Underworld – a sinister, implacable figure who ruled over the Kingdom of the Dead. Illogically he had felt a sudden unexpected flicker of anxiety.

For a while there was silence again as Mountjoy stared hard at the chart. Then he looked up. "Parents divorced?"

"No." Finn smiled, happy to register the first obvious mistake. Was that how this sort of charade worked? By fishing for information, then subtly feeding it back to you as clairvoyance? If so, David Mountjoy was going to be out of luck this time.

"One died early?"

"Nope."

"That's odd." The astrologer frowned. "Actually it's very odd. Because we've got a constellation here that clearly suggests something like orphancy, particularly paternal orphancy."

"No. My father died five years ago. My mother's still very much alive." Finn smiled again, relishing the astrologer's uncertainty.

Mountjoy tapped the chart with his index finger, then stared at the ceiling as if searching for something. "Was he away a lot, your father?"

"He was a kind of bit-part actor. So, yes, he was away sometimes." Then, without thinking, he added, "He was alcoholic."

"Ah, so that's it!" muttered Mountjoy almost to himself. "*That* kind of absence." He was staring at the chart again. "You see, the constellations show the likelihood of paternal absence. One automatically assumes that to be on the physical plane; but it can just as well be on other levels. Even if the father is *literally* there, if he isn't psychologically present – which he wouldn't be if he was alcoholic – the effect will be just the same. That seems to be the case here."

Finn suddenly felt pierced by the accuracy of the insight. Also oddly vulnerable, as if a shameful secret had just been laid bare.

Then Mountjoy had started to detour into other obscure territory, where the terminology made little sense to Finn. Mars conjunct Venus. That one he did remember because of the mythology again – the adulterous pair had been trapped by Venus' husband in a golden net, entwined and unable to escape. "A tendency towards almost obsessive sexual conquests" had been Mountjoy's gloss, followed by, "A tendency that may ultimately become self destructive." Fuck you, thought Finn. It felt intrusive. But again there had been that uncomfortable jolt of recognition. Finn's scepticism was beginning to feel precarious. Then, apparently out of nowhere, Mountjoy asked, "What sort of work do you do?"

The question was totally unexpected, but Finn couldn't help feeling a spark of relief on being diverted away from Mountjoy's esoteric territory. "I'm a money man, an investment banker," he replied calmly.

For a moment Mountjoy had frowned. Then something seemed to happen in his face, some sort of unidentifiable shift. Finn was used to dissembling – everyone in the antiquities world dissembled the whole time. He was used to reading people's looks, outguessing their lies, decoding their elaborate subtexts. But what was happening in David Mountjoy's face at that moment was quite beyond him. And it was at that moment that an achingly clear splinter of doubt slid into Finn's mind – *Was it actually possible – just possible – that Lascaris might be right after all, that Mountjoy did possess supernatural powers?*

Then David Mountjoy's face had creased into a smile. He gave a quiet chuckle. "You must work deep down in the vaults in that case!"

"What?"

"Deep down in the bank vaults."

Finn looked at him blankly.

"If you're a banker, it's the only possible explanation." Mountjoy stared at Finn and curved one thick eyebrow in a gesture of detached irony. "The only *logical* explanation that is. You see, with this Sun-Pluto conjunction, you ought to be doing something – almost anything – that's concerned with digging up what lies hidden beneath the surface. Coal-miner, for example, psychoanalyst, archaeologist, even brain surgeon – that kind of thing." He paused. "Or perhaps spy, under-cover agent, tomb robber maybe.....?"

Instantly Finn's brain had gone into red alert. Was it somehow possible that the astrologer could sense the scheme that he and Lascaris had cooked up in London? Could sense at least the deception in his presence? Just possible too that Lascaris was quite wrong – and that Mountjoy already knew *precisely* that his rituals seemed to produce sudden, unexpected discoveries…?

The astrologer leant back, disengaged from Finn's stare and gazed up at the ceiling, as if deliberately leaving Finn to hang in his own discomfort. After a long while he said, "Let's go back to Pluto. As well as Pluto, you also have Saturn directly conjunct your Sun, so their influence on your situation will be very powerful indeed. It would be unwise in the extreme to try to ignore these two planets because, in the end, they will inevitably devastate all superficiality and denial."

Finn had sat quite still. The words were vibrating in him as if Mountjoy had just prodded a deeply buried nerve. And suddenly he had felt the hairs on the back of his neck begin to bristle. What the hell had happened to his scepticism? What had started out as a kind of game was now beginning to feel dangerously out of control.

"A lot of things are about to happen," went on Mountjoy, still apparently oblivious of Finn's discomfort, as he jabbed his bony finger at the left edge of the circle. "For one thing, Uranus here is just about to move into the Second House, where he will directly oppose your sun. Uranus is the great awakener, so we can expect a lot of things to start to happen for you very soon, quite suddenly and unexpectedly."

The astrologer had pushed the computer aside then and folded his hands on the table. He had stared at Finn with those strange, opaque eyes. "With this chart," he said slowly, "a permanent status quo is not really an option. It's time for a big change." There was an almost threatening tone in his voice.

Finn had stared back, trapped in a labyrinth of feeling. He had come blithely in here – just as he had with Lascaris in London – confidently expecting a total charade. And now suddenly he feels stripped, disorientated, with all the shock of a man caught in an ambush.

He wanders out onto the garden terrace. He feels shaky now and slightly stunned, as if he has just been in a minor accident. He heads for one of the tables. What he needs right now is a drink.

EIGHT

The city of Cairo never sleeps. Even at 5 am, under the dim pools of orange sodium light, people are riding bicycles, stacking vegetable stalls, slicing gigantic water melons, strapping huge loads onto donkeys who stand with their heads bowed and their stick-thin legs spread in resignation. Lara watches in fascination as this nocturnal version of city life spools past the coach windows.

She has woken at four from a ragged sleep. The night has been splintered with strange dreams that are slow to fade back into the shadows – recurrent, shifting images of David Mountjoy. She had looked at her watch, yawned, then climbed out of bed and drawn back the curtains. The sky was still dark. She began to pull on her clothes. Far better to go for a walk in the freshness of the beautiful gardens than lie in this soulless hotel room waiting for a wake-up call.

Quietly she had opened the door. And stood transfixed. Further down the corridor Finn was emerging from a room with his back to her. He closed the door carefully behind him. He was naked, his clothes casually draped over his left arm, his fingers hooked into the backs of his shoes. A hotel key dangled like an ornament from his right hand. Unaware of her, he padded unconcernedly down the passage, unlocked another door and disappeared.

Birgit? It could only be Birgit. But *how?* She has seen nothing to connect them. No flirting, no intimate conversations, not even any meaningful glances. Within twenty-four hours! How the hell has he done it? How the hell have *they* done it? She shook her head in amazement and closed the door quietly behind her.

*

The bus finally shudders to a halt. Lara clambers out into the twilight. To her left and below her the vast spread of city lights is fading rapidly in the gathering dawn. A faint mist hangs over the Giza plateau.

"Impressed?" She looks round. Finn is standing beside her.

She frowns up at him. "By the city?"

He smiles. "Just open your eyes."

For a moment she stares around, mystified. Then she gasps and holds her hand up to her mouth in a gesture of total astonishment. "Oh my God!"

There they are, in overlapping formation, one behind the other. The Pyramids, so huge that she has been unable to see them, her retinal mind prepared for something singular, discreet, something to be easily encompassed by the eye. But these aren't buildings at all, aren't structures, surely aren't even man-made, so vast that they blot out the sky, rising like some huge geological event, connecting earth and heaven, thrown up four and a half thousand years ago by a culture that had yet to discover iron or steel or bronze or horses or concrete, millennia before aluminium or petrol engines, or compasses or lasers or steam power. Despite all the familiar images, all the photographs and picture books, *nothing* has prepared her for this. A deep sense of awe comes over her, and inexplicably she begins to cry. Then she feels an arm around her shoulders. She looks up. Finn is smiling down at her.

"The same thing happened to me the first time I came here. It's as if your brain just isn't prepared for anything so huge, isn't it?"

She nods and moves away. She's touched by his unexpected kindness. The arm had felt brotherly, but the memory of what she had seen earlier is still prickling her mind.

"Come along," calls out Mountjoy. He is dressed in a kaftan, with some kind of makeshift turban wrapped around his head like a bath towel. He looks like a random extra who has wandered off the set of *Lawrence of Arabia*. "We still have twenty minutes before the pyramids open and I want us to honour this moment with our first simple ritual." He turns and strides off purposefully away from the Pyramids in the direction of the city lights.

Finn shakes his head. "Where the hell is he going?"

"Don't ask me," says Edward. "He's a law unto himself."

After about a quarter of a mile, close to the edge of the plateau, Mountjoy stops and motions for the group to gather round him. The sun is coming up now, bathing the pyramids in flame-coloured light. Mountjoy glances over his shoulder at the Sphinx, then towards the pyramids. "We are standing here," he says, holding out both arms in one of his messianic gestures, "at the point of intersection between the energetic ley lines of the three great pyramids and the Sphinx. This is the precise point from which Imhotep, the architect of the pyramids, would have drawn his inspiration." Beside her Lara hears Finn let out an ironic puff of breath. "So let us honour the sacredness of the place and allow the psychic power of ancient Egypt to enter us. Form yourselves into a circle and when I begin the universal Omm chant, please follow me."

Lara feels self-conscious and faintly irritated by Mountjoy's autocratic manner. There is a brief moment of silence, then his voice rings out, "Ommm ...."

Reluctantly Lara takes up the chant. "Ommm ...." Within seconds she is aware of something happening in her body. It feels as if a huge bass drum has begun to reverberate in her blood, something vast and archaic of which she is only an infinitesimally tiny part. And yet – and this is so strange – at the same time she feels intensely energised, as if she has been connected to some greater power source.

As Mountjoy brings the chant to an end with a lowering of his arms, there is a long silence, a moment of total hiatus as they stand in the morning light at the foot of the pyramids. Lara can feel her whole body trembling. She glances across at Finn. He has a strange, incredulous look on his face.

"Ladies, gentlemen! Ride around the pyramids – very cheap! No baksheesh!"

Lara turns. An Egyptian in a fez and galabiya is coming towards them leading two matted, shambling camels. One of the camels draws back its rubbery, bristled lips and bares its yellow teeth in an ugly snarl. A cloud of rancid breath wafts towards them. In the background, a flotilla of coaches is beginning to disgorge its cargo of passengers.

*

It is after six when Finn comes down the stairs of the Omar Khayam Hotel. It has been a long, stiflingly hot day, full of colliding impressions – the pyramids, the surprising effect of Mountjoy's bizarre ritual, the afterglow of his night with Birgit, all somehow uncomfortably intermingled with the faintly unnerving presence of Lara. He has been glad of the long, relaxing shower to clear his head and now he is looking forward to the prospect of a cool drink in the garden.

He's pleased too to have made contact with his old friend Abdul Hassani in Luxor. Despite the necessarily guarded tone of their telephone conversation, there had been that one tantalisingly veiled hint – "Maybe I have a small surprise for you….." – that had instantly quickened his blood and stirred his dealer's adrenalin. Within three days he will be in Luxor and the waiting will be over. Then he can see what Hassani has to show him and, with the day of his own 'Solar Return', he can finally put Mountjoy's so-called 'psychic powers' to the test.

Just as he is stepping into the hotel lobby, his attention is caught by a long, black limousine drawing up outside. Cairo is a city of donkey carts and dusty taxis and sights like this are a rare event. As he watches, the near door opens and Alexander Lascaris steps out, wearing an immaculate khaki tropical suit. Instinctively Finn backs up against the staircase. From the other side appears a squat, sallow-faced Egyptian with a clipped black moustache. He is carrying a large briefcase. Side by side they cross the hall, deep in conversation and disappear into the lift.

Finn emerges in time to see the limousine draw away. He notices that he number plates are blank. He feels unnerved. But why? After all, he is due to meet Lascaris in Luxor within the next few days and it's perfectly logical that he would pass through Cairo on his way there. And the black limousine? If Lascaris is an habitual film-maker here – which he undoubtedly is – he would need to have high level government contacts and know the right people to bribe in order to secure the necessary permits. It all makes perfect logical sense. But still there remains an uneasy sensation of not quite being able to fit all the pieces precisely into the puzzle.

Still wondering, he steps out onto the long stone terrace. It is a beautiful, cloudless evening. From the tall eucalyptus trees comes the excited chatter of roosting starlings. And at this calm hour even the muted blare of the Cairo traffic sounds like a distant symphony. At the far end of the terrace he catches sight of Lara and Edward sitting in wicker chairs, deep in conversation. As he approaches he can hear them discussing the prospect of the next day's excursion to Alexandria.

"Believe me, Alexandria's a bore."

They both turn. Lara smiles up at him and gestures to the empty chair beside her. "Come and join us."

"If boring means quiet and uncrowded," says Edward, "after today's performance, that's definitely quite okay by me."

"Boring means boring. End of story." Finn settles into the chair and raises his hand to summon a waiter. "There's a tatty corniche, a few drooping palms, a hint of decadent colonial splendour à la Lawrence Durrell and some really bad sculpture from the time of Cleopatra and the Romans. Oh, and a pathetic phallic column called 'Pompey's Pillar'. Not a great advertisement for poor old Pompey, I'm afraid. And that's pretty much it. It's eminently missable."

The waiter arrives and they all decide on beer. He reels off the list of European brews – Heineken, Stella, Carlsberg ….? Or Nefertiti perhaps? "Nefertiti!" they chorus. The waiter smiles broadly at this display of local solidarity and disappears into the hotel.

"Yep," says Finn. "When you find something authentically Egyptian around here you'd better grab it and hold on tight before it disappears under the stampede of tourists."

Edward nods. "Not like the pyramids. It looks like they've been grabbed and stampeded over generations ago."

"I thought you were just being an irritating culture snob when you kept whinging on about the crowds in the beginning," says Lara.

Edward smiles. *"They have just as much right as you and I. We're tourists too, you know!"* He mimicks her schoolmistress reprimand.

"Sorry." She blushes and laughs. "Was I being prissy?"

Edward smiles. "Maybe just the tiniest bit."

Actually she had been surprised by the easy way he had just shrugged off her rebuke, as if it hadn't even touched him. She knows she has a sharp tongue and sometimes she can upset people, even when she doesn't mean to. She had been so irritated by the heat, the flies, the crowds that it had just burst out of her. But he seemed to let it flow past him, as if he scarcely noticed, a man invisibly armoured. She watches him now as he sits forward in his chair, talking to Finn.

"Being inside the great pyramid of Cheops was the worst," he says. "All those lines of shadowy figures stooping in the low tunnels, filing up and down the ramps looking like ghosts in the neon light. It was like something out of Dante's Inferno."

"Except that Dante would have kept them silent," says Lara. "Everyone was shouting at each other across the walkways and the tour leaders were waving placards and umbrellas and God knows what and screaming at the tops of their voices! It was a complete nightmare. That was when I grudgingly had to admit you might have a point." Edward raises his eyebrows in mock surprise and they both laugh.

"For me the real climax was in the burial chamber itself," says Finn. "It's probably the most sacred place in all of ancient Egypt, and we were jammed in there like a soccer crowd. And then the tour guides kept trying to demonstrate the remarkable acoustics by yodelling – as if the place was expressly designed for the Pharaoh to serenade himself in his bath tub!"

"I know," says Lara, shaking her head. "It's not that they *don't* have as much right as you and I. Of course they do. At least I'm right about that!" She tilts her chin ironically at Edward. "It's just that there's such complete lack of interest in what they're actually seeing, an absolutely mindless disregard for the spirit of the place. They might just as well have been at a circus or a football match. I think that's what finally snapped me. I'm just mightily pleased you hauled me out of there when you did."

Edward smiles. He had seen her body suddenly go rigid and knew he had to get her out before either claustrophobic panic or rage exploded in her. He had taken her wrist and forced his way towards the exit, quietly but determinedly shouldering people aside.

She laughs. "And when I finally got outside I was gasping for air like a beached fish!"

"And furious," says Finn.

"Right! And furious. But is it really going to be like that *everywhere?*"

They pause as the waiter arrives and sets down the tall flutes of beer. Finn runs his fingers down the beaded condensation on the outside of his glass.

"Most places, I'm afraid. But not quite everywhere. Either you have to get to the sites very early in the morning or very late in the evening. Or go to places which are simply not interesting to tourists."

"And Alexandria?"

"Alexandria's not interesting full-stop. But there'll be plenty of tourists. You can bet on that. It's another convenient venue for tour operators to ship unsuspecting day-trippers to.

Tourism is purely finance driven. Each sacred site becomes just a place to entertain the punters, who are usually bored by it anyway. Before long they'll probably be organising stag parties in the pyramids!" He pauses and stares down at his beer. "And that's incredibly sad because it's destroying one of the most beautiful countries in the world. And the trouble is Egypt's so poor and so damn vulnerable."

Lara glances at him, surprised by the deep, unexpected tone of hurt in his voice.

"So how are we going to survive?" asks Edward. "We elitist culture snobs who don't like the crowds."

"Well ….." Finn sets down his beer and stretches. "Number one, we can visit the museum this evening, instead of tomorrow morning with the rest of the group when it will be like a cattle market. Tonight is late-night opening, but nobody ever goes. The tourists are all in their hotels busy stuffing themselves with their prepaid dinners. We'll be nearly alone." He pauses. "*And* if you're prepared to brave the terrible wrath of David Mountjoy, I can show you some places where the tourists don't go."

"Well, the day after tomorrow is listed as a 'Day at Leisure' in the programme anyway. So that would be fine," says Lara.

Finn smiles. "Or we can always just skip Alexandria altogether tomorrow and play truant?"

For a moment they eye each other silently like three conspirators. Then, at the same moment, they all burst out laughing.

Lara smiles at Finn. "You're a bad man, Finn Connors," she says. " A very bad man indeed."

NINE

Grey threads of mist cling to the fields of cattle clover as they follow the narrow side canal that skirts the Nile. Far to their left the palm trees that border the great river lift their charcoal heads like dark fans against the whitening sky. With the sprawling, dimly lit suburbs of Cairo finally left behind, their early chatter has faded as the dawn has come up in a majestic blaze of crimson.

Lara leans half out of the open window, watching the landscape spool past, enjoying the warm tug of the wind in her hair. Up ahead a small boy in ragged pantaloons is leading two huge, heavy-footed water buffaloes across the road and down to the canal's edge. He heaves impatiently on the ropes threaded through the rings in their steaming nostrils. Beside their huge bulk he looks absurdly small, almost like a toy. Just beyond him a group of women, swathed in black, crouches in the shallows. Lines of white linen are laid out around them on the banks, waiting for the first scorching rays of the sun. The sound of their melancholy singing floats in the air.

She leans back and feels her breathing slow as a feeling of calm comes over her. Already, after just two days, she loves this country. It's so different from anything she has ever known in Europe. Every sight, every sound and colour, even its strange, exotic smells seem to open up in her a sense of spaciousness.

And she's surprised how much she has begun to enjoy this crazy trip despite her initial feeling of vulnerability. She likes the Scandinavians with their weird diets and yoga pants and crystal pendants. There's a kind of dotty gentleness about them. And yes, she definitely enjoys being the feminine link between these two attractive men, pulling the three of them closer together.

For a moment her mind wanders to her astrological reading with David Mountjoy the previous day. There had been – just as Edward had said – something so uncanny about the way he had *seen* her, almost as if he had known her since childhood. He had seen too, very precisely, the break-up that now seems to be fracturing her life. She had felt a surge of excitement, followed by a quick stab of fear, as he leant back in his chair, stared at her with those strange opaque eyes and then said very certainly, "*According to your chart, right now, here in Egypt, your fate is waiting for you*". Instantly she knew that he was right.

Looking back now, she realises that feeling had been there even on the very first evening in Cairo. Wedged into the claustrophobic taxi with Finn, gazing up at the colossal statue of Ramesses, with all the smells of diesel and donkey manure, garbage and spices churning in through the open window, she had felt something wanting to burst inside her, propelling her across the borders of who she has always been into not just a new geographical continent, but into another continent *of herself*. In some inexplicable way she senses that what is driving her now is no longer her past. No longer the decisions blindly taken, the mistakes made, the courses so carefully – and uselessly – plotted. What's past is past. What seems to be driving her now is her *future*, propelling her irrevocably further and further away from everything she has ever known.

She lets out a deep sigh and, for a moment, allows her mind to drift back to London. To Tim. What would he be doing now? Jogging in Holland Park? Or already at his chambers checking emails? It all seems so impossibly distant. Almost as if it is taking place on another planet. And yet....

It had been a grey Thursday morning.

"Go away *now*? What on earth for?"

Lara had hesitated, then very deliberately tapped the last grains of coffee into the cafetiere and cleared her throat. "I think what I really need right now is some space ....." Instantly she regretted the word.

"*Space?*"

She could picture him there behind her, his grey track-suit patched with sweat from his early morning run, black hair tousled, eyes theatrically widened in mock amazement. Suddenly her heart was beating wildly.

"It's only six weeks since we came back from an extremely expensive holiday on the beaches of Antigua, in case you've forgotten. And now you want *space*? You've no job ....."

She spun round. "*You* were the one who made me give up my job, remember?

"No children to look after ....." She gasped. *How could he?* How could he be so cruel? "And still you want space! It's not every wife who can just ...."

"I'm not every wife! I'm *me*."

He had folded his arms and raised his eyebrows in a studied look of shocked surprise, a well-practised courtroom gesture. Then, with ostentatious indifference, he crossed to the fridge, opened the door and began rummaging around. "And where might you go to get this *space* that's so important to you?"

Caught off guard, she hesitated. "I don't know ..... I just want to get away. That's all....."

He closed the fridge door and straightened. "*I don't know …..*" His voice carried the mocking whine of the playground. He cocked his head to one side and smiled down at her condescendingly. "You know what? You're like a child just running after one thing, then ….."

But she was no longer listening. Her body had suddenly gone very cold as if something just detonated inside her. "Don't call me a fucking child! As if *you'd* know what being a grown-up is!" He started to speak, but she cut him off. "No, you listen to me for once! You think you can treat me like a fucking retard, don't you? Just because people pay you ridiculous amounts of money for showing off in court and some girls are dumb enough to flirt with you. But you know what? Deep down they see the same as I do. Everyone sees it – that you're just an empty, arrogant, puffed-up, selfish windbag, oblivious of anyone except yourself, hiding like some frightened child behind all your pompous words! You're the fucking child in this house! You're ….."

His face had gone frighteningly blank. He came towards her. She backed up against the counter and closed her eyes, helpless…..

When she opened them he had gone.

She let out a deep sigh and slumped forward over the work surface. She waited until her ragged breathing slowed. Then, needing the steadying familiarity of routine, she picked up the kettle and started to fill the cafetiere. But her hand was shaking so badly that the water spilled and cascaded across the granite top. She put down the kettle and sank onto one of the high stools. She felt utterly drained. Provoking him to near violence had seemed like a kind of victory for a moment. But she knew it was a dangerous one. He was six foot three and she had seen a look in his eyes then like the blind aggression of a cornered animal.

From upstairs came the sound of the shower running, cupboard doors being opened and closed with calculated force, just enough to let her know that he was back in control and that the day was going on despite her childish tantrums. That *some people* had to go to work to earn the money to support her mews house and her smart clothes and her Caribbean holidays and …. and her bored, useless days at home.

Steadier now, she emptied the kettle into the cafetiere, waited a moment, then pushed down the plunger and filled a mug with coffee. She carried it through to the sitting room, sat down on the sofa and stared blankly out of the French windows at the limp daffodils in the terracotta tubs. A moment later, heavy footfalls resounded from the stairs. Then came the tinkling of keys being lifted from the Chinese bowl on the hall table, followed by ostentatiously casual whistling. The front door closed with a thud loud enough to shake the house.

Was this really how a marriage imploded? With no dramatically uncovered affair, or shameful secret exhumed from the past? Yet over these last weeks, a strange new element seemed to have entered her heart; something hard and inscrutable, slowly stripping her of her old illusions, peeling away all the fictions she has so conveniently invented for herself. And this new presence seemed to have a will of its own, and dangerous, corrosive weapons at its disposal. Like a recurring nightmare, a memory had kept surfacing that she had long tried to suppress – the one and only time she had gone to watch Tim in court.

It had been a damp October morning. The underground courtroom was pine-clad, neon-lit, claustrophobic with a mute, antiseptic sense of hopelessness. She had sat in the empty public gallery as he put on a virtuoso display for her, striding the floor, the lapels of his black robe clutched theatrically in both hands, wigged head deliberately thrown back to reveal his rugged profile, dark eyebrows steepled in mock surprise at each obvious lie from the pathetic, already broken figure in the dock. Yet – she had dutifully reminded herself as she felt the dismay gather inside her – weren't these precisely the qualities that had made him so attractive in the first place? The self-confidence, the dark good looks, the hint of arrogance? Watching him enjoy his own performance like some mating beast displaying, she had felt a sudden wave of disgust. And in a terrible flash of insight she glimpsed something she had always known and never wanted to see – behind all the arrogance and show lay an aching hollowness. And behind the hollowness, the suppressed rage of a needy child. It had been like opening a sacrificial animal and finding the heart rotten. Horrified, she had turned away. And made a terrible, subversive pact of silence with herself.

How much of her true self had gone underground that day, sacrificed to the so-called 'success' of the marriage! How could she have descended into such a wasted, pointless life of cruising the shops and social charity events and occasionally helping Jane out at the bookshop? How could she have allowed her career to collapse, her painting to falter, then stop altogether? How could *she* of all people have come to this? Out of nowhere, a hot cloud of shame had enveloped her, a sick, hopeless feeling of waste for these last empty years; for all the cowardly evasions, all the lost hopes and pretentious ambitions, all the unnecessary, humiliating compromises. And, in a sudden furious reflex, she had whipped back her arm and sent the mug spinning across the room. It hit the marble mantelpiece and shattered. The coffee flailed wildly across the walls and veneered the Hockney print.

"This is *my* life," she said fiercely. "*My fucking life!*"

For a moment everything went still. The stained shards lay glittering on the stone hearth. Her body was ablaze with energy. Then several things seemed to happen at once: the brass flap on the letter box clattered and she heard the sound of paper swishing across the polished wooden floor, followed by whistling and the dying thud of the postman's trolley on the cobbled mews. And, at the same moment, the strangest thought came into her mind, fully formed like a headline – *Something just opened in the Other World*. Feeling as if she was taking part in a waking dream, she walked into the hall and picked up the letters.

There were a couple of obvious bills and several of the usual thick packages for Tim. She set them aside on the marble table. At the bottom was a pale green envelope addressed to her with a foreign stamp – Denmark? – and computerised italic script. Curious, she went back to the sitting-room, kicked off her slippers and settled down on the sofa. She slit open the envelope with her thumb.

Inside was a thickly folded wedge of green paper. She flattened it on her knees. At the top of the first page was a drawing – a circle flanked by the heads of cobras and, spread out on either side, two elaborately feathered wings. Below: *Eternal Egypt – An Esoteric Twenty-one day Exploration of the Ancient Egyptian Temple Landscape*. An advertising flyer! She felt her heart dip with disappointment. Ever since she had joined that yoga class she had been inundated with such rubbish.

She ran her eye quickly down the itinerary, then flipped over to: *David Mountjoy, World-renowned Astrologer, Tarot Reader, Psychic and Expert on the Mysteries of Ancient Egypt* ….. followed by a description of the esoteric aims of the tour. The pretentious New Age language nearly made her toss the paper into the waste-bin. But some obscure instinct stopped her. She turned to the next page.

Forty-two questions to be answered from the Ancient Egyptian Book of the Dead.

Something in those archaic words seemed to silence her cynicism. Slowly she began to read, mouthing each question like a child:

> *Hast thou been envious?*
> *Hast thou told lies?*
> *Hast thou strayed from the path ordained for thee?*
> *Hast thou cared for thy body as a gift of great work?*
> *Hast thou understood that life ends only to begin?*

She felt her heart tighten. There was something so poignant, so *personal* in these questions. Why had this come today, of all days, when she felt so stripped, so utterly vulnerable? With an effort of will she forced her eyes down.

> *I am the last assessor, but mine is the question that can set thee free:*

Is There One Upon The Earth Who Is Glad That You Were Born?

She had sat and stared. And suddenly she was cut wide open by the ancient words. How could she not have seen it all before? It was as if her life had suddenly been split like a nut: one half brimmed with obvious 'success' – local girl from the Welsh borders made good, wealthy barrister husband, 'friends', Chelsea house, exotic holidays ….. How she must be envied!

And the other half? The other half was empty. Glaringly, gapingly, suddenly frighteningly, empty. She stared again at the paper. Was there indeed *one* upon the earth who was glad that she was born? She rolled over, hugging her knees to her chest. The words had opened up a pit of emptiness beyond anything she could ever have imagined. Her whole body began to shudder, the sobs bursting out of her with epileptic force.

After a long while her crying began to ease. She sat up. Strangely, she felt calm. It was as if her tears had somehow released a flow of new chemicals into her blood. Outside the window a blackbird strutted blithely on the grass, sending out the first liquid notes of its summer call. Moving as if in a dream, she went through to the study, swivelled the arm-chair and hopped up on the seat. Standing on tiptoe, she stretched to the very top of the bookshelves, until she reached the long-abandoned section of her childhood books. She selected one heavy volume, apparently at random, and pulled it down – *Ancient Egyptian Mysteries*. The top edge was thick with dust. She blew and it scattered in a theatrical cloud.

She settled down on the floor cross-legged, opened the book – and gazed in astonishment. The same round disc with its encircling cobras and elegantly spread wings stared back at her, absolutely identical to the green flyer now lying on the sofa! She frowned, unnerved by the coincidence. Then she shrugged. It must be just a standard Egyptian motif. But, at the same time, she had the odd sensation of something fitting smoothly into place.

She turned the page. A double-plate colour photograph of dawn over the Nile. Suddenly she could feel her heart thud against her ribs like a drum, as she sat and stared. The steel glint of the river filled the foreground and above, in dense black silhouette, rose a line of palm trees and the triangular, white sail of a boat. And far beyond, the distant outline of a mountain range, jagged and dragon-backed, surmounted by a vast glowing ellipse of blood red. The Egyptian sun was rising.

They have detoured away from the canal now. To their right the desert seems endless as it recedes in a series of sandy humps and hollows, already liquefying in the gathering heat. She glances sideways at Finn. He is leaning back casually, one hand on the wheel, watching the road ahead. She enjoys his easy charm and good looks, his careless disregard of convention and his open-handed way with people. There's a kind of profligacy to everything he does, so uncalculated, so totally unlike Tim. He is the sort of man you walk down the street with and, by the time you turn the next corner, he has already gathered six new friends, pulling them into the heat of his unfocused intimacy. And yet something in him feels slightly hidden. What you see is not entirely what you get. She wonders what David Mountjoy has made of his chart; but she suspects Finn won't give much away. Sometimes when she watches him moving amongst the group, laughing, cracking jokes, reaching out and casually touching others, as if they were just simple extensions of his own body, she thinks of her father – a man who had strode through life quite oblivious of the devastation he left behind him. Behind all the charm he would probably be just as ruthlessly self-centred as Tim, a lover who would quickly get bored with his new toy. And she certainly isn't going to fall for that! A casual affair on the rebound is the last thing she needs right now.

As if reading her thoughts, Finn glances across at her and smiles. She smiles back briefly, then turns to look out of the window again. Despite his almost ostentatious superficiality and that hint of ruthlessness, she can't help liking him. And

God, how much the sight of him emerging naked from Birgit's bedroom had unsettled her! That lean back and loose-limbed walk had ignited a sudden unexpected flash of female competitiveness. And ..... well, yes – she has to admit it – a stab of just plain, hot lust. Now that *has* surprised her.

"Christ!" Finn swerves to avoid a deep pot-hole. "It's a good thing we insisted on an off-road vehicle. Once you get away from the tourist areas the roads are terrible."

Lara shades her eyes and squints through the windscreen. She points at the blockish shape slowly growing on the horizon. It rises clear of the shimmering haze of the desert. "It doesn't look much like a pyramid to me."

"To my eyes it looks like part of the Manhattan skyline," says Edward from the back seat.

Finn laughs. "I promise you it's a pyramid! The collapsed pyramid of Maidum. It just hasn't looked like the proper thing for the last four thousand years, that's all. You're both spoilt from having seen the Great Pyramids at Giza first. Don't worry, you'll be impressed when you get there."

"What happened to it?" asks Lara.

"Well, it used to be just like all the others, smooth sides all round. What you see now is only the rough inner core before they put the outer limestone casing on. It was actually the very first proper pyramid to be built. That was probably part of the problem – they hadn't got the technology right. Or they just got grandiose and overreached themselves. We know from the way it's built that they kept on changing their minds. The project just got bigger and bigger as it went along. But in the end it got so big that it simply collapsed – exactly like Beauvais Cathedral. Millions of tons of masonry just poured down the sides like a sandcastle. I imagine the Pharaoh would have had something to say to the architect!"

Edward laughs. "But according to Mountjoy the problem wasn't really anything to do with the design."

"So what does *he* suggest then, from his superior viewpoint?" asks Finn with an ironic smile.

"Apparently there was a famous High Priest and Priestess here."

"Right. Rahotep and Nofret."

"Very knowledgeable for a banker," says Lara. Finn ignores her.

"Well, according to Mountjoy," goes on Edward, "they were running some kind of esoteric school out here, doing astral experiments and stuff. That's why they built the pyramid, to draw down the same cosmic energies which were being used to preserve the Pharaohs in the great pyramids at Giza."

Finn snorts. "Okay. So what happened then?"

"It seems there was a big love affair between Rahotep and Nofret and they hoped to make themselves immortal just like the Pharaohs. Apparently they pulled down enough astral power to do the job, but didn't know how to handle it. So it just blew the whole thing apart."

Lara looks at him incredulously. "Is that *really* how he explained it?"

Edward nods.

"Jesus!" Finn shakes his head slowly. "He's even crazier than I thought."

"Okay," says Lara sharply. "He may be off on his own trip there. But perhaps that's just a metaphor for something that really *has* a meaning." She pauses. "What I really don't understand, Finn, is why you would want to come on a tour like this, when you're clearly so sceptical of anything that's not strictly scientific or just plain bloody obvious."

There's an awkward silence. Finn frowns, then reaches out and ostentatiously tilts the mirror so that he can see Lara's face without turning his head. "It's simple," he says. "From the moment I caught sight of you in your skin-tight trousers at Cairo airport I had this deep inner conviction that I was astrologically fated to be with you."

"Christ, Finn!" explodes Lara in exasperation. "Aren't you ever serious about *anything*?"

"Okay," says Finn, holding her gaze in the mirror. "Perhaps I just wanted something different. I wondered what a tour like this would be like. You're not the only one who's curious, you know." He swings the car off the road onto a barely marked track that leads straight towards the pyramid in the distance. For a while they drive in uneasy silence as the car bumps its way across the desert. From the back seat Edward observes Finn and Lara, imperceptibly leaning away from each other as if to make their distance explicit.

And in her new heightened state Lara can feel his attention. Edward is quite unlike any other man she has ever met. She senses a kind of unseen hinterland in him, a private area just out of reach. All her life, all the way back to her father, she has been attracted to tall, good-looking, charismatic men. Men like Finn perhaps? But when that façade has crumbled, she has always ended up taking care of them. But in Edward there's a kind of dogged self-sufficiency, an obstinate tensile strength. She senses he is a man who doesn't need to be taken care of. But he's elusive too. She has seen how he manages to slip out of situations, not just with her, but with the others in the group. He's willing to listen but reluctant to get involved, as if he is somehow protecting himself. But when he had talked with so much passion about astrology that day in the hotel garden, there had been a fascinating, electric intensity to him. In short, he's an enigma.

Ahead of them the pyramid is coming closer, rearing up out of the vastness of the desert. Finally, wanting to break the silence before they arrive, Lara turns to Finn. "So what exactly did Mountjoy tell you about your horoscope then?"

"Oh *that*," says Finn contemptuously. "I could have got that for free out of the tabloids."

"Finn! That's completely...."

But at that moment they draw to a halt and Finn cuts the engine. In the overwhelming silence of the desert the bulk of the pyramid looms above them. From down here it looks gigantic. Its buff-coloured sides and truncated top give it the appearance of some grim mediaeval fortress. All around are mountains of debris, some sixty feet high, witnesses to its catastrophic collapse.

Finn opens the door, steps out and slams it behind him. He stands for a moment, holding up his arm against the sun. He squints towards the green line of the cultivation half a mile away, where the palm trees seem to be liquefying in the air rising off the desert.

"Strange," he mutters.

Lara comes and stands beside him. "Why? What's strange?"

He points to one edge of the gigantic pile of collapsed debris. Slowly Lara makes out the shimmering outlines of an old jeep, so dusty that it almost blends into the ochre rubble behind.

She turns to him. "Why's it strange?"

Finn shrugs. "It's just very unusual for people to come here. It's too far off the beaten track."

Edward comes and stands with them. "What's up?"

"Finn's upset that we aren't alone. This is his own private pyramid and he resents intruders."

"I just hate tourists," says Finn in disgust.

Lara pushes her dark glasses up into her hair and stares at him. She screws up her eyes against the light. "Then what the hell are *we*?"

"*We*," said Finn magisterially, "are travellers. There's a world of difference." He turns and strides off towards the pyramid. "Let's go and have a look anyway," he calls over his shoulder, "even if it *is* crowded."

"Crowded!" Lara gazes around at the empty landscape and shakes her head. "Finn, you're an impossible, arrogant son-of-a-bitch!" She shouts at his back. "You're an elitist snob! You're a male chauvinist …" She runs after him, laughing

Some ten feet above the level of the desert the black hole of the entrance gapes. Wooden steps lead up to it. An iron grille has been unlocked and thrown back, but no one is in sight.

"Aren't there any guards or anything?" asks Edward as he follows Finn and Lara up the steps. At the top he peers into the blackness of the shaft.

"The guardian probably came at sunrise to open up," says Finn, "and he'll be back at sunset to close it. Meanwhile I imagine he's got better things to do than wait for non-existent tourists to show up and give him minimal baksheesh." He puts down his rucksack on the wooden ramp, opens it and takes out a torch.

"You're well prepared," says Lara.

"Comes from being an old Egypt hand." Finn pats the rucksack. "Everything you need for a day out in Egypt is in here. Water. Two torches – just in case one gets stolen. Candles and matches for emergencies inside the tombs. An old copy of Baedeker – still the best guide book. And, inevitably, a roll of lavatory paper, again just in case." He rebuckles the canvas flap and shines his torch down the entrance shaft. The walls are black stone, polished to a glassy sheen by centuries of casual touching. A wooden ramp with handrails covers the stone floor. It slopes steeply downwards to a point where the white beam extinguishes itself in blackness.

Edward turns to Lara, remembering the Great Pyramid. "Are you okay to go in there this time?"

"Sure. This one's not crowded."

"I'll go first then," says Finn. "The ramp's even, but it's probably a bit slippery, so hold on to the handrails."

He disappears through the opening. Lara follows. Edward stands for a moment, surveying the desert as it stretches out to the north and west until it fades into the shifting haze. To his right is the clean, straight line of green where the cultivation begins. The fronds of the palms are motionless. The air seems filled with silence. Almost subliminally he registers that the jeep has disappeared now and that a figure in a galabiya is standing at the corner of the pyramid. Suddenly he feels reluctant to venture into the darkness of the shaft.

"Come on, Edward!" Finn's voice echoes hollowly up the stone passageway.

Edward sucks in a deep breath like a diver about to submerge, then turns and hurries after them. He can feel his heart pumping unnecessarily heavily against his ribs. He puts his left hand against it for a moment, as if to reassure himself.

The ramp leads sharply downwards. The air feels close and dense. Edward quickly catches up with the outline of Lara's shoulders and the bobbing of the torch as its beam sweeps over the blackness of the walls and ceiling. And still the ramp leads down and down, far below the level of the desert. The air grows colder.

Suddenly the passage levels out. They walk in silence. After a few minutes the ramp begins to climb again. The white beam swivels as Finn turns back to talk to explain, "It's built like this in order to ....."

But the sentence remains unfinished as a huge sound like the slamming of a great door echoes along the passage and a scalding blast of air spins them round and slams them down against the walkway.

TEN

All is darkness. Lara's hands fumble frantically, desperate to find anything solid. Her head is ringing like a huge pressurised bell. She wants to cry out, but something is stuck in her throat. Grit rasps between her teeth and sticks to her tongue. It clogs her nostrils and grates against her eyeballs. Her pupils feel as if they have been scorched. All she can remember is a deep thud like a huge bass drum echoing from the distance, and then something had sucked all the air out of the passage and punched her hard in the back. She puts her hand to her head. Near her right temple a lump is rising and she can feel warm blood pouring out of it. The thing in her throat is swelling uncontrollably. Desperately she clutches at her neck as the darkness begins to spin, gasping to find air. And then suddenly she vomits violently, again and again, until her throat is clear.

Able to breathe again, she struggles to a sitting position and looks around. *Nothing!* It's as if her eyes have been bandaged. As if the darkness is *inside* her. She begins to moan in a small, terrified voice. *"Oh Christ! Please. Please don't let me go blind. Please....."*

"Lara?"

The voice comes from just in front of her.

"Finn? Is that you?" She croaks out the words, then spits, trying to clear her mouth. Her lungs ache with the effort of breathing.

"Are you all right?"

"I think so. But I can't see."

"What the hell happened?"

"I don't know. Can you see anything?"

"Not a thing. I dropped the torch. Wait. I've got another." She hears fumbling. "Edward?" Finn calls out. "You there?"

"Yes. I'm okay." The voice comes from some way behind her. "I hit my head."

"Here it is." The thin white beam clicks on.

Lara blinks as the passage comes into focus. Her heart leaps with a surge of relief. "Oh, Christ!" She sighs and slumps back against a wooden upright of the handrail as the beam swings backwards and forwards trying to penetrate the blackness. The light glints off swirling clouds of dust. Finn is in front of her, almost close enough to touch. He is kneeling on the wooden walkway, his rucksack open on the ground.

She turns and looks back. Just within reach of the torch's beam she can see Edward fading and reappearing in the clouds of dust. He is sitting with his back against one of the wooden posts, holding his hand to the side of his head.

"What the hell was it?" asks Finn again.

Edward coughs, spits something out. "I think the roof must have caved in."

"But before that there was an explosion."

Lara scrambles to a sitting position. She rakes her fingers through her hair. It is caked with dust. She wipes the vomit from her lips. "There was a huge bang. It was as if someone had blown a hurricane down the passage. That's all I remember."

"Okay," says Finn. "Let's see if I can find the big torch." He swings the beam across the wooden planking. The air is starting to clear, the dust settling down on the boards like a fading snowstorm. He shines the torch into the narrow space between the edge of the walkway and the granite wall. "There it is!" He rolls over onto his chest, thrusts his right arm down into the gap, then moves closer to the edge, trying to reach in with his whole shoulder.

"Shit!"

"What is it?" asks Lara.

"Can't reach it." He presses his head against the wall and shines the beam onto the stone floor below them. "It's broken anyway. The glass and the bulb are smashed. We'll have to make do with what we've got."

Finn rolls over, puts one hand on the rail and pulls himself to a standing position. He wipes his left hand over his face, then shakes his limbs. "Nothing's broken, at least. See if you can both stand." He moves towards Lara, offers his hand and pulls her up. He shines the torch on the side of her face. "You all right? It looks like just a cut."

"It's okay."

"Edward?"

Edward has scrambled to his feet. He is holding a handkerchief to the right side of his head above the hairline, where a rosette of blood is already oozing through the material. "Yes. I'm all right. It's not serious."

Finn walks up to him, takes away the handkerchief and inspects the wound. He nods. "It's quite deep, but you'll do. Okay, let's go and see what's happened."

He leads the way, keeping the torch beam on the floor in front of them. For a few yards the wooden planking is flat. Their feet rustle on the boards, stirring up new clouds of dust. Then the gradient begins to rise. They walk in silence. After about a hundred paces the dust on the planks grows thicker, scattered now with pebbles and small blocks of stone. The blocks grow larger. Finn stops, shines the torch directly in front of him.

"*Jesus!*"

Lara gasps and clutches both hands to her mouth, trying to stifle her scream.

The whole passage, from side to side, from floor to ceiling, is filled with sand and masonry. At the level of the walkway it fans out in a gentle slope towards their feet. Lara leans against the handrail and bites hard into her knuckles as she stares at the wall in front of her. A small grey stone detaches itself and rolls silently to her feet.

"Okay," says Finn. "Let's try to find out how bad it is." His tone is matter-of-fact, but underneath Lara can hear the tremor of fear.

"How far down the passage are we?" asks Edward.

"That's the question," mutters Finn. "That's the fucking question alright." He runs his torch again over the grey-white wall of rubble in front of them, then turns. "Let's go all the way back to the burial chamber. Then we'll pace it out."

They take Lara between them as they retrace their steps, down the long slope, along the flat passage until the walkway begins to rise again, now steeply. Then, out of the darkness, two wooden steps appear and above them a horizontal stone slab, worn to a dip in its centre. They step over it into the burial chamber. Finn shines the torch upwards. The ceiling opens up and disappears into blackness.

They are standing in a square room, perhaps twenty feet by twenty. In the centre of the floor is a rectangular depression about four inches deep. Along one wall a low bench has been hewn out of the rock. All four walls, the undulating floor, the upward sloping angles of the ceiling are made of polished black granite. They stand for a moment gazing up into the darkness, feeling the weight of the millions of tons of stone above them. The air is hot and heavy, strangely inert, as if no one has been there for thousands of years.

Finn sets down his rucksack, kneels and begins to rummage inside. Then he stands up, holding a battered blue and white copy of Baedeker's *Guide to Egypt* in his right hand. He shines the torch on it and begins leafing hurriedly through the pages. His fingers slow. "Okay, here we are: *Maidum – built by ….. collapsed in ….*" He turns the page. "This is it – *The sloping granite passageway which links the burial chamber to the entrance in the north face of the pyramid measures one hundred and eighteen meters.*" He pauses. "One hundred and eighteen meter….. One hundred and eighteen meters," he repeats slowly. "I have about a sixty centimeter stride. So that would mean ….?" He hesitates. "One hundred and ninety-five paces, I think." He looks up at Edmund, then at Lara. "Are you both okay to come?"

Lara nods. Any movement would be better than sitting alone in this silent stone hollow, buried in the rock. Finn positions himself carefully on the granite threshold. "I'm going to call out each pace. If I miscount one tell me. I'll backtrack and pick it up again. Alright?"

Lara hears him draw in a deep breath. Then he stretches out his left leg and carefully places his foot in the first slightly elongated stride.

"One hundred and ninety!" Finn's voice rises, echoing down the passage. The wooden planking vibrates with each tread. "Ninety-two, ninety-three, ninety-four!" He digs the heel of his boot into the pile of sand. "One hundred and ninety four!"

He spins round. In the torchlight his face is alight with excitement. "One hundred and ninety-four! We're at the entrance! It's not the roof that's collapsed. Something must have slid down from outside. It can't be more than a metre thick! Maybe less." He begins to sweep away the lower rubble with his boot.

"How do you know your paces are accurate?" Edward's voice is taut with anxiety.

"They're accurate enough!" shouts Finn angrily. "They're fucking well accurate enough! Do you have any better ideas?"

Edward draws in a deep breath, turns and looks at Lara, then back at Finn. "So we dig?"

"Right," says Finn, regaining his composure. "There's only room for two of us at a time. We'll do a rota." He looks at his watch. "Fifteen minute shifts. Then the one on the left falls out and holds the torch. The other one takes his place. Okay?"

Edward nods and moves up to Finn's right. Lara sits down on the wooden planks and shines the torch on the grey wedge of rubble in front of them. Finn takes off his watch and passes it to Lara. "You keep time."

She sits in silence, watching them work. Almost instantly their shirts are black with sweat. She watches their shoulder muscles rise and fall as they grab boulders and blocks of stone, wrench them away and drop them with a heavy thud into the space beside the walkway. They work rhythmically, like miners at the coalface, using their cupped hands to scoop away the powdered rubble, the silence broken only by their grunts of exertion, the thud of a stone being discarded.

Within minutes Lara knows it is useless. Each space they clear is instantly filled with rubble pouring in from above. Wherever their scooped hands create a hollow, within seconds there is only smooth grey dust and pebbles. She thinks of the pyramid as she had seen it this morning, its huge granite bulk towering above them, taller than a ten-storey building, blocking out the skyline. How much has come down? It could be tons. Perhaps hundreds of tons. Perhaps thousands. *And they are trying to clear it with their bare hands!* It could take weeks for anyone to get through.

Suddenly, as if jolted by an electric charge, her whole body begins to shake. "*It's no use!*" she screams. "*It's no use!* Can't you see? Every time you clear something, more sand just slips straight in. We can't clear that with our bare hands. *We just can't!* There could be tons of it".

Finn spins round. His breath is coming in short gasps. His mouth is half open. His face pours with sweat. In the torchlight he looked like some underworld troll. "What the hell are you talking about?" he shouts.

"She's right," says Edward. "It's useless. It'll never work." He turns, wipes the sweat away from his forehead and sits down on the mound of sand. His fingers leave white streaks across his face.

Finn glowers at him. "So what the fuck do *you* suggest we do then?"

"Wait," says Edward quietly.

"*Wait?* Are you fucking crazy?" Finn clenches his fists as if he is about to hit him. Then he turns back to the blocked doorway and stares at it. "It's got to work! *It's got to!*" He begins scrabbling frantically at the mound, hurling rocks aside, throwing sand wildly over his shoulder. The air begins to fill with dust. Lara lunges towards him. But freezes. Finn has started to growl. And now, as the sand pours down, burying his arms to the elbows, the growl rises in his chest and bursts out as a terrible animal scream. It goes on and on until Lara covers her ears with her hands. Then Finn wrenches his arms clear, whips round. His legs buckle. He slumps back against the rubble, eyes closed, his mouth slackly open. A thin stream of saliva trickles from the corner of his lips. There is a quiet swishing sound as a white pebble dislodges from the top of the mound and rolls away into the blackness below the walkway.

Edward takes the torch and crouches down in front of Finn. He holds Finn's chin in his right hand and turns his head so that he is looking directly into his face. Finn's eyes are blank, unconscious, as if he was gone from behind them.

"I think he's fainted," says Lara.

Edward shakes Finn's head gently. "Look at me."

Finn gives a low groan.

"*Look at me!*"

Slowly the eyes begin to focus.

"We'll be okay," says Edward quietly, staring into his eyes. "We just need to sit calmly and wait. They'll get through to us. Thank God you had the sense to bring the water."

For a long moment the two men stare at each other. Then Finn nods, takes Edward's hand and squeezes it hard. "Right," he says. "Thanks. Let's go back to the chamber and stretch out." He pulls himself to his feet.

The air in the burial chamber is stifling. Finn picks up his rucksack and extracts two white candles, a box of matches and a large plastic bottle of water. He sets the water down on the floor, strikes a match and lights one of the candles. He holds it out in front of him. Lara notices that his hand is steady now. The practicalities seem to have calmed him. For a while they watch the small yellow flame in silence. Suddenly the flame begins to flicker, bending first one way, then another, leaning towards Lara, then righting itself, then leaning again.

Finn jumps up. "Air!" he whispers. "We've got air! There must be an air shaft."

Lara's heart crashes against her ribs. "Perhaps if we could find it ....? There may be a passage or something." She grabs the torch, swings it round the chamber, then up. Above there are only layers of overlapping granite disappearing into blackness. "Perhaps a secret passage that no one knows about!"

The two men stare at her, their faces grotesque in the candlelight. She spins round to the wall and begins to run her hands imploringly over the granite as the crushing reality of their situation avalanches through her last defences – the huge, indifferent mass of the pyramid, the terrifying fragility of her own insignificant life. Frantically she tries to force her fingers between the joints. "There must be! *There must be!*" Her whole body is shaking epileptically. And then the cry that she has been holding down suddenly rips itself free and tears its way out of her throat. Her scream fills the chamber and echoes up into the cavity above them.

Edward steps forward and slaps her hard across the cheek. She whips round and sinks to the floor, sobbing, her face buried in her hands. Edward crouches down beside her. Very gently he lays a hand on her shoulder. "There's no other way out," he says quietly. "If there were it would have been found centuries ago."

"But if there's air ....." She looked up at him imploringly. "Surely ..... surely....."

"He's right." Says Finn. "Most pyramid chambers have air vents to the outside. But they're tiny, maybe just an inch in diameter. The only way out is the one we came in. But at least we've got air. And water. We can wait for days if need be."

He reaches down and takes her hand. He pulls her up and for a moment holds her to him, straining to give her comfort. Then he goes to the broad ledge and picks up the bottle. He passes it to her. "We'd better all wash our mouths out, otherwise the dust will dehydrate us. Then just a small sip each at intervals. We need to ration it. I'll time us." He clicks off the torch and sets the candle down on the ledge beside him. Lara passes the water to Edward and sits down on the stone bench. And suddenly a huge lethargy descends on her, as if she has been drugged. "I feel exhausted," she says and slumps sideways beside Finn. Within seconds her body is rising and falling in the slow rhythm of sleep. Finn brushes a strand of hair from her face.

"Is she okay?" he asks.

"Sure. It's the aftershock. Once the huge amount of adrenalin begins to dip you're left exhausted. It's best she sleeps anyhow."

For a long time the two men sit in silence. Then Edward turns and looks at Finn. "Are you really a banker?"

Finn starts, then draws his knees up under his chin and stares at the ground. "Why on earth do you ask that?"

"Because I don't think you are."

For a while Finn is quiet, weighing his options. Strangely he feels relieved by Edward's question.

"No," he says at length. "I'm an art dealer. I buy and sell antiquities." He gives Edward a very direct look, as if challenging him.

"You mean the kind of things we saw in the Cairo Museum?"

"Right."

Edward nods slowly. "Okay ..... Now it all starts to make sense. But why all the secrecy? Why the banker cover?"

"Because," says Finn slowly, "dealing in antiquities is totally illegal here. The maximum penalty is ten years' hard labour. Not many of us Europeans would even survive that sort of sentence in an Egyptian prison. And the whole country is full of informers just waiting to be bribed. Or aggrieved middlemen who feel they should have been paid more. Not to mention all the people who may suspect what you're doing and want to blackmail you. It's a bloody minefield for people like me."

"But then why do it, if it's so dangerous?"

"Probably precisely for that very reason," says Finn with an ironic smile, remembering one of Chloe's frequent jibes: *You'd be bored if you weren't permanently living on the edge.* "And sure, the money's an attraction. Sometimes you can buy an object here in Egypt and sell it for twenty times the price on the London market. Maybe fifty times. That's a lot of profit." He pauses. "But if I'm really honest, I guess it's the excitement as much as anything. And the beauty of the objects, of course. Ask any antiquity dealer, he'll tell you the same."

"What started you in that business? It's so unusual."

Finn stretches out his legs, laces his fingers and stares up into the blackness of the corbelled roof. "Well, I left Dublin and went to London when I was seventeen. The only thing I knew then was that I wanted to deal in antiquities. It was like an obsession. But the problem was that I didn't have any money. That's a very bad combination – in the London art world a dealer with no money is the lowest form of life. The first couple of years were tough – and, frankly, pretty bloody humiliating. I had to eat a lot of shit. I used to charm the rich, stuck-up dealers into giving me something to sell on consignment. Then I'd run around the corner and flog it to the competition for twice the price. But I could never really make enough money to get properly started."

"So how did you?"

"Well, in my third year, just when I was getting really desperate and wondering if I shouldn't give it all up, I got a lucky break. There was a rumour going around the market that there had been a big find just north of Rome – an intact Etruscan tomb. Normally the *tomboroli* – they're the local tomb robbers – who found it would simply dig it up, smuggle it out to one of the customs free-ports in Switzerland and then on to the big dealers in London or Paris or New York. Everyone made money. No problems. Only this time there *was* a problem. The tomb was smack on the border between the territories of two rival gangs of *tomboroli*. Things got pretty rough. And then one of the *tomboroli* was shot. Of course, everyone was scared shitless, because they knew that now the heavy brigade from Rome was going to come in and, as all the dealers said, no-one in their right fucking mind would touch the antiquities then."

"But *you* did?"

Finn nods slowly. "Right. *I* did. I was the only stupid bastard who was crazy enough, or desperate enough, to go down there. But it paid off. I got the entire contents of the tomb – sculptures, vases, some incredible gold jewellery, the whole lot – for twenty thousand dollars. That was a mere fraction of its normal price. They were almost begging me to take it off their hands."

"And you managed to sell it?"

"Within a month. I called a well-known collector in New York – someone who would normally have been way out of my league – and he flew over and bought the whole lot for a million dollars. The established dealers were furious when they found out. As far as they were concerned, I was just a small-time runner muscling in on their big client. They tried to scare the collector off by telling him that the goods were stolen and about the murder and everything. But luckily he was a tough guy and he wasn't interested. And after that I could really go into the market and buy the best things. So with just one jump I was clean through the hoop into the big-time. I got lucky, I guess." He pauses and stares at the ground for a moment. Then he turns to face Edward. "But you know what? It wasn't really the money that counted. I recognised that even back then. For several weeks I was on a kind of incredible high. It was an experience I could never forget."

"Addictive?"

Finn hesitates. Then he gives a wry smile. "*That* would be the perfect word to describe the antiquities market."

Lara stirs and mumbles something. They both look at her anxiously, but she seems to fall back into her deep sleep. Some detached part of Edward is aware that they are deliberately using up the time, keeping the terror at bay with talk. But he is fascinated too by Finn's revelations. It's as if, pressed to the wall by their situation, he is finally putting aside his well-practised charm and beginning to show himself.

"What attracted you to antiquities in the first place?"

Finn lets out a long puff of breath and for a while is silent. He seems to be reluctantly dredging up memories, perhaps in two minds how to answer. Finally he says, "It really all began way back when I was seven. Home life was pretty bad, you know. School was even worse. I was in one of the roughest areas of Dublin. Then one day, probably out of desperation, the teacher – a Miss Flannery, a cross-eyed old bat with thick brown stockings – took the class to the National Museum." He shakes his head at the memory. "For me it was like entering another world. Everything there was made of gold and silver. And it was all so beautifully crafted and inlaid. There were bracelets of twisted gold and armlets and crowns and massive solid gold torques to be worn round the neck. And brooches and swords and daggers with inlaid scabbards and carved ivory pommels. The whole thing screamed of a life of glory and dignity and nobility and all that stuff. And all I knew then was drunkenness and beatings and cockroaches under the bloody sink. I stayed there for hours. I was completely oblivious to everything else. They only noticed when they counted us back on to the bus. Miss Flannery had to come back to get me. She was apoplectic with rage. I got strapped for it, of course, but I didn't care – I was used to that. And besides I'd discovered the one thing in the whole world that really meant something to me ….."

He pauses, staring at the ground. Edward stays quiet, silently urging him to go on.

"After that I went back every single moment I could. Entrance was free and the guards were very kind. They gave me sweets and called me 'The Little Celt.'" He smiles. "I could stay there as long as I liked. It made me different from the other boys, of course, and that could have been a problem, but I was a tough kid too – with my home life I had to be – so no one tried to mess with me. Later, as things got really bad at home I started doing drugs and nearly lost my way completely. There were gangs in our area and people wanted me in their gang because I was smart and I could fight, but somehow the antiquities kept pulling me back into that other world. Most of the people I hung out with at that time are now doing ten year stretches for robbery with violence and stuff like that. I think the museum really saved me ….."

He hesitates, as if doubting whether to go on. Then the words start to flow out of him like a confession. "My father was a failed actor and a good old-fashioned Irish pisshead. It wasn't all the time with him, thank God, but when it was he'd beat my mother up, then me if I tried to interfere. But it was my mum who really worried me. In the beginning she was all right, and maybe it was living with my dad that did it, but eventually she became a full-blown boozer, morning to night. And a so-called clairvoyant. She would lay the cards for people who wanted to know about their futures, for God's sake. And sometimes she would go upstairs with the men afterwards. She was a sort of part-time hooker, I suppose. When I was seventeen, after my Dad had left – even he couldn't stand it any longer – I came home one evening and she was sitting on the living-room sofa stark naked. The place stank of vomit. I can smell it now if I think of it. There were pools of vomit all around her, vomit all over the sofa. Vomit on her breasts. I knew I had to do something to help her, but she started screaming at me – "Get the fuck out of here you little cunt." I left and I told social services and the next week I was in London. I've never been back. I just couldn't take it any longer."

He stops and stares up into the darkness. Then he turns and says the thing that Edward has already guessed: "I've never told that to anyone in my life before." Edward holds his gaze and nods, aware that to speak would break the moment between them. He can see in Finn's face the shock and relief of a man who has at last, forced by the extremity of his situation, started to tell his story. Without our stories, thinks Edward, without attempting truthfully to tell our stories, we're just the fictions that we have dreamed.

"How do you feel?" Edward asks at length.

Finn nods thoughtfully, as if trying to take stock of his inner world. "Okay. Actually good. Surprisingly good. And exhausted."

"Me too," says Edward. "It's the aftershock. It's a chemical reaction – a big hit of endorphins. Let's try to sleep. We should save the candles anyway. We don't know when we might need them."

"Right," says Finn.

And the last thing Edward sees is Finn's giant shadow on the wall and the small plume of yellow dancing in the void.

Then Finn's breath extinguishes it.

In the blackness time disappears. Lara sleeps fitfully now, caught in a space between sleep and waking. She wonders at Edward's stillness, his apparent lack of fear. Sometimes she can hear him breathing evenly as if he has fallen into a deep sleep. Once, she finds his hand and they hold each other. His hand is dry and consoling.

Gradually she feels herself become weightless, as if she is suspended in space. Then, without warning, the panic begins to surge up in her like a floodtide, threatening to burst through and shatter her self-control. But just when she feels on the brink of collapse, some hard, terrified structure inside her seems to give way and she finds herself drifting in the darkness, suddenly inexplicably calm. She imagines herself cradled by a huge protecting arm, not crushed by the towering mass of stone above her, but cocooned by it, merged in it, as if her arms, her legs, her mind, her entire being is somehow dissolved now in the great bulk of the pyramid. She starts to breathe more deeply. The air no longer seems stale and heavy. She can feel her blood, her very heartbeat take on a slower rhythm, as if she is a hibernating animal waiting out the long stretch of winter.

She thinks of Tim, of her life in London. Both seem unreal. As unreal as if she were observing the earth from the moon. She lets them go, imagines them spiralling up like plumes of smoke into the black funnel of the corbelled roof above, leaving her with a strange, unexpected peace. Gradually she lets herself drift into the hands of Egypt.

At some point in the night, at a moment when the darkness has become their whole world, something seems to enter the chamber. Each feels it in their own way. Finn's restless sleep becomes calm. His breathing lengthens. Edward lies quiet, surprised by his own lack of fear in the face of potential death. He thinks of Kate. He can *feel* Kate. Not just the familiar pain of her absence, but the presentness of her too, as if she is suddenly there, stripping the shadows of his grief. His mind wrestles to make sense of what is happening. Thoughts bend themselves and buckle. And yet, in a place beyond thought, he can feel something quietly settle down inside him. And for the first time since Kate has gone he feels a true sense of peace.

He hears Lara shuffle beside him. He puts his arm around her and she lays her head on his shoulder. He listens to her quiet breathing. And they both pass into a dreamless sleep.

Lara stirs. Something is wrong. There's a sensation like feathers or dust moving across her bare arms. She jerks up, brushes at herself frantically. She scrabbles at the bench around her with her fingertips, trying to get her bearings. Then, with a low moan, she slumps back against the stone wall and buries her head in her hands as the realisation of where she is sinks in.

But something *is* moving. Over her hands, her face, her arms, her ankles….. *Air! Fresh, clean air slowly sliding through the burial chamber!*

She sits up, listening. Something in the quality of the silence is different. No longer so all-encompassing. Time passes. And then from the distance comes a faint scraping sound. She fumbles blindly, grabs Finn's foot and shakes it hard.

"Finn, wake up!"

A match scratches in the darkness. She sees Finn, in silhouette, moving cautiously towards the doorway, shading the flame with his open hand. His shadow is huge against the granite wall. He stops. The match gutters and goes out.

"Light!" The word seems to catch in his throat. "Christ! I think there's light!"

He strikes another match, reaches into his pocket for the candle. Edward and Lara press themselves against him as they peer down the blackness of the tunnel. Then, like a sound from another world, a voice comes echoing along the passage, calling out in Arabic.

"*Here!*" screams Finn. "*We're here!*"

Their cries ricochet down the darkness. Then Finn is off along the passage, the torch beam bobbing in front of him. "*Come on,*" he shouts over his shoulder. "*Quick! Come on! Come on!*"

ELEVEN

They come up into light and air.

At first Finn's shoulders stick in the narrow opening. Then he grips the stones on either side, pulls hard and wrenches himself free. He sucks in great gulps of air like a diver breaking surface. Blinded by the sunlight, he stumbles and leans against the granite doorway. He feels the stone warm against his back, the clear heat of the sun on his face. A titanic wave of gratitude washes through him. Slowly the world comes into focus: the ochre drift of the desert, the shimmering green of the palms, the arching, endless, *endless* blue of the sky. He blinks the glare out of his eyes. "*Jesus, Jesus, Jesus.*"

From his left he hears Lara gasp. She clutches at him, covering his face and neck with kisses. Her body heaves with sobs. Then another pair of arms encircle him. Sweat plasters their clothes to their bodies as they cling to each other, laughing hysterically like children, doubled over, overwhelmed with relief, until the tears pour down their dust-caked faces and their sides ache.

"Pliss."

They stop. Finn looks around. Below them five men, almost black-skinned, their long *galabiyas* tucked up above their knees like pantaloons, are staring up at them in astonishment. Sweat trickles down their bony legs. Shovels and pick-axes lie in the rubble around them. A small mechanical digger stands off to one side. Beside it is a squat man in rumpled army fatigues and a black beret. His round, moon-like face radiates concern. "Pliss," he repeats. "To come." He spreads his hands apologetically and gestures with his head towards a battered khaki minibus.

Finn turns, scanning the landscape. "What happened? Where's our car?"

The soldier shrugs in incomprehension. "Pliss. No car." He makes a vague, faintly hopeless gesture with his outstretched hands. "No car," he repeats and moves towards the minibus.

The police station at el-Akhmin stands in the centre of a straggling collection of mud-brick houses. It is constructed of grey breeze-blocks and a corrugated iron roof. Steel bars slat the windows. Where glass had once been a few sharp spikes now project from the rotting frames. A lugubrious soldier stands aside to let them pass through the low doorway. In the cramped room beyond, a ceiling fan revolves with a slow rhythmical creak. Its thick wiring hangs like a swag across to the window. Outside a generator is clattering noisily.

The place is sparsely furnished: a wooden desk, an old-fashioned black bakelite telephone, a two-drawer khaki filing cabinet, the lower drawer missing, and four maroon metal and plastic chairs. Every surface seems covered in a layer of dust. The soldier calls out in Arabic and a moment later an old man, bent almost double with age, appears carrying four glasses of red tea on a copper tray. He sets them down on the desk. The soldier opens the filing cabinet, extracts a pad of yellow paper, a pencil and a pack of cigarettes. He offers the cigarettes, then settles into his chair and smiles nervously. "Pliss passports."

"What for?" asks Edward.

"Pliss."

Lara sighs and collapses back in her chair. The euphoria of escape is ebbing and the exhaustion hits her now like the workings of a drug. She glances across at Edward. His eyes are sunken and black-rimmed. Dried blood cakes the gash in the side of his head. Beyond him she can see Finn's haggard face smeared white with dust. "Do we *really* have to go through all this?" she asks irritably. "A pyramid collapses on top of us and all they want to do is look at our passports!"

Finn shrugs, reaches into his pocket and hands over his passport. "I think they've got us by the balls. We'll just have to give in to Egyptian bureaucracy. Otherwise we'll be here for ever."

The soldier stacks the passports neatly on the desk, then picks up the top one and opens it very carefully, as if he is handling a rare manuscript. He stares at the first page upside-down.

"I have the feeling," says Finn, "that this is going to take a very long time. We'll just ….." But his voice is interrupted by the sound of a car drawing up outside. Its powerful engine dies away. Two doors thud like muffled gunshots. The soldier drops the passport and jumps up. He smooths down his rumpled khaki tunic and hurries from the room. For several minutes there is a rapid exchange in Arabic. The soldier is speaking loudly as if his volume has been turned up. The other voice is almost inaudible.

Then the door opens and a tall, slim man enters. He is wearing a pale grey suit and a striped silk tie. His black hair is parted in the centre and brushed flat against his skull. A cigarette dangles from the fingers of his right hand, trailing the sweet smell of Turkish tobacco. Despite this exotic detail, he brings with him into the sweltering Egyptian chaos of the room a chill blast of northern efficiency. Without speaking he moves behind the desk, wipes the seat of the chair with the back of his hand and sits down. He studies each of them carefully with a slow, demanding gaze. Lara stares anxiously back. There is something chilling about those inscrutable eyes and that unremarkable sallow face. Something that feels quietly ruthless, untouched by pity or self-doubt. Involuntarily she shivers.

There is a long, uncomfortable silence. At length he says, "My name is al-Shaikh. Firstly, on behalf of the People's Republic of Egypt, allow me to apologise for this most unfortunate accident in which you have been involved." His English is faultless, almost without accent. "Such incidents are virtually unheard of in our country but .....," he shrugs slightly, "when one is the custodian of a civilisation that is more than five thousand years old not everything can be guaranteed .....

"I don't think it was an accident," cuts in Finn. "We heard a ...."

"Please, Mr Connors ....." Al-Shaikh holds up his hand to forestall any further interruptions. "You have all had a very exhausting and trying experience. It would not be surprising if you were feeling a little confused." He stresses the last word, then picks up the top passport and begins leafing through it. His eyes flicker between the pages and the faces opposite. "We know exactly what happened. Our engineers are already at work. Unfortunately the pyramid will need to be closed for several months while we secure its safety." He picks up the second passport.

"Please," says Lara. "We'd really like to get back to Cairo as soon as possible. We're very tired."

Al-Shaikh stops and gives her a long, appraising look, clearly unused to so much dissent. "Of course, Madame," he says with exaggerated politeness. "That is precisely why I am here – to expedite your return." He glances at the third passport, then up at Finn. Slowly he begins leafing through the pages. "I am putting my car and driver at your disposal. It is air-conditioned. I think you will find it most comfortable."

"But our car ...." protests Edward

"Please, Mr Cavanagh, do not concern yourself," says al-Shaikh. "Your luggage has already been loaded into my car."

In the tense silence that follows, the ceiling fan creaks rhythmically overhead. Lara can feel the anger rising in Edward. "After what we've been through," he says firmly, "we'd much rather go back in our own car. We ...."

"I am afraid that is impossible," cuts in al-Shaikh. An unpleasant hint of steel has entered the voice. "It will be much safer this way. I do assure you."

"*Safer?*" Lara looks at him in alarm. "I thought you said it was an accident."

"I mean," says al-Shaikh slowly, as if explaining something to a slightly backward child, "that you have all had a great shock. I do not think it would be safe for you to drive in your condition."

On an instinct Lara glances sideways. Finn is leaning back in the chair with his arms folded, feigning relaxation. But she can see that his folded knuckles have gone white and a small muscle is twitching rhythmically in the side of his jaw. Everything about him seems to have gone into red alert. Suddenly she feels afraid.

"Will you be coming with us?" Finn asks, unable to conceal the tension in his voice.

Al-Shaikh gives him a long, questioning stare, as if he is interrogating him. "Sadly no," he says at length. "I must stay and attend to matters here." He gathers the passports between his hands, stacking them like cards. "There is just one other thing." He pauses, eyeing each of them in turn. "I must ask you not to mention this matter to anyone."

"*What?*" bursts out Edward, clearly unable to contain his simmering anger any longer. "We get trapped inside a pyramid and nearly die and you ask us not to talk about it!"

"Please," says al-Shaikh quietly. "I am afraid I must insist."

"And if we just decide to ignore your insistence?"

Al-Shaikh carefully aligns the edges of the passports and taps them on the surface of the desk. He waits a long time before he looks up. Then he gives Edward a cold confronting stare. When he speaks his voice is like steel. "Then we may be forced to detain you in Egypt for longer than you wish, Mr Cavanagh. *Much* longer. We have psychiatric institutions in our country for the long-term treatment of those traumatised by shock. Sometimes the patients never fully recover." He pauses, allowing his words to penetrate. "I hope I make myself entirely clear."

Lara gasps. Fear squeezes her heart, not just for the brutal threat that al-Shaikh has been holding out, but for something more intangible, even more sinister, like a barely glimpsed flash of a shark's fin in the water. Al-Shaikh holds out the passports and places them on the far edge of the desk. "My driver will take good care of you," he says. Then he rises, nods curtly and leaves the room.

Outside stands a black Mercedes 500 with darkened windows. A ring of ragged children are staring in silence from a respectful distance. Otherwise the street is deserted. The car has been freshly washed, the windows and paintwork glisten. Dark wet patches on the ground are rapidly shrivelling back into the dust.

As they leave the police station, the driver's door opens and a man steps out. He is wearing black trousers and a white short-sleeved shirt. He is built like a middle-weight boxer, his arms corded with muscle and matted with thick hair, his head close shaven. Without speaking he opens the back doors and stands waiting.

As Finn circles the car he notices that the number plates are blank. He slides in beside Lara as Edward climbs in the other side. The driver shuts the doors, then slips behind the wheel. There is a muffled clunk as the central locking snaps home. Inside the temperature drops twenty degrees. The air smells of cool leather.

Lara shuffles forward on the seat. "How long will it take to Cairo?" she asks, as if trying to strike up a casual conversation with a London taxi driver. The man turns and frowns.

"You don't speak English?"

He spreads both hands, then touches his lips with his index finger and shakes his head.

"We obviously aren't going to get much out of him," she says and settles back in the seat. The driver throws the engine into life. There is a powerful roar, then almost silence as the car slides forward and gathers speed, throwing up a cloud of dust. The ring of children parts. A knot of chickens scatter with a flurry of wings. Suddenly there is a muffled thud from outside. Lara spins round and peers through the slatted blind that shades the back window.

"Oh, God!"

"What is it?" asks Finn, craning his neck

"He hit a dog! And the bastard hasn't even blinked."

She sits back and folds her arms angrily. For a long while she is silent. Then she says, "What did you make of that whole …." But Finn's knee bangs against hers. She glances at him with an enquiring frown. Finn lifts his chin almost imperceptibly towards the stocky shoulders and thick shaven neck in front of them.

"*Speaks English?*" Lara mouths the words.

Finn's glance flickers towards the mirror. The black eyes are observing them dispassionately.

"We're all very exhausted," he says. "We might as well sleep all the way to Cairo."

He leans back in the leather seat, folds his arms and closes his eyes. Lara stares at him. His right eyelid flutters in the faintest of winks.

"Right." She settles back beside him and leans her head against his shoulder.

TWELVE

Nadia Rusedska stands in front of the long mirror and inspects herself. She has changed twice before finally settling on the scooped ivory dress that shows off the start of her suntan. She picks up a pair of long gold earrings from the dresser and holds them up. She tilts her head left then right. Too exotic. She drops them back in the padded box, extracts a pair of cut glass studs and examines them carefully. More restrained. Much more suitable. She passes the spindle through each lobe, checks the mirror with satisfaction, then takes up the octagonal bottle and dabs Dior to each side of her neck, the insides of her wrists and finally into the exposed space between her breasts. She runs her hands over her hips, smoothing down the dress, pleased it shows off her slim waist and that its cut is low enough to expose the tops of her breasts. She smiles. After all, she knows it gives him pleasure. She can tell by the way he looks at her. And the way he treats her here is so different from Europe or America. Always before she has been the dutiful student, but here he seems to regard her as more equal, perhaps simply as a woman. And she loves too the way he introduces her everywhere as 'my colleague', as if quietly bestowing on her the mantle of his fifty years of scholarship.

In the weeks before the trip she had moments of panic when she regretted her impetuous acceptance of his offer.

After all, she hardly *knows* him. At least, not in that personal way. For her he has always been some kind of icon, an unachievable rôle model, and her decision had felt reckless. But all her anxiety had evaporated the moment she saw him at Cairo airport. After years of formality it was an almost unimaginable transformation. Gone were the sober jackets and ties. Instead he greeted her in patched khaki trousers and a loose bush shirt. On the cross-town journey to their hotel she watched in amazement as he revelled in the chaos of Cairo and delighted in the ancient, ramshackle Landrover with its complicated gear-shift system. It was suddenly so clear to her that *here* was where he was truly at home. Not in New York or London, Berlin or Oxford. Not in the library or classroom. Not even on the lecture podium which he commanded with such legendary authority. She could sense how, over the years, Egypt must have sustained him in those dry academic deserts.

His Arabic was fluent, and everywhere they went they were fêted. The faces of swarthy temple guards would light up as they ran forward to embrace him like an old friend. Doors into locked tombs and normally sealed excavation stores were miraculously opened. Whenever he tried to dispense *baksheesh*, it was politely refused with a shake of the head and a dignified bow. Within minutes of their unannounced arrival at the Cairo Museum, the Director had come scuttling out to offer his services. And with each encounter he discreetly enquired about the mysterious Alexander Lascaris, dropping careful hints about the cosmetic box – but always to no avail, turning back to her with a faint shrug and shake of his head.

He was passionate about everything Egyptian. Not just the archaeology, but the teeming life and chaotic energy of the place, its colour, its history, its myths. He particularly loves the ramshackle country crossroads where the local farmers and peasants, the *fellaheen*, sit for hours, surrounded by their families and livestock, bartering food, arranging transport, swapping gossip. He has taught her the Arabic names for the numerous different kinds of palm trees and the crops in the low-lying fields and explained the ancient ways of extracting water from the Nile – the *shadouf*, a kind of bucket wheel, and the *sakhia*, driven like an Archimedes screw. From time to time he regales her with personal – and usually highly indiscreet – stories of famous Egyptologists – Gardiner, Aldred, Wenlock. He has known them all. He had even worked with Howard Carter, the legendary discoverer of Tutankhamun's tomb, who feels like a figure out of mythology.

And then there is the Nile. She has sensed from the start how it is so much more than just a river for him. Whenever he talks of it, its power to regenerate the land, its strange visceral mythology, its historical significance, his face becomes radiant, the lines in his forehead suddenly smoothed. Her heart swells to see it. And she senses it isn't only the Nile. There is a tenderness about his quiet care of her here that makes her feel so treasured, so incredibly safe, so *feminine*, as if this is a long-awaited homecoming, a birthright that has always been unfairly denied her. And now she doesn't want to give it up. *Ever.* Already, after only four days, when she thinks of the end of the trip, she feels a deep melancholy descend on her at the prospect of returning to the damp, grey Edinburgh weather, the stultifying restrictions of the museum, the small-minded, self-serving attitudes of her fellow academics.

As the days pass in his company she becomes increasingly aware of how much, over the years, Dortmann – strange that she still can't bring herself to think of him as Bernard – has formed her vision and honed her love for Egyptian art. It's an immense debt that she owes to him. As he guided her through the monuments – Giza, Memphis, Sakkara – it became so achingly clear that *this, here*, was why she has studied Egyptology in the first place. Not to fight political battles with her stuffed-shirt colleagues, or sit alone in some cramped, dingy office typing up display labels no one bothers to read.

Her mind drifts back to The Godhurst Museum, with its shiny green copper dome and spiralling mosaic-floored rotunda, the founder Sir Henry Godhurst immortalised in a marble bust that squints down from a high alcove. It had been Dortmann who had alerted her to their search for a full-time curator of Egyptology, hinting that it would be the logical stepping-stone one day to the coveted curatorship at the British Museum. He had provided the references, wielded his influence and eventually shepherded her into the job.

At first she hated the greyness of Edinburgh and its unrelenting weather. Hated her shabby, inadequately heated apartment. Hated her jealous, mean-spirited colleagues, who treated her with the casual disdain reserved for brash New World academics. And most of all she hated the uptight British men with their phoney manners and covert lechery. Except for the one brief adventure with that antiquities dealer from London – and that had been a terrible mistake – she has been living in a sexual and emotional desert.

For months she had sat in her cramped office doggedly sifting through the eight thousand uncatalogued objects brought back from Egypt by Sir Henry Godhurst in 1884. The loneliness and boredom had been intense and sometimes she even hated her mentor for steering her into this deadly provincial backwater. But gradually, as she levered open packing case after packing case in the mildewed, vaulted stores, she began to feel a grudging respect for the courage and taste of the long-dead Victorian philanthropist, who had braved malaria and banditry to assemble this extraordinarily diverse collection.

For three long years she had cajoled and charmed the finance out of reluctant government departments and grey-faced local bureaucrats. She had even slept with that creepy dyke from the National Lottery Committee, just to secure their grant. Despite the endless jealousies in the museum, she had hired new staff and technicians, stubbornly battered away at the inertia of the establishment until she could finally present the world with an array of Egyptian galleries so clear, so beautiful, so respectful of the original architecture, that even her many detractors had to give grudging praise. Even on the bleakest Edinburgh days she can feel herself straighten with pride whenever she enters *her* galleries. For all the dyed-in-the-wool conservative enemies she has made in that archaic city, for all the academic back-biting she has had to endure, *this* is her answer. An outsider she will always be in that moribund establishment. But *this* no one can take away from her.

She checks her watch. Seven-thirty. Still a quarter of an hour before Dortmann will collect her for their dinner at the Omar Khayam Hotel. She stands once more before the mirror, smoothing back her long auburn hair, placing her left hand for a moment against the side of her face. Strange how her jaw hurts this evening. In the cold and damp of Edinburgh it gnaws like a tooth-ache all year round, far worse even than in the bitterest New England winters or the freezing chill of Gdansk. But *here?* In the dry heat of Egypt? It feels like some kind of strange premonition. Very gently she puts the tips of her fingers to that small lump half way down the left side of the long bone of her jaw. It's an imperfection invisible to others. They see only her wide-awake dark green eyes, her broad sensual mouth, her delicate nose, the determination in her chin. But she knows it is there. That small, almost invisible reminder.

Just as she is about to turn she stops, arrested by the reflection of her square unvarnished nails against the sharp line of her jaw. Instinctively she closes her eyes and, without warning, the vision comes, like a shape rising through water.

The face blotched with stubble, the stench of stale whisky …. Her freshly painted scarlet finger-tips spread proudly on the kitchen table. Bloodshot eyes coming closer. The familiar, disgusting smell making her want to vomit.…*Whore! Filthy Whore!* Splatter of saliva across her face ….. Splinters of pain cutting through her head. Exploding into darkness. Then the white uniform bending over her ….. *Where are your parents, honey? Where are your parents?*

Her jaw had been wired up for months like something out of a hardware store.

She opens her eyes and stares at her unvarnished hands, then crosses to the bed and sinks down. *Why now? Why this evening of all evenings?* It feels like a touch from another world.

*

Lara has showered, washed her hair and put on the only dress she has brought, a simple white cotton smock. Despite the ordeal of the last thirty-six hours, she feels strangely refreshed and alert as if, in some secret fashion, the escape has gifted her a new appetite for life. They have agreed to meet at ten, but she has come down early and sits now opposite the lift, happily observing the passing hotel guests. She enjoys trying to puzzle out their histories and imagining the invisible vectors of their lives. A tall, distinguished-looking man, probably in his early sixties, is crossing the marble-floored hall now. He is dressed in a khaki tropical suit. Beside him walks a much younger woman, attractive, with auburn hair and elegant long legs. The man is clearly telling a story, lifting his bearded chin in emphasis, while his right hand carves shapes in the air. The girl stares up at him with an almost childlike look of pleasure on her face. Then she laughs, confidently slides her arm through his and he briefly touches her hand with his own.

Could they be lovers? As if in answer to her own question she shakes her head. There was something about the man that felt too paternal, almost too gentle, to be sexual. They pass through the glass doors at the far end of the hall and out into the night. At the same moment the lift doors slide open and Finn and Edward emerge. They come towards her side by side. For the first time she notices how much a pair they seem, in spite of their obvious physical differences, almost like two brothers who each take after a very different parent

Finn sees her first. "Wow! What a fantastic looking chick!" he says to Edward out of the corner of his mouth in an exaggerated stage whisper.

Edward hesitates for a moment. Then he smiles and nods solemnly. "Oh yes, *very* sexy. And look at those amazing legs! Have you ever seen legs like that before? Do you think we could get her to have dinner with us?"

"No problem," says Finn. "Leave this to me." He approaches her with an pantomime swagger. From the corner of her eye Lara can see Edward looking at her legs. Suddenly she feels self-conscious. She begins to blush. Then she looks down and laughs. "You two are a pair of jokers!"

"Finn's persuaded them to serve us dinner in the garden," says Edward. "By the sound of it he's organised an Egyptian banquet worthy of Farouk."

"I thought that way we don't stand much chance of running into the rest of the group," explains Finn. "I didn't think any of us would feel too much like company tonight."

Lara smiles. "Will they really serve us in the garden? Finn, you're an absolute genius!"

"Nothing to it," says Finn with a small bow. "They'll probably serve us on the Nile if we pay them enough. That's the wonderful thing about Egypt. The bad news is that nothing ever works here because there aren't any rules. The good news is that because there aren't any rules, absolutely *anything* is possible. At least with a little *baksheesh*."

Laughing, the two men take Lara between them and she slips her arms through theirs as they walk towards the open doors onto the garden at the back of the hotel. Suddenly the evening feels strangely festive. A round table has been set up under a tall palm tree. The ridged trunk and curved underside of the fronds are lit by a garish yellow spotlight at its base. Two candles in glass funnels spread their flickering light over the crisp white cloth. In the centre of each plate stands a tall flute of champagne, the bubbles flickering in the light.

Lara stops and stares at the glasses. "What's this?"

"When one has escaped death by the narrowest of margins," says Finn with a theatrical flourish, "what else would one drink but champagne?"

Suddenly her mood evaporates. Why does he have to turn *everything* into a joke? We nearly died in that pyramid, for God's sake! And yet here he is already trying to reset our emotional clocks back to zero as if nothing has happened.

Finn catches her glance and makes an ironic face as if to undercut his own remark, then he wraps his arms around them both and squeezes them hard. They sink into their chairs and raise their glasses. And for a long while no one speaks. Lara glances at Finn. He has tipped his chair onto its rear legs and is staring up at the night sky, his head thrown back, inhaling deeply as if drinking in the air. It's true, there's a kind of animal throb to him that she can't help but find attractive, even when he disappoints her with his superficiality. It just feels so unnecessary; he's worth more than that. But the problem is that disappointment is the one thing she can't bear; she has endured a lifetime of it with her father. But perhaps she has been unfair to him just now. After all, it had been his command of the situation that steadied them after the explosion.

A moment later, two white-jacketed waiters emerge from the restaurant, carrying trays on their shoulders. They spread an array of Arabic *mezehs* across the table. Finn explains the food: '*Kishik*', yoghurt pasted together with onions and butter; '*Mashi*', vegetables stuffed with herbs and meat and '*Tranaya*', deep fried fava bean balls, and half a dozen other dishes. For a while they are quiet, picking from their plates. At length Lara sets down her glass, leans forward and puts her elbows on the table. She looks at Finn. "How did you know the driver could speak English?"

Finn lifts his eyebrows in surprise. "Did he look like a chauffeur?"

"He looked like a killer to me," says Lara angrily, remembering the dog.

"I guess he was the bodyguard," says Edward.

Finn nods. "Something like that, I suppose. Only, if he was a real bodyguard, a personal minder, he wouldn't have left al-Shaikh alone. I think he was a kind of government storm-trooper. Not a man to mess with, that's for sure."

"Who is al-Shaikh anyway?" asks Edward. "Just appearing out of thin air in the middle of the desert, wearing an impeccable suit and tie and with his big, black, shiny, air-conditioned Mercedes waiting outside."

Finn shrugs. "No idea. But my guess is Secret Police. And high up. *Very* high up. Government level. That degree of sophistication doesn't grow on trees in this country."

"But why would someone that important be so interested in *us?*" asks Lara. "And did you notice? There was something really weird."

"What?"

"The driver took us straight to our hotel." She pauses. "*But no one asked us where we were staying!*"

Edward frowns. "I guess they could have checked us out somehow. Through the car hire company maybe? Or the travel agency?"

Lara looks unconvinced.

"That wasn't the only thing that was weird," says Finn. They both turn to him. He is drumming the tablecloth rhythmically with the end of his knife.

"Well ....?" says Lara.

"He knew all our names."

"That's easy. He had our passports."

"Yes, but he knew *my* name *before* he picked up any of the passports."

"So?"

"So, even if he somehow did know our names already from the car hire company or something, in order to know that I was Finn Connors and *not* Edward Cavanagh when he spoke to me, he would have had to have seen a photograph of me, *in advance.*"

They both stare at him.

"And there's another thing," goes on Finn. "He went right through my passport and didn't bat an eyeball. He didn't ask me a single innocent question."

"Why should he?"

"Because," says Finn slowly, "my passport, from beginning to end, is absolutely jam-fucking-packed full of Egyptian visas. Don't tell me he wouldn't ask about that!"

There is a long silence. Then Lara looks very directly at Finn. "So why *do* you come here so often, Finn?"

Finn glances at Edward, then leans towards Lara and folds his arms on the table. He clears his throat. "Yes," he says, "You're right. There's something I want to tell you."

It is after midnight when Finn has finished talking. The fading roar of the Cairo traffic drums in the distance. A moth has slipped into one of the wind lights and is batting frantically against the glass. Edward slides his fingers into the funnel, grasps its wings and releases it into the night sky.

It is Finn who finally breaks the silence. "I know I have already told Edward something of this, but I have now shattered the one absolute golden rule for any antiquities dealer. I have told you both the truth about my presence here in Egypt. And by doing so I have given myself completely into your hands."

But even as he speaks he is aware of all the things he had *not* told them, as if, despite his wish to be open, his dealer's wariness is too genetically ingrained to be abandoned altogether – even now, after all they have been through together. And besides, there are things he is having trouble admitting even to himself – the whole fantastical plot he and Lascaris had hatched that grey morning in Islington: how he would join the tour, and they would use Lascaris's contacts in Egypt to dig wherever Mountjoy performed his Rite of the Solar Return and smuggle any objects they found back to London, where Finn would sell them, dividing the profits fifty-fifty. Logically it's all insane. He knows that. And yet....

And yet, even though he can't explain it, there is something here that he just can't let go of.

Lara is staring at Finn. Then she nods slowly, as if confirming to herself something she has known all along. "Now it all starts to make sense," she says quietly. "And *of course* Edward and I aren't going to tell anybody. You know that, for Heaven's sake!" She is aware too of a feeling of relief, as if Finn's sudden honesty has made him more real again, more the person she wants him to be. But still something feels not quite right ….. "But then what on earth are you doing on this tour?"

Finn is rolling his wine glass uneasily between his outstretched palms. "I have a possible lead to follow up when we get to Luxor. As a dealer, if I travel in a group I'm much less obvious. My passport just slides through with all the others."

"But *this* group? Doing rituals all over the place? We're hardly inconspicuous! If you'd wanted to be anonymous you could easily have gone with Thomas Cook and totally disappeared in the crowd."

Finn shrugs. "Maybe I just thought it might be different." He smiles at Lara. "And perhaps I just knew I was fated to be with you."

Lara ignores him. "Actually," she says sharply, "I don't get what you're doing here at all! To judge from what you've said, the authorities may already be aware of you. They could put you in prison – an *Egyptian* bloody prison, for God's sake – if they caught you. And still you're here! Are you completely crazy?" She turns to Edward with a look of desperation. "You're a psychoanalyst. Can *you* explain this to me?"

"It's simple," said Edward. "It doesn't make any logical sense. It's probably bloody dangerous. But he still can't leave it alone. In short, he's addicted to the process of dealing." He turns to Finn. "Right?"

Finn shrugs. "Something like that, I suppose." He looks at Lara. "You've probably never met an antiquity dealer before?"

She lets out a dismissive puff of breath. "Luckily not."

"Well, we're pretty much all like that when it comes to the possibility of a new discovery. If you haven't experienced the excitement, you can never really understand it."

"Jesus!" says Lara and throws herself back in her chair. "You must all be nuts to risk yourselves like that." But, despite her exasperation, she feels afraid for him. There's something so blind and relentless in his character. She remembers her shudder of premonition as he had dismissively held up his sinister-looking Tarot card that first morning and smiled. She leans forward again. "But, Finn, listen. Surely this whole thing is incredibly dangerous. We nearly died in that pyramid. That must mean that that man ….. whatever his name was ….."

"Al-Shaikh?"

"Yes, al-Shaikh. He must have engineered what happened there just to get rid of you ….."

Finn shakes his head emphatically. "No. That wouldn't have had anything to do with him."

"But then, if not him, who the hell set the bomb to make the entrance cave in? It just doesn't make sense….." Her voice trails off.

Edward and Finn glance at each other. "Islamic fundamentalists?" says Edward.

Finn nods. "That would be my guess. The Maidum pyramid is on the edge of Middle Egypt, and that's their stronghold."

"Okay. But why? Why *us*?" Lara's eyes widen with shock. "Don't tell me it could equally well have been anyone – say a random group of tourists from Milwaukee!"

Finn shrugs. "Why not? It was just ….."

"A coincidence?" Lara raises her eyebrows ironically.

"Yes. Why not? Coincidences do actually happen, you know, in spite of what Mountjoy may say about synchronicity and the inescapable forces of fate and all that guff. Perhaps, just for once, it was a good old-fashioned, straightforward, no-nonsense, honest-to-God, unfated coincidence. It just bloody well happened to be us and not someone else!"

Lara looks unconvinced. "But why Maidum? And why just three random tourists? That's hardly worth the risk, is it?"

Finn shrugs. "I don't know. A good place for a trial run for something more spectacular elsewhere maybe? There's virtually no security to hamper them at Maidum – in case you hadn't noticed."

"Okay," says Lara, "but why would the Fundamentalists do that at all?"

"It's simple," says Finn. "They want to halt the tourist trade. Full stop. They blew up a couple of hotels on the Red Sea and even massacred an entire group of tourists a few years back, gunning them down in front of Queen Hatshepsut's temple in Luxor. And for a while it worked. The foreigners stayed away. But the Egyptian government just waited a few months and then announced that all the terrorists had been rounded up and executed and the place was quite safe again, and gradually the tourists started to trickle back. Also the Fundamentalists here have become more sensitive to international criticism since then. Their ultimate aim, at least for most of them, is to take power and form a radical government, not to be seen as mediaeval terrorist savages and become an international pariah like the Taliban."

Lara frowns. "I don't get it. What's the difference between shooting someone in cold blood and making a pyramid collapse on top of them? Murder is murder. The international community isn't going to be very impressed by a group that goes around blowing up tourists."

Finn shakes his head. "Don't you see? If the Fundamentalists could make it look as if it wasn't actually an explosion at all, but that the monuments themselves are unsafe – can you imagine the thoughts of the millions of tourists who go in and out of the Pyramids every year, not to mention all those claustrophobic tombs in the Valley of the Kings, if they believed there was a risk that the thing might collapse while they're inside? It would mean that something like that could easily happen *anywhere*. *At any time*. *To anyone!* Prospective tourists in London or Paris or New York wouldn't even be able to *look* at a poster of the Great Pyramids without shitting themselves with fright. You can see the headlines now:

Egyptian Pyramid Collapses,
Burying Hundreds Of Tourists Alive!

If our story hit the international press it would halt the tourist industry here overnight. And permanently. Al-Shaikh's no fool. Why do you think he went to such lengths to hush us up? They can keep the tourists coming by pretending that the terrorists have all been executed, but they can *never* guarantee that all the monuments are safe. It would be a smart move by the Fundamentalists."

"How serious would it be if tourism here failed?" asks Lara.

"You see the poverty all around you," says Edward. "Egypt has virtually no oil, not enough agriculture to feed themselves, scarcely any real industry. The population is exploding. Take away the tourist trade and pretty soon the economy would collapse."

"But what on earth would the Fundamentalists hope to achieve from that? Wouldn't it just make things worse?"

"Egypt is on a political knife-edge," says Finn. "The place is a hot-bed of dissent. If you have no functioning economy, then pretty soon you'll have a revolutionary situation, swiftly followed by an Islamic Fundamentalist government, like in Iran. At least that's what the Fundamentalists hope. I can't imagine ....." He breaks off. A waiter is approaching them across the lawn. Most of the lights in the restaurant have been switched off. The palm trees are now in darkness. The waiter swiftly clears the table. Edward reaches into his pocket and hands him a note

"*Shokrun, shokrun!*" The man smiles broadly, bows to each in turn, then gathers up the tray and disappears into the hotel.

"Do you think al-Shaikh was serious about his threat?" asks Lara.

"About putting Edward in a so-called loony bin for life? Oh yes, he was serious all right. He's not the kind to joke."

Lara leans forward, puts her elbows on the table and pushes both hands through her hair, scraping it tight to her skull. "There's another thing that spooks me," she said nervously. "Why are those two Egyptians following us everywhere?"

"What Egyptians?" asks Edward. "Aren't there always Egyptians hanging around a group, just being curious, or trying to sell something, or hoping for *bakhsheesh?*"

"But the same two *everywhere?*" insists Lara. "Giza, the museum, Memphis. I even saw them outside the hotel this evening! Like they're the group's personal minders or something – but always hanging back, trying to be inconspicuous." She turns to Finn.

"I suppose they could be extra security," he says. "The Egyptian government's paranoid about tourists getting attacked." But even as he speaks, he is aware of the lack of conviction in his own argument. He has seen them too and – he now realizes

– has tried to brush them aside. But another part of his mind knows all too well that the Egyptian authorities would *never* normally assign two men to such a small, insignificant group. And certainly not in plain clothes. Something isn't right. In the back of his head an alarm is starting to sound.

The last of the restaurant lights go out and they are left with the white tablecloth, the two candles burning in the glass funnels and the faint spread of stars above. Their faces look ghostly in the dim light. Beyond the Nile the Cairo traffic hoots and rumbles. For a long while they sit in silence. Speech suddenly seems to have exhausted itself. There are too many questions, too few answers. The terror of the previous night is still too close, too vast to be absorbed.

And in the stillness comes the realisation that, in some way they cannot yet articulate, the events of the last thirty-six hours have changed their lives for ever. Like sole survivors from a battle, they are set apart from the world now by that experience and joined to one another by a silent bond. Something that can never be broken.

At length, Finn clears his throat. "There's something else." He looks embarrassed. "It's weird… my watch stopped in the pyramid."

Edward raises his eyebrows. "Two o'clock?"

"Right."

"Mine too."

They look at Lara. Slowly she nods.

"I wondered about it too," says Edward. "But then I realised it was just the blast. It must have been around two o'clock, mustn't it?"

"That's what I thought at first," says Finn. "But then I realised that today's the eighth. Right? And the date on my watch had moved on!"

They both stare at him in bewilderment.

"Don't you see? That means that all our watches stopped simultaneously at two o'clock *this morning*. While we were trapped in the burial chamber."

Lara's eyes widen with shock as she remembers that strange feeling of some presence entering the chamber. She turns to Edward. "Is that really possible?"

"I don't know," he says slowly. "It seems so."

"Dear God," whispers Lara. "*What kind of a country is this?*"

PART TWO

I am like Osiris, my desires fragmented.
I am the pieces of myself, a man longing for union.

The Egyptian Book of the Dead
ca 1500 BC

When they pulled out my brains through my nostrils with long-handled scourers, when they eviscerated my belly and took out the contents, when they drained my blood and packed my body with natron and herbs — rosemary and juniper, myrrh and sweet-smelling frankincense — I, Akhenaten, Pharaoh of Egypt, watched from above.

From my vantage point I saw that treacherous priest Amenmose as he carried in the four jars of the forbidden gods of the old way — baboon-headed Hapi for my lungs, the jackal Duamutef for my belly, the falcon Quebshenef for my long intestines and he of the human face, Imsety, to receive my liver — and I knew then that the oracle of the High Prophet of the Aten would be fulfilled: that the old ways would come again and the corruption of the priests of Amun would seize hold of the land. I saw then the vision — the city of Akhetaten, beloved of the light, laid waste; the houses and gilded palaces crumbled into dust; the great temple of the Aten destroyed; the fields sown with salt; the Nile choked with grief and the heresies of the many gods imposed once more upon Khmet, the black land of Egypt.

But what he did not know, that fat treacherous priest, whose sweat I could smell as he laboured in the heat of the panther skin, his body dripping with ointments, was that I, Akhenaten, denied my place amongst the Immortals, could see every deed and every creature on the face of the earth. From this blackened pit above the Western Desert, denied by an act of treachery the daily rising of the Aten, I see into the hearts of men.

And here amongst the rocks I await the fulfilment of the prophecy: that when a new force arises in the East I shall be released from this accursed tomb and my time shall come again.

THIRTEEN

"Hey, Mister!"

A small girl in blue pantaloons and a ragged patchwork top stands boldly in front of Finn, barring his way. Her thick chestnut hair is bundled back from her face and clamped in a pink plastic clip in the shape of a butterfly. Her enormous brown eyes survey him steadily. In her right hand she holds up a chicken by its legs, offering it to him. The animal protests with a pathetic flap of its wings.

"*La shokrun*," says Finn politely.

The girl blinks in astonishment to hear a European speaking Arabic. Then she bursts out in a peal of excited laughter and steps aside, casually stroking the chicken with the back of her left hand. Finn watches her spin round and shoot off down the narrow street, still laughing, the unfortunate chicken clutched like a rag doll. He shakes his head and smiles. He would have liked to make her happy – but what the hell would he do with a live chicken? The girl waves as she dips into an alley and disappears.

The air of the Luxor bazaar is thick with the scent of hot dry earth, warm donkey shit, spices, burning charcoal and apple-scented tobacco from the many *shisha* pipes in the makeshift cafes. Between the mud-brick houses the heat is stacked like something solid. An old woman, swathed in black like an ancient crow, crouches in the dust, holding out an arthritic hand to offer a pile of tiny silver fish spread across the raffia mat on the earth in front of her. On the far side of the street a bull of a man with a glistening scimitar-shaped moustache stands behind a heavy wooden trestle. He gives Finn a broad smile and pulls a long string of intestines from a bubbling copper pot and swings them playfully in the air, laughing. Behind him dark swarms of flies circle hungrily around the carcases of sheep and goats that hang from polished steel hooks. There's something surreal and shocking about their carmine flesh and plastic-bright eyes protruding from their flayed skulls in broad daylight.

Next comes the street of the spice sellers, their tables piled with neat mounds of pumpkin and watermelon seeds, sesame, cardamom, turmeric, dry brown sticks of cinnamon and brilliant yellow heaps of saffron. Then the knife grinders, spraying sparks and the copper-merchants busily polishing their stock of gleaming dishes. Blacksmiths and mechanics are stripping machinery and welding metal frames in the deep gloom of their cavernous shops. A small boy in a long ragged shirt rushes up to Finn, gesturing excitedly to a stall where a line of trussed goats are bleating pitifully and scrawny chickens strain their necks through the holes in cramped bamboo boxes in a vain attempt to peck the dried earth. Behind them, in the darkness of a café, figures are hunched over backgammon boards, puffing on long-stemmed bubbling *hookahs* as they click the counters around with lightning speed. The seething energy of the place, the heat, the noise, the smells make Finn feel faintly giddy.

Towards the end of the long central alley he halts and looks around for a moment, trying to get his bearings. To his left a gaunt one-legged man sits on the beaten earth in front of a pile of sugarcane. Beside him lies a wooden crutch crudely cut from the branch of a tree. The man glances up briefly from his work of stripping the cane with a long curved knife as Finn passes and disappears into a narrow alley. Almost instantly the noise of the market is left behind. To his right an unbroken wall of mud-brick rises two storeys, throwing the passage into dense shadow. Thirty yards away the alley ends abruptly in a rough wall of breeze-blocks piled high with garbage. The air is thick with the smell of rotting vegetation. On the other side of the narrow street stands a row of dilapidated shops, their windows thick with dust. Finn strains his eyes in the sudden gloom. The first shop is empty, half boarded up, the bleak interior strewn with rubbish.

He pauses outside the second. Crude bead necklaces and earrings lie scattered across a rough wooden shelf. A few of the beads look ancient, but most are clearly plastic. At the right end of the shelf a mummified cat is propped against a cardboard box, its body trapped into a tight brown cylinder, which makes it look like a bandaged sausage. The desiccated face and bulging eyes stare out pathetically. Above the door, inscribed in shaky black lettering are the words, *Hassani Antiques* and an uncertain representation of a sphinx.

Finn moves to the doorway and peers into the gloom. Behind the counter a thick-set man in a crisp white *galabiya* sits on a wooden stool. He is threading beads onto nylon fishing twine. His round moonlike face has the mournful expression of a sad clown. As Finn steps inside the man glances up. The widely spaced, intelligent brown eyes inspect Finn carefully. He frowns for a moment as if trying to catch a distant memory. Then his mouth splits into a broad smile, lifting the edges of his thick black moustache. The eyes light up. "Aaah, my friend!" he says slowly. "My friend! So you came!" He circles the end of the wooden counter and comes forward, his arms outstretched. He clasps Finn in a heavy embrace and kisses him on both cheeks. Finn can feel the rubbery softness of the man's skin and an exotic smell of sandalwood and spices. Hassani steps back, holds Finn at arms' length for a long moment and studies him. Then, apparently having seen enough, he gestures to a low bench against the back wall, covered in a thick Persian rug. He settles down and arranges his white *galabiya* about him.

He shakes his head slowly. "My friend! It's a long time since we see you. Too long! Far too long! Tell me *everything*." He pats the rough carpeted space between them as if inviting the news of their long separation to come and settle there. "It seems you no longer find time for us." The eyes twinkle in mock complaint. "You are too grand for us humble people in Luxor now perhaps?"

"Of course I came," says Finn. "I said I would...."

Before he can continue a young boy with a heavily pock-marked face emerges through the bead curtain behind the counter. He is carrying a round copper tray with two glasses of red hibiscus tea. He bows deeply as he offers them. Finn takes the scalding hot drink and holds it just long enough to be polite, then hurriedly sets it down on the concrete floor. Hassani, apparently impervious to the heat, keeps his thick fingers wrapped firmly around the glass.

"Not too grand," says Finn smiling, "but your government doesn't make life easy for people like me nowadays. They don't issue any more permits. You can't export anything legally. They've even started putting dealers in prison and their spies watch everyone like hawks. I heard in Cairo that only last week two dealers were arrested." He pauses and glances at the dusty shop window. "I wouldn't be surprised if we were being watched even now."

The corners of the Egyptian's mouth turn down sardonically. "You mean my one-legged friend on the corner?"

Finn nods. "Possibly."

"It is true. But do not be concerned. He is a clever man. The Antiquities Police pay him, of course. But I pay him better. That way he never sells any sugar cane, but he fills his belly well. And he never reports me." Finn laughs. Hassani smiles, then he rises and moves slowly behind the counter. "But first let us play our old game. What toy can we find for you today?" He stares down through the glass top of the counter at the jumble of objects on the dusty shelf below.

While Hassani sorts through the antiquities spread out before him, Finn inspects his surroundings. Nothing has changed. The place is a time warp. The heavy mahogany display cases, each with a delicate circular ivory handle, must be at least eighty years old. The glass fronts are thick with dust. The shelves are littered with fragments of undecorated pottery, battered coins, splinters of coloured glass and faience.

On the peeling wall behind the counter hangs an oval mezzotint of an Egyptian dressed in a fez and grey *galabiya*. The sharp eyes, angular nose and heavy moustache echo the features of the man now bent over before it. Below the photograph hangs a large square sepia print of the same man, identically dressed, standing with a dapper figure in a three-piece suit, a spotted bow-tie and grey homburg hat. A thick overcoat is draped over his left arm. In the background the boulder-strewn escarpment of the Valley of the Kings is clearly visible. Finn recognises the fleshy, arrogant features of Howard Carter, the legendary discoverer of the tomb of Tutankhamun.

Abdul Hassani's father and grandfather had both been licensed dealers of antiquities in Luxor. His grandfather, a man of unbribable honesty, had overseen Howard Carter's unruly gang of Egyptian workmen at Tutankhamun's tomb. The Hassanis had a proud tradition, not so much merchants as gentlemen-connoisseurs, on friendly terms with Egyptologists, excavators and the stream of aristocratic collectors who had passed through Luxor since the start of the Twentieth Century.

But in the last decade everything had changed. In a sudden fervour of nationalism, the Egyptian government had banned the export of all antiquities. As a result the open market had virtually ceased. The old-fashioned dealers were reduced to selling off the remains of licensed stock, and the occasional clandestine transaction. But the real market had merely gone underground and passed to a new generation in Cairo, mostly immigrants, Armenians and Greeks, younger men with hard faces and Swiss bank accounts. And enough money to bribe the necessary politicians and police. Meanwhile, the stately line of shops in the corniche below the old Winter Palace Hotel, where *Hassani Antiques* had been installed for seven decades, had been converted into gleaming modern boutiques selling brash gold jewellery and imitation Swiss watches. Tucked away now with his Edwardian furnishings in this makeshift concrete bunker behind the market, Abdul Hassani could have dwindled to a pathetic figure. Yet he retains his dignity. No one ever refers to him as Abdul. He is either 'Mister Hassani', or simply 'Hassani' to his intimates.

"Here we are!" Hassani removes a square tray from the case. He straightens and hands it to Finn. The tray is lined with faded red velvet, so worn in places that the dark mahogany shows through. On it are arranged at least twenty small representations in coloured faience of the scarab beetle, the ancient Egyptian symbol of rebirth. Finn picks up each in turn, examines it closely, turning it over to see the hieroglyphs on the flat underside. Finally he sets the tray down on the bench, selects a small chipped scarab from the bottom left corner and holds it up between thumb and forefinger.

"How much?"

Hassani claps him on the shoulder. "Bravo! I see you have not lost the eye!" He taps the dark pouch under one of his lower lids. Finn laughs. It's an old dealer's game, the simplest way of assessing a client's knowledge. As Hassani once said, if a man can't pick the real scarab, then a forgery will satisfy him just as well.

"But have you seen what these people can do nowadays?" exclaims Hassani, shaking his head in aggrieved wonder. He picks up an unbroken scarab in brilliant blue faience and turns it over. The underside is precisely etched with the cartouche of Queen Hatshepsut, the only female Pharaoh in Egypt's three thousand year history. He passes it to Finn. Finn balances the small object in the palm of his hand. "It's a great rarity," he says. "It would be worth a lot of money if it were real." Then he tosses it like a dice. "But the glaze is too even and shiny. And look ....." He holds it up between thumb and forefinger, allowing the light to shine through the hole that pierces it from end to end. "The hole is the same thickness all through. It's been done with a mechanical drill. The ancient ones are drilled from both ends till they meet in the middle. So the hole always gets a little narrower in the centre."

Hassani smiles and sips his tea. "You know your onions," he says. "These days the people know nothing. Nothing! The ones who used to come, they were like you. We sat and drank tea. We discussed. We took our time. And they knew. They *knew*. But now ....." He waves his hand dismissively. "They know nothing. They *see* nothing. All these professors, these so-

163

called university archaeologists. If they come at all they treat me like a *fellah*." He uses the Egyptian word for peasant. "They only know how to read books. And if they dig something up, they measure it, they weigh it, then send it for scientific tests. But they never *look* any more. No eyes! No eyes!" He gestures to the tray. "They could not choose the real scarab if it had a big label on it." He chuckles ruefully. "But, at least, that way I sell a lot of forged scarabs – for a good price. Probably all are now in museums in America." He sits back and sips his tea thoughtfully. "It's only you that knows the antiquities now. You and the old Professor."

Finn frowns. "Old professor?"

"You know him," says Hassani, drawing his thumb and fingers together at the point of his fleshy chin. "Beard. Tall. Speaks Arabic. German, no?"

"Dortmann?

"Yes, yes! Dortmann! Old. But still he has the eyes. And a gentleman," he adds sadly. Then he sets down his glass. "Now just the tour guides send me their tourists. They come with cans of Coca-cola and dress ... Pah!" He sniffs disdainfuly. "They know nothing. *And* they do not want to spend money. It is not even a pleasure to sell them a forgery. The tour guides want ten per cent. Sometimes even twenty per cent!" He spreads his hands in despair. "I tell them ten per cent of nothing is nothing!" He pauses. "Look." He gestures imperceptibly with his head towards the street.

Two figures are peering through the dusty window, shading their eyes to try to penetrate the gloom. They hesitate. Then they enter, glance suspiciously at Finn, and ignore Hassani altogether. They start peering into the cases, whispering, bent over the glass-topped counter, their noses almost pressed against its surface. They are both wearing shorts and multi-coloured singlet tops. The woman's thighs bulge like dough. The bearded man has a large Nikon slung over his shoulder.

Hassani rises. "May I be of service?" he asks politely.

"We want …..," the woman starts, but the man cuts in. His voice has the sledgehammer consonants of northern Germany. "We want antiques. But genuine! Understand? Only genuine. No fakes. Understand!" The tone is belligerent. Hassani nods.

The woman shuffles her feet nervously. "That one!" She prods the glass counter with her forefinger. "Show me!"

Hassani opens the back of the case and extracts a large scarab carved in a shiny, speckled black and white stone. He lays it carefully on the counter.

The woman picks it up and turns it over in her plump hands. "How much?"

"Fifty Egyptian pounds," says Hassani calmly.

The couple whisper together. The man looks sharply at Hassani. "Is it genuine?" he asks suspiciously. "Remember – no forgeries!"

Hassani smiles. "Madame chose the piece. Not I. No, it is not genuine. It was made last week by a fellah on the West Bank. Good is it not?"

The woman stares at him in disbelief. "Fifty Egyptian pounds! And not genuine! Why so expensive?"

"Because," says Hassani patiently. "The stone is diorite. It is very hard and it takes much time to make." He picks up the scarab carefully and replaces it in the case.

The man says something to the woman. They turn and hurry out through the door, whispering angrily to each other.

"You see how it is," said Hassani with a shrug. "Every day the same." He sits down again, allows his fingers to play with the scarabs on the tray, rearranging them.

"Have there been any finds at el-Amarna recently?" asks Finn casually.

The fingers stop for an instant, then continue. Hassani remains looking down at the tray. "Why you ask?" he says at length.

"Oh, I don't know. I heard a rumour." There is a long silence. The cries from the market ricochet along the narrow alley. "And when we spoke on the phone you said you had something of interest.....?"

For a long while Hassani remains quiet, still adjusting the scarabs on the tray, as if nothing has been said. Then he looks up and gives a small smile. "Perhaps you like to come dine with me tonight?"

Finn starts to speak, then hesitates. "Tonight may be difficult. I'm with a group".

"A group! *You?*" Hassani frowns.

"It's a long story. But I'm less obvious that way. The police would never look for a dealer on a package tour. Tomorrow would be better."

Hassani nods. "Tomorrow is good, in'sh Allah. Only," he adds, "do not carry your hopes too high. The best will be the food."

Finn smiles and rises. "Thank you." He reaches down, picks up the genuine scarab and holds it up between his fingers. "How much?"

Hassani's hands flutter out of the sleeves of his *galabiya* like two dark birds. They wrap around Finn's hand, closing it over the scarab. "It is a gift," he says simply. "I am happy to see you. Please come for eight. You stay at the Winter Palace Hotel?"

"No. The Sobek, outside town."

"I will send the boy to fetch you."

FOURTEEN

Some three miles south of the town of Luxor, set on an island joined to the river bank by a narrow causeway, lies the Sobek Hotel, named after the ancient crocodile god whose creatures used to inhabit these shallow waters. It consists of a group of small, single-storey villas spread in an enormous garden of date palms and towering eucalyptus trees, acacias and tamarisks, multi-coloured bougainvillea, hibiscus and oleander, mimosa and pink-flowering camel's foot tree.

In the days before the Aswan high dam, much of this low-lying island would have been flooded by the summer inundation. To prevent this, it has been buttressed by a steep bank that falls away to a watery plain some fifty yards wide before its reeded edges give way to the Nile. In this broad space fishes creep into shallow pools, fishermen push their boats in amongst the reeds and water buffalo are tethered under the low spreading acacias. Bee-eaters swoop and chase amongst the ochre bulrushes and white ibises stalk the margins, investigating the muddy banks. And beyond this lies the Nile, sliding, swirling, changing colour at each hour of the day, rose-pink, silver-white, at evening gun-metal grey.

Lara is instantly entranced by the place. Her cottage is at the furthest end of the garden, fronting directly onto the river, so that nothing separates her from the view across to the lush farmland of the far bank and, further downstream to her right, the castellated lion-coloured cliffs that rise to a sharp line above the Valley of the Kings. To her left a low wall divides the hotel from the surrounding cultivation. Some twenty yards beyond this lies a rambling low-built, mud-brick farmhouse. To her delight, part of the wall has collapsed and the farm children run freely in and out of the hotel garden in their brightly coloured *galabiyas*.

She watches now from the top of the bank as a troop of children make their way in single file across the marshy land below. At their head is a girl of perhaps twelve in a bright red smock. Her pale auburn hair falls about her shoulders as she walks with a quiet, determined step through the waterlogged grass towards the river's edge. In her right hand she holds something that looks like a wire-mesh frying pan. The smaller children chatter excitedly behind her.

Lara smiles. The girl looks like the Pied Piper. She envies her grace and simple authority. Twelve years old, and already a woman! How differently the women move here, compared to the sharp staccato rhythms of Europe. Here they seem to glide, as if nothing could shift them from their silent purpose. How fragile, how unsubstantial she feels beside them, as if every puff of wind might blow her over. Even this little girl seems more a woman than she is.

She watches as the girl places the wire mesh down amongst the thick reeded grass close to the river. She steps back. The other children form a semi-circle behind her, cramped into poses of frozen excitement. For perhaps twenty seconds the silence holds. Then the girl shoots forward, grabs the wire pan with one hand and in a single movement flicks up a writhing silver fish which hangs for a moment in the air, then falls into the hollow formed by holding up the front of her dress. The ring of children hop with delight and clap their hands. Still holding the fish in her dress, the girl moves forward again, drops the wire net into the shallow water and turns to glare at the children. Immediately they fall silent. Then she jumps back, her cotton dress drawn up around her thighs, innocently exposing her slim brown legs.

"Enjoying the game?"

Lara starts. She hasn't noticed Edward making his way along the top of the bank towards her.

"I was envying them." There is a wistfulness in her voice.

He looks at her questioningly. "Envying?"

"Yes. The little girl in the red dress. She has such dignity and grace. Like a real woman. Yet she still has all the unselfconscious joy and energy of a child."

He holds up his arm against the sun and gazes at the scene below. After a while he says thoughtfully, "Yes, I know what you mean. The older girls here especially, even though they stay children, it's as if they've somehow already been received into the guild of women."

"The guild of women.....Hmm." She turns the phrase over in her mind. "I like that."

At a sudden whoop of excitement they look round. Another fish is being flicked into the air. It flashes silver in the sunlight.

"I was wondering if one of these days you'd like to take a ride in a *felucca*."

She frowns. "A *felucca*?"

"The boats."

"You mean the beautiful boats with the triangular sails? Can we really do that?"

"Sure. But not right now because in half an hour David Mountjoy is stampeding us into a special evening ritual in the Luxor Temple."

169

She claps her hands and smiles broadly. "I'd absolutely love to!"

"Now *you* look like a child who's been received into the guild of women."

Her smile fades. "Oh, I don't think I ….." She stops.

"What is it?"

"Oh, nothing." She shakes her head. Absurdly, tears begin to prickle her eyes and she looks away. But Edward stays staring at her, his head slightly tilted to one side. And instinctively she knows that he has understood the words she hasn't uttered. And, for a moment, her heart opens to him.

*

The group has gathered in the central court of the Luxor Temple. It is evening and the lights illuminating the surrounding colonnade have been switched on, giving the place a theatrical feel. Twilight is gathering over the western escarpment. There are few visitors now and those that remain stand between the huge columns, watching. There is an air of expectancy.

Lara stands a little apart from the others. From the very first morning she has been startled how swiftly her initial scepticism for these rituals has evaporated. Somehow they give a rhythm to each day, like the steady peel of church bells through a Mediterranean village. Each morning and evening, as they move through the patterns Mountjoy has taught them, it feels as if her cluttered life is somehow being re-ordered, creating space for something calmer to surface. Compared to this, her days in London seem a random series of meaningless, disconnected events.

David Mountjoy claps his hands. Standing on tip-toe, he raises both arms in the manner of a lay preacher. He waits for the murmurings to go silent. "We are standing now in one of Egypt's most sacred places," he intones. "For this is the Solar Court of the Temple of Luxor, the centre of the worship of the great god Amun. It was built by the Pharaoh Amenhotep III in the Fourteenth Century BC." He pauses. "That is almost *three and a half thousand years ago.*" He carves up the words, emphasising each one with an abrupt theatrical tilt of his bearded chin, as if this somehow conveys the enormity of the time-span. At the back of the group, Finn and Edward exchange smiles. "Here, *on this very spot*, the ancient priests of Amun would have carried out their rituals, chanting the praises to their deity....." He pauses dramatically and looks around. "Today we shall take up that tradition. So let your voices resound!"

They take their places, hands linked, in two concentric circles, Kai and Birgit, selected for the day by their Tarot cards, on the outside, facing inwards. The excited chatter from the watchers in the colonnade fades. There is a moment of silence. Then Mountjoy starts, the first low sound, slowly swelling: "*Raaa..... Maaa ..... Taaa ...*" The circles begin to revolve in opposite directions, slowly taking up the chant. "*Raaa ....Maaa ...Taaa .....*" and, as the note grows and lifts, Lara feels herself being absorbed into the hypnotic world of sound and movement. Gradually the ritual gathers pace, the two lines of figures crossing and intersecting diagonally. Each crossing pair pauses, faces each other, clasps hands then moves on. Now it is Lara's turn. Suddenly she is face to face with Edward. For a moment they are isolated in their own world. She looks into his eyes. Their hands touch. For that split second everything is still. Then they move on. But, in that instant, surrounded by a pool of silence, she has felt something that has been trapped inside her suddenly shake loose. He has looked at her with such intensity that there, in the centre of that ancient courtyard, she has felt more naked than she has ever done with any man. And she knows he has seen it.

The group circles around Kai and Birgit. A final chant goes up into the sky. A smattering of applause breaks out from the onlookers. The ritual dissolves. David Mountjoy gestures for the group to gather round and arrange themselves on the ground. "Story-time," murmurs Finn to Edward.

Into the silence Mountjoy begins to speak:

In the beginning of the World, Sky lay upon Earth and she conceived and gave birth to two sons, Osiris and Seth; and two daughters, Isis and Nephthys. To Osiris was given the rich soil and the crops, the vines and all the seeds, flowers and fruits. He loved the Nile, flooding the land and making his crops grow. To gentle Isis was given rain and dew and all the moist places of the earth. Her breath was the breath of life and without her no seed could sprout, no plant could grow.

But Seth, the younger brother, was quite different. His hair was as red as the desert. He sent the scouring hot winds and searing sandstorms that withered the crops. He loved the bitter salt waters of the sea. Sometimes he took the form of the fearsome crocodile or the raging hippopotamus, trampling all in his path.

Nephthys was the dark sister of Isis. She inhabited the night and loved the dark and waning moon. When they grew up, Isis married her brother Osiris – as the Egyptians often did – and Nephthys married Seth.

Osiris was a gentle ruler. He took care of the people of the earth and taught them how to plough the fields, how to plant the crops and how to bring order and justice to their lives. But Seth was jealous of his brother's gentle powers and one day he trapped Osiris. He cut his body into fourteen pieces and scattered them throughout the land so that they could never be found.

When Isis heard this she was overcome by grief and began to hunt all along the Nile for the scattered parts of her beloved husband. After many months of searching, she recovered all of them, except one – his penis, which had been eaten by a fish. And she cunningly reformed the body of Osiris, putting together the pieces and giving him a penis fashioned from clay. Now Isis had beautiful rainbow-coloured wings and she hovered over him and breathed life gently back into his nostrils until he became a man again and she was able to conceive a son by him. And this was the young god Horus, the soaring falcon, who would one day grow up to avenge his father's murder and rule in his place.

So Osiris went down to reign in the Kingdom of the Dead. Isis and Horus could hear him crying out in anguish from the depths of the Underworld. And they called down to him in despair: "Why do you stay so long in the Underworld, Osiris? Arise and pour forth your waters again and bring us back life." For three days and three nights they cried out to him. But Osiris could not rise. And ever since that time, Horus has reigned over the Earth as the great hovering falcon in the light of the sun. And Osiris has remained below, ruling in the Kingdom of Darkness.

And though Osiris cannot truly rise, yet it is to him, hidden in the darkness, that the crops go when they die, so *that they can be reborn the next year. It is he who, from the Underworld, makes the Nile flood and brings fertility back to the land. Without his silent, invisible power nothing can grow and nothing is healed. Unable to rise himself, it is he who sends healing and rebirth to the world above from his place below in the Kingdom of Darkness.*

Mountjoy folds his hands in a gesture of completion. The group dissolves. Lara waits, then walks alone towards the unlit part of the colonnade. She leans her back against one of the sandstone columns, slides down until she was resting on her haunches. Something in the story has moved her deeply. The court is silent now. Bit by bit the lights are going out. She cradles her arms around herself and gazes up at the night sky.

So many things seem to be happening at once: Edward, the ritual, that sudden, searing sense of nakedness as he had looked at her.... And now something in this story has opened doors inside her. It's so strange the way these myths, conceived thousands of years ago, so deceptively simple, almost like fairy tales, can contain something that touches the very centre of her.

"Are you okay?"

Startled, she looks up. David Mountjoy is standing beside her. She hesitates, aware of her ambivalence towards him. But then she gestures to him to join her. He sinks down beside her. Perhaps sensing her confusion, for a long while he is silent. Then he says, "Things are really happening for you here, aren't they?" It isn't really a question.

For a while she is silent, wondering if she really wants to go into this conversation, to have her mood disjointed. Then she nods. "Yes, almost too many things too fast. Everything seems to be suddenly changing for me and it's hard to make sense of it all. I love it here. Egypt is *so* beautiful. There's a richness to this country that really touches me. When I sit beside the Nile or listen to that story that you just told, I feel how incredibly *poor* we've become in the north. How everything there seems so thin by comparison. It's almost as if we've lost our roots in Europe and what might give sense to our lives has died up there. But *here* it still exists." She hesitates. "And, at the same time, it feels as if my old self is somehow crumbling away. And that's so scary!" She hesitates. "You know, when you read my horoscope I thought it was….."

"Bullshit?"

She puts back her head and laughs at this unexpected response. "No, not exactly. It did make sense. But it also felt somehow not quite attached to me, as if I didn't fully recognise it as my own. But now it feels as if, in some strange way, my horoscope is actually working itself out in me, and I can't stop it, even if I want to."

For a while he is quiet. Then he says, "I think you're starting to sense what a mystical country Egypt really is. It always feels to me as if the earth's psychic crust is thinner here. And, of course, that can be frightening if you're sensitive to it. But it can also be magical because, if we can open our hearts and respond, then everything we see around us becomes a kind of glowing doorway into another world."

She nods, remembering that intense feeling of spaciousness as she watches the slow, steady flow of the Nile. "Yes, I think I start to understand that now."

"But, of course," goes on Mountjoy, "when we experience those special moments here, moments when, as the ancient Egyptians used to say, '*The gates of the horizon swing open*', we also become painfully aware of how scattered and fragmented we normally are, especially in our western culture. I think that's part of what that story of Osiris is actually about – that we're *all* wounded in some way, all dismembered Osirises struggling to put together the scattered bits of ourselves and rise and become whole again."

She nods, then her brow furrows. "Look..... This is probably going to sound crazy. But... Me, Edward, Finn – there's something really strange about us, isn't there? I don't mean strange individually, but..." She looks up at the night sky, searching for the right words. "I sensed it right from the start, when I first met them. I think that at first I tried to explain it away logically. After all, they're both attractive men, both interesting in their very different ways. But the bond between the three of us feels so..... I don't know... so *immediate*, so *intense*, as if we've known each other for years, instead of just a few days. And it dawned on me just now when you told that story.... It's as if, in some bizarre way it's *our* story, isn't it?" In the dim light he is watching her closely. He stays silent. "How is that possible? That myth's at least three thousand years old. How can we be living it out now in the Twenty-first century? It's crazy!"

Mountjoy shakes his head. "Perhaps it's not so crazy after all. Man has been living out myths since the beginning of time. It's part of the human condition. What's important is to discover which myth you're living in and to understand it and try to cooperate with it."

Which myth you're living in? And suddenly, without warning, she can feel the other part of the myth, the part she hasn't wanted to notice, push itself forward. Somewhere out there there must be a Nephthys, a dark, sinister sister. And Seth, some kind of threatening, destructive force. And with a sudden jolt of memory, Finn's Tarot card comes back to her – the solid mediaeval tower shattering under the bolt of lightning, the tiny figures being hurled pitilessly through the air like rag dolls. And with the memory comes a terrible sense of premonition. She turns to him. "Something bad is going to happen to the three of us here in Egypt, isn't it?"

He spreads his hands. "I don't know." He catches her anxious look. "*Really* I don't. I'm an astrologer, not a clairvoyant. There's a big difference." He hesitates. "What I do know from your horoscopes is that, at this moment, all three of you are being offered some kind of chance to break out, to shatter your old lives, if you like. That's why you're all in Egypt together at this precise time. Fate has brought you here to open you up to new beginnings. That much is obvious to me. But what will happen exactly in physical terms – *that* I cannot see. And, in many ways, it will be up to the three of you. We always have the choice to change our fate."

She can feel the anxiety inflate in her stomach like an air bubble. She thinks of Finn's stubborn cynicism, Edward's protective introversion, her own inability truly to give herself to anything, to anyone. Surely these things are almost genetically ingrained, too intractable to change? She stares at him and a sense of foreboding creeps over her. "But what if we just *can't* break out of our old lives? What if it feels impossible, just too hard to do?"

For a long time Mountjoy doesn't answer. Then he says quietly, "What I do know is that not to choose when a choice is demanded of us – that is the worst choice of all."

FIFTEEN

As soon as Finn sees the boy with the pockmarked face standing in the far corner of the entrance hall of the Sobek Hotel, half obscured by a potted fern, he instinctively checks to see if they are being watched. A small group of Italians is seated round a low table laughing and drinking wine. The bored clerks at the reception desk are chatting amongst themselves. Otherwise the place is deserted.

As Finn starts towards the door, the boy turns and disappears into the darkness. Outside a horse-drawn *caleche* is waiting. The horse snorts impatiently and shakes its head, making the heavy harness jangle. Finn places one foot on the creaking metal step and climbs in. The boy jumps up onto the bench beside the driver. Then the whip cracks and they are off at break-neck speed into the dark, hooves clattering noisily on the tarmac. At first all is blackness, except for the spread of stars above and the faint glow of Luxor staining the sky ahead. But quickly they are through the first mud-brick outposts and clipping along the main tourist street, gaudy with neon from the shop fronts. The Nile is obscured by a cliff of concrete hotels to their left.

In the square at the end of the market street they draw to a halt. There are fewer people here. The air smells of warm horse manure and spices. The boy jumps down and moves quickly between the empty stalls. Finn follows. When the boy reaches the turning to Hassani's shop he turns left instead of right. The one-legged sugar-cane seller has gone. Only the scuffed earth and scattered debris of stripped cane show where he has been. A brindled cat, all shaggy fur and bone, lies in the dust suckling a cluster of kittens. The boy waits at the corner, then disappears down a narrow alley. Finn follows through the twisting maze of streets. There are few lights now and he stumbles as he tries to keep up on the uneven ground. It is hotter here away from the Nile, the heat trapped in the narrow passageways. Somewhere close by a dog is barking furiously.

Suddenly the boy stops in front of a peeling wooden door. He knocks sharply twice and holds out his hand. Finn fumbles in his pocket, drops twenty piasters into the waiting palm and immediately the boy turns and disappears at a run into the darkness, leaving Finn to listen to the fading slap of his bare feet on the earth.

For a long while nothing happens. Finn has lost all sense of direction in the narrow alleys and is just beginning to wonder if the boy has duped him, when the door is flung open. Hassani stands there, resplendent in a maroon *galabiya* edged with grey. The whitewashed room behind him is patched with hangings in strong Bedouin colours. In the centre stands a long table draped in a floral cloth. A low bench, obscured by rugs and cushions, runs all around the walls and in one corner a 1950's vintage television-set rests on the floor, wired to a tangled flex which spirals upwards and disappears through a hole in the ceiling.

"Welcome! Welcome!" booms Hassani. He smiles broadly, ushers Finn inside and closes the door. The room is lit only by candles. Their warm amber glow gives the place the feel of an

Aladdin's cave. At the far end an open doorway is obscured by a plastic curtain. The harsh glow of neon seeps round its edges and Finn can hear muffled whispers in the background.

Hassani escorts him to the bench and sits down. In front of them an elaborately fretted wooden frame supports a round copper tray. A small boy with tousled black hair, probably no more than seven years old, scuttles out from behind the curtain carrying glasses of the obligatory *khakade*. Hassani raises his glass in welcome, then sits back and crosses one ankle over the other knee. Finn stares in amusement as the maroon *galabiya* rides up to reveal long, thick woollen socks and impeccable black English brogues.

Hassani catches his glance. "Ha! You like my shoes?"

Finn smiles. "Isn't it a little warm? Those socks and shoes were designed for London, not Luxor!"

"Not at all! The evening is cool." Hassani gestures towards the door as if indicating the thirty-degree heat that lies trapped in the alley beyond. "The shoes," he goes on, "were made for my grandfather by the finest boot-maker in London. Look!" He reaches down, unfastens the laces of the left shoe and takes it off. Then he grasps a candle from the low table and holds it up. In the flickering light Finn can just make out the faded outline of a royal crest. "See!" says Hassani triumphantly. "By appointment, boot-maker to His Majesty King George the Sixth!"

He puts down the heavy brogue on the rug and begins to wriggle his thickly stockinged foot back into it. "My grandfather," he goes on, "had one pair sent from London every year until I was twelve years old."

"Then what happened?"

"The shoemaker died." Hassani spreads his hands. "Two years after that my grandfather died." He pauses. "It is a different world now. A very different world," he adds sadly. "All plastic clothes and rubber trainers."

With a flash of neon the curtain is drawn aside and the boy emerges, staggering under a tray stacked with copper dishes. He begins to spread them over the thick covering on the table.

"But tonight," says Hassani, rising, "we will show you an old-fashioned Egyptian feast." He pulls out a chair for Finn, then seats himself opposite.

The meal takes nearly two hours. The first course is a kaleidoscope of small dishes: tzatziki, tabouleh, hummous, keftedes, babaganoush and others that Finn can't even identify. Eventually the boy clears away the empty dishes and replaces them with an enormous copper platter bearing pigeons stuffed with heavily seasoned wild rice. Finally comes an array of sweet pastries. At odd moments, the edge of the curtain behind Hassani is furtively drawn aside and Finn is aware of being under the scrutiny of several pairs of eyes, followed by hushed whispers and stifled female giggles.

As the evening wears on Hassani becomes ever more expansive, telling stories of the spectacular antiquities that have passed through the hands of his father and grandfather before the new export laws had come into force.

"Now....," says Hassani angrily, "they try to turn us into criminals! They make everything undercover. The secret police – they persecute us, then they steal and line their own deep pockets! And leave us with only the rubbish to sell." He pauses and glances slyly at Finn from under his long black lashes. One of the boys appears from behind the curtain, but Hassani waves him back with a flap of his hand.

"Only sometimes," he goes on slowly, "the rubbish has surprises that no one notices."

He rises, levering himself up on the table, then crosses to the low bench against the wall. He gestures Finn to follow. There he stops, lifts up one of the heavy rugs, fumbles underneath and pulls out a battered cardboard box fastened with string. Carefully, moving his thick fingers with the delicacy of a seamstress, he unravels the heavy knot and folds back the lid.

Finn leans forward, straining to see the contents, but the box appears to contain only items of old clothing bundled together. Carefully, one by one, Hassani removes these and drops them on the floor. Then he reaches deep into the box, turns with a bundle of cloth cradled against his heavy body and lays it on the table. He folds apart the wrappings and steps back.

Lying on the table is a brightly painted mummy mask. Or, to be more precise, half a mummy mask, for the whole right side of the face has been broken away. For a moment Finn stares in silence, not wanting to let his disappointment show. After all the theatre, is this really the 'surprise' Hassani has promised him? The object is unquestionably ancient, made from cartonnage, a primitive form of papier maché, that would once have covered the face of a mummified body. But the crude drawing of the eyes and lips and the gaudy, slip-shod colouring show that it dates from the period of Rome's occupation of Egypt, the final years of a decadent civilisation, when craftsmanship declined, religion gave way to superstition and the art degenerated into crude parody. He shifts uncomfortably as he looks down at the pathetic wreck on the table-cloth, wondering how to escape without offending his host.

"Do you know how they made the cartonnage for these mummy masks?"

Finn glances up and is surprised to see Hassani smiling almost mischievously at him. He picks up the mask and turns the fragment over in his hands to reveal the discoloured, starchy material on the inside. "It's a bit like sticking bandages together. In the time of the Roman occupation they used old papyrus scrolls. There were plenty of them lying around after the Egyptians left and they weren't any use to the Romans, because they couldn't read the hieroglyphs anyway. In fact the majority of the papyri that scholars study today is taken from the backing of masks just like this."

Hassani nods silently, then prods the edge of the mask with his finger at a place where the layers of cartonnage are frayed and separating like a broken wafer. "Lift here," he says.

Curious, Finn takes the topmost layer between his thumb and forefinger and lifts it gently. About an inch folds back. He can see the clear black markings of a hieroglyphic inscription from an earlier period, long before the arrival of the Roman invaders.

"A little further," urges Hassani.

Taking care not to break the delicate fibres, Finn peels back another few millimetres. And suddenly what he sees makes the breath catch in his throat. For a full minute he stares down at the tiny exposed segment of ancient papyrus.

"Interesting, is it not?" says Hassani.

Finn nods in silence. At the left edge of the tattered fragment of papyrus, just where it remains stuck to the mask, is unmistakably the royal title of a Pharaoh, enclosed in the sacred oval-shaped cartouche. Though faded, the blood-red ink of the cartouche stands out against the black of the other hieroglyphs. Finn tries to trace the tiny characters with the nail of his little finger, but they are too small and too faint. Hassani reaches into the pocket of his *galabiya* and passes over an old-fashioned magnifying glass with a slender ivory handle. "I think this is what you need," he says.

Finn peers through the glass. For a moment the hieroglyphs swim, then straighten themselves into focus. He lets out a low whistle. "*Akhenaten?*"

"Just so, my friend."

For a moment random memories splinter Finn's brain – the sudden shock of his Tarot card ….. the little faience box Lascaris had shown him, also containing the cartouche of Akhenaten… And something else, something he can't quite see, lodged under the eaves of his mind. He forces his attention back into the present. "Where did you get it?"

Hassani shrugs. "I have friends." The words echo in Finn's head like a small explosion, recalling Lascaris's exact same phrase as he had sat with him in his house in Islington three weeks before. He crosses the room, feeling unsteady, as if he has just escaped a minor accident. He lays the mummy mask down on the thick rug. Then he drops onto the bench. In the silence he can hear the ragged pulse of his own breathing.

"Friends anywhere in particular?"

"Middle Egypt." Hassani pauses and allows himself the beginnings of a smile under his thick moustache. "El-Minya, to be precise."

"El-Minya?" Finn runs a hand over his jaw. "So it *could* come from el-Amarna. It's right next door."

Hassani nods. "It is possible. The man who brought it was a *fellah* – a peasant. He comes from there. But they are always very secretive. They trust no one. They tell you nothing."

Finn leans back against the cushions. It's true, Roman burials *had* been found at el-Amarna, the doomed capital of Akhenaten. The place had been abandoned shortly after the Pharaoh's death, when Tutankhamun had declared him a heretic. But over a thousand years later Roman invaders had reoccupied the site and, as they dug foundations for their houses, they might have found the older tombs from the time of Akhenaten. And in the tombs would have been funerary papyri to accompany the dead. So the Romans could have reused the papyrus scrolls to make their own mass-produced mummy masks. After all, they had no other use for them ... "Yes, it would make sense," he muses. "Who knows what might have happened? That's the weird thing with archaeology. We try to make it into logical patterns, but we don't allow for the sheer, unpredictable randomness of what might have happened over the course of three thousand years." He looks up at Hassani. "So we've got a small fragment of an Eighteenth Dynasty papyrus, which mentions the name of Akhenaten ....." He pauses. "But we don't know what it says. And we don't know where the rest of it is. Right?"

Hassani nods. "Just so, my friend."

Finn spreads his hands. "It could be just some boring standard inscription that happens to mention the king's name as part of a prayer or something. In which case it's not particularly valuable. But ..... it could just possibly say something *new* about Akhenaten. Something we didn't know before. In which case ..." He lets his voice trail off for a moment. "In which case it could be massively important."

"You cannot read more?"

Finn shakes his head. "I can decipher a standard text, but this is a complex private document. It would need a specialised Egyptologist."

"And you do not know someone who can?"

"Not here. Chicago House up the road, where the American archaeologists live, probably has people who could read it. But as soon as we show it to them, we know what will happen."

Hassani nods. "They would immediately inform the authorities and the mask would be confiscated. You would be arrested. So would the *fellah*. My shop would be closed. My house would be so covered with police it would look like flies on a carcass. It would cost me all my money not to be arrested too. And ...," he spreads his hands in despair, "in six months it would be on the European art market. And I would see the Chief of Police here driving around in a new Mercedes."

Finn laughs and gets to his feet. "Let me think about it. Maybe I can come up with something. I just need the right person." He looks down at the mask. The single eye is crudely outlined in black and white. The centre of the cheek is circled with rouge. The gilding is cracked and faded and the surface is flaking. It probably wouldn't be difficult to pull away the layers from the back, but there are no guarantees how much more of the papyrus might be there. And to ask for help here in Luxor would be very dangerous. Once the circle of the secret is widened it could too easily touch the wrong people. "In any case," he says, "from one fragmentary bit of papyrus we're unlikely to learn much." As he speaks, he is aware of a gnawing sense of frustration. The papyrus could hold something momentous. Some sixth sense is telling him that. "The real question is," he says at length, "where's the rest of it?"

"Aaah," says Hassani. He has risen too, and stands now with both arms extended, as if to indicate the enormity of the possibility. In his maroon *galabiya*, with the wide sleeves hanging loose, he looks like some enormous tropical bird caught in the candlelight. "So many things can happen in two, three thousand years. Fierce floods come down out of the ravines behind el-Amarna. The mask gets broken. One part gets washed here. Another there." He gestures with his open palms. "Maybe five kilometres away. The plain at el-Amarna covers over five thousand hectares. *Five thousand hectares!*"

Finn nods. He can feel the weight of disappointment press down on his earlier excitement. "It's would be like looking for a particular grain of sand in the desert," he says.

"True, my friend. But we Egyptians also say that when a man takes one step towards God, then God will take more steps towards him than there are grains of sand in the desert."

Finn raises his eyebrows in question. There seems a message in Hassani's enigmatic words.

"We also say," goes on Hassani, " 'In'sh Allah' – as Allah wills it. This is not Europe. Strange things can happen here. So whether it is by your God or mine, it has all been written. It is all fate, my friend. *Kismet.*" He pauses and smiles. "So we shall have to see what Allah's fate has in store for us."

He extends an arm to escort Finn. As if at a prearranged signal, the tousle-haired boy shoots out from behind the curtain and stands waiting at the open doorway.

*

The air has cooled and a light breeze is stirring from the Nile. Finn listens to the sharp clip of the horse's hooves and the rhythmic creak of the caleche in the darkness. He has enjoyed the long evening with Hassani. But now his mind is lasered to that one moment when the liquid shiftings of the magnifying glass had stilled and the ochre-red cartouche of Akhenaten came into focus. He had felt a surge of excitement like the sudden workings of a drug to see the tiny clue of that inscription, with all its unravelled mysteries, all its silent possibilities suddenly exposed three and a half thousand years after it had been written.

He leans back in the leather seat and stretches. It isn't the money that drives him in this crazy profession. It is *these* moments, these electric flashes, holding out the promise of discovery and adventure. It's a sensation like no other, almost erotic in its intensity..... The caleche bumps. The old metal springs squeak noisily. They have turned off the tarmac road onto the long causeway that leads to the hotel. Finn cranes his neck and looks up at the stars.

Hassani's final words come back to him: '*In'sh Allah*' – the phrase can be heard a hundred times every day in Egypt – *If it is the will of Allah*. He has always thought of it as part of the lethargic fatalism of a country whose people wait hopelessly for events that will never happen. But perhaps this time .....

The caleche draws up outside the hotel. He pays off the driver and goes through the glass doors into the lobby. It is one o'clock. The place is deserted except for a bored-looking clerk behind the reception desk, smoking a cigarette that smells suspiciously like marijuana. He hands Finn his key, together with a white envelope. Finn turns it over. His name is scrawled across the front in black ink.

"Who brought this?"

The clerk shrugs. "A boy."

"An Egyptian boy?"

He nods.

Finn thanks him, turns and slits open the flap with his thumb. Inside is a single sheet of typed paper.

Meet me in the gardens of the Old Winter Palace Hotel.
Tomorrow evening. Six o'clock.

It is unsigned.

He slides the page back in the envelope, rips it into small pieces, then drops them into his pocket. He remembers Hassani holding up the fragmentary mask in the flickering candlelight. *It is all fate, my friend. Kismet.* Is it possible, just possible, that Lascaris could be right about Mountjoy's apparently miraculous powers?

And, with a light step, he makes his way through the gardens to his room.

SIXTEEN

Finn slips through the narrow side gate set in the high brick wall, eases past the snoring guard slumped in his deckchair and into the gardens of The Winter Place Hotel. Here palms and banyan trees tower up more than a hundred feet, throwing broad purple shadows across the carefully watered grass. Thick borders of scarlet hibiscus and peach-pink azalea line the neat gravel pathways that radiate out from the ornate central pond with its clumps of papyrus. In the fading evening light their colours glow as if lit from within. Overhead the air is filled with the chatter of birds beginning to roost.

He has taken care not to enter through the front of the hotel and be slowly observed by Lascaris as he descends the broad stone steps into the garden, as if that might have exposed him to an assassin's cool inspection. Christ, he thinks, I'm becoming paranoid. All the same, he can't quite shake the feeling. Slowly he makes a circuit of the garden, checking for watchers, but it appears to be deserted, except for the single figure at the very centre, dressed in white.

Alexander Lascaris is seated on a wooden bench overlooking the circular pool. He is wearing a white linen *galabiya*, edged at the hem and neck with black braid. On his head sits a cream panama hat with a black band. White loafers complete the ensemble. At this moment he has his legs crossed, his hands folded, as he stares straight ahead as if contemplating the thick clumps of papyrus. Finn approaches from behind, relishing his moment of surprise. "Nice hat."

Lascaris starts, then steadies himself. He turns and studies Finn coolly for a moment. Then he smiles. It's that same infectious smile that Finn remembers from that grey morning in Islington, the eyes crinkling in ironic amusement as if everything is a game. Without a word he rises, takes the hat from his head and sweeps it low in a theatrical bow. He holds it out to Finn. "It's a Number One."

"A *what?*"

"A Number One. Didn't you know? Panama hats have five gradings. Number five is the coarsest, like a beach hat. But Number Ones ...." He holds the hat lovingly between his hands and slowly twists it into a long, tight cylinder. "Number Ones are only produced to order for special occasions like weddings. They have to be made in damp, dark conditions underground to preserve their suppleness. They take at least four months to complete."

"Must be charming for the workers."

"True, but even more charming for the wearer." He removes a gold signet ring from the little finger of his left hand and draws the tightly rolled hat through it in a single unbroken motion. Released, the hat instantly springs back into perfect shape. "That," says Lascaris triumphantly, "is how you can tell a Number One."

Just as Finn is about to respond, he becomes aware of Lascaris glancing towards the hotel. Finn follows his gaze. Two men in western suits are descending the stone steps. They walk quickly towards the hotel offices on the north side of the garden and disappear behind a hedge of hibiscus. For a moment Finn's brain feels scrambled. Then his heart gives a jolt. The one on the right, surely, is the sinister character from the police station at el-Akhmin – al Shaikh? What the hell is he doing here? Trying to force down the anxiety, he takes the hat from Lascaris and turns it over, buying time to steady himself.

"Very impressive," he says at length. Casually he hands back the panama. "How long are you staying here?"

"Oh, I shall be around for several weeks. Or at least until something interesting happens with our little plan."

"Several weeks! Don't the locals get suspicious? People usually only stay a day or two here, maximum a week. The antiquities police are constantly on the look-out for any unusual behaviour. The hotel will notify them for sure."

Lascaris shrugs. "It's no problem. I'm well known here as a film maker. As far as the authorities are concerned, I'm simply researching another film. It will take as long as it takes. They will give me no trouble." He takes Finn by the elbow. "Shall we walk a little? It's a pleasant evening for a stroll."

For a while they walk in silence. The air is beginning to cool and with the lengthening shadows comes an oasis-like calm. The sounds of Luxor are distant. "And how goes Mr Mountjoy's astrological tour?" asks Lascaris at length.

"I am surrounded by people who meditate at frequent intervals, do not eat meat and drink their own urine for breakfast."

Lascaris smiles. "Ah! They tell me that is good for the soul."

"Yours or mine?"

"In this case, yours, I suppose. Has anything of interest occurred?"

"Not yet. Apart from the minor incident of getting trapped inside a collapsing pyramid." Lascaris says nothing. Finn frowns. Did Lascaris think he was joking? "But if anything's going to happen, at least according to your bizarre theory about Mountjoy, it should be the day after tomorrow."

Lascaris raises his eyebrows in enquiry. "Why the day after tomorrow?"

"Because," says Finn slowly, "In case you had forgotten, the day after tomorrow just happens to be my birthday."

"Ah yes, of course," says Lascaris as if he has suddenly become absent-minded. "Does Mountjoy know that?"

"*Of course* he knows that!" snaps Finn, suddenly irritated by Lascaris's casual obliqueness. "He knows everybody's fucking birthdays. He knows their time of birth. He knows their place of birth. He knows their ascendants and descendants. He knows their meridians and conjunctions. For all I know he probably knows the workings of their small intestines."

"And where is the group scheduled to be when they celebrate this grand ritual of your Solar Return?"

"Apparently we were going to go to Dendarah, but the programme's been changed – a terrorist scare or something. So we're taking a two-day trip to el-Amarna instead."

Lascaris stops dead. "El-Amarna!" He looks disgusted. It's the first time Finn has seen him ruffled. "But there's nothing there! It's just a barren plain. There can't be anything to be found there!"

"Except beautiful faience cosmetic boxes …" Finn watches him carefully.

"But that doesn't come ….!" Lascaris stops himself, folds his arms. "There can't be anything much at el-Amarna," he repeats. "We both know that. It's just a deserted site. An ancient rubbish dump. It was completely razed by Akhenaten's successors after his death." He shakes his head morosely.

"Right. Well, this is where we test out your crazy theory about David Mountjoy."

"*Our* crazy theory," corrects Lascaris. Suddenly he stops and seems to brighten, as if he has just remembered something. "By the way, I met two of your colleagues in the hotel this morning. I'm sure you must know them."

"Colleagues?" asks Finn warily. He is uncomfortably aware of Lascaris constantly being half a step ahead of him and he doesn't want any more shocks.

"Yes, the celebrated Professor Dortmann and his companion, the charming Doctor Rusedska. They're staying here at the hotel." For a moment Finn feels disorientated, his brain racing to catch up. Nadia and Dortmann together? *Here?* But Lascaris is already talking: "I must say she is a most attractive young woman – the longest legs I've ever seen. And apparently a most talented Egyptologist, the new rising star in the firmament everybody says. Probably Dortmann's successor in the world of Egyptology. But he seems *very* well aware of that ....."

The last words are packed with unspoken meaning. Dortmann and Nadia an item? It seems highly unlikely. Not from what he knows of the old professor. But still, with Nadia anything is possible....

Suddenly Finn becomes aware of Lascaris observing him with a strange predatory intentness. He has seen that look before sitting on the sofa in Islington that morning just after Lascaris had handed him Mountjoy's absurd green programme..... And, as he gropes towards an answer, something that has been nagging at his brain for weeks like an undiagnosed pain, suddenly crystallises: Lascaris hadn't been surprised at the coincidence with his birthday! He hadn't been surprised *because he already knew his date of birth!* At the time Finn had wondered, then dismissed the idea. But now...

They have reached the stone steps. Lascaris stops and holds out his hand. "I'll meet you here the evening after you get back. Same time. Let's hope Mister Mountjoy can pull more than just the proverbial rabbit out of his astrological hat."

They shake hands and Finn watches him patter up the stone steps. Half way up he stops, swivels and gives one of his infectious smiles. "Oh ..... and *do* enjoy your Solar Return. It's all in a good cause, you know. You will be very much in my thoughts."

Screw you, thinks Finn. But he can't help smiling as the curious figure in his Number One panama hat and white *galabiya* disappears into the hotel through the broad French windows.

Finn walks in the garden for another ten minutes, keeping well away from the offices where he has seen al-Shaikh. Then, when sufficient time has elapsed, he exits through the garden gate, down the narrow side-street, circles the hotel and comes back in through the front door. No sign of Lascaris. He approaches the reception desk in the opulent entrance hall.

Professor Dortmann? Yes, sir. And Doctor Rusedska? Yes indeed. The receptionist in a black tail coat turns to inspect the line of pigeon holes with keys. He turns back. "It would appear," he says apologetically in impeccable English, "that the Professor and the Doctor are out." Finn thanks him.

As he goes back down the broad steps, the question is still reverberating in his head: Dortmann and Nadia here together in the heat of August? Why? Uncomfortably he remembers something Mountjoy had said – *Synchronicity is meaningful coincidence.* He brushes it aside. The receptionist had inspected *two* keys, so probably Lascaris's lurid innuendo is pure speculation. And, although he certainly doesn't relish meeting Nadia again – especially in Dortmann's company – her presence here might just be a windfall.

He crosses the street, passes the line of waiting caleches, ignoring their drivers' invitations, and threads his way through a knot of children trying to sell a grotesque plastic bust of Akhenaten. He sits down on the concrete parapet that borders the river. The incident with the birthday is still nagging at his mind. And he can feel a wave of anger coming up now – with Lascaris. But also with himself. How the hell did he ever manage to get involved in this whole crazy, possibly dangerous, plan? With al-Shaikh prowling around, what had felt like a harmless escapade back in London has suddenly taken on a real edge of threat. He shrugs irritably. Probably the whole thing will come to nothing anyway. A complete waste of time and money.

Erratically his mind jumps to Lara. It's strange how much he seems to miss her when she's not around. An odd sense of desolation washes over him. *Stop it!* He thinks. *Don't go there!* I'm not for her. I'm a wrecker. It's what I always seem to do to people. And besides, there's so obviously something going on between her and Edward, even though neither of them seems aware of it. He digs the heel of his boot into the dust and looks out across the river. The sun has just set behind the mountains of Deir-el-Bahri. The Valley of the Kings is already sunk in deep violet shadows. Above him the chatter of roosting birds in the trees is reaching a crescendo.

"Please mister! Wanna buy scarab? Please. Very cheap! Please! *Please!*"

Finn stares at the flat ceramic beetle in the grimy outstretched hand. The boy is no more than seven, with a long face and serious brown eyes. The eyes hold a look of silent desperation. Just below the hairline runs a long diagonal sore. A fly is crawling up and down its length. The boy makes no effort to brush it away. It's like a sign of defeat, a mute acknowledgement that for him things can never change. Finn reaches into his pocket and holds up a one pound note.

"Two," says the boy.

With an exaggerated show of reluctance, Finn takes out another note and hands it to him. The boy grabs the notes, passes over the scarab and shoots off down the road, hopping excitedly on one leg. He turns the ugly scarab over in his hand. It is made of cheap plaster, gaudily painted in acrylic blue, a disastrous, shoddy pastiche of everything that was once great in ancient Egypt. He loops his forefinger around its curved edge, draws back his arm and sends it skimming with all his force through the evening sky towards the Nile. Jesus, he thinks, what a fucking mess we all make of things!

Then he stands and crosses the road towards the Luxor Museum. Once inside he turns right towards a small doorway guarded by a bored-looking attendant with a pile of crumpled tickets on the table in front of him. Finn pays another five pounds. The long, narrow room is deserted. No tourist ever bothers to pay the extra to come in here. In the sudden silence it feels tomb-like, as if he is sealed off from the outside world.

Twelve statues of deities line the walls, each one perfectly preserved, as if they have just left the sculptor's studio. It's a time warp, as if he is falling back through three and a half thousand years and suddenly stumbling into the presence of the gods. These are the sculptures found in perfect condition in the secret chamber under the Solar Court of the Luxor Temple, the chance discovery made in the exact same spot where ten days earlier David Mountjoy had performed the ritual of his own Solar Return. *Pure coincidence?* Or could it just possibly, as Lascaris claims, be an event orchestrated by some unseen force, something totally beyond his normal comprehension?

Slowly he makes his way down the long gallery. There, at the end, gazing imperiously down the length of the room is the celebrated statue of Amenhotep III, the father of Akhenaten, possibly the most beautiful ancient Egyptian sculpture ever found. Finn stands there, gazing up, as the Pharaoh rises majestically above him, his left leg thrust aggressively forward, caught in mid-stride for all eternity. The crisply pleated kilt clings to his narrow hips and powerful thighs. Each line and detail has been carved with almost superhuman precision. Utterly lost in his concentration, Finn feels his breathing slow. And for an hallucinatory moment it seems not so much the stone effigy of the Pharaoh standing before him, but the god-king himself, gazing out untouched by the passage of three and a half thousand years, still breathing with the power of the immortals .....

"Mr Connors!"

Disorientated, Finn jumps. Then he turns.

"What a most pleasant surprise!" Bernard Dortmann is holding out his hand in greeting. "But I fear we have disturbed your contemplation." He smiles in apology. Then he gestures courteously to his right. "You know Doctor Rusedska, of course."

"Yes, we've met." Nadia shakes his hand briefly and looks ostentatiously over his shoulder.

"And this is Doctor Saad al-Jawad, the newly appointed director of the Luxor Museum." A gaunt, nervous-looking Egyptian dressed in ill-fitting western clothes hovers beside them. He bows low as he shakes Finn's hand but, despite the servile gesture, Finn catches a flash of cold enquiry in the eyes.

"Such an honour to have the great Professor here." The Egyptian smiles obsequiously up at Dortmann. "And of course our distinguished – and *most* charming – colleague from

Edinburgh." The eyes run over Nadia with more than casual interest.

"It is truly Egypt's greatest masterpiece," says Dortmann, turning back to the statue. "Red quartzite is the one of the rarest of all stones. It's used for a mere handful of royal sculptures. It must have held some esoteric significance of which we are now sadly unaware."

"Do you know the real story of how this group was found?" asks Finn, wondering if the professor could shed more light on the strange events of the discovery.

Dortmann spreads his hands. "All the reports, although almost incredible, are apparently true. The Egyptian Antiquities Service was trying to stabilise one of the temple's columns, when suddenly – whoosh!" He throws out his arms in a theatrical gesture. "Thirty yards behind them the ground just opens up. And the next minute the workmen are staring down into this deep pit with the Pharaoh Amenhotep staring up at them." He smiles. "It's one of those strange events that makes ancient and modern Egypt so fascinating. Egyptology isn't just laborious excavation or the painstaking decipherment of obscure inscriptions. There's so much more to it." He turns to Nadia. "Is that not so?"

She beams a smile up at him and nods. Finn watches them closely, trying to see if there is anything there to support Lascaris's prurient claims. Nadia catches his inquisitive glance and lowers her eyes.

"Was it just pure coincidence?"

Dortmann shrugs. "What else? Of course, there must be a rational explanation. Probably the work on the column had upset the equilibrium of the soil. I don't know. But still, I enjoy the mystery." Finn smiles. Although he has known the elderly professor for many years, he has never seen him so relaxed and expansive.

Dortmann glances round at al-Jawad, but seeing him deep in conversation with Nadia, he leans forward and goes on in a quieter voice, "Anyway, it's a wonderful Egyptian story. They struggle to do one thing and make a complete mess of it – the column is now in danger of collapse. But, as a result, while they're all looking the other way, they achieve something far more spectacular – purely by mistake!"

Finn laughs. The museum director turns to look at him and, in a strange synaptic flash, Finn notices how close he is standing to Nadia and how she has not backed away, as if encouraging some kind of complicity.

"But we must not interrupt you further," says Dortmann. "To break in on a man's communion with Amenhotep III is already unforgivable."

"No, no." says Finn hurriedly. "I was just leaving anyway. I have to get back."

"Do you stay long?" asks Dortmann.

"Another ten days, although tomorrow I'm making a two-day trip to el-Amarna."

"Doctor Rusedska and I are staying at the Winter Palace Hotel. Perhaps you would care to dine with us one evening?"

"I would like that very much," says Finn.

"Then shall we say Thursday? Eight o'clock?"

Finn thanks him and shakes his hand. He looks at Nadia. She gives the briefest of smiles, then ostentatiously turns to face the statue.

On the way down the steps into the hot night air, Finn shrugs off Nadia's obvious snub. He can hardly blame her. But still, if he could only just win her round…. Now *that*, he thinks to himself, as he crosses to the Nile, would be my kind of synchronicity.

SEVENTEEN

It is still dark as the group straggles aboard the bus in ones and twos. They are all dressed in white *galabiyas* to celebrate the ritual of Finn's Solar Return at el-Amarna. A forced display of hilarity fails to conceal the general air of self-consciousness. Birgit has tied her blonde hair back in two bunches like a schoolgirl. She pauses on the platform beside the driver to do a brief pirouette. There is a smattering of ironic applause. The giant Kai has obviously been unable to find a *galabiya* long enough to fit his huge bulk. The robe hangs halfway down his shins like a nightshirt, exposing a pair of ancient white trainers and half-length maroon socks. Lara comes and sits in the window seat in front of Edward. She looks shy and demure in her white smock She turns to him.

"Ready for the great adventure?"

Edward sniffs. "We look like something out of a fancy-dress Thousand and One Nights! Thank God only the night porter was around to see us."

Finn arrives last. He grimaces at them, slides in beside Lara and settles back noisily in his creaking seat.

"You look rather grand," says Edward, leaning forward and folding his arms on the seat back. "A bit like a desert sheikh."

"I feel bloody ridiculous."

Lara smiles at him. "Actually," she says, "he's right. You look good like that. A sort of latter-day Lawrence of Arabia. And, by the way, Happy Birthday!"

Finn grunts non-commitally. His eyes are heavy-lidded with sleep and thick stubble lines his jaw. Another busy night with Birgit? wonders Lara, trying not to let the thought percolate into her feelings. Playfully she stretches out her hand and draws it down the red-blonde stubble on his cheek. "And what a great shave!"

With deliberate slowness Finn turns and looks at her and, for a long moment, their eyes lock. Then Lara turns away, aware that she is starting to blush. Why on earth did I do that? she thinks. I'm behaving like a teenager! She swivels round and stares out of the window. From the corner of her eye she can see Edward observing them.

From outside comes shouting in Arabic. Then the driver climbs in, slams the door and kicks the asthmatic engine into life. Above them the air-conditioning grilles belch out clouds of condensation. Lara sighs in relief and settles back in her seat.

They ride in silence until the dawn comes up, illuminating the dense swathe of vegetation to their left and the broad expanse of the Nile beyond. To their right rocky hillocks and the tops of isolated palms appear out of the early mist. Lara turns round to Edward, but his eyes are closed and he seems to have fallen back into sleep. Finn is staring out of the window, studying the passing landscape. She leans towards him, wanting to re-establish their normal easy contact.

"You've never told me what Mountjoy said when he did your astrological chart."

Finn turns. "Oh, that!" He waves a hand dismissively. "It was a bit like the end-of-term assessment with the headmaster. Must try harder."

Lara frowns. "Try harder in what way?" She knows she is being insistent, but his constant evasiveness around anything serious has begun to irritate her.

"Oh, I don't know," says Finn. "Frankly, I've forgotten most of it. All those trines squared Uranus conjunct Neptune stuff doesn't mean much to me." He hesitates and runs his finger hesitantly along the seat back in front of him. "The one thing I do remember for some reason is that there's a funny set-up between Pluto and Saturn and my Sun. Mountjoy seemed to think it was some kind of big deal – 'A challenging conjunction.'" He mimics Mountjoy's reedy voice with its northern inflection.

Lara looks at him in surprise. "That's strange. Edward told me he has something very similar. Apparently Sun-Pluto conjunct is about having two sides to your character. One side is shining, extrovert. The other's dark and sombre. And usually one part is not being expressed."

Finn snorts. "Well, that might be true of Edward, but no one has ever accused *me* of not expressing anything!"

Lara looks at him quizzically. "Hmmm ..... I wonder," she says slowly. "I really wonder." Finn appears to ignore her and for a while they are silent. Then she asks, "Do you think that night in the pyramid has changed you?"

Finn stares at her in surprise. "Why do you ask? In what way?"

"Oh, I don't know. I was just thinking about it." She hesitates. "I mean ..... we almost died in there. Hasn't it had any effect on you at all?"

Finn shrugs as if to dismiss the question. "I'm pleased to be alive if that's what you mean. It sure beats the hell out of the alternative." He drums his fingers on the seat back. It's obvious that the conversation is making him uncomfortable, but she isn't going to let him off the hook this time by colluding in his jokes. "I don't know," he says reluctantly. "It happened. It wasn't fun. I'm alive. That's pretty much it. I'm a literal kind of person, you know. Too much introspection's not my thing. I think my 'inner eye', as Mountjoy likes to call it, must be myopic. Frankly I don't get most of what he's on about."

"Or don't want to get it?"

Finn shrugs. "Maybe. Who knows?" He pauses. "If you really want to know, Mountjoy went on and on about me living my life too literally. 'Plundering Pluto, the god of the Underworld'….." He etches the inverted commas in the air with his forefingers. "Instead of searching for his hidden riches. Some shit like that." He glances at Lara, not wanting to provoke her again. "'Refusing the depths' was the precise phrase, I think." He pauses. "You know, I somehow have the feeling he doesn't quite buy my investment banker routine. He kind of dismissed it, as if he already knows it's phoney."

"How did that feel?"

"That he was seeing through me?"

"Right."

"Actually, a bit weird. I hadn't quite expected it. But he probably gives the same routine to everybody. The more he can put them off their stride, the more in control he is." He catches her dismissive look. "Okay, to be honest, it felt bloody destabilising." He pushes his hand back through his hair.

"Do you think he knows you're a dealer and everything?"

Finn shrugs. "I doubt even his extra-terrestrial information sources are that good. Still, it's an unnerving thought…." And suddenly, he realizes that he has never actually asked himself exactly what Mountjoy's role in this whole weird business really is. It's as if his resistance to the man has blinded him to this obvious question. Is he really just a naïve, self-important New Age freak? Or is it just possible that he knows precisely what his rituals seem to provoke – at least according to Lascaris? And if so, what does he do with that knowledge?

"Did he say what would happen if you didn't stop 'Plundering Pluto' as he put it?" Lara's voice cuts across his thoughts.

Finn lets out a short puff of breath. "Well, if you really want to know, he said that the god would rise and avenge himself and I would be imprisoned in the Underworld. Something like that."

"Christ!"

"My thoughts precisely. Not wildly encouraging, is it? Somehow I don't think I'm his favourite pupil."

For a long while Lara is silent. She is intensely aware of the anxiety that had just crept over her. Aware too of how right Mountjoy is about Finn having two sides unreconciled, constantly at war. "It sounds to me," she says slowly, "like he saw you were keeping the lid pretty tight on one part of yourself that doesn't normally see the light of day."

Finn shrugs. "Now you start to sound like Mountjoy. Or Edward. That's far too psychological for me." He points out of the window. "We're nearly there." Then, seeing her look of concern, he puts his arm around her shoulders and gives her a squeeze. "Don't worry," he says. "I'm a survivor. Pluto's not going to get me just yet."

*

It is after nine when they finally step off the bus. The freshness of the morning is already fading. The still, dry heat is beginning to build. The riverbank here slopes sharply down to an unsteady wooden landing stage. The far bank is dotted with a line of palms. Beyond them a vast, empty plain shimmers in the early light. It stretches out to a distant barren escarpment, which closes off the space like a giant amphitheatre. The sun is already well clear of the ridge, bleaching out the sky.

The usual boat for the crossing is found to be unserviceable and instead they board a square raft made of planks lashed together, supported on a clutch of empty petrol drums. A young man with a long scar down his left cheek sits impassively on an upturned wooden crate, his bony hand resting on the throttle of a small outboard motor. When they have all clambered aboard he gives a sharp pull on the starter cord and the engine splutters into life.

Edward sits down beside Finn. "Nervous about the ritual?"

Finn shrugs. "No. Why should I be? It's just a fancy-dress tea party."

But despite his attempt at indifference, Finn is aware of a mounting sense of unreality, as if he has somehow been *conveyed* here to el-Amarna, rather than determining the course of his own journey.

As the unsteady raft nears the far bank, the deserted landing stage suddenly explodes with children. They shoot from behind palms and hibiscus and catapult out of mud huts and wooden shacks. The air rings with shouts as they run towards the water, pushing each other into the dust, holding out beads and plastic scarabs, multi-coloured hands of Fatima and grimy Coca-cola bottles.

A moment later a thick-set bull of a man, dressed in khaki fatigues, lumbers out of a wooden kiosk. He picks up a long bamboo stick and begins flailing it across the ground. The screams spiral as the children try to jump it like a skipping rope, only to have it crack viciously across their shins and ankles. Within half a minute the landing stage is clear. As the group disembarks, the children watch from a safe distance, stretching out their hands in silence. Lara feels her heart lurch. They look so poor and dishevelled, far more ragged than the children in Luxor. Their arms and ankles are stick-like. Their eyes look like porcelain against their blackened faces. Flies circle and cluster at sores and open wounds. A little girl with a mane of matted auburn hair bursts forward, holding out a crude wooden statuette. Instantly the uniformed guard lashes out with his stick, sending her scurrying back to the safety of the crowd.

Under the palms at the top of the bank stands a rusting tractor with a tall vertical exhaust pipe, like a ship's funnel. Hitched to the back is a low farm trailer with raised sides. A torn canopy of red and green cotton has been stretched across a wooden frame to provide shade. Down either side run low benches. The policeman gestures for them to climb aboard and casually holds out his hand for *baksheesh*. When everyone is on the tractor starts up with a belch of black smoke and an explosive clattering from the engine. And they are off, bumping across the uneven ground in the direction of the distant rock-face. A posse of screaming children, now beyond the reach of the policeman, follow in desperate pursuit, holding out their wares, their thin legs kicking out frantically behind them. Within seconds they are left behind, standing in a swirling cloud of dust. All around the sun bounces off the huge amphitheatre of sand and rock, welding it into a shimmering haze of white.

None of the group notices the man in the black *galabiya* and white *tarboosh* crouching in the shade of the palm trees, playing with a long string of amber worry-beads.

*

Finn, Edward and Lara are standing on a narrow ledge, trying to keep within the band of shade thrown by the rock-face above. Far below them the vast featureless plain of el-Amarna stretches out until it dissolves in a flickering mirage. The glare of the sun is merciless. All around sand and dust, rock and scree, scorching, barren, lion-coloured, shimmer in the haze. The Nile, barely visible in the gathering heat, seems shrunk to a thin silver glitter. The cultivation is at its narrowest here, the swathe of green less than twenty meters wide, barely clinging to the edges of the great river. It looks like a moonscape, majestic in its austerity.

"This is what we came to see," says Finn, spreading his arms towards the view. "Not those boring second-rate tombs along the ridge that Mountjoy seems so excited by. I hope they take another half hour in there and leave us in peace."

Lara leans back against the rock, and slides down until she is resting on her haunches. She stares out across the plain. There is something profoundly moving in the silence and the uncompromising grandeur of the place. "It's magical," she whispers. "Absolutely magical." Finn settles down beside her and stretches out his legs.

"Why here?" asks Edward.

Finn glances up at him. "You mean why did Akhenaten build his capital here?"

"Right. The other great Egyptian sites like Karnak and Memphis are all located in fertile places. That makes good practical sense. But this ….." He gestures towards the plain. "It's just a giant dust bowl!"

Finn nods. "Every Egyptologist who's ever come here must have asked themselves the same question. Akhenaten says in his records that he was 'divinely directed' to choose this place. You can't really argue with that."

"Divinely directed .....?" murmurs Edward. "I wonder what he meant by that. He must have felt a special energy here, something quite different from just practical necessity. Some kind of spiritual power presumably...?"

Lara hugs her knees to her chest and rests her chin on them. "It has the most incredible atmosphere," she says. "It's almost hypnotic, somehow other-worldly. From up here I think I can begin to understand why Akhenaten became the world's first monotheist. Everywhere else in Egypt the great river dominates, with its constant flooding and ebbing and all its fertile fields and swamps and exotic animal life. So then that whole baroque mythology of gods with crocodile bodies and falcon heads and so on seems completely right, as if the lushness of the place just gave rise to the gods naturally. But here .....!" She spreads her arms. "All you have here is the desert. Everything else is obliterated by the light. It makes me think of those early hermits in the wilderness – Saint Simeon and Saint Jerome. I'm sure Akhenaten must have had some of those ascetic qualities."

Edward nods in agreement. "Here there's only one thing that really matters." He points at the sky. "The great disc of the sun. In the face of that, everything else just falls away. Imagine how it must have felt in the days before electricity. Each evening the sun disappears, dropping below the western horizon in a ball of flame, plunging the world into complete darkness, leaving you only with your faith that it will reappear. Then, the next dawn it rises again, huge above the escarpment. It would completely dominate your life. Here I can easily imagine becoming a sun-worshipper and abandoning all other gods. You're right, the place *is* hypnotic. You can almost feel the power of it taking you over." Suddenly, despite the heat, he shivers. "And somehow you can feel the presence of Akhenaten too. It's as if he's never truly left. Still the presiding spirit."

For a long while they sit in silence. The plain is full of white light and stillness. And, as they sit there, a wave seems to wash through them, welding them together in an intimacy beyond their bodies. Lara glances at Finn and Edmund to see if they are feeling it too. And suddenly a deep sense of gratitude wells up inside her. Tears begin to prickle her eyes. She reaches out, takes their hands and squeezes them.

"This is a good time," she says quietly. "*A good time*. I know it will stay with me all my life. Thank you both."

Finn starts to speak, but a sudden burst of noise to their right cuts across the moment. The group is emerging from a rock tomb further along the ledge. There is a heavy clank as the guardian pushes shut the metal gate.

"Come along you three!" booms Mountjoy irritably. "It's already eleven-twenty. We've only got quarter of an hour to Finn's Solar Return!"

They rise. Once clear of the shade, the heat hits them like the open door of a furnace. The rocks along the pathway down to the plain are too hot to touch with the naked hand. They are all slightly drunk with fatigue from the early morning and the burning light and the power of the place.

As the tractor bounces across the rutted plain, back in the direction of the river, the group chatters excitedly. "Please!" shouts David Mountjoy above the clatter of the engine. "We are in the sacred precinct of the city of el-Amarna! I would ask you all to remain silent until we have reached the appointed place of the Solar Return."

Lara turns to Finn. "Appointed place? What's he talking about?"

Finn shrugs. "No idea."

Mountjoy rises, holding on to the swaying canopy. His eyes sweep backwards and forwards, scanning the horizon. Suddenly, about two-thirds of the way towards the Nile, he glances at his watch, leans over, taps the driver on the shoulder and gestures for him to stop. The tractor slows to a halt. The engine shudders, gives one last sharp explosion and falls silent.

Without a word, Mountjoy dismounts and walks towards a line of tall palms some two hundred yards to the north. Between the trees and the tractor are a few scattered remains of ancient mud-brick walls. He begins to walk backwards and forwards in the barren space between the line of collapsed walls and the palm trees, circling and weaving like a cat trying to find a resting place. There is no wind. Nothing moves. The white pacing figure begins to shimmer in a mirage. Suddenly he stops. For a full minute he stands motionless. The group is silent. And gradually in that bowl of welding light the silence seems to expand until it roars in their ears. David Mountjoy holds up both arms and beckons them forward.

As Finn steps down off the trailer into the rutted sand, he is hit by a strange sense of isolation, as if he is suddenly cut off from the rest of the world. His brain scrambles for a reassuring hook of logic. *After all, isn't this precisely the moment he has come for? Exactly what he and Lascaris had wanted?* But nothing can dispel the anxiety that is rising in him now like a floodtide.

At first he feels absurd lying in the dust with the staring faces and white gowns ranged in a circle above him. They are at the very margin of the shade cast by the line of palms. The slightest movement of any frond exposes him to a laser-flash of sunlight. Slowly the two circles begin to revolve, moving in opposite directions, hands linked. Finn closes his eyes, trying to shut out the spinning sky above, the steady thud of feet, the swelling nausea.

He struggles to focus his mind on the pressure of the ground under his back, the heat against his face, the swaying palms at the edge of his vision….. *Anything* to prevent the sense of dislocation that is creeping over him. But the rhythmical stamping is becoming hypnotic. He feels himself drift and grow weightless. His mind begins to slip and scatter, splintering into random thoughts – Mountjoy's tangled beard, Lascaris's thin fingers on the cosmetic box, the black claustrophobic walls of the pyramid at Maidum ….

David Mountjoy lets out a low, throbbing sound. Gradually the group picks it up.

"*Ommm* ….. *Ommm.*"

The sound swells in Finn's ears, dies away. Swells again. It seems to penetrate his eardrums and enter his skull. It surges through him, unbinds his muscles, sucks him helpless into its rhythm. His arms and legs begin to vibrate to the thud of footfalls. Hands lift him, circle him, binding him to the rhythm. White light strobes his face. He can feel himself spinning faster and faster, shattering his last desperate efforts at control. Until something that has been gathering inside him all morning, all week, all …… suddenly finds its channel, pours through his body, obliterating his mind …..

The glittering dome above him pulses and swells, grows brighter. And splits open in a blinding flash of white.

In the distance a cock crows. He gazes up at the palms and the clear blue-white of the dawn sky. In his body he feels the slow rising of the sun. Its heat throbs like a pulse in his blood. Down the long street between the tall white houses are lotus flowers and cobra heads, red, green,

cobalt blue, raised against the sky. Figures scuttle past,
hurrying towards the square. Sand under his feet, greased
leopard-skin against his chest, a film of sweat and scented
ointment on his shaven head, sharp smell of incense in the
nostrils. Up ahead a deep groan swells and falls, the sound
of ten thousand throats. Expectant. Hungry. He steps
into the square. Into the ring of light. Into the heartbeat
of the ten thousand. The groan rises to a roar. His limbs
begin to shudder, unleashed by the god. The line of bronze
trumpets is raised. The gilded curtains of the tabernacle of
the sun begin to part. The groaning lifts him on its swell,
roars in his ears. The axe is raised. The light blinds him.
The blood-red disc rises behind the rim of the mountains.
And suddenly, unleashed, something flies out from the
ravine, comes rifling across the plain directly towards him
until it pierces his body and splits the sky. And he is falling
… Down …. Down ….. The flung spars of him shatter
and dissolve, absorbed into the darkness…..

Painfully Finn opens his eyes. The world seems blurred. There
is an ache in his throat and a terrible sense of dislocation, as
if something that has always been hard-wired in his brain has
come loose and is turning in the wind. Lara's hand brushes
the hair off his forehead. Her grey eyes are filled with concern.
"Are you alright?"

He nods and eases upwards, supporting himself on his
elbows. He looks around at the faces. Slowly they come into
focus, creased in anxiety. Directly opposite him stands David
Mountjoy, feet apart, arms folded, a smile of satisfaction on his
lips. Finn's vision begins to circle again. He feels another hand on
his shoulder, then Edward is supporting him upright. "Christ, I
thought you'd screamed yourself into extinction," he said.

Finn looks dazed. "Did I scream?"

"As if you were never going to stop."

Slowly, with Edward's help, Finn climbs unsteadily to his feet. His whole body seems insubstantial, as if he has no bones. He is aware of Lara's soft touch on his left arm. His head rings, his eyes ache, his throat feels as if something solid has been dragged through it. He feels nauseous. Edward supports him across to the palm trees. He slumps down, props his back against one of the ridged trunks. The group has become a shimmering mass of white.

Finn lets out a deep breath and shakes his head. "That was something!" he says. Then he gives a faint smile. "It's a helluva way to spend my birthday, isn't it?"

"Oh Finn!" says Lara and holds his head for a moment against her chest, caught between exasperation and relief.

EIGHTEEN

By the time Lara comes downstairs Edward is waiting for her in the desolate hotel lobby. For a moment he stares at her in surprise. She is wearing a pair of loose, dark blue linen trousers and a white shirt buttoned at the throat and wrists. A blue headscarf covers her blonde hair and is fastened at the nape of her neck. In the austerity of the scarf her features are accentuated, her high cheekbones more prominent, her grey-green eyes seem enormous. As she walks towards him there is a fluidity to her movements he hasn't noticed before. It's as if the loose-fitting clothes have given her permission to be more at ease with her body. For the first time he feels a shock of sensuality in her presence. He raises his eyebrows in enquiry.

"All covered up, I see."

"Well, when we drove through the town I noticed that all the women were swathed in black from head to foot. I just felt it would be better not to flaunt myself here."

He nods. "Have you seen Finn?"

She hands him a folded piece of paper. "I found this pushed under my door when I woke up."

He glances at it.

Something I need to do. Meet you in the hall around eight for 'dinner'. F.

"What on earth would he have to do *here?*"

"Exactly what I thought. He's a man of mystery all right."

He shrugs. "Well, shall we go for a walk anyway?"

"Sure. Anything would be better than staying in this shitty hotel."

"How's your room?"

"It's a dump. It has cockroaches. There's an arthritic fan that squeaks so loudly I can't sleep and the shower dribbles like an incontinent dog."

"Mine too. I guess it's the price you pay for getting off the beaten tourist track in Egypt."

For a while they walk in silence. El-Minya has clearly seen better days. Set on a rubbish-strewn side channel of the Nile, its once stately colonial houses are badly decayed and crumbling now. Their long French windows are smashed, the heavy wooden slatted shutters split and peeling, the classical cornices crumbling to dust. The air smells of stagnant water and garbage. Some of the old houses have disappeared altogether, replaced by half-finished concrete shells where the empty floors are packed with makeshift dwellings of wood and cardboard.

Lara shakes her head in despair. "They look like Bedouins marooned in some god-forsaken urban desert." On the shattered pavement a group of boys is playing football with a tin can. They stop to stare at the foreigners, their black eyes filled with suspicion. Lara smiles at them. The boys gaze blankly back. "It feels as if we're a totally alien species to them. They don't even beg."

"I don't think they're very used to tourists here," says Edward.

"Why not?"

"There aren't many famous archaeological sites in the area, and anyway it's pretty inaccessible. I think everyone normally

216

skips this bit and flies direct from Cairo to Luxor. Also, from what I hear, this is the hotbed of Islamic Fundamentalism. If a tourist is going to get assassinated anywhere, this would be the place."

She blows out a small puff of air. "That's encouraging!"

"I'm sure we'll be fine, so long as we don't stray into the back quarters." He stops and looks up and down the street in desperation. "Perhaps we should go down to the river. At least that hasn't been tarmacked over yet."

She nods and takes his arm as they clamber over a low concrete wall, where a few rusting spikes indicate the shattered remains of a once decorative wrought iron railing. They pick their way through the dust and scrub until they find a patch of coarse grass. Lara sinks down and folds her legs under her. Beside her Edward circles his arms round his raised knees and stares glumly across the water. A hundred yards to their right, where a metal bridge spans the canal, two boys are leaning over its parapet dropping stones into the water. Despite the occasional traffic, they can hear the faint plop as each pebble breaks the surface. The sun has sunk behind the houses at their back, casting the canal into deep purple shadow. Ahead of them the eastern sky is still a clear pale blue. Lara glances at Edward, aware of being alone with him for the first time since they had talked in the hotel garden in Cairo. Without the safety of their comfortable triangle she feels suddenly vulnerable. She wonders if he is sensing it too.

"It seems a long way from the beautiful Nile," she says, wanting to break the silence.

"I suppose even the Nile has to have its slum."

She turns to him. "Didn't that whole thing with Finn this morning strike you as incredibly weird and unlikely? Not just the ritual itself, but that something like that should happen to *him* of all people. And that scream that came out of him! It was terrifying. It was as if something was being ripped out of his soul."

For a while Edward is silent. Then he says, "Perhaps he's not the most unlikely person after all."

"Hmm….." She turns this over in her mind. Not for the first time she's aware of him giving voice to something she has sensed about Finn, but not quite been able to articulate. "Why do you say that?"

"Well, despite everything he does to put you off the scent with all his jovial camaraderie and charm and stuff, if you look closely you can see that he's actually incredibly sensitive and intuitive."

She frowns. "How can you tell?"

"Just watch how he is with people. He senses exactly how they're feeling and what they want. Everyone in the group loves him, even though he constantly makes fun of their beliefs. I suppose that's how he's managed to glide through life so successfully – people just can't help being attracted to him." He smiles. "At least until they have an affair with him, I imagine. When we were in the temple at Karnak, I wandered off with him alone for a while. The way he talked about the monuments and the sculptures was incredibly sensitive. He even became quite emotional at one point, although of course he tried to conceal it." He sighs. "But for some reason he limits himself. It's as if he's been given a real gift with that sensitivity and he's chosen to turn it into a party trick instead."

For a while Lara is silent. She can sense the truth of what Edward is saying and yet she doesn't quite like it. "He's a big contradiction, that's for sure," she says at length. "But there are two things I still really don't get about him. Firstly, why is he so rebellious around Mountjoy? It's almost childish. And secondly, what on earth is he doing a tour like this if he doesn't believe in astrology anyway? It's beyond me!"

"He said he wanted to be in a group so that he would be anonymous as far as the Egyptian authorities are concerned."

"Anonymous? On *this* tour, doing rituals all over the place! And if he's trying to fade in to the background he's certainly not making a terribly good job of it."

"I don't think Finn could fade into the background even if you turned him into a chameleon." She laughs. "But you're right, there seems to be a kind of running battle between him and Mountjoy, and I don't quite understand why. Perhaps he's just a natural rebel."

"Well, maybe. But it still doesn't explain what he's doing on this tour if he doesn't believe in what Mountjoy does anyway."

"I suspect he believes more profoundly than either you or I," says Edward flatly.

She stares at him in amazement. "Finn? Are you kidding me?"

"No."

"Then *why*? Why does he behave like that?"

"I think there's a Celtic part of Finn that's so hyper-intuitive and psychic that it actually scares the hell out of him. So he tries to shut it out. And yet it keeps calling to him. And I suspect that Mountjoy sees that too. And that's what really pisses him off about Finn – that he keeps pushing this psychic, intuitive side away."

"You mean he's schizophrenic?"

Edward smiles. "No, I mean he's normal. We all do that to some degree. Finn's just a rather extreme version of normal. But then he's a rather extreme version of pretty much everything."

She laughs. Then she says, "But why would anyone want to shut down a quality like being intuitive or psychic? If you deny being a potential child molester or something, now that I could understand. But why do it with something that's a gift? Can you, Mr Psychoanalyst, please explain that to me, because to my simple mind it doesn't make any sense at all."

Edward straightens his legs and leans back. "Well, think about it. If you're an exceptionally bright kid born into a working-class family of low intelligence – which was Finn's situation – and you show yourself to be much smarter and more sensitive than your peers, then the chances are you'll be ridiculed, ostracised, probably bullied and beaten up. The same would happen if you're highly intuitive and everyone around you is totally different. You just don't fit in, right? So what do you do? You learn to be just like the others. Or you pretend to be. You learn to be *normal* – at least in their terms. That way, at least, you get to survive. And pretty soon you come to believe that that's the way it *really* is. You literally *can't* access your intelligence or your intuition, even if you want to. It's simply gone into the unconscious and become unavailable."

"Is that what you think happened with Finn?"

He pauses for a moment, thinking. "When we were trapped in the pyramid, he told me some things about his childhood. I don't think it was very easy for him. I got the impression he had never talked to anyone about it before, but I suppose the pressure of the situation somehow forced it out. His mother was some kind of ditzy psychic, a part-time hooker and an alcoholic to boot. An extremely scary person by the sound of it. So that would almost certainly make him want to deny that he himself has an intuitive, psychic side, however strong it may be. Otherwise he'd be afraid of ending up just like her. And so he doesn't want to be mixed up with any of that stuff at all. But that doesn't mean it doesn't exist in him. And if you repress something like that deeply enough for long enough, you can bet that one day it will erupt in some explosive way at an inconvenient moment. And then the effect may be quite shattering, a bit like a dyke suddenly bursting."

"Like the ritual this morning?"

Edward nods. "That's my best guess."

"Or like when he lost it in the pyramid at Maidum?"

"Yes, that too, I suppose."

"But what happened in the pyramid doesn't seem to have affected him at all! I tried to get him to talk about it in the bus, but he wouldn't go there. It's as if he's just dismissed it, all the fear and everything. Remember him ordering champagne afterwards, as if we had been invited to a party?"

Edmund sighs and nods. "I know. He's repressed it. Or tried to repress it. And frankly I find that worrying." He pauses. "Particularly in view of his Tarot card."

Lara stares at him anxiously. She remembers the image of the tower shattered by lightning and her jolt of fear when Finn had held it up, smiling, clearly trying to dismiss it.

"What do you mean?"

For a while Edward is silent. "I don't know," he says at length. "There's something so strange about this whole country….." She frowns. "Well, don't you feel it too? Not everywhere. Not in the crowded tourist places, of course. But when one is alone, like this morning on that ridge overlooking el-Amarna. Or where we did the ritual. Or in the pyramid at Maidum – even before it collapsed. Mountjoy's right: it feels as if one is never quite alone here. As if *they* are always watching – the ancestors, the invisibles, the gods…. whatever you want to call them. They're somehow always present. Then one really can start to believe in synchronicities and Tarot cards and all those sorts of things that we would normally dismiss back home. For example, the ritual this morning was hypnotic. Actually the whole place felt hypnotic. It almost felt as if Akhenaten was still watching." He stops and runs a hand through his hair. "That may sound crazy, but no-one can say that the spot Mountjoy chose was just some purely random place in the desert. It *vibrated* with energy. We all felt it. I could sense that something very strange was going to happen to Finn….."

"How?"

He hesitates. "In the bus, all the way to el-Amarna, I could feel a growing sense of….. I don't know….. foreboding. I was as if something was beginning…." Suddenly he stops and shrugs. "But it's probably all just fantasy. Sometimes I can let my imagination run riot." He sits up and clasps his bare ankles. Almost physically she can sense him pull away. It's as if he feels that by talking too much he has somehow exposed himself. She feels a quick stab of disappointment. Then a flash of irritation. *Why does he always have to play this stupid game of leading you into intimacy, then slamming the door shut and leaving you feeling excluded? How can someone so psychologically wise be so blind to their own failings?*

She watches him stare across the canal, his arms wrapped round his shins like a shield. There's a rigidity in the set of his shoulders, almost like a stubborn child. She hunches forward beside him, matching his hardened posture. After all, she can close up too. They sit like that for several minutes in awkward silence. A line of ducks steeples to their left, then flights down, wings outstretched, skidding onto the glassy surface of the canal. Slowly her irritation subsides. *Why am I always so sensitive with him?* she thinks. *It's ridiculous – two grownups sitting here side-by-side sulking! About what?* Without turning her head, she asks quietly, "What makes you so sad?"

For a while he doesn't answer. Then he says, "Is it that obvious? I thought I was anonymous here. A man with a profession but no past." There is a faint sting of bitterness in his voice. He stays staring out over the canal.

"Is that how you want it?"

Silence.

"Of course, we can leave it like that … only it seems really sad to me. That's all, especially when you're with friends. And lonely too."

He shifts slightly. "My wife died some time ago." His voice is without emphasis.

"I'm sorry. Obviously I didn't know." She hesitates, glancing at him. His face is impassive. "How long ago?"

"Just over four years."

"I see." Only she isn't at all sure that she does. How long does grief take? Can it really thread your life for ever? Can you go about your daily business for a whole lifetime, wearing it like clogs on your feet? Can you surround yourself with it like a self-imposed stockade as he seems to do?

"What was her name?"

"Katherine. Kate."

Kate. She tries to imagine her there with them beside this desolate canal. Blonde? Dark? Beautiful? Ordinary? She searches for her image, as if it might provide an explanation of who he is. Aware too of a feeling of which she feels ashamed – the presence of a rival. God, it's as if her mind has no propriety! She gropes for the right words, not wanting him to close her out again.

"How did it happen?"

"Cancer." He turns to look at her now, his face unreadable. "In the end it was peaceful, even uplifting in a strange sort of way. She was so incredibly tender with everyone around her. That's what I remember most ….." His voice trembles and he stops. In the half darkness the boys have dropped something big into the canal. The splash reverberates across the water, followed by suppressed whoops of delight and a fast clatter of feet on the metal bridge. She waits for the silence.

"And how are you with it now?" she says gently, trying to draw him out.

"Me? I guess I'm okay. What would you say?" He cranes his neck and looks up at the sky. Then he smiles.

She keeps her face impassive. But suddenly she is angry again at his patronising attempt to brush her off with a smile. Yes, she may have prodded too hard – she knows she can do that – but still, she feels played with and her anger gives her courage. "Well, since you ask, I'd say that you've cut yourself off from life. That you're a man who lives in a bubble. That you like to dig into other people's emotions, but never show your own. And you seem to enjoy that, as if it makes you somehow superior and powerful. And I find that very sad." Her voice is like a lash.

He stares at her. She bites her lip. Yet her anger feels right and she isn't going to back off now. She stares back. Then his eyes soften and she knows she has touched him. He nods slowly. "You're right, of course. I think I've learnt to live pretty skilfully cut off from people. In many ways it's easier. Certainly safer." He shrugs. "Perhaps I've always done it. I just didn't think anyone had noticed. But, of course, *you* did."

Her anger begins to ebb and she has noticed that stress on *you*. But still, four whole years like this! She feels a numb ache in her heart. She has a sudden vision of him, a solitary man, wading in a dark lagoon, forever unable to reach the far shore…

She shakes herself to clear the image. Then she lies back on the grass and stares up at the sky, where the first stars are piercing the indigo. She wants to break the spell that he can cast over her with his kindness and understanding. She doesn't want to be tied to the ebb and flow of his feelings. She says, "Do you remember the story about Isis and Osiris? I was thinking…"

But her words are swallowed up by noise. A convoy of four open army trucks, packed with khaki-clad soldiers, rumbles by. The air is filled with the clatter of engines and the stench of diesel. Some of the soldiers point at the foreigners and shout. Others turn and stare with mute curiosity. A young soldier in the last truck stands up and shouts out something in Arabic as he waves his rifle above his head.

Edward scrambles to his feet and holds out his hand. "I think we'd better be getting back. I don't think this is a good place to be hanging around in the dark."

She takes his hand and allows herself to be pulled towards him and for an uncertain moment they stand facing each other.

NINETEEN

In the narrow dirt street that runs behind the Hotel Ibis a donkey cart draws up. There is the sound of metal shutters being raised, then two heavy wooden crates are pulled from under sacking and manhandled into the empty garage.

Amir Salim's back bows under the weight of the boxes. He bends his knees and sets them down very gently on the concrete floor. Behind them water melons are stacked against the wall, and beside the watermelons lies a pile of car tyres, wrenches and a jumble of rusting mechanical parts. Squatting, Amir pauses to wipe the sweat from his face with the hem of his grey *galabiya*. Then he turns and raises his head to the man seated on the donkey cart. The man nods, cracks his whip and the cart jerks forward. Amir listens to the muted thud of the donkey's hooves on the street until the cart reaches the corner and is gone. The metal shutter rattles down. He hears the click of a heavy padlock being fastened on the inside. He rises and faces the tall figure dressed in black.

"*Allahu akbar* – Allah is great!"

The man stares at Amir in the cold blue of the neon light, running his black eyes up and down his body. Then he returns the phrase, "*Allahu akbar!*" He has the upright bearing of a village elder, a man of perhaps sixty. But closer to, despite the deep lines that ridge his forehead and groove his upper lip from the corners of his mouth to the wings of his thin nose, you can see he is only half that age.

Amir rises from his crouching position, rubs his hands and smiles. The other man continues his silent inspection of the boxes and the stack of water melons which glisten a sickly blue-green in the harsh light.

"Do you have it all?"

"Yes! Yes! Everything." Amir grasps a wrench from the floor and levers open the top of one of the crates. The wood creaks and splits as the nails come free. He clears aside a layer of straw with the flat of his hand. Underneath are three motor gears, glistening with grease, the ridged teeth just touching. Carefully, he lays these aside on the oily concrete floor and brushes away the next layer of straw. The light glints off the barrels of two rifles lying side by side.

"AK 47s!" says Amir excitedly. "The best! Almost as new as the day they were made."

The tall man nods. "And the explosives?"

"Here." Amir taps the top of the second box. "Detonators, remote control. Everything is here." He chuckles. "With this. And these," he lays his hand lovingly on the rifle barrels, "we kill many of those godless foreigners who desecrate Mohammed's country, like the ones who arrived this evening." He smiles broadly, showing a line of uneven nicotine-stained teeth. He starts to rise, but before he is fully upright the other man has taken two steps towards him. He raises his right arm and swings it in a vicious arc, catching Amir across the cheek with the back of his hand. Amir staggers, then collapses backwards amongst the watermelons. He puts his hand to his face. He can feel the groove cut by the silver ring. He takes his hand away and stares in shock at the blood.

"You fool!" says the standing figure. "Will you never understand? There will be no killing. Not now. First we will frighten these foreigners from our land. Bit by bit we will destroy the pagan tombs that make them flock here." He gently touches the back of his right hand. "Then, without their whores' money to fill their pockets, this godless government will collapse and the time of true Islam will come again *In'sh Allah*." He pauses and fixes his black eyes on Amir's face. "But for now there will be no killing. Now it is our task to be disciplined, to await orders. Fear not, my friend, our time will come." He pauses. "Do you have the spades for tonight?" Amir Salim nods. "That will be your work. Nothing more. Do you understand?"

Amir stares dumbly. He stretches out his hand and lays it flat on the wooden crate beside him. Then he nods.

TWENTY

Gusts of hot wind tug at Finn's hair as he strains his aching thigh muscles and forces down the metal pedals. The chain is rusty and slips, the springs in the saddle have gone and the hard ridged plastic chafes his thighs and feels like a rod of iron in his groin. Once clear of the streetlights he begins to relax. He allows his ragged breathing to slow. The moped he saw would have been faster, but the noise of its engine too great a risk. This way, at least, he has passed almost unnoticed out of the sleeping town. Only one old man, standing motionless, bent over a stick, has turned to observe him.

Gradually his legs begin to move more easily. His senses are wide awake, plucking every sight and smell and sound from his surroundings with hallucinatory clarity – the liquid snorting of a water-buffalo in the long grass, the smell of hay and honeysuckle and manure, the metallic drumming of frogs in the marshes. After several minutes the Nile comes into view, gleaming like a line of steel in the light from the high watermelon slice of moon. There is a slight downhill gradient now and he allows the bike to glide. From here to the landing stage is about seven miles. He knows that a little before it a cluster of mud-brick houses stands to the right, encircled by palms. In the aftermath of the ritual, while his body had felt sick and disorientated, his brain – or at least *some part of* his brain – had become calmly detached, noting every minutest detail with photographic clarity, recording precisely everything he would need for what he already knew would be his inevitable return.

Only occasionally does the knife-edge of logic try to slide in. *What the hell am I doing here?* he wonders. Simply trying to prove Mountjoy wrong? *Or to prove him right?* whispers a quiet voice in his head. He lets it go, mere spindrift on the surface of his mind. Dimly he is aware of being quite outside of *what* or *why*, drawn forward in the grip of an illogical certainty, operating at a remove from himself.

A strange memory keeps invading his mind, stubbornly refusing to leave, like a drumming refrain. Brigitte? Had that been her name? Yes, Brigitte, leading him giggling up the narrow staircase in Kilburn, smelling of cats and ammoniac damp, to see Mr Cameron, 'Psychic Reader of Past Lives'. He had done it for the laughs. The dense fug of the room comes back to him now. Mr Cameron in frayed tartan carpet slippers with hooded eyes and sparse hair, like a seedy Dickensian bank clerk. Remembers too the soft drone of the voice – *I see you ….. I see you …..* It was then that the laughing had stopped. In the space of forty minutes, watery-eyed Mr Cameron had 'seen' eight of his past lives. Each, with unerring accuracy, had laid bare an unmistakable aspect of who he, Finn Connors, now was. Not all of it welcome. But one 'life' above all now bores in on his mind:

> *"I see you in a beautiful city beside a river. It is The City of Light. I see white lotuses and cobra heads. You hold your face up to the sun. You are a sun-worshipper. A priest. A prophet. Your soul aches for the beyond ….."*

Up ahead a dog starts to howl, the sound outlined by the silence of the night. And a moment later the houses come up on his right looking big and silvered in the moonlight. He presses down hard on the pedals, aware of the tension building in his stomach. The shirt sticks to his back with sweat. And suddenly there it is – the dust track leading to the landing stage. He dismounts, slides the bicycle in amongst a thick tangle of reeds and walks down to the water's edge.

The river looks huge, the smudged outline of the far bank impossibly far away. In the moonlight he sees a piece of driftwood spin round, then disappear rapidly downstream, pulled by the current into the darkness. For the first time doubt rises in him. He pushes it aside and makes his way quickly through the rushes. The ground is waterlogged and he can feel the river, warm as blood, slop round his ankles and fill his shoes.

Like an animal with a homing device, he finds his way straight to the boat. The tiny outboard is still in place on the stern, just as he had seen it this morning. He unties the rope and pushes the boat towards the edge of the Nile. He is thigh deep now and can feel the power of the current tugging at him. With one last heave he thrusts the tiny vessel into the stream and hauls himself aboard, his weight almost capsizing it. At the same moment the pull of the flood drags him from the bank, sucking him towards the centre of the great river.

For a moment he feels a flutter of panic. He scuttles to the back, crouches down, flips open the choke and pulls hard on the starter cord. Nothing. He pulls again, feeling the trail of sweat cold against his spine. The motor coughs and dies. At the third attempt he pulls so hard that he feels something snap in his forearm. The engine explodes into life, the sound colossal against the silence of the night. Quickly he throttles back, swivels the steering arm and begins to guide the boat upstream straight into the current, but angling it towards the far bank. Once in the centre of the river his brain begins to click with practicalities. Are there night guards on the far bank? What about all the begging children, where do they sleep? It would surely be safer to take the boat far upstream, cut the engine and then try to manoeuvre it on the current in silence.

The far bank is coming closer now, the line of palms clear and black against the night sky. He shuts the throttle. The engine coughs and dies. And suddenly he is aware of the silence around him – the immense darkness of the river, the spread of the encircling desert, the vast dome of the sky, velvet black and studded with stars. Despite the heat he shivers.

The little boat drifts precisely as he had hoped, the current ferrying him towards the east. About a hundred yards above the landing stage the bow slaps and grates on the mud. He leaps out, grabs the sodden rope and pulls the boat ashore amongst a thicket of rushes. He wades through the reeds, up to his knees in mud, until he reaches the landing stage. Here he pauses and listens. One minute. Two minutes. Nothing. The concrete guardhouse and adjoining mud huts stand blackly above him. Slowly he edges forward, remembering the pile of tools he had seen thrown carelessly behind the hut, hoping his wet footprints will dry before anyone wakes to see them in the dawn light.

Moving swiftly now, he circles the buildings. The tools are still there. He crouches down and begins to finger through them, afraid to use the torch here, moving each object centimetre by centimetre. From the far side of the river comes the continuous yapping of a dog. His back aches. He has damaged something in his right arm and the pain is intense.

His fingers run silently across rusted metal and splintered wood – a hoe, a pickaxe, some primitive form of rake. Then he finds what he is searching for – the broad flat surface of a shovel, heavily encrusted with dirt. With infinite care he pulls it from the pile. He curses – the handle is broken! There is barely a foot of rough wooden shaft, terminating in a jagged end. Better than nothing.

Within minutes he has picked up the marks of the two broad tractor ruts in the sand, heading east towards the escarpment. The light from the quarter moon is feeble, but his eyes are accustomed now, scanning the landscape like a nocturnal animal. The barren plane looks vast and lunar in the silvered light and ahead of him the mountains rear up black in an immense semicircle. For perhaps half a mile he follows the tracks easily. Then he pauses. The deep parallel ruts are confused now, suddenly scuffed and buried by footprints and divots, clearly indicating where the group had alighted from the trailer. With his heart thudding in his chest, he turns and faces north towards the line of palms.

There they are – the telltale tracks of the twenty-two pairs of feet as they had followed David Mountjoy. Even in the half-light they are clearly visible in the sand, like a sudden flutter of wind on a calm sea. He follows them, a man in a waking dream, dimly aware that some slippage has occurred in his brain, leaving him no longer the author of his own narrative. Something else has come in and is propelling him now back towards that place.

Suddenly he stops. The jumbled spread of tracks begins to arrange themselves in a pattern around him – a circle, the perimeter clearly pounded by feet. Beyond lies the smooth undulating sand of the desert. His stomach lurches. He is standing on the precise spot where his ritual has taken place. He can even see the outline of his body, where he had lain sprawled in the sand. He stands and waits, not knowing what he is waiting for. And then, without warning, something in his brain begins to flicker like a compass needle. *Right .... left ..... forward .....* Suddenly the needle spins through three hundred and sixty degrees – and stops. Instinctively he drops down on one knee and presses the palm of his hand to the ground. And slowly, very gradually, he can feel a clear growing pulse from the earth begin to vibrate up through his arm, like a message from another world.

He turns and reaches for the shovel. Then freezes. Something has flickered at the edge of his vision. Adrenalin pours like a tidal wave into his stomach. He drops down and lies flat, trying to slow the seismic thudding of his heart. Surely it had been just a trick of the brain, a hallucination in the half-light? He peers into the darkness, straining his eyes towards the palms outlined against the silvered background. But no – there it is again! And this time there is no mistake – two black figures moving between the trees, tall and pyramidal – men in *galabiyas* coming directly towards him.

Driven by adrenalin, Finn's logic clicks in. Their unbroken strides show no attempt to hide, so they must be unaware of him. He looks round. Less than a hundred yards away, beside the place where the tractor ruts disappear, is a grove of palms. Grasping the shovel in his right hand, he begins to crawl as fast as he can, flattening himself to the earth. Every few meters he turns his head. The two tall figures are clear of the trees now, crossing the open plain directly towards the circle.

When he reaches the palms he stops and crouches, his chest heaving with exertion. His hands are cut and bleeding. The blood thuds in his head like a bass drum. The two figures have stopped. One is pointing at the ground. For a long while nothing seems to happen. Then, clear across the desert silence, comes the unmistakeable smooth rasp of a spade being slid into the earth.

For over two hours Finn watches the figures bend and straighten in unison, looking like senseless mechanical toys in the dim light. Then they pause and seem to confer. They move to their right and begin again. Despite the danger, despite the pain in his arm and a numb, gathering sense of dread, he stays, held to the place as if by an invisible magnet, trying to control his frustration, until a feint line of grey across the top of the eastern escarpment jolts him back into reality. Then fear kicks in. It would be madness to cycle into town in broad daylight. The place had been crawling with soldiers. He would be picked up and interrogated immediately. And then .....? With a last glance at the stooping figures, he turns and, bending as low as he can, starts back towards the river.

He pushes the boat out from its hiding place amongst the reeds, scrambles aboard and, with his left arm, pulls hard on the starter cord. With the first heave the motor bursts into life. In the silence the sound seems immense. He throttles back, pulls on the steering rod and aims at where he hopes the bicycle will be. As he moves out into the stream he feels a huge surge of relief. It is as if his normal faculties have suddenly been restored and he is released from the sealed world of a nightmare. He can feel his whole body begin to relax.

Halfway across the engine splutters and dies. He pulls the torch from his pocket, unscrews the cap of the engine block and shines the beam in. The bare slicked metal stares back. *Christ, how could he have failed to check the tank?* He spins round, desperately looking for the oars, but as he does so he drops the torch and the light goes out. Trying to calm the rising panic, he begins to feel his way along the bottom of the boat, tearing his hands on the rough wood, until he reaches the bow. And it is only then that he understands. There are no oars. *The boat is empty*. Absolutely, completely, fucking empty! And he is adrift and as isolated as if in space, being carried by the surge of the current into the darkness. For a moment fear freezes him, the nightmare prehistoric fear of a man deprived of all sense and boundary. Then, with one last surge of will, he forces his right foot onto the slippery gunwale and dives into the blackness.

*

Dawn had been a livid grey as Finn stumbled back through the open door of the hotel, exhausted, unseen. He had swum blindly, his muscles driven by a force beyond himself. But it was the surge of the current that had carried him downstream almost to the outskirts of the town and dumped him unceremoniously in the stinking mud. Shoeless, shivering, oblivious of the risk of bilharzia, he had staggered ashore. He had been, he thought later, lucky.

With his clothes still wet he tumbled onto the bed and stared up at the ceiling. The image of the two black figures bending and straightening in the moonlight loomed over him. And then suddenly, a thought of absolute certainty speared its way in from beyond the confines of his exhausted brain – *They had been digging in the wrong place!* He sighed with relief.

Then sleep pulled him under.

*

Tap, tap, tap.

Finn groans and turns over.

TAP, TAP, TAP!

He sits up and looks at his watch. Six-thirty! What the hell is going on? He climbs off the bed, aware of the dull ache in his right arm and an overwhelming sense of exhaustion clinging to his body like lead. He goes to the door and slides back the heavy bolt. Edward stands there, fully dressed, his hair dishevelled.

Finn squints at him. "What is it?"

"I don't know. They're waking everybody. They want us out of the hotel as fast as possible."

"Who do?"

"The police. Or the army. It's crawling with them downstairs. You'd better hurry up."

"Okay."

Finn shuts the door, scrambles his belongings together and rams them into his bag. He runs down the stairs, zipping the bag as he goes. Halfway down he hears a scream, then shouting in Arabic, a man and a woman, then another man joining in. He takes the stairs two at a time.

Down in the hall a woman dressed in full black *chador* and a man in a *galabiya* are in furious argument with the hotel owner. Beside them two small boys sit on cardboard boxes crying. David Mountjoy comes running through the front door.

Finn grabs him by the arm. "What the hell's going on?"

"I don't know." Mountjoy's eyes look wild. "They want us out of here right away. I think we're the only foreigners in town. The soldiers are panicking."

"Has something happened?"

"I don't know! I think they may have uncovered a terrorist cell or something. That's the most I can get out of them. They're going to give us an armed escort back to Luxor."

Out in the street soldiers are patrolling in combat gear. One stands either side of the entrance, automatic rifles at the ready. Two more are prowling on the far side of the road. The group is already crowding into the bus, their bags being tossed into the gaping hold in its side. Finn throws in his bag and begins to climb the steps.

Suddenly a sound like the thud of a gigantic bass-drum fills the air, blocking out everything else around them. The ground shakes and the air is squeezed tight, like a huge bulge of pressure in a confined space. Followed by an awed, all-encompassing silence. And into this silence tinkles the sound of cascading glass.

Then everything seems to happen at once. From all over the town terrified, high-pitched screams break out. Car horns and alarms shriek; the turgid water in the canal heaves and explodes over its concrete banks, and a huge, swelling cloud of dust rises from behind the hotel.

For a moment everyone stands transfixed. Then the soldiers begin shouting at the group and pushing them frantically up the bus steps. "*Yala! Yala!* Go quick! Go Quick!"

And within seconds the bus is careering down the narrow street, swerving wildly to avoid the dazed pedestrians.

TWENTY-ONE

The overloaded local bus from el-Minya to Assiut bumps off the tarmac and shudders to a halt. The driver cuts the engine. There is a hushed moment before the door clatters open and two soldiers, barely more than teenagers, step into the cabin, cradling automatic weapons. Yassin Zahawi shifts the black briefcase on the floor between his feet and inspects the new arrivals. They look nervous and he can see that their safety catches are off. Three other soldiers are standing outside holding AK 47s. The two young men begin moving silently down the aisle, opening cases and checking identities. Outside, the other soldiers have thrown open the baggage hold and are pulling out suitcases and cardboard boxes. There have already been two roadblocks since leaving el-Minya. Clearly this is no routine search.

Zahawi begins to calculate: the weapons can't have been found, but perhaps the police have already uncovered Amir's corpse. In this heat it is hard to conceal a body for long. Or could there have been another violent incident altogether? A bomb or another murder? El-Minya is overflowing with young, ill-disciplined and heavily armed revolutionaries, each with their own agenda, never willing to subject themselves to authority....

The soldiers are coming closer. An old woman at the front starts to whimper.

Young Amir had always been a dangerous liability, childish, over-enthusiastic, lacking the necessary discipline. If the police had got him he would have crowed like a cockerel. Killing him had been a necessary act in the service of Allah, drawing the blade across his throat the only solution, the knife now safely consigned to the silence of the Nile....

One of the soldiers stops beside him. Zahawi holds open his briefcase with his left hand, careful to keep his right concealed. The young man begins blindly fingering through the textbooks and lecture notes. Zahawi can smell stale sweat and fear and American tobacco. He passes over his identity card. The soldier glances at it, then hands it back with a respectful nod and moves on.

Zahawi sits with his head bowed while he allows the thudding in his blood to settle. He swivels the silver ring on his right hand. The hand is badly bruised and swollen from the punch he has given Amir – easy to explain for a farmer or mechanic, less so for a university lecturer in economics – but the young soldier hadn't seen it. Though he dislikes western clothes, he has deliberately chosen them this morning – brown trousers, white shirt and trainers – to signify his academic status and put him above the reach of any normal soldier's mindset. Who would suspect a trusted government official, a senior employee of the Ministry of Education?

Yet it is hard these days for Yassin Zahawi to be absorbed into the anonymity of the crowd. As a student he had weighted twenty kilos more and his fleshy face had been insignificant. But time and events have defined his features, carved out the cheeks, cut deep deltas around his eye sockets. His jaw and nose have taken on a desert cragginess and the black eyes send a message now that is almost impossible to conceal. After Izat's death, his face, like everything else in his life, has become clarified.

That one moment in the Cairo city morgue had changed everything. They had tried to stop him seeing Izat's body – the body of a criminal, they said. *The body of an eighteen year-old apolitical auto mechanic,* who had been caught up in a mistaken police raid, then shot in the back 'while attempting to escape'. But with Sayed Gamal's belligerent legal manner and the forged police permit they had forced open the rusting steel door and pushed their way past the confused and frightened attendant into that concrete hell-hole smelling of formaldehyde and death.

Zahawi's breath froze as he pulled back the blood-stained sheet. *Shot while attempting to escape .....* The eyes were open, staring at some unseen horror. The face disfigured and swollen as if it had been inflated with air. The black tongue protruded from the mouth like a half-swallowed fish. One eye was so badly bruised it looked ready to pop from its purple socket at any moment. Across the throat ran a scarlet stripe like a tyre mark. *Shot while attempting .....*

He had felt a scream start to rise in him in that moment, a scream beyond the borders of control, a scream that might go on forever..... And it was then that something inexplicable happened. Something – he later realised – that would alter the course of his life forever. A hand was silently placed across his mouth. The scream, instead of bursting out to shatter the morgue, went inwards, channelling its way to the very centre of his heart. And gathered there in a silent well of pure hate. Rocket fuel. Enough to last him a thousand years. It had been the hand of Allah.

From that moment his window onto the world had swivelled. Everything became simple. Where once he had seen career and advancement, money, DVDs and one day a Mercedes and a wife in smart western clothes and children at university, he now saw only the brutality and greed of western government terrorism, the way they bombed and gassed and raped and massacred, all in the name of 'peace' and 'liberty' and 'democracy'. In an instant the scales literally fell from his eyes, allowing him a terrifying vision of a huge wave of evil and corruption sweeping from America across the earth, carrying all the servile nations of Europe with it, polluting and destroying everything in its path. He saw the arrogant stupidity of the West, its false claims and brutal lies, concealing a culture so rotten, so corrupt that it was infecting the whole world – an empty creed of power and greed and materialism that seduced and devoured and left behind a blighted, barren landscape of pollution and spiritual despair. Against this he would fight forever and die willingly in the service of Allah!

His own government, which tortures and kills and rapes its own people, has sold out to the obscene 'American dream', with its sordid promises of easy sex and Coca-cola and satellite television for all. He has witnessed all this in his year of study in Boston and now on the streets of Luxor and the shameful beaches of Hagudar and Sharm el-Sheikh. He has *forced* himself to look at how the West is turning his country – his beautiful, devout country – into a plaything, a bauble, a money machine, a technicolour whorehouse. With arrogant disregard and mindless greed, billions and billions and billions of dollars are being poured into the trivialities of a few over-fattened lives, all of them gorging like pigs, while more than half the world starves. Their politicians shout of 'liberty' and 'justice' and 'democracy' and 'war on terror', while every day in the streets of Baghdad and Fallujah and Gaza children are being killed, women murdered, hands and feet and heads blown off and scattered carelessly around like playthings. Why can't they see the truth, these westerners? *Why can't they see?*

There is only one way to make them see – the way of Allah and the way of the gun. The truth cannot remain hidden forever. You might as well try to blot out the face of the sun with mud. Once he could not have contained this incandescent rage, this radio-active fury that burns day and night in his heart. But he has learnt, with Allah's help, to keep silent, to be a servant of a higher cause. Above all, to wait.

And the ways of Allah are mysterious, not his to question. In the weeks before the arrival of the bearded Englishman they call 'The Magician', he has silently obeyed the orders, studied the workings of the art market on the internet, read about the price of Pharaonic antiquities at auctions in London and New York. *A million dollars for a single statue!* Enough to feed a starving Egyptian village for a hundred years! Enough to pay a thousand university teachers! This much too he now understands – how many black-market AK47s one small statue can buy. And even though last night has yielded nothing, slowly, with Allah's help, their time will come…

He gives a rare smile as the shantytown on the outskirts of Assiut begins to slide past the window.

TWENTY-TWO

Lara sits on the coarse grass in front of her cottage, gazing out across the river, lost in the view. Already, after only a few hours back in Luxor, the events at el-Amarna seem far away. Even the shock of the bomb has begun to fade. It's as if it has all happened in another, more fantastical world.

She loves the evenings here, especially these pre-sunset moments when the whole landscape is flooded with an even light. As the West Bank sinks into darkness, the heads of the distant date palms begin to emerge with hieroglyphic clarity, like giant fans against the crimson sky. To her right, the first call of the evening muezzin breaks out. Soon it is followed by others. They echo down both sides of the river until the whole valley seems overarched by a cathedral of sound. She leans back, her arms braced, her fingers spread like starfish on the coarse grass. She knows that she is falling hopelessly in love with this country.

She loves its colour and its heat and its noise. She loves the sounds and smiles of the people, their rich flowing vowels like running water and the sharp, guttural stops. She loves the insistent wailing of the muezzin, the constant hooting of cars, the cries of the caleche drivers, the irrepressible surge of life constantly spilling out of dark doorways into the streets. Everything about it makes her feel more alive, more *herself,* than she has ever felt in the familiar drab greyness of England. Despite the chaos and the dirt, despite the rawness and the grinding poverty, despite the occasional casual brutality, she finds Egypt a gentle country.

She puts her head to one side and smiles as she remembers that hollow sense of fear as the aeroplane door had shut in London, sealing her off from the safety of her past. Only five days ago and yet it seems so utterly distant, like another – far less real – existence. In these last days she has experienced again and again a strange sense that something in this country is actually *waiting* for her.

As she watches the steady flow of the river now, the story returns to her of how Seth had chopped his brother, Osiris, into fourteen pieces and scattered them throughout the land of Egypt. And how Isis had so lovingly and patiently searched right here, along these marshy banks, until she had been able to reform his mutilated body. She lets out a sigh. Is Mountjoy right? Is that what I'm doing now? she wonders – searching for the scattered pieces of myself? Hoping to repair something that has always felt lacerated and destroyed beyond help? As Mountjoy had talked of the terrible mutilation of Osiris's body a pain had cramped her stomach. She can feel it starting again now. Instinctively she pulls up her knees and squeezes them hard to her chest.

Five miscarriages! Christ, no wonder I need healing! Five miscarriages. And who really cares? She can hear her mother's strident Sunday-school voice: 'You must be strong, darling, for Tim's sake.' And her father? But, of course, he wasn't there. He would never be there. And Tim? 'We can always try again. No good crying over spilt milk.' He had actually used that phrase! Actually, unbelievably, used the fucking phrase, as if she was some disappointed school girl who had failed to win the prize. Christ, she had felt lonely, lying there, bleeding in that desolate hospital corridor, stinking of shit and antiseptic, cradling herself, knowing that she had lost her baby *yet again*. No wonder I need to put the scattered parts of myself together again, to feel the embrace of Isis's rainbow-coloured wings. What a beautiful, gentle image!

In the twilight an unexpected memory drifts to her – that brief moment in the Cairo Museum, when she had rounded the corner of the dusty wooden display cases and come face to face with a statue of the goddess Isis, seated on a throne, suckling the young god Horus on her lap. The evening sunlight had slanted in from one of the high upper windows. Finn and Edward were still some yards behind. After all the macho figures of warrior Pharaohs, this still, primal image had come as a sudden shock. She stood silent, almost winded by the intimacy and naturalness of the scene – Isis, the goddess, full-breasted, giving life to her son, like the young mothers she has seen squatting beside the banks of the Nile. As she faced the statue, there had felt something unfair about Isis's uninhibited, buxom naturalness, like a birthright that has been denied her. And a terrible feeling of inadequacy and shame washed through her. David Mountjoy had talked of her fate. Is this her fate – never to be able to take part in this natural, silent, all-consuming ritual as other women do? Is something in her so broken and incomplete that she can never fully be a woman?

She sits now with her jaw clenched, tears prickling her eyes. She stares blindly across to the far bank as it sinks into darkness. From this vantage point she and Tim look like two children adrift in a leaking boat, clinging to each other in despair. And of the two – she can now see – he is by far the more afraid. She shakes her head. How could she have been so blind at twenty-three to have backed into a marriage, not really looking at Tim at all, totally unaware of what she felt or what she needed, just blindly following her own ruthless social ambitions, trying to tell herself that she was in love? She knows now that for years she has been secretly digging tunnels under her marriage as if, all that time, her soul has been preparing the necessary means of escape.

The muezzin dies away, leaving the silence tangible. The echo now seems carried in the darkness of the river. The upper lip of the sun dips behind The Valley of the Kings. For a moment the whole ridge flames crimson, then dies into blackness. And suddenly a very distant memory surfaces as if through water – an image from the picture book of Egypt that had so fascinated her as she sat in front of her grandmother's fire: the sky goddess Nut arched above the earth, supported only on her hands and feet like a child doing push-ups. Her slim body formed a canopy over the fertile land; her long indigo dress was studded with hundreds of silver stars. She had flipped over the page. Now the goddess was eating the sun! *Actually swallowing it whole and digesting it!* With her finger she traced the night's passage of the orange disc down inside the long arched body. She turned the page again – and stared in wonder and disbelief. *The goddess was giving birth to that glowing crimson ball!* With all its energy and heat it was emerging from between her legs. She gazed in horrified fascination. And instinctively her hand slid down between her own legs, searching for comfort. And comfort is what she feels here in Egypt. It's as if the universe is no longer holding her responsible for her failings. At least, not responsible in that terrible, cramping, soul-destroying way....

A soft rustling behind her right shoulder startles her. She turns and looks up. Finn is standing there, clearly uncertain of his welcome. She smiles and pats the grass beside her. It's strange how, despite all her reservations about him, all the disappointment she can sometimes feel, something in her heart always lifts when he appears.

"You sure?"

She nods and looks back over the river. He settles down beside her and crosses his ankles. For a long while they are silent. At length he draws his legs in, as if to rise. "I didn't want to butt in ….."

"No, don't go. I like it that you're here. It feels peaceful." She pauses, surprised how easy it is to say that to him. "I was just thinking that I don't want to go back"

"We've still got another twelve days."

"I mean *ever!*"

He stares at her, startled by the vehemence of her tone. And suddenly he sees her silhouetted shoulders begin to shake. He slides towards her and puts his arm around her. She pushes her face into his chest and begins to cry in deep moaning sobs that seem pulled up out of the depths of her belly, like someone vomiting up their pain.

He sits, his arm tight around her, her body pressed against him, aware of a strange, aching sensation in his chest. He holds her until she grows quiet.

TWENTY-THREE

"The location cannot be propitious." Lascaris crosses the legs of his cream tropical suit. It is early evening and they are sitting on the broad stone terrace overlooking the gardens of the Winter Palace. Finn is vaguely aware of a change in his companion. Something about him feels subtly different from their last meeting, as if there's an extra tension, like a bow that has been more tightly strung.

"I haven't told you where it was yet."

Lascaris picks up his almost empty glass of whisky, drains it and signals to the waiter. "You don't need to," he says with studied casualness. "You were observed."

Finn stares at him in disbelief. It takes a moment for the surprise to sink in. *"Observed?"* Then he adds drily, "I see. And may I know what else your observers observed while they were at it?"

The waiter returns, sets down two fresh glasses, a bottle of mineral water and a bowl of ice. Lascaris turns to him and begins speaking fluently in Arabic. Finn understands just enough to know that he is asking the man about his family. The waiter's face lights up as he holds out his hand to indicate the heights of his children. Lascaris raises his eyebrows in mock astonishment, holds up six fingers and says something that makes the waiter laugh. Then he reaches into his pocket, folds a note and places it on the silver tray. The waiter smiles broadly and bows. He certainly knows how to turn on the charm, thinks Finn, remembering how Lascaris had calmly reeled him in when they had first met in London.

Lascaris casually pushes aside the bowl of ice with the back of his hand. "It's death to take the ice here," he says. "The water has probably come straight out of the Nile." He uncaps the water bottle, adds a splash and sips the whisky, then places the glass back on the polished wooden table. "It seems the famous ritual of your Solar Return was something of a spectacle. I gather you went on quite a 'trip', as they say." He etches the inverted commas in the air with his forefingers and gives one of his infectious smiles.

Finn ignores him. He picks up his glass and takes a long swallow. "It's certainly a bloody weird place for buried treasure – if that's what's supposed to be there...." He hesitates, aware of all the things he is instinctively not telling Lascaris – his disastrous night-time adventure, the two Egyptian figures digging in the darkness....."Up in one of the ravines," he goes on, hoping his hesitation has gone unnoticed, "or even beside the cliff tombs, there I could imagine something being buried. But right on the edge of the ancient city? There can't be much left there. So the whole thing will turn out to be just as crazy as I thought it was on day one. I should have followed my instincts and stayed in London, instead of messing about here, eating vegetarian food and dancing around in circles. You know, in some places the Egyptians actually gather to watch us! They must think we're completely out of our fucking minds."

Lascaris smiles. "I hear the dancing around was actually rather elegant. Apparently the Egyptians enjoyed it. I suppose these are the trials we must go through to achieve our aims."

Finn scowls at him. "*I* must go through, you mean. You're just sitting here drinking scotch and having a bloody good time from what I can see."

Lascaris chuckles. He clearly finds Finn's discomfort amusing. "It is true, that for the moment, I seem to be getting the better end of the deal," he says in a conciliatory tone, "although I hear you have the compensation of having two remarkably beautiful girls on your tour." He pauses, apparently just remembering something. "Thinking of beautiful girls, did you ever make contact with Doctor Rusedska? I think she's something definitely not to be missed."

Finn looks at him enquiringly. It feels as if Lascaris has some kind of agenda, almost trying to match-make them. But before he can respond, his attention is caught by an elderly American couple, tall and elegantly dressed, coming down the steps of the hotel. The tickertape of Finn's dealer's brain instantly sizes them up: old money, almost certainly from the South, Georgia or the Carolinas. Between them walks a slim, strikingly pretty girl of perhaps thirteen or fourteen – presumably their granddaughter. Her long blonde hair cascades loosely over her thin cotton dress. He turns back and sees Lascaris's eyes slide over the girl in a look of pure desire. And suddenly he's aware of how little he knows about this man with whom he has become so dangerously involved. Aware too of how mercurial Lascaris can be, turning you first one face then another, always trying to pull you into collusion with his charm, but giving nothing away.

"I have acquired a detailed map of the site." Lascaris cuts across Finn's thoughts. "The place where the ritual occurred appears to be just beyond the excavated area. It seems the archaeologists who worked there in the fifties stopped digging at that point, and no-one has returned to it since. So it's virgin territory."

"Why did they stop?"

Lascaris shrugs. "I suppose there are just more exciting places to dig. As you know, that area was resettled later by the Romans. There's almost certainly nothing of Pharaonic times left. Probably just squatters' debris."

Finn frowns. "You seem extremely well informed."

Lascaris shifts forward in his wicker chair, his face suddenly sharpens. "Do not forget that I am a professional researcher. I make my living by finding out about such things." His right hand darts up to play with the gold earring. And, just for an instant, Finn catches something in Lascaris's look that he had never seen before, something that has slipped from behind the charm. Perhaps it's even *part of* the charm. Not greed exactly, but something almost diabolic, like a gleeful flash of malice. He knows it is a warning moment, a glimpse of fin in the water. Then it's gone and Lascaris settles back in his chair and smiles at him. "Anyhow," he says calmly. "We will investigate the place tomorrow night."

Finn stares at him in disbelief. "*Tomorrow night?* Just like that! How the hell will you manage that up there in Middle Egypt, surrounded by soldiers and crazy, rifle-toting Fundamentalist terrorists?" But his brain is already clicking into other channels. *Tomorrow* night? So whoever the two dark figures were digging on the plain at el-Amarna, they couldn't have been Lascaris's men. *Then who ...*? And suddenly he sees David Mountjoy's enigmatic smile as he had lain there, sprawled in the dust at el-Amarna, his mind fractured by the ritual.

"That, Mr Connors, is my problem," says Lascaris. "As I told you in London, I have friends here." He drains his glass. "It's probably better we don't use the telephone from now on. Our business is too sensitive now and there are too many ears in this town. Meet me here in the hotel lobby in two days' time. Then we shall see the results of David Mountjoy's supernatural talents. Let's hope for a surprise. Shall we say four o'clock in the afternoon?"

TWENTY-FOUR

"My God, what opulence! I can hardly believe we're still in Egypt."

Lara's eyes widen in amazement as she stares round the vast colonial entrance hall of the Winter Palace Hotel with its grand sweeping staircase and gilded columns, oil paintings hanging from silk sashes, the long striped sofas and the circular marble table at the centre surmounted by a huge blue and white vase filled with lilies. Beside the polished mahogany reception desk porters in red brocaded jackets and black Turkish trousers stand quietly in attendance.

Finn smiles. "It was bought a few years back by some smart French company like Louis Vuiton, who spent a fortune tarting it up. Back in the old days it was just tatty Victorian splendour coming apart at the seams. Actually I think I rather preferred it that way."

"It looks like high-class Parisian chic to me," says Edward, "with just the faintest added whiff of pseudo-Arabia. I suppose that's exactly what kept our great-grandparents from dying of home-sickness while they were wintering down here – reconstructed aristocratic Europe, without too much full-on squalid Egypt to ruin it all."

Lara laughs. "Yes, you can almost see the women floating through in their crinolines, preparing their parasols to protect their delicate complexions while taking a gentle ride in a *caleche*. It makes our humble set-up at the Sobek look a bit down-market, doesn't it?"

"Don't deride our shabby little hotel," says Finn, "because we've got something that they haven't. We've got the Nile gliding right past our front doors. Here there's just hundreds of hooting tourist boats and hordes of taxi-drivers screaming for baksheesh and belching out fumes smack outside the entrance. Believe me, we're the lucky ones."

"Are you sure your friend won't mind that we've come?" asks Lara, turning to Finn.

"Dortmann? Of course not. I phoned him when we got back from el-Amarna and he was delighted. When he's not doing his academic work he's very sociable. And he *particularly* enjoys the company of beautiful women." He nudges her gently.

"Oh piss off, Finn. You're….."

"There they are!" interrupts Finn. Then in a whisper, "Brace yourselves for Nadia."

Dortmann and Nadia are descending the broad sweep of the staircase side by side. When Dortmann sees them he raises his hand and smiles. Beside him Nadia is dressed in a cream dress scooped low at the neck. For a moment a startled look passes over her face and she ostentatiously slides her arm through Dortmann's as if for protection. The ormolu clock above the reception desk softly strikes eight.

Finn makes the introductions. The two women shake hands at arm's length, eyeing each other warily. Nadia's face looks defiantly closed and Edward's brief nod to her is perfunctory almost to the point of rudeness. Finn stares at him in surprise. For a moment an awkward silence settles between them. Then Lara breaks it. She turns to the professor. "I believe I've seen you before," she says.

His eyebrows shoot up in surprise.

"Weren't you at the Omar Khayam Hotel a few nights ago?"

He nods. "Yes, that's right. We went there for dinner. Such a beautiful situation in the middle of the Nile, though I fear what they have done to the old palace is not too sympathetic in terms of restoration."

Finn heaves a sigh of relief as Lara effortlessly defuses the atmosphere with her charm.

"You and Finn seem to be old friends," she goes on brightly.

"Indeed Mr Connors and I have known each other for many years. In the old days, whenever he was in New York, he would invite me for an excellent lunch. It was an event I always eagerly anticipated. And even now he takes the trouble to make the long drive into the Oxfordshire countryside to visit me." Nadia glances at Finn with a look of angry surprise. "Only a true friend continues to visit one," goes on Dortmann, "even as one declines into boring academic senility."

Lara gives him one of her most magical smiles. "That, I would say, seems highly premature."

Dortmann inclines his head graciously.

"Professor Dortmann is not only one of the world's foremost Egyptologists," says Finn, "He's also one of the few distinguished archaeologists who will deign even to speak to anyone as morally suspect as an antiquities dealer like myself."

Dortmann raises his shoulders and spreads his hands in mock despair. "A clear case of personal preference overcoming rigid academic dogma, I fear."

They all laugh, except for Nadia, whose face remains fixed.

"Are you the Professor Bernard Dortmann who wrote the book on the Pharaoh Akhenaten?" asks Edward.

Dortmann turns to him with a look of quizzical interest. "I see that my fame – or perhaps infamy – goes before me. Am

I, by any chance, in the presence of a fellow Egyptologist? The book is hardly what you would call popular reading."

Edward smiles. "I'm afraid not. I'm just an ignorant layman who happens to have blundered into your field. But I found the book fascinating. It managed to be both scholarly and very human at the same time. It was if you were somehow getting right inside the character of that strange man, a bit like Freud did with Leonardo da Vinci."

Dortmann stares at him for a moment in surprise. Then he smiles with undisguised pleasure. "What sort of 'layman' may I ask?"

"A psychoanalyst."

"A *psychoanalyst*? That is of great interest to me. We must talk further. And your compliment is most kind though, I fear, a little too generous. The book is now somewhat out of date. There have been so many discoveries, so many new theories, in the meantime."

"It remains by far the best written and most scholarly book on the Amarna period," cuts in Nadia sharply. She looks defiantly around. In the awkward silence that follows, Finn exchanges glances with Lara. Then he says, "Professor Dortmann was also the moving force behind the new museum here in Luxor."

"Really?" Lara smiles at the professor. "That's wonderful! It's so beautifully done. So much better than the tatty chaos in the Cairo Museum."

Dortmann purses his lips and inclines his head in a gesture of self-deprecation. "I was only peripherally involved. There were tens of thousands of objects that could have been displayed. I merely helped the Egyptian archaeologists to make the selection." He pauses, lowering his voice conspiratorially. "Though, to tell the truth, I expect that Mr Connors' practised dealer's eye would have made a much better job of it!" This time they all laugh.

Finn smiles and glances quickly round the group, aware that he feels uncomfortably responsible for the success of the evening. Lara's naturalness and charm have found an easy match in Dortmann's irrepressible enthusiasm and old-world courtesy. Nadia's haughtiness he had expected, but Edward seems strangely ill at ease. Right now he is staring round the entrance hall, as if trying to abstract himself from the group.

Suddenly Dortmann says, "Would it be unforgivably rude of me if I asked the three of you to excuse us for a moment and take your drinks on the terrace? There is a book in my room that I would very much like to show to Mr Cavanagh. If that is not an imposition?" he adds, turning to Edward.

"Not at all," says Edward. "I would be delighted."

Dortmann takes Edward by the arm and leads him towards the staircase. "It's such an opportunity, you see…"

For a moment Lara, Finn and Nadia are left uncomfortably alone. Then Nadia says, "I'm afraid I've just remembered I have a telephone call to make." She turns brusquely and walks towards the stairs, following the two men.

Finn and Lara are left staring at each other. "Well!" says Lara, raising her eyebrows. "This is going to be quite an evening!"

"Don't mind her. She'll simmer down. She gets like a defensive cougar when other women are on what she considers her territory. She's just put out because the Professor is so obviously already a fully paid-up member of your fan-club." Before Lara can rebut him he takes her arm. "Come outside. I'll show you the gardens. They're quite spectacular."

Out on the terrace, the night air is filled with the scent of jasmine and honeysuckle. Spotlights illuminate the towering palms and banyan trees and the oleander-lined paths. In the distance the muezzin is starting up, calling the faithful to prayer.

"How beautiful!" said Lara.

"It was all laid out in the 1870s at the height of colonial splendour. Let's explore it a bit before we have a drink. If I know the Professor, once he gets carried away on some intellectual hunt, it could take quite a while. Just give him something that interests him and he instantly sheds forty years. In New York he was famous for exhausting his students."

"I think Edward may have some of that quality too, so we could have quite a wait on our hands."

They descend the broad stone-steps and begin walking along the gravel pathways. At length they come to the circular pond filled with lotuses and papyrus – the same pond that Lascaris had been observing three days before. Lara sits down on the bench and gazes up at the night sky. Then she turns to Finn. "What on earth do you think was up with Edward?"

Finn shrugs. "No idea. Weird, wasn't it? He's normally so polite. It was as if he just wanted to get out of there. At least until Dortmann swept him off."

"And you?"

Finn hesitates. "Me?"

"Yes."

"Meaning?"

"Have you slept with her?"

Slowly he turns and looks at her, his eyebrows raised in ironic enquiry. "Who?"

Lara sniffs derisively. "Don't give me that bullshit, Finn Connors. You know who."

"How the hell did you work that one out?"

"Easy. You completely ignore her. The same way you do with Birgit. Is that what you always do with the women you sleep with – ignore them? I'm bloody glad I'm not one of them!"

Finn laughs uneasily. Then he glances at her. She is staring at the pond. Having fired her shot she's apparently content to let their conversation lapse. Above them the sky is a deep indigo, bleached violet at its western edge. The muezzin has reached its crescendo and is beginning to wind itself into silence. Unexpectedly, a moment of total peace settles between them. Finn is intensely conscious of the scent of Lara's perfume, something between cut grass and wild flowers. And as he inhales it his mind drifts off erratically.

Even as a teenager in Catholic Dublin girls had always come easy to him. Once, to pass the time on a long-haul flight, he tried to count the number of women he had slept with but lost track after forty. Mostly he can't remember their names, let alone their faces. But, sitting here now, he can suddenly feel the futility of all those so-called 'conquests'. It's as if all his life he has been trying to fill up a hole through which the wind has been blowing. But why, for God's sake, is he thinking abut this now, sitting here in these exotic gardens, the evening filled with the scent of jasmine, beside a woman he has never even slept with? He doesn't understand this. All he knows is that she is utterly different all the other women he has ever known; somehow both more innocent and more knowing at the same time. He can't explain what he feels about her, least of all to himself. It's a feeling of... intimacy? Intimacy without desire? *Is that even possible?* He glances sideways at her and in the half-light he sees her delicate profile and suddenly, without warning, he's aware of something inside him, something hard and archaic, beginning to come apart.

It's a strange, physical sensation, as if his heart is literally opening and he doesn't know what to do with it. Struggling to find his voice, he says, "Why do I always feel so incredibly well when I'm with you?"

She turns and stares at him, her eyes narrowed. She's inspecting him for irony. But his look is clear and open in a way she has never seen before. There is a strange, stripped moment between them as they stare at each other. Then slowly her face splits into a broad smile. "Do you?" she says, in a slightly puzzled voice.

"Yes. Otherwise I wouldn't say it."

"Then that's easy to answer."

"Why?"

She slides along the bench until their arms are touching. She begins to rub slowly up and down like a playful cat. "It's because I know you," she says simply. "And *you* know you don't have to play any games with me. I know who you are – and I know what you're worth. And you don't need to sleep with me to prove it." She pulls back and laughs at the look of shocked surprise on his face. "My God, I thought you were supposed to know all about women! You know what? You may be full of bullshit a lot of the time, Finn Connors, but you're still a lovely man in spite of it."

He stares at her, for once totally lost for an answer. Then he smiles, puts his arm around her and squeezes her hard. She rests her head on his shoulder. Is this what it's like to have a brother? she wonders as she leans into him, feeling the warmth of his body, enjoying the uncomplicated comfort of his presence. The older brother I always longed for.

Suddenly Finn says, "I think I'd better be getting you back inside before we start getting too serious – and that would never do!"

He rises and pulls her to her feet. She laughs gaily and, as they walk back towards the hotel, she slides her arm through his. As they arrive on the terrace, they meet Dortmann and Edward coming out of the entrance hall. Nadia is seated in a wicker chair to one side with an ostentatiously bored look on her face.

Dortmann leads the way down a long corridor, hung with watercolours of Egypt and lit by crystal chandeliers, to the dining room, where the headwaiter, resplendent in white tie and black tailcoat, is obviously expecting them. He bows low to the Professor, formally addressing him in French, then leads them to a round table set against the long windows overlooking the floodlit garden.

Dortmann swiftly arranges the seating: Lara on his right, then Edward, then Nadia between Edward and Finn. Nadia stands rock-still when Dortmann indicates her place on the far side of the table and for a moment she seems about to protest. Then she shrugs and moves reluctantly towards her chair.

"I have taken the liberty of ordering a traditional Egyptian meal," says Dortmann. "I do hope that meets with everyone's approval. This is not the most ethnic of restaurants in terms of ambience, I fear." He runs his eyes ironically over the pale green silk walls and crystal chandeliers. "Apart from the waiters in their fezzes and *galabiyas*, we could equally well be dining on the Cote d'Azur. But the chef here is famous and there is no better Egyptian food anywhere in the country."

A waiter appears with a bottle of white wine, pours a little for Dortmann to try, then begins to fill the other glasses. Dortmann raises his glass. "Welcome to you all!" He smiles and glances at Lara and Edward. "And a special welcome to our two new-comers to Egypt." He sips the wine, savouring it for a moment, then sets down his glass. "Though if I may say so, you both already seem extremely well-attuned for novices.

Many people coming here for the first time are rather shocked. They reel under the strange hieratical nature of ancient Egypt, the vastness of its monuments, the enormous gulf that seems to separate the ancient world from our own, its curious beliefs about the afterlife and so on." He pauses. "And then, of course, there is the dirt and poverty of modern Egypt. It's often too much. Many people hate it and simply never return."

"I don't think I could return often enough," says Lara. "Of course there *is* poverty. And yet, amongst all the dirt and chaos, there's a surprising sense of ..... I don't know ..... dignity?" Dortmann holds his head to one side, listening carefully. He nods slightly. "The people are always so impeccably dressed," she goes on. "And even if their surroundings do look squalid – at least by our standards – you hardly ever see a dirty *galabiya* or turban, even in the poorest areas." She pauses, as if embarrassed by her own eloquence. Edward smiles at her in encouragement. "And amongst it all, even amongst the dirt and the chaos, the people seem to have such a sense of calmness. It feels like something we've lost in the west. If I think of all the commuters scrambling in the London underground in the rush hour, then I think *we're* the ones who look shabby and drab and crushed by our surroundings." She glances across at Nadia who is staring ostentatiously around the room. "I'm sorry, I seem to be rabbiting on."

Dortmann smiles. "It sounds refreshingly passionate to me. If this is what you would term 'rabbiting'," he pronounces the word as if savouring an exotic delicacy, "then please rabbit on some more."

Lara's cheeks colour, but she smiles back at him. Nadia leans forward and folds her hands on the table in front of her. She stares at Lara. "I don't think you can have seen the City of the Dead yet." Her voice is edged with sarcasm.

Lara hesitates. "No....., I... What's that?" She glances round the table.

"It's a huge cemetery on the outskirts of Cairo," says Finn. "Most of the poor from the countryside who have flooded into the city and can't find housing have settled there. It's a kind of vast shanty-town for ....."

"*A quarter of a million people* living amongst the graves!" cuts in Nadia. "Once you've seen that, it takes the romance out of poverty."

Lara flushes. "I wasn't trying to suggest ....." But at that moment two waiters arrive with enormous round copper trays and begin spreading dishes filled with mezes across the table.

"A prize for anyone who can name each dish!" declares Finn, clearly trying to distract the conversation. "Except, of course, for Professor Dortmann, who can probably name them all in at least five languages!"

They all laugh except Nadia, who eyes Finn angrily.

For several minutes they are preoccupied with discussing and passing round the food. Then Dortmann clears his throat. "At the risk of being tiresomely curious, may I ask our two new-comers what you have enjoyed most about your visit so far?"

His glance settles on Lara. She hesitates, her eyes shifting for a moment to Edward, then to Nadia, but both seem preoccupied with their food.

She spreads her hands as if lost for an answer. Then she says, "I don't know. It's hard to explain. I just love it here. I love the vegetation. I love the colour. I love the view of the mountains on the West Bank." She pauses. "Actually, to be honest, wherever we are in Egypt, I think the thing I always love most is the Nile. I could sit and watch it all day. There are some moments when I seem to lose myself in it. It feels almost as if it's somehow flowing *through* me."

She stops and shrugs, suddenly self-conscious again. Her glance shifts to Edward. He is gazing at her with such intensity that she almost gasps and for a moment she loses her thread.

"... don't you think, Miss Rostock?"

She wrenches her glance away. What has the Professor just said? Confused, she shoots out a hand for her wine and knocks over her glass. She watches the stain spread slowly across the white table cloth. "Oh God, I'm so sorry ..." she stammers. She looks up. Nadia is smiling

Dortmann gestures to the waiter. "That's absolutely no problem. I was just saying that I find your answer a most graceful one. And interesting. I too love the Nile, and believe in its power to transform us." He breaks off a piece of pitta bread and chews it for a moment, as if ruminating. "Elsewhere rivers are merely useful economic lifelines. They simply cut through the land, dividing it in two. But Egypt is quite different. Here the river *unites* the land. Here the river is the centre. It has been said that Egypt is the gift of the Nile ....."

"Herodotus, the sixth century Greek historian," cuts in Nadia. She glances defiantly round the table, then smiles at Dortmann.

Dortmann nods. "And he is right. Egypt without the Nile would literally not exist. That is part of this country's magic." He turns to Edward. "But tell me, as a psychoanalyst, what do you make of the tomb paintings you've seen; all those depictions of the dead man's worldly goods – his flocks and herds, his servants and children, not to mention his politically incorrect, totally undersized, obedient little wife? Don't you feel that it must indicate an excessive fear of death – a primitive desire to take it all with them? I'm sure your Dr Freud would doubtless have called it a conspicuous display of anality. Hardly a spiritual view of things." He gives a small, playful smile.

Edward shakes his head emphatically. "No, I don't think so at all. Those paintings are so full of vitality and sheer delight in life. You've only got to look at them to know that they couldn't possibly have been made by men dominated by a fear of death. What they suggest to me is something quite different. They seem to show a world that's so beautiful, so alive and intense that it somehow burns right through into eternity. It's as if the hereafter is right here and now – *and it is enough in itself!*" He taps his forefinger on the tablecloth for emphasis

Lara nods. "That's exactly what I feel when I sit beside the Nile. It's such a sensation of completeness, a kind of quiet abundance." She turns and looks at Edward. "You're absolutely right – it's a feeling of 'This is enough', a kind of plenitude. I don't think I've ever really felt that anywhere else."

Nadia sits forward and thrusts out her jaw. "Enough for *what?*"

Lara pauses, then turns calmly and looks at her, this time clearly ready to hold her ground. She shrugs. "Just enough."

"Just so," says Dortmann nodding slowly. "Just so." He smiles warmly at Edward.

Nadia puts down her fork and leans back in her chair as if formally withdrawing from the conversation. Finn's eyes have been moving backwards and forwards, watching the interplay. The Professor is smiling broadly, clearly relishing the conversation. Suddenly Finn feels a pressure against his lower leg. He stays still. No mistake. The pressure increases. He holds back a smile and reaches casually for his wine glass.

"I would also be intrigued to know," Dortmann is saying to Edward, "what you made of all the funny little tricks you see in the tomb paintings, like the crafty way they lure the cattle across a river with a decoy for example. Or how they drive the fish into the nets ….."

Nadia drops her napkin and leans sideways to pick it up. Under the tablecloth Finn feels a hand on his thigh, just above the knee. He glances at Nadia, who was sitting upright now, a slight smile on her lips, her other hand playing casually with her earring.

".…. Don't you find these almost comic scenes slightly unseemly for a tomb?" The hand slides to the inside of Finn's leg and moves slowly upward. He glances across the table. Lara is observing him with wide-eyed curiosity.

"Well .…." Edward sits back and takes a sip of wine. "Strangely enough, those scenes didn't feel out of place to me at all. In fact, it occurred to me that when man does those kinds of tricks, using his cunning intellect, he's actually expressing his special place in creation – a little above the animals and a little lower than the angels, as Thomas Moore put it. And then he's being most true to his nature. And I believe that's what the Egyptian artists were celebrating so beautifully."

He stops, moves his eyes from Dortmann to glance around the table. Then he laughs self-consciously. "I'm sorry. I seem to have been rather holding the floor."

Dortmann sets down his glass. "You have just," he says slowly, "expressed an idea, after only one week in Egypt, which I have been struggling to get into my writing for the last forty years! So please do not apologise. Unless it is to my sense of scholarly envy."

Finn and Lara laugh. Lara glances at Nadia and is surprised to see a smile on her face. Her food is almost untouched. At a sign from Dortmann, the waiters clear away the mezes and set down in the centre of the table a large copper dish piled with kebabs. The air is filled with the scent of rosemary and coriander.

Dortmann gestures for everyone to help themselves. For a while there is an easy silence as they all concentrate on selecting the food. At length, Dortmann says, "Being here with you all and talking like this takes me back to my very first visit to Egypt. I was just now remembering it. That first trip was almost overwhelming." He leans forward and rests his chin on his hands. "I knew then that I would return here again and again. But it was also a peculiar mixture of joy and sadness. I think that every time I come to Egypt I realise that the Bible is right: that we – at least in our western society – really have been cast out of Paradise, and now we only see through a glass darkly. But the ancient Egyptians *didn't*. They really saw the world with a kind of pristine clarity and joy. And when I came here and encountered their art and this ancient mystical landscape, it was as if for a moment the scales literally fell from my eyes and I too saw clearly for the very first time."

"And afterwards came that sense of loss and sadness, of being cast out of Paradise?" asks Edward.

Dortmann looks at him gravely and nods, as if the two of them are sharing a mutual secret. "Just so. Yes, I believe that a sense of absolute loss also enters the soul at such moments. Maybe that is the price we have to pay for the beauty. But perhaps what Egypt still gives us – even if only in flashes – is a small view back into that Paradise. A view into what Rilke called, 'The self-delighting soul'. *That* is still available to us. Especially here beside the Nile." He pauses and coughs, perhaps surprised by his sudden openness in company. Then he turns to Edward. "If you have time while you're here, Mr Cavanagh, it would greatly interest me to discuss this further. I've long been fascinated by the psychology that must underlie our strong emotional reactions to ancient Egypt. Perhaps you would even consider collaborating with me on an article?"

Edward smiles broadly and nods. "I would be delighted to."

*

It is almost midnight. The driver cracks his whip and the *caleche* lurches forward. Bernard Dortmann stands at the top of the long flight of stone steps waving them off. Behind him the lights from the hall of the Winter Palace glow amber in the darkness. Nadia has already disappeared inside.

Lara turns to Finn. "What a lovely man! How long have you known him?"

"Ever since I started dealing. For years he was the central figure for the antiquities market in North America, a kind of *eminence grise*. All the collectors there consulted him before they bought anything. Most of the museum curators too. His word was law. If you didn't get his seal of approval you couldn't really sell an object."

"That must be a tricky position. I imagine he'd have to be both art expert *and* diplomat."

"Art expert certainly. He's the best in the field. And diplomat? Well, he can be – when he wants to." He pauses. "But there's something that's always struck me as even more remarkable about him. In that position of influence he'd only have to hold out his hand for a bribe and all the dealers would flock to him with fists full of cash. A lot of other academics do that. But in all the years I've known him, there's never been the slightest whiff of corruption."

Lara sniffs. "Corrupt? *Him?* It would be pretty hard to imagine!"

They are nearing the end of the brightly lit avenue of hotels and tourist shops. The concrete high-rise buildings gradually give way to mud-brick houses and sporadic street lamps. For a while they are silent. The hooves click in the darkness. Then Lara says, "But, my God, *she's* something else! What's going on between the two of them?"

Finn shrugs. "No idea. She used to be one of his star students in New York. I can't imagine they're an item. She wouldn't be his type. Not elegant enough. I got the feeling you might fit the bill much better." He nudges her gently.

Lara ignores him. "And what was going on between *the two of you* at the table?"

Edward, who has been gazing out of the carriage at the passing procession of dimly lit doorways, turns to look at them.

"How do you mean?" asks Finn.

"Oh, come on, Finn!" says Lara. "Don't fob me off with that!"

The sickly glow of an overhead sodium light momentarily illuminates the smile on Finn's face. "Well, okay," he says reluctantly. "Let's just say it's been an occasional thing between us. She may not be everybody's cup of tea, but at least she's sexy. Don't you think so, Edward?"

Edward has turned away again and is looking sideways out of the carriage. He doesn't answer. Finn prods him with his foot. "*Edward?*"

"What on earth is it, Edward?" says Lara irritably. "Why have you been acting so strangely all evening?"

Edward finally turns to face them. "I can't really answer," he says reluctantly.

"Why on earth not?" insists Lara.

"It's professional."

"It's *what?*" chorus Finn and Lara.

"Professional."

A long silence.

"Okay, I get it ….." says Lara slowly. "She's a patient of yours, isn't she?" Edward doesn't reply. "….. And ethically you can't admit it unless she does. Right?"

Finn bounces forward on the leather seat. "You mean a *therapy* patient?" He stares in disbelief.

"Only you know you can't keep a secret from the two of us for long," says Lara.

Edward nods reluctantly. "Something like that."

"Oh, great!" says Lara. "So Finn's screwing her and you're therapising her and no one's supposed to know anything about it. Christ, what a nest of vipers I've been sitting in! No wonder it felt so uncomfortable when she was there. Poor girl! Now I almost start to feel sorry for her."

"That's probably why she was so quiet and withdrawn," says Edward. "It's hardly surprising."

The carriage bumps off the tarmac road down onto the causeway to the hotel.

"Noooo," says Lara slowly. "She was quiet and withdrawn because she was so concentrated on trying to undo Finn's trousers."

There's a moment of shocked silence. Then all three of them burst out laughing.

They are still laughing as they carry their drinks from the bar out to the terrace and settle into the cane chairs overlooking the Nile. The restaurant has closed, the lights are dimmed. They are alone.

Finn leans forward. "Is she *really* your therapy client? And you run into her here! What an absolutely bizarre coincidence! It's almost enough to make me think that all Mountjoy's talk about fate and synchronicity isn't total bullshit after all. But what's wrong with her? Is she really crazy?"

Edward laughs. "Not everyone who goes into psychoanalysis is barking mad. But I ....." He hesitates and stares into his drink, clinking the ice against the side of the glass. He is clearly weighing something in his mind. At length he glances up at Finn. "Look, in a way, I shouldn't even be saying this at all….. I'm sure you know what you're doing, but ….. my impression is she could be quite unpredictable."

"In what way?" asks Lara, her face suddenly creased with concern.

Finn cuts in. "Sure she can be difficult. Everybody knows that. But she's highly intelligent and a brilliant Egyptologist and she's bloody good at her job. She's completely galvanised that whole moribund museum in Edinburgh. Everyone respects her for it. Even the ones who don't particularly like her." He smiles. "And there are quite a few of those around."

Edward shakes his head. "Unfortunately, intelligence and doing a good job don't have very much to do with it. Certain kinds of psychological damage are very often precisely what can fuel an exaggerated drive for achievement. Probably most of the best paid jobs in the City are held by people like that. What I'm talking about is something like a deep, unhealing wound that has its origins way back in childhood. In some situations this can lead to quite irrational behaviour. Sometimes even dangerous."

Lara sits forward, her chin on her knuckles. She frowns. "What sort of situations?"

"Principally if the circumstances of the original trauma are in some way recreated."

Lara shakes her head in incomprehension.

"Look," says Edward. "If, for example, there's been some kind of childhood abuse – violence, sexual or whatever – and then years later someone quite innocently re-enacts a relatively trivial detail that accompanied the incident – even something as small as a gesture, a movement, a form of words – then this can retrigger the original sense of being abused.

And the perfectly innocent person suddenly *stands in* for the perpetrator."

"And then?"

Edward shrugs. "Well, then they get the full force of the rage stored up against the original abuser. Only it's not an adult's rage; it's a *child's* rage. That's the problem – it knows no bounds. And when it's allied to the physical strength or the mental cunning of an adult, that's when things can get really dangerous. Technically it's what we would term borderline psychotic behaviour."

Lara stares anxiously at Edward. "Jesus, does that mean what I think it means?" Edward doesn't answer. "And in this case what *was* the original trauma?"

Edward spreads his hands. "You realise that ethically, even if I knew the answer to that, I couldn't tell you. But, in any case, I don't know. I've only seen her twice, then she just disappeared." He looks at Finn. "I don't *know* any of this. It's absolutely *not* a professional opinion – I hardly know anything about her. It's just a gut reaction. All I'm, saying is – treat her carefully. Otherwise I think she could be real trouble."

"Did you hear that, Finn?" asks Lara, putting her mouth close to his ear.

"I heard," says Finn wearily and lies back in the chair. "The problem is," he drawls, "forbidden fruit is almost always irresistible."

"Christ, Finn!" explodes Lara. "Don't you ever give up?" But then she laughs, despite herself.

TWENTY-FIVE

At four o'clock in the afternoon of the following day, Finn finds
Alexander Lascaris seated on a long striped sofa at the end of
the hallway of the Winter Palace Hotel. The low table in front
of him is stacked with papers, a bulging leather briefcase sits
on the floor at his side. As Finn approaches, Lascaris rises and
holds out his hand.

"What's all the paper for?"

"Our film."

"Our *what?*"

"It's better you look like part of my film crew. The
antiquities police watch everybody around here. If we're
observed just wandering round the garden in conversation
too many times people may start to wonder. Does anyone in
Luxor know you're a dealer?"

"No," says Finn, aware he is not only lying about Hassani,
but also concealing his fears of al-Shaikh.

"Good." Lascaris pushes a pile of papers across the glass
table towards Finn. "Take a seat and sort through this while
we're talking. That way it will look as if we're discussing a film."

Finn picks up the bundle of pages. "What is it?"

"A script for a documentary that never got made."

Finn begins leafing casually through the pages. Suddenly
his hand stops. He stares at a document in Arabic carrying
an official stamp at the bottom. "What's this?" He holds it up.

For a moment Lascaris looks startled. Then he calmly takes the piece of paper and drops it into his briefcase. "That must have got into the wrong place." He gives Finn one of his infectious smiles. "It's just a permit for filming at the Pyramids."

Finn thinks to question him further but holds back, knowing he will get nowhere. Instead he says, "Did your people find anything?"

"They did." Lascaris picks up one of the papers, holds it out to Finn and taps his finger on it, as if indicating something important. "Although I rather wish they hadn't."

"Why?"

"Just as I said, there's nothing of interest to be found at el-Amarna. Least of all in the resettled Roman areas. If it had been Luxor or Denderah or even Abydos there might have been something worthwhile. But el-Amarna!" He shakes his head in disgust.

"But they *did* find something?" insists Finn.

Lascaris takes more papers out of his bag and places them on the table. "Oh yes, they found something alright. Unfortunately. I will show it to you. You will know its value better than I. But even my rudimentary knowledge of the antiquities market tells me that it's not worth more than ten percent of the bribes it took to dig it up and transport it here through all the security checkpoints."

"I guess Mountjoy just had an off day," says Finn casually. He leans back. He can feel a swirling mixture of disappointment and relief, knowing that the whole bizarre escapade is about to collapse. A sense of release too, as if he has just eluded some unseen danger.

Lascaris glances at him from under his dark lashes. "It seems our Mister Mountjoy can guarantee finding *something* – but not its financial value – which is not particularly helpful.

Perhaps we should have thought of that before we started." He begins to gather the papers together into piles. "Later we can discuss whether we should persevere with the whole project or just abandon it. But for now come up to my room and I'll show you this wreck of antiquity." He taps the edges of the thick stack of papers against the glass table-top and hands them to Finn. "You carry these."

Finn frowns. "You have it in your room?"

Lascaris looks at him in apparent surprise. "It's quite safe." He rises. "Sometimes I have half a ton of cinema equipment in my room. They know me here. No-one ever bothers me."

Lascaris' room appears unoccupied. Finn glances around. No papers, no hairbrushes, no clothes. It's as if Lascaris is actually living somewhere else. Lascaris crosses to the cupboard, opens the door and bends down. Finn tries to see over his shoulder, but the lack of space between the bed and his crouching body makes this impossible. He hears the scrape of a key, followed by two metallic thuds as heavy locks flick open. Then Lascaris emerges holding a bundle of white cotton. He lays it on the bedspread and begins pulling back the wrappings.

Finn waits impatiently, aware of the adrenalin pumping in his stomach. Despite Lascaris's discouraging words his dealer's curiosity is bubbling. It could be anything – a fragment of some destroyed wall painting perhaps. Or a heavily encrusted bronze figurine? Or even some rarity, which Lascaris wouldn't necessarily recognise as valuable…

Lascaris pulls aside the last piece of cloth.

And suddenly Finn feels winded, as if he has been punched in the stomach. Staring up at him is the black outlined eye and half the face of a Roman period mummy mask. The *right* half of the face. He crouches down, pretending to inspect the mask. He needs time to steady himself before he can face Lascaris. *Could he possibly be mistaken?* But the break is in the right place, the colouring seems identical. His brain wheels. *Five thousand hectares ..... How is it possible? Who could have .....? Hassani?* In the Middle East cross-cultural messages are hard to decode. He knows that from bitter experience. Gifts, loyalties, friendships are all stamped with a different currency here. But *Hassani?* Not to trust Hassani would be like not being able to trust the ground under your feet. Better to believe in Mountjoy's absurd claims about fate and synchronicity. But still ...... Suddenly he feels sick with anxiety.

"Not much of a prize for all our hard work, is it?"

"No," says Finn curtly. He doesn't trust his own voice. He runs his fingers gently over the splintered surface and along the broken edges in a play of inspection, trying to buy time. Gradually he feels his pulse return to normal. He rises. Still gazing down at the mask he says, "No, you're right. It's a piece of junk. Almost worthless."

He turns. To his relief Lascaris has his back to him, staring out across the gardens. Finn notices the slender fingers drumming like a pianist's on the window ledge. Suddenly Lascaris spreads his arms theatrically. "What on earth shall we do with it? Perhaps I should just crumple it up and dump it in the Nile."

"No!" Finn pushes a hand back through his hair as Lascaris turns to look at him enquiringly. "I don't believe in destroying *any* antiquity – no matter what its value," he adds more calmly. He glances down at the mask again, avoiding Lascaris's eyes. "Occasionally I have clients for such things – first-time buyers who want something inexpensive. Sometimes they go on to be serious collectors. It's an investment." He looks Lascaris in the face. "I'll give you two hundred dollars for it. That's probably as much as I can sell it for in London on a good day."

Lascaris shrugs. "If you wish. It's all yours." He bends and begins recovering the mask in its wrappings.

As Finn goes down the broad staircase, the bag under his right arm, he becomes aware of something clicking in the recesses of his brain. Everybody in the antiquities world distrusts each other; treachery is the common currency. So why has Lascaris so unhesitatingly given up the mask for a mere two hundred dollars? Somehow it feels too easy.

He tries to brush his disquiet aside. After all, to a relative layman like Lascaris, the battered mummy mask wouldn't look as if it was worth anything. Probably he had thought Finn crazy to have given him even two hundred dollars.

He steps out of the hotel into the sunlight, suddenly relieved to be out of Lascaris's orbit. He turns right in the direction of the old Luxor village.

*

In the long silence Finn listens to the slow grating of the ceiling fan.

Hassani begins to click the row of amber worry beads in his left hand. Then he picks up the battered piece of cartonage mask that Finn has laid on the floral table covering and examines it. A large split runs from the top of the forehead, down through the eye and across the crudely painted cheek. Much of the outer colouring has peeled away, exposing the crumbling white gesso beneath. He turns the mask over, peers briefly at the back. Finn watches his face closely, but it betrays nothing. Then Hassani crosses the room, slides out the cardboard box from under the bench and pulls aside the ragged cloths. He takes out the battered mask that Finn had seen four days before. Then he returns and picks up the other fragment. For a moment he looks like a magician, standing with a piece of the mask in each hand. Finn's breath catches in his throat. He can feel his heart pumping against his ribs.

Hassani holds the two pieces at arm's length. Then slowly he draws them together. Reassembled, the face looks even less impressive than it had when split apart. The expression is pudgy, blank, the colouring gaudy and tasteless. It is a third-rate antiquity of no beauty and little value. But the two halves fit perfectly together. Of that there can be no question. Finn lets out the breath from between his lips with a low sigh.

Hassani looks at him over the top of the mask. "Is the papyrus on the back of the other piece also?"

Finn nods. "Yes, as far as I can see. We'll have to be very careful separating the layers, but it's definitely there. So we have nearly all of it, except for the little bits lost in the break."

Hassani sets the two fragments down on the table, draws his thick index finger along the line of his black moustache. "My friend," he says slowly. "You know I never ask such questions but ...." He hesitates. "This time I need to know – for your sake. Where you get this thing?"

Finn shrugs. "It doesn't really matter." Hassani stares at him. Finn feels uncomfortable under his unwavering gaze. "Okay," he says. "It comes from el-Amarna, of course."

Hassani spreads his arms. "Five thousand hectares. *Five thousand hectares!* A particular grain of sand – remember? And you find it in four days!"

"Like you said, perhaps it was the will of Allah!"

Hassani doesn't smile. "And you dug it up yourself and

carried it single-handed past all the check points from Amarna to Luxor with no help?"

Finn glances down. Hassani's presence is like a rock, irrefutable, and, for a moment, he feels ashamed of having doubted him. But still ….. in this business one never reveals one's sources or contacts to anyone. *Ever.*

"My friend," says Hassani quietly. "Sometimes, even in our world, it is safer to speak than not to speak. Maybe someone put this there, specially for you. Maybe you are walking into a trap."

Finn looks up at him. He has the uncanny feeling that Hassani has just been reading his mind. "Okay," he says at length. "I have an associate."

There is a long silence.

Then Hassani says, "The cinema man?" It isn't really a question.

"*Who?*"

"The cinema man." Hassani runs both hands lightly over his head, as if to indicate Lascaris' bald skull.

"How did you know?"

Hassani shruggs. "He came five days ago." He sees Finn's enquiring look. "Luxor is a small place. In my business we have to be careful. We sit. We wait. We watch. We stitch the pieces together." He makes a threading gesture with his thick fingers. "That is how we learn things."

"You know him?"

Hassani pulls out one of the heavy wooden chairs that flank the table and sinks into it. He gestures to Finn to do the same.

"He comes to Luxor many times. For many years." There is something reluctant about Hassani's manner, as if he doesn't like – or doesn't trust – Lascaris.

"It's his job," explains Finn, feeling uncomfortable, as if he is having to defend Lascaris in the face of Hassani's condemnation.

"Why does he need *you*?" asks Hassani.

"That's easy. He has the contacts here, but only I can sell what he finds. He's not a dealer."

"The selling is done in London," says Hassani bluntly. "Not here. He doesn't need you here. Here is dangerous."

Finn drums his fingers on the table. "Okay. He needs my expertise with the objects then. To authenticate them."

The Egyptian raises his thick eyebrows almost to the line of his cropped hair. "He needs *your* expertise to tell him that an antiquity that has just been dug up out of the ground is not a forgery!"

Finn coughs. "Well, like you said, it could have been a fake put there especially for him. A set-up. Such things have happened before. You know that."

Hassani is silent. He stays looking at Finn with his eyebrows arched. Then he says, "Put there for *him*? Or put there for *you*?"

Finn sits back and runs a hand through his hair. There is a prickle, a stirring at the back of his mind. He remembers his vague sense of unease when he had visited Lascaris that grey morning in London. And again just now, as he had come down the stairs of the Winter Palace. Some part of him knows that Hassani is right: the pieces of the jigsaw aren't fitting together properly. Or perhaps fitting together *too* well? But still, the mask *is* genuine and so is the papyrus that backs it. There is no doubt about that. So what is the problem?

In the long silence that follows, Finn listens to the soft clicking of pigeons strutting on the flat mud roof above. He sighs. "Okay. I'll be careful. But in any case, my business with him is over. He thinks the mask is worthless. I paid him two hundred dollars for it. It's all finished." He pauses. "Can you keep both pieces for a couple of hours? I have to go to a Son et Lumiere performance at Karnak. I'll collect them on my way back. I may have a safe way to get the papyrus read."

"You show it to the Professor?"

"Something like that."

Hassani doesn't reply. He remains staring down at his thick folded hands shuffling the worry beads.

"What is it?" asks Finn. "Don't you trust me?"

Hassani sighs. "My friend, of course I trust you. But be careful. Be very, very careful. This is a dangerous country. Even *you* do not really know Egypt."

TWENTY-SIX

Lara steps off the wooden jetty down into a white felucca. The young boatman, who identifies himself as Jamal, gives her his hand and steadies the shallow boat against the dockside with his bare foot. The broad planking inside is painted a brilliant sky blue. The low bench that runs around the edges is scattered with brightly coloured cushions. Everything is spotlessly clean.

Lara and Edward move quickly to the stern where a canvas awning has been rigged up against the sun. Jamal heaves the boat off with his foot, then scuttles to the mast and pulls on a thin grey rope. With a series of soft snaps, the knots that furl the sail to the diagonal mast pull free. Despite the stillness, the triangular sail flaps then fills, billowing out so that the felucca turns and slides effortlessly towards the centre of the river.

Out in the middle of the Nile the world feels stilled. The thin sail seems to gather wind from nowhere, propelling them rapidly upstream away from the last straggling mud-brick houses. The town of Luxor fades to a distant blur. Edward leans back against the awning, suddenly aware that this is the first time he has been alone with Lara since that difficult evening beside the canal at el-Minya. And again he feels uncertain and strangely ill at ease. For a long time they are silent, listening to the slow creak of the ropes and the soft wash of water under the stern. They glide past fields of clover and date palms. Water buffaloes are cooling themselves in the muddy shallows, sending up rainbow arcs of water as they flick their long tufted tails. A line of women with tall earthenware pots balanced motionless on their swathed heads, moves silently along the bank. Further downstream a rowing boat is becalmed in the shallows. A young boy stands in the stern, beating the water with an oar to drive the fish into his net. The hollow slapping sound reaches them distantly, as if disconnected from the action. A calm lies over everything.

Edward turns to Lara. He watches her grey-green eyes as they dart around, taking in every detail. He sees the pulse in her throat, the lifted line of her small breasts as she cranes her neck to inspect the patched sail and the swaying top of the bowed mast. And suddenly he aches to touch her, to press his mouth to that slow beat in her throat.

Even without turning, Lara can feel the intensity of that gaze. She's surprised that she has no urge to deflect it. Instead she sits quite still, allowing it to travel over her, enjoying its slow, sensual slide across her body. She lets her hand over the edge and trails it in the warmth of the water.

"Welcome!"

Startled, she looks round. Jamal is smiling at her. "Welcome! In Egypt we say, "Put your hand in the Nile and you will return.""

Her face lights up. "Oh, I do hope so. Thank you." She turns to Edward. "Isn't it beautiful? I keep wanting to say 'Biblical' to describe it, but of course it's much older than that. Actually it looks exactly like the scenes in the tomb paintings."

"It's probably virtually unchanged since the time of the earliest Pharaohs five thousand years ago."

They are skirting a flat bank of reed and sedge in the centre of the river. A red-legged moorhen struts jerkily amongst the shallows and sparrows flit between the cottony heads of the bulrushes. The air is alive with the clicking of small birds. Suddenly a cluster of ducks, disturbed by their arrival, explodes from behind a curtain of reeds. They squawk frantically as they bat their wings, their orange feet slapping the water as they struggle to get airborne. Lara laughs and turns to watch. She throws back her head. A ray of sunlight slanting through the cotton awning caresses her throat. The water is like silk against her wrist. She feels lost in the day.

"You're very beautiful."

Startled, she turns to look at him. And she can see now the intensity of his gaze, no longer camouflaged. The hunger of a man coming back to life. She holds his eyes, afraid of what is suddenly happening between them, but more afraid to let go. She can feel the struggle in him, as if he is playing some kind of internal Russian roulette. For a strange instant she remembers the myth of Osiris, struggling to free himself from the underworld. Within half an hour they will be back on land, gathered up into the anonymous familiarity of the group. And she knows that with that one apparently innocuous phrase he has opened a door into his private stockade. Suddenly this small pocket of time feels very precious.

"I want to know you better," she says quite openly. "And it seems that's not a very easy thing to do."

He smiles. "Am I so secretive? Try me."

She hesitates. "Well, for example, that night in the pyramid ….." He frowns, obviously taken aback by this apparent non-sequitur. "I didn't understand what was happening in you, the way you managed to stay so calm, as if you weren't at all afraid. You didn't explode like Finn and I did. And I don't really understand that." She looks him straight in the eye, willing him to stay with her. "And if I'm to know you at all, I somehow need to know what's going on in you. What makes you tick if you like. It's hard being so close to a mystery."

There is a long silence. She can feel the hesitancy in him, as if he mistrusts her intentions. At length he says, "Of course I was afraid. Like all of us. When I saw that wall of sand I was absolutely terrified. But by the time we were back in the burial chamber the fear just seemed to have evaporated. I can't explain it rationally. I just somehow accepted the situation as my fate. Perhaps I'm just a fatalist."

For a while he sits staring down at his hands, his shoulders slightly hunched, as if weighing a decision. When he turns to her there is a look of resolution in his face. His voice has gone quieter and she can sense him picking his words carefully, like a man edging forward on precarious stepping stones, afraid he may lose his balance. "I think that in the night, while we were trapped in the pyramid – perhaps it was at that moment when all our watches stopped...." He shrugs. "Anyhow, at some point, I had the strange impression – it was *more* than an impression – that Kate came to me." He hesitates. "You see, I've always tried to think about her death as positively as I could. Not just focussing on the pain and the loss, but also how the grief has somehow made me a stronger person – more compassionate, more resilient, a more profound therapist, less afraid and so on. At least less afraid of death ....." He stops and lets out a long puff of breath before going on. "But it seems not less afraid of life. And I think that's what she came to tell me. In some way to release me."

She can sense how hard it is for him to make this raw confession. His voice has gone hoarse, as if something solid is being dragged through his throat.

"Release you? From what?"

"From a kind of mistaken loyalty to Kate. From a grief that has clearly outrun its real purpose, that has become self-indulgent and self-serving. And I think I saw then that, if they really love us, what the dead want is not for us to cling to them. They want to push us away from them, *back into life*."

She nods but stays silent. She's afraid to jolt him from the sleepwalker's path he seems now to be entering. But his voice has trailed off, and she senses him edging away again, as if this much exposure has been too long.

Jamal has tacked them back to the centre of the Nile. He heaves the wooden tiller all the way over to one side, bringing them about in a graceful arc, then pulls the sail tight. And suddenly they can feel the surge of the huge river under the keel, carrying them back downstream, like being pumped along a giant artery.

"And did you feel released?"

He meets her eyes now and she sees uncertainty. He sighs. "All I know is that on this trip there have been moments with you and Finn – especially with you – when I've felt more alive than I've ever done before."

"More alive than with Kate?"

The words are out of her mouth before she can stop them. His face hardens, all trace of the earlier softness is suddenly gone. She bites her lip and turns away. *Christ, how could I have asked such a question? How could I? Why am I so damn needy around men? Especially around him?* She sees the pain in his eyes. For a moment he holds her gaze, then he shrugs and looks away. And he is gone again, his face impassive, remote. It's an almost physical movement, like a steel shutter being drawn down. She feels a deep, familiar ache in her heart. *If only he…..*

"Come along you two!" David Mountjoy's voice booms irritably across the water. "The bus is here to take us to the Son et Lumiere at Karnak. We're all waiting."

She spins round. They are less than fifty yards from the hotel landing-stage. Jamal moves forward, agile as a cat, flicks the rope free from its housing and pulls hard, gathering the loose sail against the diagonal boom. Noiselessly he guides the felucca alongside the dock with his foot.

*

Lara sits on the wooden benches ranged above the Sacred Lake. Already she's bored by the Son et Lumiere. She hates the statues absurdly lit in blues and greens, the booming voice of the narrator retelling the familiar story of Isis, Osiris and Horus, the naïve gasps of the crowd. She withdraws into her own world, needing to unpick the tangled skein of her feelings. She knows she has behaved stupidly in the *felucca*. And now she feels confused and, yes, angry. She hates it that Edward can make her feel this way with his constant disappearing act. It's like some kind of crazy game between them, where his elusiveness keeps her constantly striving towards him. She feels played with. And some part of her wants to smash his obstinate self-sufficiency, his stubborn ability to turn away and be lost in his own private world. Somehow he always manages to withdraw and leave her feeling marooned, washed up helpless on the bleak shores of *his* bloody emotions.

She closes off her ears with the flat of her hands, trying to block off the pretentious, treakly voice retelling the story of Isis bringing back life to Osiris. Is that what *I'm* really doing? she wonders. Constantly hovering around him, trying with my woman's wings to fan life back in to him as he lies there stubbornly inert, too afraid to be caught in the current of another's emotions, as if that might risk some kind of extinction for him? *Why am I trying* yet again, *hoping against*

288

hope that I can be the one to succeed where all others must have failed …..? Of course, a psychotherapist would probably tell her it's all about trying to regain the love of her absent father. But, right now, she doesn't want this kind of superior, patronising explanation. In fact, right now, she couldn't give a fuck about it.

She shakes her head. Subliminally she's aware of something tugging at her attention. She drops her hands and glances up. To her left, in the row below her, Finn has turned and is staring at her. His face, caught for a moment in the strobe of lights across the monuments, is lined with concern. *Somehow* he has picked up her distress. She nods in recognition, then sits back. But already she feels calmer. It's as if there is something in Finn's matter-of-fact directness that holds more tenderness than all Edward's complicated, supersensitive twists and turns. She remembers how comforting it had felt when he had held her as she had cried uncontrollably that evening beside the Nile.

But she knows too that he's wounded in his own way. She thinks of Birgit, Nadia….. and the scores of others that must have come before them. It feels as if he is constantly giving away his real strength through these indiscriminate seductions, somehow demeaning himself. It's as if some part of him remains adolescent. There's something uncertain and immature behind his charm and macho bravura. A familiar bitter taste of disappointment rises in her. She sighs.

There's something so strange about this triangle into which she has unexpectedly fallen. Something that feels almost older than themselves. Something fated? Or ancestral? The words seem to make no sense. But, in a place below the level of her mind, she can sense that Mountjoy is right. Here, in Egypt, her fate is waiting for her.

TWENTY-SEVEN

Nadia Rusedska gazes out over the gardens of the Winter Palace, her elbows resting on the broad sill. It is evening and in the twilight the azaleas give off a final glow as if lit from within. The air is filled with the scent of jasmine. As she turns back to the room she catches sight of her clouded reflection in the long window. In this half-light, with her long hair falling over her shoulders and her low-cut, ochre-coloured dress, she can imagine herself as a princess leaning from the crenelated battlements of a castle. She smiles. Despite her outer toughness, fairy tales have always been her life-blood, her inner secret. She loves their magical ability to transform poverty into riches, ugliness into beauty, to make the impossible possible. Ever since childhood they have helped to keep her inner turmoil in check. And in these last days, travelling with Dortmann, she has had the constant feeling of actually taking part in a fairy story, living in a blissful world where everything unfolds just as it should, and someone finally sees how truly special and lovable she is.

She hated to run into Finn Connors in the museum. He felt like an intruder from another, far uglier world. She recognised him at once. Even from the back and twenty yards away his fair hair and loose-limbed stance had been unmistakable. All down the long sculpture gallery she felt herself trying to withdraw, like a mollusc pulling back into its shell for protection. Yet with every step, humiliatingly, she could feel her body react to him as if it had a chemical life of its own. Instinctively she moved closer to Dortmann, seeking his protection.

Her sex life has never been prudish; she does what she wants with her body. But still, she can't explain what happened at that dull Egyptology conference in Leiden the previous year. Amongst the tweed jackets and grey suits, Finn had stood out exotically in his jeans and check shirt. His energy was a complete mismatch with everything around him. No one knew exactly what he was doing there. As a dealer he was an outsider, almost a pariah, amongst the academics. And he didn't seem to care.

It was on the second evening, bored, that she wandered into the almost deserted hotel bar. He caught her eye, rose politely and gestured to the empty stool beside him. To this day she can't understand what made her – without hesitation – cross those four yards of carpet and sit down next to him. He had been drinking a vodka martini, a novelty in her world. The first taste burnt her throat and brought tears to her eyes. But when the second glass arrived she began to enjoy it. An hour later they had walked together arm-in-arm up the main staircase and gone directly to her room. She hadn't even bothered to check if they were being observed.

When she woke the next morning the bed beside her was still warm. She stretched and smiled, enjoying the feel of her body. Then suddenly she sat up and stared around. The room was empty. The bastard had left without a word, not even a note. For three days the rage in her stomach was all-consuming.

She hasn't seen him since then. Until now. God, how she hated that boring dinner! They had all chatted so brightly, snobbishly ignoring her, as if she didn't belong there, while they stole Dortmann's attention. Particularly that snotty English girl with her haughty manner, so coyly flirting with Dortmann and treating Finn like her private property. And what an appalling shock to run into that psychotherapist, *here* of all places, two thousand miles from home! It was as if the universe was conspiring to play jokes on her. She remembers all too well her two sessions with him: how he had annoyed her with his prodding and questioning about her anger. It had felt as if he was sniffing for blood, wondering why her relationships never lasted, wanting to know all about her father. Two sessions of that had been more than enough! She lets out a long puff of breath, wanting to clear the whole memory from her system. At least this time, what she has done with Finn under the table has been on *her* terms. She has shown him that – and cut that snotty English bitch right out. She turns and runs her hands over her hair, rearranging it carefully. Dortmann will call for her in half an hour.

The telephone beside the bed jangles. She glances at her watch in surprise, then crosses the room and picks up the receiver.

"Nadia?"

It isn't Dortmann.

"Who's that?"

"Nadia, it's Finn."

"Finn!" She wavers, then starts to put down the 'phone.

"Nadia, it's important. I need to speak to you."

"No!"

"Don't worry, it's not about us. It's a business matter. I need your help." She doesn't answer. "I think you'll find it ..." He pauses, his voice drops lower. "..... *Interesting. Very* interesting. I don't want to say more on the 'phone."

Silence. She cradles the receiver against her shoulder and sinks down on the bed. She can feel the little hooks of him digging into her. He knows just how to slip behind her defences, even as she watches him do it.

"Why should I?"

"I promise you, you won't be disappointed."

Another silence.

"*I promise*," insists Finn.

"Where are you?"

"Downstairs."

"That was confident of you," she says acidly. She pauses. She can hear her own irregular breathing. "I'm in room 109, first floor to the left of the staircase. And Finn, ….."

"Yes?"

"It's only business, right? Otherwise I shall scream and kick you out."

"It's only business."

The line goes dead. She sighs. Why has she said yes? *Why?* She bites her lip angrily. Then she shrugs. At least it sounds intriguing. And, let's face it, she has nothing to lose. Perhaps he might even have some information about the little cosmetic box that the strange Maltese film-maker had shown her. After all, Finn is one of the great information gatherers in the art market. It's part of his success; he can charm almost anybody into giving away their secrets. She will hear whatever it is he has to tell her and then he will leave. If he tries to lay a finger on her she will scream and have him thrown out. She stands up, glances in the mirror above the small wooden dressing-table and flicks her hair back behind her ears.

There are two soft knocks on the door. Finn is standing there holding a large plastic bag. In the top of it she can see a folded striped *galabiya*, the usual banal tourist fare. He smiles, slips inside, closes the door and bolts it behind him.

"What the hell are you bolting it for?"

"Don't worry," he says gently. "I'm not going to assault you." He lays a hand on her arm as she reaches for the bolt. She draws it back as if he has scorched her. "You'll understand in a minute why I wouldn't want anyone bursting in."

For a moment they stand facing each other in silence.

"Been shopping?" she asks sarcastically, gesturing to the bulging bag in his right hand. Without answering, Finn moves to the bed and begins to unpack the bag, pulling out the covering of *galabiyas* from the top and dropping them one by one onto the floor. Within seconds the two halves of the cartonnage mummy mask are lying on the white linen cover of the bed.

Nadia stares at them. Then up at him. "I thought that, at least, you had better taste than *that*." Her voice is filled with calculated disdain. "That's just a Romano-Egyptian lump of shit! You know bloody well it's illegal to handle antiquities here. The whole place is crawling with secret police and informers with their hands out for baksheesh. And yet you come bursting in here trying to involve me in something bloody dangerous – all for a piece of crap like that!" She gestures at the mask in disgust. Apparently unconcerned, Finn sits down on the bed, picks up one of the pieces and turns it over. "Do you really think I would have bothered you if it wasn't important? Look."

Nadia stays motionless.

"Come on. You know I'm not going to mess you around."

Reluctantly she moves over to him. With his thumb and forefinger Finn gently lifts back the frayed brown edge of the backing. Nadia frowns, then lets out a little gasp. She sits down beside him and bends closer over the mask. There is a long silence. When she looks up her eyes are wide with amazement.

"But this is an Eighteenth Dynasty papyrus!"

"Right. And that's not all. Take another look." She picks up the other section, turns it over and expertly slides her nails between the two layers of cartonnage. She begins to peel away the top section. Finn can see that her hand is trembling slightly. He smiles to himself.

"It'll take time to do this properly," she says. "I don't have the proper tools here. I'll have to apply heat and use a sharp, flat instrument. Probably a nail file will do."

"You'll have to be careful. If it starts to tear ….."

"Look," she says sharply, "when I was a student I spent a whole summer's internship separating papyri in the Boston Museum. I know what I'm doing."

Her nails continue to prise apart the layers of the wafer-like material. Finn holds his breath. More and more of the carefully drawn black hieroglyphs come into view. Then a blank space broken only by the ends of two apparently random lines.

"Damn!" says Nadia. "It's really stuck together here. This is where I'll have to use heat and do it millimetre by millimetre. It could take hours." She points with the nail of her little finger. "I don't know what's going on under here with these two single lines. They can't be hieroglyphs. It's really weird." She goes back to studying the black markings of the inscription.

Finn watches her silently. He can feel the pulse of excitement in her. His gamble has been right. We're two of a kind, he thinks. From somewhere deep in the building a gong booms.

"Can you read it?" he asks at length.

She nods. "I think so. At least most of it. But it's complicated. And I haven't got the right books here." She runs

295

her nail down one of the columns. "It's not a standard text. It's some kind of private document." The finger stops. "Yes! Here's the name!"

Finn picks up the other half. "No, the cartouche with the name is *here*."

"No, no. Not the Pharaoh's name." Nadia bends deeper over the mask. "The name of the owner of the papyrus ..... the Vizier Amenmose," she pronounces slowly. "High Priest of Amun, steward of the King's estates ... High Priest of Amun in the Eighteenth Dynasty. Christ, he's someone really important!"

"*Amenmose?*"

"Yes." She turns to him. He looks shaken. "What is it?"

"I have a statue of him in my gallery."

"Amenmose, the High Priest of Amun from the Eighteenth Dynasty? The same guy? *Really?*"

Finn nods.

"What a bizarre coincidence!"

Finn rises and walks towards the window. He pushes his hand back through his hair. He tries to concentrate, but his mind is elsewhere, focusing in on the statue in his Chelsea house. On that cryptic line in the inscription ..... *That act most cherished, most secret, known only to the king's heart* ..... And then the morning of his visit to Lascaris, the strange feeling as he had stood on the doorstep, a sense of premonition. Suddenly he feels unsteady, as if the ground is stirring under his feet.

"Oh, come on Finn! It's not *that* unusual. Tombs often get broken up and scattered when they're discovered. The contents of some of them are spread through half the museums of Europe and North America."

"Hmmm."

"But there's something really funny here."

He turns and goes back to her. She is pointing at the oval ring on the other fragment, containing the blood-red hieroglyphs of the cartouche of the king. "This is the cartouche of Akhenaten."

"I know."

"Well, Akhenaten was a monotheist. Right? He banished all the old gods, including the god Amun. So how come you get a High Priest of the god *Amun* on a document of Akhenaten's reign? That would have been heresy, punishable by death. It doesn't make any sense." She pauses, frowning. "Hmmm. Perhaps it's a very clever forgery."

"No!" Finn snatches up one of the pieces, turns it over and over in his hands. Slowly his agitation subsides. "It's *not* a forgery," he says emphatically. "I can smell forgeries. This is as genuine as they come."

He picks up the second half and joins the two together. "Besides, what forger would hide an important private papyrus inside a fifth-rate piece of crap like this? It was just a miracle that it got noticed at all."

"*A miracle?* Specially for you, Finn Connors?" Nadia looks at him ironically and raises her eyebrows. "Perhaps you're being set up."

He sniffs. "If so, then they're out of luck. It's already mine and I paid next to nothing for it. I just need to establish what's in the inscription and whether it's worth all the money and hassle to have it smuggled back to London."

Nadia gives him another ironic smile. "And just exactly how ….," she asks slowly, "do you propose to do that? Are you going to go to Egyptology night school while you're here or something?"

Finn stares at her hard. "Look. If this is an important papyrus, how would you like to have it in your museum at a bargain price? Not a Getty Museum price or a Metropolitan Museum price. But a price just specially for you."

"Oh, right! And the price gets fixed only *after* I've read the hieroglyphs for you? You must think I'm simple."

"You'll just have to trust me."

"Jesus! You've got to be joking."

Without looking at her Finn begins wrapping the mask. He manoeuvres the pieces carefully back into the bag, covers them with the *galabiyas* and slides the package under the bed.

"What the hell do you think you're doing?"

"Think about it," he says casually. "I'll leave it with you overnight."

There is a long silence. Nadia stares at the floor. The faint hum of the town can be heard in the stillness of the room. She can feel herself being tugged in different directions. She knows she should throw him out – and the mask with him. Suddenly she looks at her watch. "God! I'll be late for dinner!"

She jumps up and moves towards the door. Finn follows. She reaches out, but before her fingers can touch the lock, he grips her by the upper arm and turns her round.

"No!" She tries to spin away, out of his grasp, but his mouth is already on hers. He backs her slowly up against the door. She wrenches her mouth away. "You bastard! You fucking bastard!"

He kisses her again, presses her hard against the woodwork. And then, as if they have all the time in the world, he begins to pull up the loose ochre-coloured dress. He feels her arms slide up and around his neck.

*

Bernard Dortmann is sitting on a checked sofa at the far end of the long bar, holding a glass of white wine. When he sees her he rises and summons a waiter.

She hurries over. "I'm so sorry to be late. I lay down and I must have dozed off." She drops her gaze and adjusts her dress nervously. It is over a year since she has last made love – Edinburgh is hardly conducive to sex – not since that long night in Leiden. And now she feels utterly naked under his gaze. Can people tell that you have been having sex just by looking at you?

"It has been a very long, hot and tiring day," says Dortmann as he swirls his wine, making small opaque patterns against the glass. She looks up and meets his eyes. He smiles. She breathes an inward sigh of relief. What has happened upstairs – both the contents of the plastic bag and the hard pressure of Finn's body as he pinned her to the door – feels like part of some lurid, pornographic dream that seems unattached to her. At least unattached to that part of her that is sitting now so demurely and happily with the elderly Professor.

Dortmann starts talking about the recent excavations at Karnak. She nods politely. What if he had come to collect her from her room as he sometimes did in the evenings? That would surely have destroyed everything that these last ten days have meant to her. She feels herself begin to colour at the thought. She has never blushed in the normal way; her face betrays nothing. But lower down, her throat and chest can suddenly erupt in scarlet welts as if she has been stung by a jelly-fish. She leans forward and clasps her hands under her chin, drawing her arms together. God, if only she hadn't worn such a low-cut dress!

Dortmann glances at her, then turns and summons the waiter, saying, "Why don't we take our drinks into dinner?" He busies himself with signing the bill, then chats in Arabic to the waiter, a handsome, dark-skinned man dressed in a brilliant white *galabiya*. Without glancing at Nadia, Dortmann rises and escorts her into the dining-room. She's pleased to have her back to him. As they sit down he begins to explain that the waiter is a Nubian, from the extreme south of the country. His voice runs on smoothly. She senses him deliberately putting her at ease. She smiles, inwardly leaning back into the comfort of him.

It is only towards the end of dinner, as the waiter is laying out the plates for fruit, that she feels composed enough to broach the subject that has been ricocheting in her head ever since Finn's departure. She selects a mango and begins paring away the skin. Then she takes a deep breath and looks him directly in the eye. "Finn Connors telephoned me before I dozed off," she says casually.

"Oh?"

"He has some antiquity that he wants to show me, some fragments of a papyrus apparently." She pauses, trying to gauge his reaction. Dortmann remains impassive. "I have a strange feeling it may be connected with the Amarna-period cosmetic box that I was shown in the museum. The one I told you about." He nods. "I wanted to ask your advice about what I should do."

Dortmann frowns. "Why do you think they're connected?"

"He was rather guarded on the 'phone. But he gave the impression that it was something very special – *and* of the reign of Akhenaten. Two significant finds of the same date in such a short space of time seems like too much of a coincidence." She hears her voice tremble slightly. She shrugs and concentrates on the mango. "Perhaps it's just a totally irrational hunch...."

"My advice?"

"About whether I should look at it or not. I know it's illegal to trade in antiquities here. As a scholar I could be compromised. Or worse."

Dortmann sits back and dips his fingers into the finger bowl. He moistens his lips, then dabs them with his napkin. "You are an academic not a dealer," he says slowly. "True, it is illegal to deal in antiquities here, but not to study them. Mr Connors is a professional, he knows the risks and he knows how to look after himself. If there were ever any questions, you would simply say that he had told you that the papyrus belongs to an old private collection, that it is officially registered by the state and therefore legal. That you were deceived by an unscrupulous dealer was not your fault. You would be totally in the clear. Is that not so?"

Nadia smiles and nods. Dortmann begins to speak again, but breaks off as the waiter returns to give them clean napkins. He watches the waiter retreat to the far end of the room, then unfurls the new napkin and spreads it carefully over his lap. "That is the basis on which I have been looking at objects in this country for the last forty years. If the Egyptian government wishes to forbid all trade in antiquities I cannot stop them." He runs his hand down the side of his beard and gives an exasperated sigh. "But almost the only possibility of survival for most ancient objects dug up by chance here is precisely that they *do* have a financial value. Take that away and they become merely a problem to the finder – and he will simply drop them in the Nile just to get rid of them. You cannot, in a country where much of the population lives in abject poverty, expect a peasant farmer who ploughs up a statue to hand it over to the government for free, and then watch for years while they excavate his field without giving him compensation. It probably represents more money than he can earn in his entire lifetime! At least through the work of people like Finn Connors the statue survives, even though self-righteous archaeologists may not care to admit the fact."

"So you think it would be alright for me to look at it?"

Dortmann pushes aside his plate, leans forward and clasps his hands on the white table-cloth. "The golden rules are these: Look. Look and comment, if you wish. But do not buy. At least not here in Egypt. If you buy the object later in Europe, then you will forget that you have ever seen it here."

The waiter moves to clear the adjoining table. Dortmann's voice drops. "Above all, never carry an antiquity yourself. Never try to take it out of the country yourself. And never, *never* have an object in your sole possession. That way it becomes your responsibility."

Nadia coughs and looks down at her plate. "No, of course not." She pauses. "If it were interesting enough, or if I couldn't understand it properly – may I show it to you?"

Dortmann picks up his glass of wine. He looked at her over the rim, then smiles. "Under the above conditions that I have just stated – you may."

*

He sits alone on the terrace overlooking the darkness of the gardens. He will stay here for more than an hour. He sleeps little these days, the legacy of age and the return of the old wound in his spine. It had been just after eight when he had gone to her room to collect her. He had raised his hand, but before he could knock, he had heard a sharp gasp from the other side of the door, followed by sounds that were unmistakable. He had turned and walked quietly down the stairs. He had been surprised, but not shocked. Life has become too short for such judgements now. And he has made too many of them before. The price always too high.

He has seen her blossom in these past days. Her shaded eyes have cleared, her smile broadened, her skin has begun to bloom. He is under no illusions: neither of them can change their pasts, nor eradicate the other's hurts. But he is old enough now to settle for qualified redemptions.

His mind skates back over the past week. Two days out from Cairo. Dinner.

You really believe there's a god in the Nile don't you?

The green eyes had settled on him. And suddenly he feels vulnerable again as if, by that single question, years of carefully layered protection have been sliced away. Her hand slides over the table and touches his.

Other times, other places.

The tiny white-washed mud-brick house on the great bend in the river where he had spent two winters with Kathleen while he had excavated at Abu Ghurab; where Imogen, their first daughter, had been conceived and they had been in love and the world had looked full of hope.

The Nile, always the Nile.

He has returned winter after winter, to excavate, study, write. It has brought him reputation and respect, given him a safe identity to wear. But in himself he knows he has returned because this is the one place where inner balance can be restored. The balance of the slow swirling movement of the river. The balance of the steady procession along its banks, figures swathed in Bedouin robes, donkeys, sand-coloured camels and black water buffaloes, a place unchanged over thousands of years, the gift of Egypt. Without this, he knows, chaos might otherwise have engulfed him.

He takes his pipe from his pocket, pulls the tobacco into it with his middle finger, watches the flame dance against the darkness. From the first moment he came to Egypt, he had instinctively known that this was a place where the gods still walked. They have threaded his inner life like living beings for more than fifty years. The goddess Maat with her beautiful white feather, 'Living in Truth'. The great soaring falcon, Horus, the eye of the sun, 'All in order'. And Seth, the flame-haired god of destruction, who inhabits the scouring desert wind, the salt sea, the uncontrollable trampling rage of the hippopotamus. He knows Seth well.

He has returned to Egypt again and again in those dark years, the 'Years of Seth', as he now calls them, following Imogen's tragic death, the years of endless recrimination with Kathleen, before she had packed her bags and moved to California with one of his students – the ultimate betrayal – leaving him bewildered with a six-year old daughter, Elena, who stared at him silently with her immense brown eyes.

He had come here then in search of the 'Right Ordering' of ancient Egypt that seemed to desert him in his outer life. And he has tried – *really* tried – in those years to bring right order to Elena, growing up motherless in New York City. He has tried with his unskilled heart overflowing with love and with the rigid ways of an academic brought up in pre-war Germany.

And he has failed. He remembers their last terrible fight, in the small living-room of their cramped Upper East Side apartment where her teenage clutter spilled across his files and photographs. Standing in the middle of the room, her face contorted with a rage that cut his heart, she had hurled his "order" back at him as rigidity, unfairness, obsession and – most painfully – lack of love. Her final contemptuous jibe, the most comical – "A man who even orders his spice rack alphabetically!"

He had no words with which to reply, no way to reach her. Instinctively, like a man grasping at the wreckage, he had looked at his watch. *Looked at his watch*! The black hands frozen against the white dial. Seven-twenty-five. In twenty years at the university he has never been late for his lecture. He leaves without a word, the heavy click of the apartment door echoing behind him.

When he reopened it twelve hours later, determined to apologise, to try to make things right for her, he found the apartment swept bare of Elena. Every trace of her, every piece of evidence that she has ever existed in his life, had been systematically expunged.

A single thought crystallised for him at that moment: mother, wife, two daughters – the four women he has ever really loved – all are now gone. The sense of failure, a whole life's failure, settles on him like a heavy grey shroud. He knows that, no matter what he may achieve, he will never step clear of it.

The soft globes of light along the terrace click off. He leans back, knocks out his pipe into the ashtray.

She will be twenty-six by now. Wherever she is. It has been eight years of aloneness and regret. And small, hesitant moves towards redemption – whatever that may mean. Eight years of silence, except for that one enigmatic photograph, postmarked Denver, looking determined and uncomfortably like her mother.

He sits, listening to the soft movement in the eucalyptus trees, in the darkness beside the Nile.

TWENTY-EIGHT

Nadia balances the tray carefully against her left hip. As she raises her hand to knock, she can see that it is trembling. She hesitates for a moment, then taps lightly twice. For a while there is silence. She can hear the sounds of a tour group assembling in the hallway below, the feint clatter of plates from the dining room. Then Dortmann calls out, "Enter".

The room smells of his pipe tobacco. On the bedside table stands a line of books buttressed at each end by a thicker volume laid horizontally. He is seated in an arm-chair beside the tall French windows onto the balcony. A book is open on his lap. She feels foolish standing there, holding the tray covered with her breakfast napkin. Suddenly she wishes she hadn't come. But now there is no way back. Dortmann looks at her in surprise, then quickly rises and puts the book down on the table. "Well, this is a pleasant early morning intrusion!"

She can feel the blood rise, starting to blotch her throat and neck. There is no good way to start this conversation. She stares down at the white linen napkin, then up into his face. "I lied to you last night." She bites into her lower lip like a child. The words have come out more defiant than apologetic.

Dortmann's brow contracts. "Ah!" Silence. "Do you want to tell me about it?"

She nods. "It's about Finn Connors. He didn't just *talk* about an object, he brought it with him. And I kept it!" The words rushed out of her. "I just couldn't tell you last night. It seemed too late. It was already upstairs under my bed ….."

Dortmann smiles. "Yes."

"Sorry?"

"I said yes. I imagined that was pretty much what might have happened."

She stares at him. For a moment she feels strangely deflated. Then a flood of relief and gratitude washes through her. She wants to put her arms around him. Instead she stands clutching the tray, holding back the tears that prickle her eyes. Damn! Why does she always act so foolishly with him, as if she's fifteen again?

"And you've brought it to show me?"

"Right."

He rises and moves towards the bed. The bottom sheet has been smoothed flat, the bed-clothes folded back with military precision. He pulls up the sheet, picks up the white linen bedspread and arranges it carefully over the top. Nadia sets down the tray and very gently she lifts off the napkin.

"Ah! A papyrus!" He removes a pair of gold-rimmed spectacles from his shirt pocket and sits down on the bed. He gestures for Nadia to sit beside him. The brown flakes of papyrus lie on the wooden tray between them like a collection of last autumn's dried leaves. There are a few small holes and gaps, but mostly the ragged edges fit together perfectly. On the left side the two mysterious lines now explain themselves.

"And a map!" Dortmann strokes the end of his short beard. "That is rare. Rare in the extreme."

"But they do exist ….?"

"Maps? Oh yes. They do exist. It was a map like this which led us to the ancient silver mines in the Sinai desert."

She watches his eyes scan rapidly backwards and forwards across the lines of black hieroglyphs, his brow furrowed. He looks up.

"Did Connors bring it like this?"

"No. It had been used as backing in a cartonnage mask of the Roman Period. I've been up all night removing it."

He smiles thinly.

"It couldn't be a forgery, could it?"

"By no means." Dortmann shakes his head slowly. "By no means. As I'm sure you've seen, it carries here the cartouche of Akhenaten. And here another reference to him – 'The Accursed Heretic'. And over here ...." His finger moves across the papyrus. "We have the name of the owner ...."

"Amenmose?"

"Precisely. But then it becomes complicated ...." He rises, crosses to the table and picks up one of the heavy volumes that serve as a bookend. Nadia recognises Gardiner's 'Egyptian Grammar'. He sets it down on the bed beside them. "We may need this." He bends low over the papyrus. "Some of the determinatives are missing because of the broken edges, which will make it difficult." Nadia nods. "So let's take it very slowly and see what we can do ...."

His voice trails away.

Nadia's heart is thudding against her ribs. His forefinger moves slowly backwards and forwards above the wrinkled flakes of papyrus. His lips move soundlessly as he mouths words to himself. Occasionally he makes notes on a pad of paper beside him. Outside a coach draws up. A chatter of Italian voices. A faint rumble. A cloud of acrid blue smoke billows up to the level of the window. In the distance a donkey brays ecstatically. The sound descends slowly, rhythmically into silence.

It is almost an hour later when Dortmann finally looks up. For a long while he stares at her without speaking. She fiddles nervously with the tufted pattern on the bed-spread.

"Do you have *any idea* what this is?"

She shakes her head. "Not really. I got the names and some other pieces, but then it got very difficult ...."

Dortmann nods. "Yes, the style is highly oblique. Almost as if the writer didn't want to be understood." Nadia frowns. "He would have taken this papyrus into his tomb as a record of a momentous event that was intended to remain a secret between himself, his Pharaoh and the gods for all eternity." He unhooks his spectacles and lays them on the bed cover. He looks pale. "It is highly probable that we are the first to share that secret for three and a half thousand years."

He passes his hand over his forehead, then picks up the glasses and looks down. Nadia can hear the tremble in his voice as he reads.

I, Amenmose, Vizier of the Great King, High Priest of Amun, intimate of the palace, noble of first rank amongst the Sole Companions, one pure of heart, say:

In the fourth year of the reign of the Great King, who lives forever, in the second month of winter, on the third day, the King commanded me to His royal presence in the city of Amun, Ipet Isut, great and fair.

On this day the King bade me alone of all His courtiers to take the body of the Criminal of Akhetaten, once called Akhenaten, from its resting place in the home of his royal ancestors, where it defiles the sacred ground of those

Immortals. And he commanded me to take the Accursed Heretic to a secret place behind The Beautiful Temple of the South in the dwelling of Ra-Harakhte, opposite the rising of Sothis in the time of the Inundation; and there to bury him according to the approved rites and to seal in the infection of that accursed place so that no man may know of it, and that the Heretic may rest there as long as the heavens bear the sun.

And I did not neglect the deed the Great King determined. I have done this according to His command, for He is the one who leads me. And I have kept the King's secret wish to my heart so that He and I alone above the earth know of this. And no man shall disturb the accursed Heretic of Akhetaten, so that he may not go forth amongst the Indestructables through all these millions of years. This has been decreed by the Gods.

This deed I have done in purity of heart, the bidding of the Great King, giving praise to the God Amun Ra, Lord of the Thrones of the Two Lands, I, the Vizier Amenmose, beloved of the King, living in truth, justified.

Nadia stares at him. In the silence she can hear the clock on the bedside table ticking. She feels faint, as if there is insufficient oxygen in the air to breathe. She struggles to keep her voice calm. "But it doesn't say on whose instructions."

"It can only be Tutankhamun." He points to the papyrus. "Four years after the death of Akhenaten. Tutankhamun was Pharaoh then. Subsequent Pharaohs always referred to Akhenaten as 'The Heretic' or 'The Criminal of Akhetaten', which is the ancient name for el-Amarna."

"And 'The home of his royal ancestors'?"

"That has to be the Valley of the Kings, where they must have buried Akhenaten, at least temporarily, in the mysterious Tomb 55. And then Amenmose moved him on Tutankhamun's orders. There's no other possible explanation."

"But why move the body and rebury it at all? If Akhenaten was a heretic, why not destroy the mummy altogether? After all, they destroyed his city, erased his name, defaced his statues! It doesn't make sense."

Dortmann rises, goes to the window and looks out. For a long while he is silent. Then he shrugs slightly and turns back.

"We have the monuments of ancient Egypt all around us. And we have fragments of secondary information like this." He gestures towards the papyrus. "And then we have guesses. That's what Egyptology really is – a thin fabric of guesses that we string between the standing monuments. And then we try to convince ourselves that it's the truth. We like to think that we know what they did and why they did it. We pride ourselves that we can burrow inside their hearts and souls." He smiles ironically. "In fact these guesses, which fill tens of thousands of scholarly books, tell us quite a lot about ourselves – but very little about ancient Egypt. I don't believe that we can ever truly enter into their minds. Or into the mind of the Vizier Amenmose."

"But still," persists Nadia, "there must be some logic behind it ….." Her voice trails away. Her fingers scratch spiral patterns on the bedspread. "He says that they reinterred the mummy 'Behind the Beautiful Temple of the South in the dwelling of Ra-Harakhte'. What does that mean?"

"The Beautiful Temple of the South? I've no idea. That's an expression I've never heard before. It's a complete mystery. Probably deliberately so. Ra-Harakhte was the falcon god of the sun on the horizon – in this case the setting sun, so it must mean a point on the horizon where the sun sets at the time of the rising of Sothis."

"What's that?"

"Sothis? It's Sirius, the Dog Star. It appears in mid July. Its rising was vital for the ancient Egyptians because it heralded the annual flooding of the Nile on which they depended for their irrigation. So it seems to mean that the new tomb was at a point on the horizon where the sun sets in the middle of July."

Nadia frowns. "But *which* horizon? The Nile flows through Egypt for more than a thousand miles! So, depending on where you're watching the setting sun, it could be anywhere on the west bank of the river. Absolutely *anywhere!*" She throws her hands up in despair.

Dortmann extends his index finger and points at a section of the primitive map where a black line makes a series of identical right-angle turns, as if indicating the crenulations of a castle's battlements. Nadia stares at him in incomprehension.

"Look out of the window," he says quietly. She turns. Through the open doors onto the balcony, she can see the swaying fronds of the palms that border the Nile. Beyond lies the opalescent swirling expanse of the river. The far bank is at its clearest now, the moment after the early morning mist has been burnt away and just before the heat begins to melt the air and turn the vista into a liquifying haze. The ochre saddled ridge-top of the mountains is outlined sharply against the sky. Lower down lie the rich green swathe of the cultivation, palms and acacia, fields of sugar-cane and millet.

She shrugs in incomprehension and turns back to him. "I don't....."

"Look again."

She stares. Stares so hard now that the view begins to swim like a mirage. The cliffs blur and shift. The green seems to sway and melt. And suddenly something she has overlooked presses itself out of the shimmering brown rock-face, just above the line of green – the rhythmical, gap-toothed façade of the mortuary temple of Queen Hatshepsut. The white of the limestone columns, the shadowed blackness of the spaces between. The blood begins to pump in her head. The landscape around fades. The temple forces itself forward, filling all her vision. Light, dark. Light, dark. In, out. In, out.

She glances back at the rhythmical indentations on the papyrus. "Oh God!" she whispers. "The Beautiful Temple of the South." She turns to him. *"Behind Hatshepsut's Temple."*

For a long while she stays staring out of the window, lost in a world of her own, spun out into a place where there is only the glint of gold. Golden sandals and head-dresses, golden sceptres and caskets, golden masks and gilded statues. Gold everywhere. And *she* is there! It's a ferocious, almost narcotic, excitement. A feeling like the moment when Finn Connors had seized her wrists and forced her back against the door.

Dortmann glances at her. Occasionally her hand moves abstractedly to her hair, adjusting a loose strand, pulling it back and refastening it into the tortoiseshell comb at the nape of her neck. She seems wrapped in some sort of trance. Suddenly she turns to him. "Do you *really* think it could still be unplundered? Imagine – the intact tomb of Akhenaten, untouched and unseen for three and a half thousand years!" Her voice trembles with excitement.

And now he understands her strange, abstracted silence. He remembers his own tumultuous feelings when he had seen the first sepia photographs of Tutankhamun's tomb. Howard Carter standing there, flashlight in hand, dressed in a three-piece suit, staring at the heaped mountain of golden statues, caskets, jewellery. And beside him the enormous gilded shrine containing the gold sarcophagus of the boy-king, untouched, unseen for thousands of years. He remembers reading of the first overpowering smell of cedar-wood and incense as the door of the tomb had been opened, that sudden time-warp into an unimaginably distant past. Even in the photograph it had been like stepping into the presence of the gods, touching an energy beyond the human. An energy which has burnt in him like a flame through five decades of careful scholarship. And now he can see that *she* feels it.

Her eyes are alight with excitement. As if reading his thoughts she says, "Do you remember what Howard Carter said when he broke through the blocked-up doorway to Tutankhamun's tomb and shone his torch in? Lord Carnarvon asked him what he saw. And he just said: 'Marvellous things. *Marvellous things!*' What an unbelievable moment! The first person to witness that sight since the guardian of the Necropolis had wedged the last brick in place in one thousand three hundred and twenty-seven BC!"

She stares at him, imploring him to share her excitement. But he holds himself back. For he is no longer twenty-nine. He can smell danger in the situation. As she clearly cannot. And her ignorance is in itself dangerous, for he knows the darkness of Egypt's other side.

She comes forward and stands in front of him. "Don't you think it *is* possible that the tomb has never been found?"

For a long while he stays silent. At length, reluctantly, he says: "In three and a half thousand years almost anything can happen. But, yes, there is a chance – even if it's only a very small chance – that we could be talking about an untouched royal burial, but….."

Nadia cuts in, "And compared with a very minor Pharaoh like Tutankhamun, Akhenaten's tomb would be ....."

"The question is ...." says Dortmann gently, "what do we do now? This is not just a trivial chance find we're talking about. This could be a discovery of major international significance, something that happens perhaps once in a century. It would be highly unwise to go running off on some wild personal adventure." He pauses, watching her carefully. "Egypt is a most beautiful country but, under the surface, it can be extremely dangerous. The authorities here are absolutely ruthless. For you to get mixed up in this could end with you sitting in an Egyptian prison and destroying your entire life."

Nadia nods. She stares at the floor. She hates the practical tone of his voice, summoning her back into a reality that has always disappointed her.

Of course he's right! But can't he feel the excitement too? This once-in-a-lifetime, once-in-a-century chance to be there! Doesn't he know that this is what archaeology is really about? Not the cataloguing of potsherds in some dusty museum basement. Surely he, above all people, who has taught her everything, who has cared for her so much in these past days, surely he must feel it too! And yet he is choosing to lecture her in this calm, reasonable voice.

Suddenly she hates his age and wisdom. She bites her lower lip. "Right," she says quietly, her eyes still fixed on the floor. "Right."

*

Bernard Dortmann sits gazing across the Nile to the mountains of the West Bank. It is over an hour since she has left, closing

315

the door in silence behind her. He feels drained, disorientated, as if his blood has begun to circulate in the wrong direction. The moment she had stared down at her feet and muttered, "Right," with the stiff finality of a disappointed child, he had felt her pull away from him, had felt it physically. A desertion that leaves him feeling like an empty shell, a seventy-two year-old body, wrinkled and beginning to blotch, stuffed with decades of useless learning, waiting to be gathered up and blown away by the desert wind. And, worse, he has done it to himself. Once again he alone has provoked the irrevocable. By withdrawing into that tight, reasoning part of himself – *no matter that he has done it for her own good* – he has crushed her dreams and trampled on his own. And suddenly he is back in the apartment, the brown eyes blazing at him, then dying away. The double click of the door latch behind him. Memory folding on memory.

*

Nadia sits in the shaking caleche. Her eyes stare sightless at the passing houses. She has showered and changed. How could he *not* understand? Why will no one ever follow her dreams? Why, in the end, does *everyone* betray her? She sinks her fingernails deep into the palms of her hands and draws her feet into the shade of the leather canopy. She glances at her watch. Five to twelve. She is almost an hour late for her meeting with Finn Connors.

316

TWENTY-NINE

Finn is lying on a sun lounger in the shade of a clump of tall eucalyptus trees. The far bank of the Nile is slowly disappearing in the sweltering midday haze. The group has taken a day's excursion to the temple of Dendarah, leaving him some space that he badly needs. Ever since that terrifying night in the pyramid and then the crazy ritual at el-Amarna he feels as if the dial of his senses has been turned up, so that he has become like some wary nocturnal animal, alert to the slightest signs of danger. The fact is that in these last days, there has been some kind of slippage in his brain, as if some dark side of Egypt is trying to force its way in. Strange dreams and bizarre waking images are seeping through now. In the night he sees his Tarot card floating before him – the toppling mediaeval tower struck by lightning, the helpless burning figures, like tiny incendiary dolls .....

He shakes his head, pulls himself upright. trying to clear his brain. Christ, he thinks, if I go on like this I'll end up believing all that David Mountjoy supernatural crap. What I needs right now is some hard logic. He folds his hands behind his head and takes a deep breath. So:

Item One: Two pieces of the same battered cartonnage mask of minimal value turn up in separate finds. Strange but not unique. Different parts of a single object are often found at different times long distances apart.

Item Two: The mask is backed by pieces of a much earlier papyrus. Nothing unusual about that. Tens of thousands of papyrus fragments have been recovered in just this way.

Item Three: A young Egyptologist will shortly arrive to explain the contents of the said papyrus. In all probability she will reveal nothing of real interest, just a standard invocation to the gods to assist the owner's journey into the next world. Thousands of such worthless papyri turn up on the market every year.

Item Four: Total value of one battered mummy mask, plus fragments of an uninteresting papyrus? Probably around five hundred pounds maximum. Insufficient even to cover the bribe to smuggle it safely through the customs at Cairo Airport.

End of story.

Footnote: The fact that the previous evening I made love to – no, *fucked* – the young Egyptologist up against her hotel door is an irrelevance. Without that I could never have persuaded her to the dangerous task of storing the mask overnight.

For a moment he allows his mind to wander back to Nadia, her fingers frantically unfastening his shirt, clawing at his back …. He reaches out and picks up the glass of beer from the table beside him. He notices that his hand is unsteady. Logic doesn't seem to be helping much. And deeper in the recesses of his mind he's aware of the one very inconvenient fact that logic is trying to excise from the record altogether: that the second half of the mask – the part that completes the papyrus – has been found precisely at the place where David Mountjoy had conducted his ritual of The Solar Return and where his mind had temporarily seemed to buckle and lose its boundaries – exactly as Lascaris had predicted in London. And *that* is making him more anxious than anything.

He looks at his watch. Twelve o'clock. Nadia is almost an hour late. *Where the hell is she?* Could anyone possibly have caught her with the mask? He has chosen to meet her here to be as far away as possible from the watchful eye of Lascaris or any prowling member of the antiquities police. For a moment he feels panicky, remembering his shocked surprise at seeing al-Shaikh in the gardens of the Winter Palace.

On a sudden instinct he glances over his right shoulder. Nadia is making her way across the lawn towards him. She is wearing silver sandals and a white linen dress. There's a jauntiness to her walk. She smiles and waves as she approaches. He rises, trying to regain his equilibrium; Nadia isn't someone you deal with when you're off-balance. For a moment there is an awkward silence as they face each other. Then he frowns at her quizzically. "You look pleased with yourself."

She sinks down on the edge of the opposite sun lounger and pulls her dress up above her knees, displaying her long brown legs. "I'm exhausted. I've been up all night working."

Finn sits facing her. "I hope it was worthwhile. Where's the Professor? Has he given you the day off?"

She eyes him coldly. "I don't need days off. Do you want to know what I found out or not?"

"Only if you want to tell me – which you obviously do."

She lets out a small puff of breath. "You know what? You're so fucking cool one day you're going to freeze to death."

Without waiting for a response she reaches into one of the deep patch pockets of her dress and takes out a handkerchief. She slips her fingers between the white pleats and extracts a small piece of paper folded into a tiny square. Carefully she smooths it out on her bare knees.

319

Despite her casual manner, Finn can see that her hands are trembling. The paper seems to contain some fifteen lines of transposed hieroglyphs and below them tightly written script. He watches her through half-closed eyes. "So?"

She taps the page with her forefinger. "If I'm right, what's in here will make every antiquity you've ever bought or sold look like Portobello Road bric-a-brac."

"You deciphered it all?"

"Pretty much." She hesitates. "With a little help from Dortmann."

"*Dortmann? You told Dortmann about the papyrus?* Jesus, are you crazy?"

"Finn, I had to. Some of it was incredibly obscure. I could never have done it by myself. Don't worry, he's safe. I know he would never do anything that might harm me."

Finn is on the edge of the lounger now. Their knees are almost touching. "You'd better be right."

"So? Do you want me to read it or not?"

He nods.

He can hear the tremble in her voice as she begins: "*I, Amenmose, Vizier of the Great King …..*"

When she reaches 'Ipet Isut' she looks up at him. "Do you know what that is?"

He stabs a finger in the direction of Karnak. "Five miles down the road. The Most Sacred Place.'"

"Hmm."

He smiles. "Even ignorant dealers without doctorates in Egyptology can learn a thing or two along the way."

She ignores him, goes on, tracing her forefinger along the lines of script as she reads. All the way down to the final words,

" *… Beloved of the King, living in truth, justified.*"

320

She stops and looks up at him, her dark eyebrows arched. But Finn doesn't meet her stare. He runs his hand down the side of his jaw and lets out a slow puff of breath. "Jesus, that's incredible! He has to be talking about the burial of Aknhenaten. I don't think there can be any other way to read it. Can there?"

Nadia shakes her head.

"*The tomb of Akhenaten!*" he says in a whisper. He looks across at the cliffs of the West Bank. "But where? *Where?* It's incredibly vague. It would seem to indicate somewhere over there. But the West Bank is huge. It took Howard Carter seven years of searching just to find the tomb of Tutankhamun, even though he already knew he had to look in The Valley of the Kings." He pauses. "But since Akhenaten was a heretic I doubt they'd have buried him *there*. The papyrus seems to say that." He spreads his hands. "So it could be anywhere over there. Anywhere on the West Bank at all, come to that. You could search for a thousand years and never find it. Ten thousand!" He lets his hands collapse beside him, remembering the same sense of hopelessness as he had stared at the first half of the mummy mask in Hassani's house. *A grain of sand*, Hassani had said... And then 'the miracle' of the other half had happened. Or had it.....? For a moment he feels sickeningly unsteady.

Nadia is watching him closely. She gives a small smile, reaches into her left pocket and pulls out another, tiny square of carefully folded paper. She spreads it out on her knees. "There's a bit more," she says quietly. She leans forward so that Finn can see down between her breasts. He puts his head on one side and looks at her. "You're enjoying this, aren't you?"

"It certainly beats the hell out of a rainy Monday morning in Edinburgh typing up display labels."

He points to the paper. "What's that?"

"It seems to be a map."

"Yes, but what's that squiggle?"

Nadia leaves a long silence. "Dortmann," she says at length, "thinks it represents Queen Hatshepsut's Temple."

Finn's eyes widen. He grabs the paper and stares at it, then across at the West bank. "Yes," he says quietly. "*Yes!* He's right. Of course he's right! So it must be somewhere in that area. But still there's nothing else on the map." He looks at her intensely. "What does Dortmann think?"

She gives a small shrug. "He seemed to dry up at that moment. I think he may have been regretting the whole thing. Maybe he thought he might get me into trouble if he told me more. I don't know ….. perhaps he just didn't have any more ideas."

"Can you ask him again?"

She shakes her head. "I know him. When he doesn't speak, he doesn't speak and that's the end of it. If he wanted me to know more he'd have said so. But I don't think he does. I think he's trying to protect me."

"So now what?"

"Finn," her voice is throaty with excitement. "*Dortmann* didn't tell me more… But I think *I* know."

He eyes her warily. "Tell me."

She clenches her hands on her bare knees, leans forward. "There's an underground passage that runs from Hatshepsut's Temple in the direction of the Valley of the Kings. It seems the ancient Egyptians gave up before they completed it, so it never got used. It's closed now and almost nobody knows about it, not even most Egyptologists. I only know because I saw a reference to it last year in some obscure excavation report I was filing."

Finn frowns. "But they'd never bury him in a disused passage. He was a Pharaoh for God's sake!"

"Yes, they would!" She taps him on the knee. "Look, digging tombs by hand is incredibly hard work in this rock. If the ancient Egyptians could somehow save themselves the job of doing that they certainly would."

Finn nods doubtfully. "So?"

"Akhenaten was a heretic. Right? But still, he *was* a Pharaoh, so they needed to provide some sort of reasonable burial for him. That left Tutankhamun and his priests with a tricky situation. They had to find a suitable place to put him, but they certainly weren't going to invest all that time and manpower for *his* tomb! And because he was a heretic they obviously didn't want him in the Valley of the Kings. That would have been a desecration. So they needed some existing unused cave or hole in the rock outside the Valley that would be suitable."

"But still they would never use a passage!"

"Why not?" She claps her hands and moves forward on the sun lounger. "Listen. Suppose they buried Akhenaten at the very end of the unfinished passage, then made the roof cave in behind them as they left, so it looked like it didn't continue any further. Then all the conditions would be satisfied." She raises her right hand and ticks off the points on her fingers. "They didn't have to go to the expense of digging a tomb for the despised heretic. They buried him on the West Bank in the City of the Dead, as custom dictated. But *not* in The Valley of the Kings which would have looked like blasphemy because of his heretical, monotheistic views. And then they simply entombed him forever by blocking the entrance behind them with a collapsed roof!" She smiles triumphantly.

Finn threads his fingers together and rests them on top of his head. As an archaeological theory it's pretty convincing. But still, somehow Nadia's sledge-hammer logic doesn't feel quite right. Something else is stirring under the eaves of his mind. He leans back against the striped cushion. "'As long as the heavens bear the sun,'" he murmurs. "That's a quote from one of Akhenaten's own prayers."

The smile fades from Nadia's face. "What the hell has that got to do with anything? Haven't you been listening to me?"

Finn shakes his head slightly. He is staring out across the river, as if barely aware of her presence. "I'm not sure," he says quietly. "But why would Amenmose, who was a *traditional* priest, use a *heretical* quote of Akhenaten's in his own burial papyrus? And they also use Akhenaten's royal cartouche at one point, even though by then he was branded a heretic. None of it makes sense. I don't get it."

Nadia shrugs impatiently. "Perhaps it was just a mistake by the scribe."

Finn shakes his head. "No. It's got a strange flavour to it, that quote. A mockery, deliberately using it out of context like that. A kind of ancient 'Fuck you.'"

He leans right back and closes his eyes, trying to focus on something that is just beyond the fringes of his brain. "Akhenaten worshipped the sun. Under his rule all the other gods were banished. Its daily rising was the perpetual renewal of the one and only great god. Everything depended on it. *Everything.*"

He pauses. It is midday. Egypt seems to lie in abeyance under the glare of the sun. Even the bee-eaters and carrion crows are stunned into silence.

"Akhenaten's great hymn to the sun," he murmurs to himself.

With his eyes still closed, he sees for a moment the huge dust-bowl of el-Amarna lit by the rising sun. Then the vision fades. And there is a sudden flash of white houses, palm-shaped capitals in blue and red. The distant wailing. The giant carved image of Akhenaten, long-jawed, belly swollen, raising his hands to the rising sun, beckoning.

He grips the arms of the chair, shakes his head, forces his eyes open. "Jesus! Not again!"

"What is it?" Nadia's voice rings with genuine concern. "Are you all right?"

Finn pulls himself upright. He feels nauseous, just as he had at el-Amarna. For a long while he is silent. Then, "It's okay," he says quietly. "It's okay."

He leans back again but keeps his eyes open, wary of the dark. But in the blackness something has come to him, something from beyond the borders of his mind.

"It's okay," he repeats. "Now I know."

"Know what?"

Silence.

"*Know what?*"

"It's not in the passage."

She arches her dark eyebrows ironically. "And how the hell do you know *that?*"

He sits up and swings his legs round so that he is facing her again, his shoulders hunched forwards.

"Let me see if I can get this into words." He stares at the ground for a moment. "What was the most important thing for Akhenaten?"

She shrugs. "The sun, I guess."

"Yes. But more specifically."

"The rising sun?"

"Right. The sun was Akhenaten's one and only god. That was his great revolution. No other gods. He believed it with fanatical intensity. And the moment of greatest power was always when the sun made its appearance above the eastern horizon. For him it was a kind of daily resurrection."

"So?"

"That had always been important for the ancient Egyptians, of course. That's why the Pharaohs are traditionally buried on the *west* bank of the Nile – so that their tombs face the rising sun. But for Akhenaten it wasn't just important, it was *the* crucial article of faith. The rising sun, his sole god, would call him back to life – whether in this life," he pauses. "Or *'As long as the heavens bear the sun.'*"

She stares at him. "You mean call him back *after death*? A kind of literal resurrection? A belief that he might actually return?"

"Just think about it – if you're Tutankhamun and you're trying to overturn a revolution and restore orthodoxy – what do you do? You have to uphold tradition and bury your predecessor on the West Bank. After all, Akhenaten *was* a Pharaoh. But you also have a terror that he may somehow return and wield his heretical power in *your* reign."

Nadia frowns. "I don't get it."

"Look," Finn's voice is sharp with urgency. "If the spirits of your ancestors rise each morning with the sun and *support* you as Pharaoh – as would always have been the case in the past – that obviously only adds to your power. But ..... if one of them is suddenly, somehow trying to undermine you, trying to overturn everything you do, then it would be a catastrophe. Not just for your reign, but for all your descendants."

"A kind of eternal curse on the whole subsequent house of the Pharaohs?"

Finn nods. "Right. And you can imagine how that would have terrified Tutankhamun! The Egyptians thought of the rule of the Pharaohs as being eternal. It's mentioned in all the inscriptions – 'These Millions of Years.'" He pauses. "So how would you follow tradition *and* stop Akhenaten rising to destroy your royal house?"

Nadia pushes both hands back through her thick auburn hair. Instinctively she turns to look across to the West Bank. In front of them a white-sailed felucca is drifting downstream, the sails hanging loose.

She turns back to him. There is a look of astonishment on her face. "You mean bury him where he can't see the rising sun?"

"Exactly! Akhenaten was buried on the West Bank all right, just as custom dictated. But unlike other Pharaohs' tombs he's facing *west*! *Away* from the rising sun. In that way his spirit can never rise."

"A kind of living death ....." She shivers slightly. "So you think he's on the other side of the mountains? That's the only way the tomb could face west."

"It has to be."

Nadia snatches up the piece of paper lying on the cushion beside her. She runs her finger along the black lines of the hieroglyphs. The finger stops. "You're right! It doesn't say 'behind'..... *behind* Hatshepsut's temple. It says *beyond*." She lets out a puff of breath. "But what the hell is beyond the mountains?"

Finn shrugs. "I don't know. The Western Desert. No one ever goes there. As far as I know, there's nothing. Just sand and maybe a few Bedouins."

Nadia edges forward on her seat. "So you'd have to cross the mountains. They're not that high. Just a long walk – if there are paths." She taps him urgently on the knee. "Finn, I want to come with you!"

"*You?*" He stares at her. Her eyes are glittering with excitement. Suddenly he is jolted into reality. Something in her intensity feels dangerous. He remembers Edward's warning: *Treat her carefully, otherwise...* He moves his knee sideways so that her hand falls away. "Anyhow, I haven't said I'm going."

"*What?*" She eyes him with disbelief.

Finn rakes a hand back through his hair. "Do you have *any idea* what we're talking about here? Any fucking idea at all? Buying an antiquity that some peasant has accidentally stumbled across while ploughing his field is one thing. But we're talking about the possibility of an unplundered Pharaoh's tomb and not just *any* Pharaoh, but *Akhenaten*, the most celebrated Pharaoh of all time! That's potentially billions of dollars worth of antiquities."

"So?" She lifts her eyebrows in mock surprise. "That's exactly what I told you. This will make everything you ever bought or sold look like junk."

Finn snorts in exasperation. "Look, I can't go running around the art market with a two ton solid gold sarcophagus inscribed all over with the name of Akhenaten, for Christ's sake! I'd have The Art Squad, Interpol, UNESCO, not to mention the Egyptian government all over me within minutes! This is *serious*, for fuck's sake."

"There'll be more than just a gold sarcophagus in there," she says coolly. "Other things to be sold."

"It doesn't matter!" he shouts, suddenly erupting. He looks around but no one is near them. He hunches forward and goes on more quietly, "Look, whatever's in there will almost certainly be inscribed with Akhenaten's name. The statues will all have his features. Every single object will be unmistakable. You just can't sell that stuff on the market! Everyone will know immediately that you've found Akhenaten's tomb." He pauses. "Besides, it's just not right. This isn't just some casual minor find. This could be an *untouched royal burial*! Don't you understand what that means? It needs to be properly excavated. You're an Egyptologist, for God's sake!" He slaps his hand on his thigh in exasperation.

Nadia tosses her head and lets out a snort of disdain. "Since when have you been so ethically scrupulous?"

Finn leans back, braces his arms on the padded seat. "Look," he says at length. "First of all, we have no idea where the tomb is. Right?" Nadia remains impassive. "Secondly, even if I were, by some miracle, to find it, it's probably already been robbed three thousand years ago like all the others. And, thirdly, I can't just stroll over to the West Bank and say to the nearest guard, 'Hi, I'm Finn Connors. I'm an antiquities dealer. I'm looking for the lost tomb of Akhenaten. Can you help me?'" He throws up his hands in despair.

Nadia allows a long pause. "No," she says at length. "But *I* can help you."

"You? *You*! A young, tall, beautiful, pale-skinned European woman! That's all the help I need! You think you wouldn't attract anyone's attention wandering around the mountains of the West Bank with a pick and shovel over your shoulder? You must be out of your fucking mind!" He stops. "Anyway, you talk about *my* ethics! You're the one who's supposed to be the respected museum curator and archaeologist – a selfless custodian of the past for future generations!"

Nadia shrugs as if to indicate her complete disinterest. A hoopoe has alighted at the end of their chairs and begins strutting amongst the coarse grass. Nadia watches as it raises its striped fan-like crest. She turns and stares out at the West Bank. The heat has burned the mountains into a taupe-coloured mirage. Suddenly she spins round. Her eyes are sparkling. She leans forward. Finn can feel the electric intensity of her.

She places a hand on his knee. "You're right, Finn. *Of course* it's complicated." Her voice is soft now, persuasive. She hesitates. "All we know is that *there* – right over there …." She

329

lifts her chin towards the mountains. "..... there may well be an undiscovered, unlooted Pharaoh's tomb – the first since Tutankhamun's in 1922! Probably the very last one left to be found! *And we are the only ones who know!*"

Her eyes hold his. Finn feels as if he is being jerked on the end of a line. There is something narcotic in her intensity; narcotic but dangerous.

She goes on quietly: "Do you remember that evening at that boring conference in Leiden, when we sat at the bar? It wasn't your good looks that made me go to bed with you. It wasn't your charm." She shakes her head slowly. "Oh, no ..... it was your passion. When you talked about the ancient world, about dealing, about antiquities. The hunt. The chase. The moment of discovery. I could feel the electricity in you. It was the purest of all aphrodisiacs. I couldn't wait for you to take me upstairs."

She pauses, holds his eyes fast. Her hand grips his knee.

"Well, just over there lies the most incredible archaeological discovery anyone could ever make. *Ever!* Greater than Schliemann uncovering Agamemnon's golden mask at Mycenae. Greater than Howard Carter shining his flashlight into Tutankhamun's tomb. Can you imagine that moment when you step over the threshold where no one has stood for three and a half thousand years!" She pauses. "*And now you're hesitating!*" She narrows her eyes. "Is it possible that you just don't have the balls for it?" She lets her hand drop disdainfully from his knee.

Finn leans back, trying to disengage from her stare, struggling to free himself from the drug he can feel being silently injected under his skin. His throat is dry. "What the hell's in it for you that makes *you* so excited? What do you *really* want?"

330

Nadia holds his gaze, raises her jaw slightly. "What I want right now," she says coolly, "is for you to take me back to your room and fuck me."

*

Finn watches as she stands naked in front of the full-length mirror, running a comb through her long hair. Her left foot is turned slightly outwards, like a ballerina. Her buttock tenses then relaxes as she shifts her weight.

He reaches round and touches his left shoulder-blade carefully, feeling the tracks her finger-nails have left in his back. He runs his tongue around the inside of his lower lip. It feels bloated, as if he has just come from the dentist, and he can taste blood. It had been good. Perhaps too good. There has been something about her frantic excitement that has unnerved him, almost as if it came from beyond the borders of desire.

She turns, picks up the white dress from the floor and steps naked into it, shrugging her shoulders forward. Finn registers the lack of underwear. How planned was all this? Then she comes towards him with that fluid walk, fastening the thin strap behind her neck. She stands beside him for a moment and runs her hands over her hips, smoothing down the linen. She sits on the edge of the bed and looks at him.

She smiles slowly. "So just what *are* you going to do about the tomb?"

"Not a lot."

"Don't bullshit me! I know you. I know when you're lying."

"I doubt that."

She starts to say something, then bites her lip. "Look, Finn," she says more softly, her eyes cajoling him. "All I want is to be able to help."

"Meaning?"

"To come with you."

"Why? I've already told you, if I found anything interesting I'd offer it to you first. What more do you want?"

He swings his legs out of the other side of the bed and stands up. The narrow space between them feels claustrophobic. And whatever he is going to do about the tomb, he certainly doesn't want Nadia mixed up in it. He can smell danger in her excitement. He crosses the room, picks up his bathrobe from the back of a chair and pulls it on. "Anyhow, I haven't said I'm going to do anything ....." He knots the belt. "And even if I were, you're still not coming with me. Just because you fucked me don't think ..."

She comes towards him, her eyes blazing. Instinctively he steps back.

"You fucking ..." She lunges forward, raking his chest with her nails. He tries to hold her back but she slips past his guard. She scratches him again, bites him hard through the cloth into his upper arm. He grunts, pushes her back as hard as he can. She staggers, collapses on the bed, then rebounds immediately, flying at him in a frenzy of tangled hair and nails. She lunges at his eyes, kicks wildly at his groin. Finn pulls away, raises his right arm and slaps her hard across the face.

She stops and stares at him. Her left hand creeps up to touch her reddening cheek, then moves slowly to the line of her jaw. For a frightening moment Finn sees her face go completely blank, mask-like, as if she is gone from behind it, replaced by something robotic and insane. Her lips are working silently. Then she looks up into his face and narrows her eyes in a gaze of pure hate. Within seconds she is out of the door, the slam reverberating behind her.

Finn sits down on the end of the bed. The crash of the door rings in his ears. He puts his fingers to his chest. Blood. Blood everywhere.

"Shit!" he says. "Shit! Shit! Shit!"

*

Nadia flings open the door to her room and slams it behind her. For a moment she freezes. Something about the room feels different. She stands motionless, taking in her surroundings, her senses bristling. The bed has been made. The windows are open. A fresh sprig of oleander stands in the white jar on the dressing table. Of course! Just the maid.

She crosses to the cupboard, opens it, then pushes aside the spare pillows on the top shelf. She reaches up and pulls down the plastic bag. She sifts aside the piled *galabiyas*. The black and white eye with the split running through it stares up at her. She lets out a deep sigh of relief, bundles the *galabiyas* back in and lays the bag carefully on the white bedspread.

She slides open the top drawer of the dressing table. There is a strange smell, slightly sweet, like someone's heavy perfume. Gently she slides her hands between the stacks of underwear, feels around for the soft dry flakes of papyrus. Her body tenses. She pushes the heaped piles aside, her fingers moving faster. Could she have made a mistake? She slams the drawer shut, pulls open the one below and takes out the blouses one by one, shakes them, drops them onto the floor. Then back to the top drawer, her hands scrabbling frantically now, throwing things aside, finally ripping away the silk paper she has placed at the bottom to protect her clothes.

The grain of the wood stares back.

Her body goes ice cold. Beneath her dress a trickle of sweat is making its way down her spine. *Who?* Who could have known? Or guessed? Who could have gained access to the room?

For a terrifying moment the walls seem to close in on her. Her throat feels choked. She runs to the window, places both hands flat on the marble sill and leans far out, breathing hard, looking for a way to escape. Then, on a sudden instinct, she raises her left hand and places the fingers to the line of her jaw, caressing the old wound. She remembers the night Finn had come to her room, how he had ruthlessly used her, so calmly pushing the mask under her bed before pressing her hard up against the door.…."You fucking bastard," she whispers.

Gradually her breathing slows as something crystallises in her brain. A faint smile comes to her lips. She crosses to the bed and picks up the telephone. Very deliberately she begins to dial. She hears the voice of the hotel operator.

"Can you please connect me with the Luxor museum ….?"

PART THREE

I am what is left when the rest disappears. I am the face
in the flowers, the masts of ships, the sails filling with the
gods' breath.
From one land to another I carry you in myself.
I am Osiris rising.

The Egyptian Book of the Dead
ca 1500 BC

In the great City of Light, built from the desert at my command, I knew time by the rising and setting of the Aten, by the crowing of the cock, by the lengthening of my fingernails and the workings of my bowels. Such are the ways of the flesh, even for a god-king. But now, deprived of light and blood and outer sight, unable to pass to my rightful resting place beyond the horizon of the Aten, time has neither length nor breadth, only a continuous presentness. Here, trapped between the Two Worlds, the rise and fall of empires, the destruction of civilizations, the flowing of the Nile are all as one to me, as I wait for the time of my release from behind the double doors, as foretold by the High Prophet of the Aten.

I had wanted details from that sycophantic priest with his treacherous smile. What good is prophecy, I asked, if you cannot anchor it in time? But he gave a sly look and shook his shaven head as if to remind me that even the Pharaoh is subject to the workings of prophecy. I sensed then that treachery was growing all around me. Even there right at the very heart of my court, disaffected people wanted the return of the old gods. Later, when the news of the plotting reached me, I had him killed, that sweating, faithless priest, poisoned, then his bloated body dumped in the Nile for the fishes to eat. But still his prophecy remained.

But what he didn't know, our fat prophet now food for the fishes, was that, though deprived of time, the Aten had endowed me with a knowledge of proximity. The footfalls of fate, I call it. A sense of the future coming closer. It reminded me then of the tremors of excitement in my children, Meritaten, Ankhesenpaaten and little Tutankhaten, whose very name would later be betrayed, as we approached them step by step, only half hidden in the rushes beside the Nile; I and my beautiful queen, Nefertiti, so full of grace, who would also one day betray me…

What I sense now, as I used to feel in my blood waiting for the Aten to make His appearance each morning above the eastern mountains, is Destiny about to be fulfilled – the approach, as the prophet had said, of a people undiverted by the many gods and the seductions of the world. A people that can set me free.

Even now, here in the darkness, I feel each footfall coming closer.

But do they know, those who are approaching, that they are the agents of a greater fate?

THIRTY

Finn's boots thud down onto the flimsy plywood floor. He looks around. He is standing inside a wicker basket where the sides reach almost to the level of his chest, the upper edges bound by a thick strip of heavily worn leather. The basket is divided into three. His section – the largest – is no more than six feet by four. All around the inside runs a white rope, looped to provide handholds. At one end a khaki canvas pouch contains two water bottles and a plastic thermos flask. He had expected something far more reassuringly high-tech. But, as the basket creaks and groans under his movements, it doesn't feel reassuring at all. It feels uncomfortably like standing inside a giant Victorian picnic hamper.

Captain Naguib, who has been fiddling with the primitive-looking controls above his head, turns to him. "Ready?"

Finn shrugs. "As much as I'll ever be."

Naguib flashes him a broad smile and cocks a jaunty thumbs-up. Then, with his other hand, he pulls on the wooden lever above his head. A huge sheet of flame shoots up into the multi-coloured dome with a thunderous roar. The basket bobs and sways. The helpers cling to the ropes, trying to hold them steady.

"Chocks away!" calls out Naguib.

The hands let go. The balloon rises silently into the air.

Finn gazes down. Already the figures below are beginning to look absurdly small as the ground slides away.

It had taken him less than five minutes after Nadia's explosive departure to determine his course of action. It was almost as if her violence had acted like a catalyst to his reeling brain. It wasn't anything he could really call a 'plan' – there was no logical sequence from start to conclusion – rather an instinctual pull towards the next step. And then he would see.... After all, despite the possible dangers, with such a tantalising fragment of knowledge, what else could he do but go forward?

At first his request had been quite beyond the comprehension of the Egyptian boy manning the cramped office of Luxor Balloons in the line of shops below the terrace of the Winter Palace Hotel. Each time Finn tried to explain that he did *not* want to do what the tourists always do, he wanted to do something different, the boy wiped his hand over his oiled hair, pulled out the brightly coloured brochure and patiently begun, in fractured English, to explain all over again. Suddenly the boy had stopped in mid-sentence and looked over Finn's shoulder. Finn turned. An Egyptian in his mid-thirties, wearing an impeccable pale grey *galabiya* was standing in the open doorway. He had closely cropped black hair, a square head, a thick black moustache curled into sharp points and intelligent dark brown eyes. A rapid exchange in Arabic followed.

The man's looked at Finn with amused curiosity. He bowed slightly. "Captain Naguib at your service, sir. I am the proprietor and chief pilot and of Luxor Balloons."

Finn explained his request for the fourth time.

"Over the mountains and into the Western Desert, eh?" The man raised his eyebrows in surprise. "You are an adventurer, sir."

"I'm a journalist," explained Finn. "I want to write a piece for the London Times and take some photographs. Obviously Luxor Balloons would get a good mention."

Captain Naguib ran a forefinger over one side of his waxed moustache. "We do not normally cross the mountains. The collection of the balloons is too difficult over there. Here beside the Nile the pick-up truck can follow easily and be with you in ten minutes." He left a long pause. "I fear it would be expensive. *Very* expensive. You would have to take the balloon as a private hire."

"How much?"

Captain Naguib spread his hands apologetically. "Eight hundred English pounds."

"And if I give you good publicity in my paper?"

Captain Naguib sighed, showing a row of immaculate white teeth below the moustache. "That would be agreeable, but not at all necessary. But, because you are an adventurer, I make it six hundred." He held out his hand. "And fifty," he added as an afterthought.

Finn shook his hand.

"And the collection is extra," said Naguib casually.

"How much?"

The Egyptian shrugged. "That all depends where we come down. We charge by the hour. In any case, the trip may not happen. To cross the mountains we need east wind. And it must be early, before the thermal currents make it too rough. East wind in the early morning is not usual here."

Finn wrote down his hotel and room number and handed it to Captain Naguib.

*

Two days later, in the darkness before dawn, the telephone jarred Finn awake. He scrabbled for the receiver.

"Mr Finn, we have east wind! Chocks away!"

"*What?*"

"Captain Naguib at your service, sir. You wish to come? We start to make ready on the West Bank."

Less than an hour later the battered mini-bus that had collected him from the deserted landing stage on the West Bank shuddered to a halt. Below lies a piece of waste ground just beside the ruins of the temple of Ramesses II. The sun is just up and the western mountains are bathed in flame-coloured light, slashed with tall black shadows. A yellow and orange striped balloon lies half-inflated on the ground. A generator thuds in the still air as two enormous fans attempt to breathe life into the sagging material. Its top edge billows gently with the growing pressure.

Finn pulls his ruck-sack out of the van, slides the door shut and scrambles down the bank. A dozen men in *galabiyas* are tending the fans and pulling on the ropes. A clutch of children watch from a distance. Two thin white dogs sniff suspiciously at the flapping edges of the balloon.

Captain Naguib emerges from the group and comes towards him. He is dressed in black trousers laced tight at the ankle and a black flying jacket decorated at the shoulders and cuffs with elaborate gold-braid. A white silk scarf is knotted at his neck. In the hot air from the fans it billows out behind him, making him look like a World War II flying ace from a dated Hollywood film.

"You are a lucky man, Mr Finn. We have perfect conditions. Good east wind."

"I don't feel any wind."

"Trust me." Naguib takes Finn's arm and steers him towards the basket. "In fifteen minutes the balloon is ready. Then you see. First I show you the landing procedures."

Silently the balloon gains height. The circle of figures below hold up their arms against the early sun. Already they look small. The children wave excitedly. Finn waves back. Despite the stillness, the balloon begins to veer towards the Western Mountains. Naguib sends another burst of flame up into the huge striped dome.

From up here the full expanse of the plain of Luxor is laid out beneath them – the emerald fields of barley, wheat, maize and cattle-clover, orchards of lemon and orange and banana, dark brown squares where the sugar cane has already been harvested and burnt off, all criss-crossed by the gridlines of irrigation canals and bisected by the broad, shimmering steel track of the Nile, with its borders of tall sycamores and eucalyptuses standing up black in the early light. In the fields brightly coloured figures are already at work, tiny dots of yellow and blue, moving amongst the squares of cultivation like scarab beetles. For a moment Finn feels deeply moved by the sight of this ancient landscape, surely one of the sacred places of the Earth, barely changed since the times of the earliest Pharaohs, except for the distant blur of the modern town, now sprawling south along the east bank in a line of rectilinear hotels and azure swimming pools.

Slowly they begin to cross the borders of the cultivated land. Beyond lies ochre rock and sand, the multi-coloured shapes of the painted mud-brick houses of the village of el-Gourna and, coming closer, the huge horseshoe escarpment encircling Queen Hatshepsut's Temple, which stands out clear and rectangular at the foot of the towering rock face.

Finn feels his heart quicken. *Not behind, but* beyond. Beyond *Queen Hatshepsut's Temple…*

Gradually, the East Bank disappears in the blaze of early sunlight and a haze begins to gather over the river. All is silent except for a faint singing of cables overhead and the occasional roar of flame as Naguib pulls on the primitive wooden handle.

They breast the escarpment and, for the first time, Finn begins to appreciate the sheer scale of the mountains. Seen from the ground the ridges appear stacked vertically one above the other, like a theatre backdrop. But here broad expanses of plateaus and ravines unexpectedly open out, stretching to the furthest distant ridge, which seals off the Nile valley from the Western Desert.

Cut in behind the rock-face of Deir-el-Bahri, he can see the narrow gorge of the Valley of the Kings. The openings of the tombs are clear dark squares scattered against the sand-coloured earth. Further down is the black rectangle of the car park and the first tourist busses making their way snail-like along the ribbon of the tarmac road.

Finn feels a tap on his shoulder. Captain Naguib, white scarf billowing, is holding out a plastic mug of black coffee. Finn accepts it gratefully and cups his cold hands around it.

As they drift towards the second tier of mountains the thermal currents grip the balloon, pulling them higher. And suddenly they are above the topmost ridge, gazing down onto a huge boulder-strewn plateau and, in the distance, as far as the horizon, a desolate moonscape of flat-topped mountains and canyons.

Finn crouches, removes the binoculars and camera from his rucksack and slings them round his neck. He sweeps the binoculars up and down the featureless plateau. There is nothing to be seen except endless steps and shelves of grey and sand-coloured rock and occasional meandering lines of white pebbles, the legacy of millions of years of flash-floods. At the northern end he can just make out the dark mound of the ruined temple of the god Thoth, just as the books had indicated. The air is cold. He zips the windcheater up to his chin and shivers, then snaps off a few photographs.

Slowly they drift over the desolate plateau until they hang above its furthest westernmost edge. Finn grips the binoculars tight. His mouth is dry. If there is going to be anything, surely *here* it must be, facing west, away from the rising sun, nestled in the deep gullies between the domed ridges that spread out like giant lion's paws; or carved into one of the sheer sandstone rock faces that fall from the lip of the plateau. Or perhaps there will be nothing visible at all in this vast geological expanse, everything man-made long ago buried under twenty-five centuries of accumulated sand and debris.

He tries to refocus the binoculars, cursing his numb fingers. *Just anything unusual,* he thinks. *Any clue at all. Whatever it may look like…..*

He moves the focus further south. Rock, gullies, slides of white stones and pebbles are banked between the ridges like huge snow-drifts. Far below swallows twist and cartwheel amongst the ravines. The piping of their cries rises up to him. The sheer scale of the place is overwhelming. *A grain of sand in the desert,* Hassani had said. This was like a grain in a thousand deserts! Nothing to distinguish one stretch of rock from another. *Hopeless.*

He clenches his eyes tight to clear them and gives the ridge one final sweep with the binoculars. *Christ, what a waste of time and money!* Suddenly he stops and tracks back. Could he be mistaken? Perhaps it was just a trick of the light. He swivels the eye-pieces, frantically trying to sharpen the focus.

Just under the lip of the plateau in a deep crevasse, blocked with a slide of rocks and pebbles something has caught his eye. *There, near the top of the mound of debris!* It isn't the size that's different. Not the colour. It's the shape. *A right angle! A perfect white right angle. The corner of a block of masonry.....?*

The balloon is moving away. The shape begins to fade. He snatches up the camera, spins the telephoto lens, snaps off a dozen pictures. The ravine, above, below. All around. The only faint hope of ever identifying the place again – if it isn't totally buried by the next fall of stones from the plateau's edge. He lowers the camera and leans against the rim of the basket. Despite the cold he is sweating.

"Nice view." Naguib's voice startles him.

For the first time Finn turns and surveys the landscape behind him. Out here, beyond the mountains, he had expected desert, unbroken, undulating drifts of sand. Instead there are ridges of grey and buff-coloured rock and the meandering beds of wadis stretching out on all sides. Nothing moves. No house or patch of green, no road. Not even the white track of a donkey path. A total wasteland.

"Where do we land?"

"Nag Hamadi. The nearest road."

"Where's that?"

Naguib gestures vaguely towards the western horizon.

"How far?"

"By balloon one hour. Maybe one hour and a half. By car nine hours.

"*Nine hours!*"

"Yes. Here is no road." Naguib swings his arm in a wide arc towards the north. "Only *there* is road. Is good?"

"It looks like I don't have much choice. And big baksheesh, eh?"

"You got it." Naguib flashes a broad smile, guns an enormous sheet of flame up into the balloon and cocks a thumbs up. "No worries," he says happily.

Finn leans his elbows on the smooth leather rim and stares down at the unbroken desolation below. The excitement is throbbing inside him like an electric charge. At the same time, practicalities begin to flicker across his mind. The obvious person to turn to for help is Lascaris. After all, isn't this precisely the opportunity they have planned for? But something in him instinctively draws back. And he realizes too that he has no clear sense of how things will now unfold. Only an absolute certainty that he has to take the next step – whatever that might be.

*

It is dark by the time the collection truck drops Finn back at his hotel. He is wedged tightly between the silent driver and the sleeping Captain Naguib who has snored all the way from Nag Hamadi. He is exhausted and his back aches. On the flat truck behind him is the furled balloon, the wicker basket and the eight silent attendants, who now queue up for baksheesh. He nudges Captain Naguib awake with his elbow.

"Shall I come tomorrow with the money?"

"Tomorrow no good. I go to Cairo to talk to Americans about a new balloon." He starts to count the days off on his fingers. "Come Thursday," he says.

Finn climbs out over Naguib's recumbent body. "How do you know I won't be gone by Thursday?"

"You?" Naguib smiles sleepily. "You won't leave without paying me." He closes his eyes and goes instantly back to sleep.

Once back in his room, Finn drops his ruck-sack on the floor and lies down on the bed fully clothed. Within seconds sleep pulls him under.

THIRTY-ONE

It is early evening and purple darkness is swallowing the West Bank. At the sudden fall of a shadow across her book, Lara glances up. Edward is standing at the edge of the small terrace, watching her. In these last days, ever since that afternoon in the felucca, they have scarcely spoken. She has turned away from him mainly out of anger, but also from a need to protect herself, not wanting to be drawn into that vortex of feeling that he can induce in her. But as she looks at him now, standing there so clearly uncertain of his welcome, her heart begins to open.

"Can I join you for a while?"

For a moment she hesitates. Then she says, "Sure" and gestures to the empty chair. She holds up a squat bathroom tumbler. "Glass of wine?"

"Thanks."

She rises and disappears into the room. A moment later she re-emerges with a bottle wedged under her left arm, a glass in the other hand. "It's not very cold, I'm afraid."

"That's okay."

She sets them down and half fills the tumbler. Then she sinks into her chair and leans back. Starlings are beginning to settle into the eucalyptus trees. The sun is a deep orange disc suspended above the rock face. There is still a quarter of an hour before it will set.

He leans forward and cups his hands around the glass. "I wanted to talk to you. Is that okay?"

She nods.

"Do you remember the story of Isis and Osiris?"

She looks at him in surprise. "Yes, of course. Why?"

"I went to the museum yesterday evening. I was looking at a papyrus that showed a scene after Isis had put Osiris' dismembered body back together again. Osiris was stretched out in the Underworld, wrapped in a cloak, so that he looked just like a mummy. Isis was shown as a bird hovering above him, directly over his genitals. She had these beautiful rainbow-coloured wings and she was desperately beating them, trying to fan life back into him. I couldn't take my eyes off it. I must have stayed there for half an hour. It was the most touching thing I've ever seen. And the saddest." He hesitates. "Sad because, in spite of everything she was offering, he remained inert. He just wasn't able to respond."

He looks away for a moment. She knows it is a confession. The words have felt pulled out of him, extracted from a deep place by a huge effort of will. She waits for him to continue.

"I realised then that all my life I've only truly really loved two people. At least until now. My mother and then Kate." He gives a small shrug. "And in both cases I've lost them. And each time, it felt like more than just the loss of a single person, more than just normal grief, but a kind of total inner collapse ..... It's hard to explain ..... It's what Freud called 'an overthrow or an extinction.'"

He stops and runs his finger slowly round the rim of the glass. It makes a faint squeaking sound in the silence. He takes a deep breath.

"After Kate died I tried to commit suicide. It wasn't meant as a dramatic gesture. I intended to die. But I made a mess of it and they found me and got me back to life." He pauses. "I'm pleased I came back. At least now I am. But afterwards, when I picked up my life, somewhere deep down I think I made a decision that I would never really love again. Not in that way." He gives a small ironic smile. "I could be professionally touched, of course. Touched by my therapy clients, for example. That was something different. That felt safe. But deep down I knew I was standing aloof, while things just went on all around me. I learnt to construct a life where nothing and no one could ever really touch me again. Not in that deep way. And I was good at it. I thought no one had noticed."

He hesitates. The sun is balanced on the topmost lip of the ridge. The landscape is fading into darkness. Then he looks at her very directly. "But *you* did. I sensed it the very first time you looked at me. I somehow sensed it wasn't just a chance meeting. You were there for a reason. And your noticing – the fact that you really seemed to see me – opened something up in me. It was an incredible feeling. But, at the same time, it felt frightening, too exposing. That's why I had to keep shutting down. It felt as if I had suddenly arrived at some threshold that I had always craved, and then, right there on the doorstep, I panicked, as if there might not be enough oxygen on the other side to breathe or something crazy....." The words are tumbling out of him. "Of course it must have felt to you as if I was deliberately playing with you. No wonder you got angry and withdrew!"

She nods. To their right the muezzin has started up. The starlings are settling into silence.

He gives a small, ironic shake of his head. "It seems Egypt isn't a very good place for me to hide. I think the gods here just won't allow it."

For a long while she is silent, watching night spread itself on the far bank, trying to absorb what he has just said. During these past days anger has closed up her heart. Now she can feel its warmth begin to pulse again. She senses how much it has cost him to say these things. Suddenly she wants to reach out to him. After all, hasn't she, in her own way, been hiding just as much?

"There are a lot of things *I've* kept hidden too," she says quietly. "Things about me that you don't know. Things that I'm ashamed of."

He hesitates. "Like?"

"I killed five people." Her voice is flat. She is staring towards the Nile.

"*What?*"

"I've had five miscarriages."

"But that's not ....."

"No, I know. But that's how it felt. Not murdered them with my own hands, of course. But killed them just the same. Five small people. They chose to come onto the earth through me and my body rejected them one after the other, so that they all died. Just like it's always rejected everything. When I was a teenager, all the other girls were swelling and sprouting, but nothing seemed to want to happen to me. At school they called me 'Littletits'. And my periods were always irregular. And then, when I got married, there was this constant failure. Time after time after time after time! I was a freak, incapable of really being what nature had made me. Oh, I've made what my mother would call 'a good fist' of it. I've really tried." She stops and turns to him. In the twilight she can see his eyes searching her out. "But I've never, ever in all my life felt like a real woman. *Not ever.* Not fully." She holds his gaze. "I've never said this to anyone. Certainly not to my husband. Not even really to myself." She pauses, sucking in a short breath. Then she says simply: "I can never be more naked in front of any man than I am with you now."

For a moment they are silent. She has emptied a well that has been festering in her all her life. Then she stands and faces him. Her head tilts to one side. She extends her hands in a ritual gesture of offering. He stares at her.

Is it wise?

Does it need to be?

*

She opens her eyes. Night. A black fly crawls across the thin shaft of light thrown on the ceiling. Through a gap in the curtains she can see the dark scarlet of a hibiscus illuminated from a lamp outside. She has no way to place what has happened. Not with her mind. There has been something beyond them in their love-making, like a touch of death. With the desperate thirst of a shipwrecked man finding water, he has bought her to orgasm again and again. And she has given herself completely, erased her own being, so that no spaces have been left in her. Yet, in some way that only her body understands, what has occurred between them has nothing to do *with him* at all. For her, there has been one overwhelming image in the darkness, one all-enveloping sensation unforming her identity: the summer flooding of the Nile, carrying the fertile black earth, swamping the fields, filling the canals, soaking the flatlands, washing over her, covering her deeper and deeper. Drowning who she has always been. Bringing back life.

At some point in the night someone knocks on their door. They stay silent, holding their breath. The footsteps retreat.

She reaches for him. Their bodies join, then separate. Then join again. Till she feels lost in him completely.

*

First light returns her to herself. She slides silently from the bed, glances down at his dark hair on the pillow. His face is turned away, the sheet drawn up high as if protecting himself again. She pulls on her clothes, carefully opens the door and steps out of the room.

The coarse grass springs against her feet. There has been a heavy dew. The moisture slips under her soles, presses up cold between her toes. Pockets of thick mist hang over the Nile. She settles down on a patch of bare earth at the edge of the garden under an acacia tree. She hangs her legs over the edge of the bank and stares at the river. A large thicket of reed is being ferried down the middle of the flow, revolving slowly. A stately white egret stands motionless on its crown.

Below her the slow eddies form, cling together, shift, swirl. And then disperse, taken back into the flood. Her mind unshackled, her life spreads out before her. Old happenings, hard, tight, stored like knots in her body, seem to loosen and dissolve in the slow passage of the river. She feels its endless shifting, its endless constancy. Its ancient gentleness and forgiveness. And for a moment she feels weightless, absorbed into the timeless flow of the Nile. Fully at peace, enjoying her body. A woman.

She looks round, sensing his approach. He sinks down beside her, puts an arm around her shoulders. She leans against him, feeling the warmth of his body.

At length she says, "I was feeling grateful."

"Grateful for .....?"

"For *this*." She lifts her chin towards the river. "For last night. For my body. And even ….." She hesitates, then nods slowly. "Yes. Even for the miscarriages. Every single one of them!"

He tightens his arm around her, holding her close. She gives a deep sigh.

"I think my body knew all along why it kept rejecting something that my mind was trying to force on it, trying to do what the world expected of me – to be the good wife and mother, the perfect Mrs Raven with two perfect children." She sniffs ironically. "It's as if my wise soul and my wise body were outsmarting my stupid, driven brain. I'd always thought my body was somehow defective, constantly letting me down, unable to give birth, turning me into a failure. And then just very quietly, sitting here this morning, watching the flow of the river and feeling so at peace in my body, I could suddenly its wisdom. It felt like a wisdom far older than me, a kind of knowledge from elsewhere. And I knew then, just absolutely *knew*, that now I could conceive and carry a baby full term – when my body knows it's right ….. Isn't it strange – I had to come to Egypt to learn that?" She shakes her head in wonder. "My body is so much wiser than my mind."

"And that's what you're grateful for?"

She shrugs. "Sure. Why not? That alone was worth coming to Egypt for. Yes, I feel grateful for that. Grateful for *everything*. Without exception. For the past. For the future….."

He smiles. "You can see the future?"

"Nope!" She puts her head on his shoulder, fitting its shape to the line of his collar-bone, the curve of his neck. "And I'm grateful for that too. Because that means I have to start to trust in life."

From their right comes the clattering of breakfast being laid out on the terrace in front of the hotel. The mist is shifting and the sun beats against the cliffs above the West Bank, dissolving the contours. She pulls her bare feet up under her, crosses her ankles and in one graceful movement rises like an Indian dancer. She smiles down at him.

The smoothness of her brown thighs is level with his gaze. He sees the faint smudged birthmark the shape of a butterfly, the sprinkling of tiny translucent golden hairs, the soft indent where her shorts have pressed into her as she sat. She is standing with one hand on her hip, her haunches flexed, the slight swell of her belly revealed below her T-shirt, suddenly full of sensuality.

And in that moment he knows he has lost her.

Not *because* of me, he thinks, but *through* me. *The gods have worked through me.* And in our moment of greatest closeness she has stepped away into her own world. The world that Egypt has kept waiting for her.

THIRTY-TWO

Hassani sits silent, staring at the floor. His hands are folded in his lap. Slowly he begins to click the amber worry beads between his fingers. Then he raises his head and calls out in Arabic. From behind the curtain comes the sound of scraping metal, followed by the opening and closing of a door. A moment later, a boy appears carrying a tall glass Arabic water pipe in one hand, and in the other a small metal bucket with a pair of tongs hanging from a chain. He carefully sets down the pipe and removes the brass lid. Then, manoeuvring the tongs, he extracts four glowing coals from the bucket, places them on a circular platform on the top of the pipe and covers them with a piece of tin foil, moulding it roughly to their shape. Instantly the room is filled with the smell of dusty charcoal and an aroma of spiced apple. Hassani picks up the white mouthpiece at the end of the long transparent tube.

"I didn't know you smoked."

"I don't. Only for big thinking." He gives a wry smile. "And big trouble."

He offers the pipe to Finn. Out of politeness Finn accepts and takes a cautious pull at the mouthpiece. The acrid smoke of the *sheesha* burns the back of his throat and makes his head swim, but he knows that the conversation will flow more easily if they are both smoking. Besides, to refuse would be an insult. He hands the pipe back.

"It's apple," says Hassani. "Better than honey. The honey pipe's no good for the throat."

"You mean *this* is good for the throat?"

Hassani smiles. "*Very* good."

They both laugh.

"I need your help."

Hassani nods. "What I can do, I will do. You know that." The water in the clear base of the pipe gurgles as he inhales deeply. "But now is no good time. Things are not right." Finn looks at him enquiringly. "Luxor is a village, but it is also a spider's web." He lays down the pipe and his hands begin to move slowly in flat circles. Then he extends his right thumb and forefinger as if plucking at a string. "You pull here. I put my ear to the ground ....." He leans over, his left hand cupping his ear. "And I listen *here*. Usually I hear everything. *Everything* that happens in Luxor." He leans back against the wall. "But this time I hear nothing. All these things – the cinema man, the professor, the mummy mask, a crazy balloon ride into the western dessert..... This time the spider's web is silent. That is very strange. *Very* strange. I do not like it." He pauses. "The only thing I hear is that a man from the Secret Police is in Luxor. A very important man. And *that* I do not like at all."

He draws on the pipe. A bubble breaks softly against the glass. He takes the mouthpiece from his lips, inspects it, then wipes away a bead of spittle with his forefinger. "You know what I think?"

Finn shakes his head, aware of a growing feeling of anxiety hollowing his stomach.

"I think you leave it alone. Leave the Pharaoh to sleep. It's better that way. Better for him. Better for you." He pauses. "*Much* better for you. Searching is not the hard part, my friend. When you find the tomb, *that* is when your troubles will begin." He regards Finn seriously, his head tilted to one side. "In Arabic we have a word – *nafs*. The *nafs* are what drive a man. They are the things from which he cannot rest. Every man has his own. But if he cannot find a way to be at peace with them, they will pursue him. They will hunt him down and maybe make him do crazy things." He pauses. "And in the end they may destroy him. That is my fear."

He offers the pipe again. This time Finn shakes his head. He is already feeling dizzy.

"You take my advice?"

Finn shrugs. "I don't know."

"*I* know," says Hassani. He smiles sadly. "You *don't* take my advice. You will go. You are a good man." He pauses. "A good man, but a little crazy." He taps the side of his head.. "You cannot do this alone. Not here in Luxor. You need donkeys. You need spades. You need workers. You need guides. You need the silent men, the ones who will not talk. You need to know when to give baksheesh. And who to. And how much. Do you know these things?"

Finn shakes his head.

"And if I don't help you – who helps you?"

Finn shrugs. "The cinema man maybe ?"

"That is what I feared." Hassani removes the pipe stem from his mouth and lays it on the divan beside him. "Then it's better I help you."

"We can do it together."

Hassani raises his eyebrows slightly. "You talk of money?"

"Yes."

The Egyptian shakes his head. "That is kind, but no money. I help you is all. Even if I'm crazy doing it. But no money. This I don't touch with the end of my finger." He sticks out his left arm and extends the little finger. Then he rises. "Meet me this afternoon in the public garden. Five o'clock. In the middle is a big tree. You will find me there. It's better you no longer come here or even to my shop. Our friend with the sugar cane has too many eyes in the bazaar. He will get suspicious." He rubs his thumb and forefinger together. "And very greedy."

*

The Luxor Public Garden was conceived as an enlightened piece of colonial urban planning. But this worthy enterprise of a green and pleasant place is now a desolate patch of dusty ground wedged between the busy road of the corniche and the mud-brick shacks of the bazaar. The seats of the benches have all been ripped away, leaving only upright concrete slabs like tomb-stones and the occasional protruding metal bar. Dogs nose amongst the rubbish piled against the back wall, pitched over from the bazaar. But, at the centre, a clump of grand trees, eucalyptus and camel-foot and bombax still rise in defiance of the surrounding man-made squalor.

When Finn arrives he finds Hassani, dressed in an immaculate white *galabiya*, slowly circling an enormous spreading bombax tree. His hands are folded behind his back as he twirls one of the crimson waxy flowers between his fingers. Finn falls into step beside him.

"It is all arranged," says Hassani in an even voice, as if about to explain the rules of a game. "About half a kilometre beyond the wall to the south of your hotel is a thick clump of reeds on the river bank. At nine o'clock tomorrow morning a boat will be waiting there. It will ferry you directly across to the West Bank. There is farmland, well south of where the tourists go. A pick-up truck will be waiting for you."

"What if I'm seen?"

Hassani shrugs. "Then you are seen. The authorities do not like foreigners to wander from the beaten path. It makes them nervous. They are very afraid of a terrorist incident, which will destroy their tourist business. But it is not illegal. You are just a very annoying individualist tourist."

Finn nods.

"Still, it is best if you keep your head low when you are in the truck. The driver's name is Ahmed. He is a good man. He will accompany you all the way. You can trust him."

Hassani pauses, glances over his shoulder, then continues his measured pace.

"He will take you to a house that stands alone to the south of the village of el– Gourna. In the house you will put on Egyptian clothes." He catches Finn's look of surprise. "It would be better. Local people, and especially Bedouins, take the mountain path often. But for a European to ride there would attract too much attention. You will go by donkeys ....."

"*Donkeys?*"

"That is a problem?"

"I just hate donkeys. It's a childhood thing. Too many freezing cold rides on the beach."

Hassani smiles thinly. "The climb will take about four hours. And four hours back. I hope that after that you will ache enough not to want to return there. *Ever.*" He pauses, glances at a gaunt figure in a dark blue *galabiya* squatting on his haunches against the railings. He turns back. "A donkey is essential. You will be travelling in the heat of the day. No Egyptian would walk. The paths are very uneven and they are dangerous. The ravines are deep and many men have died there. A donkey is always more sure-footed than a man. In the end, please believe me, you will praise him ..... 'Sir Donkey.'"

361

Finn smiles, but in the same instant he can feel his stomach cramp with fear. Is this the precise moment when Lascaris' wild dream, so tantalising and seductive in the safety of London, begins to crystallise into harsh reality? He feels a flash of panic, like a swimmer who has drifted carelessly on the tide, suddenly realising that he is now helpless in the grip of the current, being pulled further and further away from the safety of the shore.

"There is a guard-post about half-way up…"

Finn runs a hand through his hair, trying to quell the anxiety that is rising like an air-bubble in his stomach. "Will they try to stop me?" he asks, hoping that his voice sounds normal.

"It is more to prevent terrorists coming in from the desert," says Hassani. "They will not be so interested in local people going out. It can easily be avoided." He shrugs. "In any case, mostly the guards sleep. It's no problem. Not with Ahmed to guide you."

"And when I'm on the top?"

Hassani shrugs. "When you are on the top, my friend, it is all up to you. It is your crazy idea, not mine. But you will have with you Ahmed and two other men, *fellaheen* – farmers. They too are silent men and strong. They may be of service." He pauses. "And you may need protection."

There is a long silence. Finn turns to face his companion.

"How safe is it?"

"It is unsafe," says Hassani simply. "It is very unsafe. This is an unsafe country. This is not Europe. Here anything can happen. But the three men I give you, you can trust. And they are not greedy. Not by Egyptian standards."

A flower from the tree overhead has dropped into the dust in front of them. Hassani stoops to pick it up. He blows away the dust and holds it to his nostrils. "No smell. They are so bright they do not need it."

"It's beautiful," says Finn, feeling as if he is inhabiting some kind of dream world, where nothing is quite real.

"Yes. But not native to Egypt."

"I didn't know."

Hassani nods. "Like the eucalyptus and many of the trees we have here now. This is from India, I think." He pauses. "It would be more secure in darkness, of course." He spreads his hands. The wide-sleeved robe billows around him. "But if you search for a grain of sand you need at least daylight."

He goes on walking in silence. Finn senses the conversation isn't over.

"There is one other thing ....." Hassani clears his throat. "You may find this strange. There is a young boy who lives on the West Bank. His name is Abdul. Abdul Lakim. I knew his grandfather. Old Lakim was what the local people call a 'far-seer.'"

"A clairvoyant?"

"Yes. That is your word. You may find all this primitive superstition....."

Hassani hesitates, but something in the seriousness of his tone sweeps away normal Finn's scepticism. "Go on."

"Last month his father brought the boy to me. He had found something. To the untrained eye it looked just like a piece of broken limestone. This long." He holds his thumb and forefinger about an inch apart. "On the market not worth five piastres." He pauses. "The back was smoothed, and the front curved. There were two incised lines, clearly from a hieroglyphic inscription, but so damaged that you could not read it."

He falls silent, as if unwilling to continue.

"Tell me," says Finn.

"I cannot be sure, but I think it was from a large shawabti

figure. You know, the little statues of servants they put in the tombs to do the work for the dead man in the next life?"

Finn nods.

"And because of the strange curve in the front, I think it could only be a servant figure for Akhenaten with the belly distended like the Pharaoh himself."

Finn lets out a low whistle. "But where could such a thing possibly be found – except in the tomb?"

"No, no!" Hassani speaks quickly. "Not *in* the tomb. That is not necessary. The ancient Egyptians were like the modern Egyptians. Clean, but not tidy. They often dropped and broke things before they put them in the tombs. That was what led Howard Carter to the tomb of Tutankhamun – he had picked up fragments inscribed with the Pharaoh's name lying on the ground *outside* the tomb. My father told me the story."

Finn nods.

"So ....." goes on Hassani slowly. "Not *from* the tomb but from *near* the tomb."

"But where did he find it?"

"That is the problem ..... *That is the problem.*" Hassani mouths each word emphatically. "He forgets ....."

"*Forgets?*"

"Yes. And sometimes later he remembers things." He pauses. "He is not like other children. He is strange, wild. They cannot keep him in school. He wanders. Wanders for hours. Sometimes he is gone all night and no one is sure where. Along the river. High into the mountains. It is thought locally that he too has the gift."

Finn feels the small hairs on the back of his neck begin to bristle. "But *you* ..... what do you think?"

Hassani draws in a deep breath, then exhales it slowly

through his pursed lips. "I have seen the boy," he says slowly. "The eyes are strange. Like his grandfather's. Seeing but not seeing ..... It is possible."

"But what's this got to do with ....."

Hassani puts a hand on Finn's arm. "My friend," he says gently, "you have not been up on the plateau. It is enormous. *Enormous.* When you look from the balloon you think you see a small pebble. But when you stand on the plateau it becomes a boulder as big as a man. If you wish to find a grain of sand in such a place, you need more than a donkey and a few photographs ..... The boy will also ride with you."

"What about his parents ..... will they ..... ?"

"The mother is dead. Three years ago. Pneumonia from bilharzia. But the father ..." He hesitates. "The father may need to go with you. That is a problem. But without the boy you will find nothing."

Finn watches Hassani's hesitation.

"What is it?"

"The father ..... the father is not from here. He is from Middle Egypt. El– Minya. The father," he says emphatically, "I do not trust and do not like. He has deep pockets. The only way to deal with such a man is to fill his pockets till they burst. Only that way can you hope to buy his silence. It may be a very expensive donkey ride for you."

Finn shrugs. "I'm getting used to that." He pauses. "Should we take spades and equipment – in case we find something?"

Hassani shakes his head. "Not with the boy's father there. It is too dangerous. I will tell him that you are a crazy English milord who wishes to go exploring. That he may believe. But with a spade it will be too obvious. In his eyes you will immediately become a tomb robber. And then his pockets will get deeper than even you can afford."

The two men stop and face each other. "Why are you doing this?" asks Finn.

Hassani hesitates and for a moment Finn sees a strange look pass across his face, a look of bafflement mixed with a kind of tenderness. Then it is gone. Hassani shakes his head. "Truly, my friend," he says. "I do not know."

They are silent.

"And now," says Hassani. "We will part. If anybody asks you, we have talked of the weather, of my father, of my grandfather, stories of old Luxor. You will go through that gate in front of us into the bazaar. I will go *there*." He turns his head in the direction of the corniche. "I will speak to that man."

"Why?"

"He is not from Luxor. I would like to know who he is."

Hassani breaks off and moves in the direction of the gate. The gaunt figure in the blue *galabiya* rises, walks rapidly towards the Nile and disappears behind a line of tourist buses.

Just as Finn is about to enter the narrow passage into the bazaar, a movement to his left catches his eye. In the far corner of the garden, behind a screen of straggling oleanders, two figures are walking side by side, heads bowed, deep in conversation. Finn freezes. *Lascaris and Mountjoy?* Quickly he draws back behind the tall bombax tree. As he watches, they stop and face each other; then Lascaris takes a small package, wrapped in brown paper, from the leather bag slung over his left shoulder, and hands it to Mountjoy. Without further conversation the two men shake hands and part.

But of course they know each other! thinks Finn, trying to calm his thudding pulse. Lascaris had freely admitted as much at their very first meeting in London. *So why do I feel so shaken? And what might be in the brown package.....?* Slowly, as his mind gropes to find an answer, he becomes sickeningly aware of the threat that now seems to surround him on all sides, as if there is no truly safe place to put his next step. And no one he can really trust.

He leans back against the tree and gazes up into the thick lattice of its branches.

THIRTY-THREE

Finn shifts uncomfortably on the back of the donkey. The animal is undernourished and its spine, even through the thin layers of blankets, feels as if it is made of steel. The short staccato steps are sending a growing message of pain up through his buttocks and into his hips and spine. He's not sure how much longer he can go on with this.

Several times he has tried dismounting, but the pitiless heat reflecting off the rock makes the walk unbearable. Hassani was right: the winding path is treacherous with loose stones, and the ravines are sudden and precipitous, opening up from behind a boulder or hillock and dropping sheer away into purple shadows hundreds of feet below, leaving Finn with a giddying sense of nausea. Twice, while he walked, he had slipped and fallen, cutting his hands badly. After that even the hard back of the donkey seems preferable.

He pulls up the wide sleeve of his *galabiya* and looks at his watch. Two-thirty. It is now almost four hours since they set out from the crumbling mud-brick house tucked in against the cliff face to the south of Queen Hatshepsut's temple. So far they have met no one. Ahmed, the driver, heads the column. They have passed some half a mile to the south of the isolated guard-post, a crude concrete box perched on the edge of a ravine above the Valley of the Kings. It was shuttered and looked utterly deserted. The donkeys move with a hypnotic tread. Whether crossing the open plateaus, or negotiating the narrow paths, their pace never varies.

They are a party of six. Five men, five donkeys. And a boy.

Ahmed is small, lightly built, with a dark open face and smiling eyes, a natural comic. The two farmers may be twins, identically thick-set, broad-faced with heavy black moustaches. Both wear sky-blue fellaheen robes and tan-coloured skull caps bound by thin white cotton turbans. The brown tasselled ends of the turbans stick out like cockatoos' fans. They smile broadly at Ahmed's jokes, but hardly ever speak.

The fourth man, the boy's father, is narrow-faced, his long jaw and sallow skin quite different from the dark tan of most faces in southern Egypt. A smudged bruise in the centre of his forehead indicates his devotion to prayer. He seems a man set apart, humourless, unsmiling. From Hassani's description, Finn had expected shifty-eyed furtiveness. Instead the man seems to stare right through him with a cold, demanding interest that makes Finn feel glad of the unseen cloak of Hassani's protection.

The boy seems like any normal Egyptian eight-year-old, with a plain oval face and wiry black hair cropped close to the skull like a cap. Dressed in a cream and brown striped smock that reaches to his ankles, he walks barefooted, apparently oblivious to the razor-sharp chippings of flint and limestone. Occasionally he rides on the donkey behind his father, but more usually he walks. Often he disappears into shadowy hollows or behind vast boulders and is gone for several minutes. The father never once looks back. Finn has tried to read the boy's eyes, remembering Hassani's words, but each time he searches the young face, the boy turns away, leaving Finn feeling like an intruder.

From time to time Finn's mind drifts to Edward and Lara. He feels strangely bereft without their company. Should he have told them the whole story before he left? Prudence, at least, would have dictated someone left behind who knew, just in case… But something had held him back, possibly a wish to protect them from this whole dangerous affair. And, as his thoughts wander, his mind suddenly veers to an image he has been trying to excise from his brain. Two mornings earlier, rising shortly after dawn, he had seen Edward and Lara, sitting side by side, gazing out across the Nile. They had been unaware of his presence behind them. But in that one glance their body language had told him everything. And while his mind struggled to be reasonable, generous – *what right had he to be troubled?* – an unexpected pain had shot through him. He had turned away, fighting back a growing sense of desolation.

A rough grating sound up ahead rouses him from his thoughts. A clatter of pebbles bounces down the steep path and knocks against the stick-thin legs of his donkey. Finn looks up. Ahmed's donkey is heaving its hindquarters over the lip of a sharp ridge. A moment later Finn follows. And emerges on to the plateau.

Christ! Hassani had been right. The view from the balloon had given no idea, *no idea at all*, of the scale of the place. It's gigantic, barren, the vastness broken only by huge sand-coloured boulders and low knobbly crags.

Finn dismounts and walks some distance away from the others. He takes the small stack of photographs taken from the balloon out of the deep pockets of his galabiya. Quickly he shuffles through them. They bear no relation to anything he can see. He had deliberately shot one with a distant view of Karnak Temple for orientation. He finds it at the bottom of the pack and walks to the plateau's edge. It is two o'clock.

The whole valley is shrouded in a shimmering blur. Even the Nile itself is only just visible, a meandering steel-grey track in the haze. There is no way he can see the temple in this light. He rips the photograph in two and drops the pieces into his pocket. The four men stand staring at him in silence. The boy is scratching at a stone embedded in the ground. The heat shrouds the plateau like an oven. The sunlight bounces off the naked rock.

And suddenly Finn has an hysterical urge to laugh, to cry out into the overwhelming silence at the sheer absurdity of it. Here he is, standing on a mountain top in forty degree heat, dressed like T. E. Lawrence, with four men and a little boy on donkeys, his bones aching and his buttocks raw. And he has absolutely no fucking idea of where he is or even what he is doing here!

He presses down the laughter, uncomfortably aware how close it feels to real hysteria. He gazes round at the plateau. *Nothing.* Absolutely nothing distinguishes one square meter of rock from another. Then he turns and gestures for the others to dismount. He begins walking towards the far western edge over which he had glided so smoothly two days before. From the corner of his eye he sees the boy follow at a distance.

For an hour and a half Finn prowls the western lip of the escarpment, consulting the photographs, trying to find some feature that will match, some rock formation that will suddenly click into place.

But it's hopeless. Each ridge, each crevice and boulder looks like every other. As indistinguishable as two grains of sugar. *Or two grains of sand.* And besides, the photographs had been taken from five hundred feet in the air and facing *towards* the ridge. From where he is standing now everything looks completely different. Even if he were directly above the tantalising right-angle of white stone he would probably not recognise it. And perhaps the whole vision, that sudden apparent regularity in the tumbling geological chaos, had been an accident, just a trick of the light. Something he had *wanted* to see, a small spectral clue formed by his brain. By hope. And greed.

He pulls his *galabiya* higher over his neck, wraps the cotton shawl Arab-style round his head and sinks down wearily on the lip of the escarpment, resting on his heels. Mixed with the disappointment and the sense of absurdity he can feel too a cool breath of relief. *When you find the tomb, that is when your troubles will begin.* Perhaps Hassani is right. What disasters might have followed if the whole mad dream had turned into reality? If Lascaris had been right, and Mountjoy really could ...? Perhaps it's better this way.

He takes one last look over the vast dead panorama that peters out into the Western Desert, then levers himself up and turns.

The boy is standing ten feet behind him. For the last hour he has tracked Finn like a distant shadow, following some thirty yards behind. Twice Finn has tried to approach him, but each time the boy had started and run away. But now here he is, staring bold-faced, straight at him, unmoving. On an instinct Finn stays completely still. *It is thought he too has the gift.* Slowly, watchfully, the boy comes closer. Finn remembers standing in the woods that backed onto his grandmother's house, hardly daring to breathe, while a small roe deer had approached him, shifting its head from side to side, warily inspecting his unmoving shape with one eye, then the other.

The boy is within three feet of him now. Suddenly he looks up, directly at Finn. And Finn sees the eyes. Black, motionless, unseeing. Eyes from elsewhere. For a long moment they hold each other's gaze.

And then the boy is off, running wildly along the escarpment edge, loose stones flying from his heels. Until he plunges over the lip and disappears. Finn follows him, stumbling on the rough ground. He reaches the place where the boy has gone over the edge. His chest is heaving. Below, the rock face descends in narrow splintered shelves, split by sharp fissures. The space down to the next shelf some thirty feet below is sloped by a long drift of sand and scree.

The boy is standing half way down this huge pile, buried up to his knees in the loose shingle. He stares up at Finn as if in invitation. Finn scrambles over the edge, drops down onto the slope. Immediately he sinks in up to his thighs in the scree. Slowly he starts to make his way laterally down towards the boy. But with every step he is fastened to the groin in the shifting mass of sand and pebbles. His *galabiya* has ridden up. The scorching stones scratch his legs and fill his boots.

Vaguely he wonders about the danger. Could these huge piles of shingle shift? Could they be dislodged like snow drifts and avalanche into the valley hundreds of feet below, taking him and the boy with it, burying them forever?

The thoughts scud in and out of his mind. But his legs seem driven by a force beyond himself. Sweat pours down his chest inside the *galabiya*. His lungs burn with the effort. He nears the boy, stumbles and falls forward, burying his face in the shingle. Red hot it burns his skin. He tries to brush it away and looks up.

And there, just above the muted grey-brown of the shingle, is a perfect white right-angle, about eight inches broad and showing perhaps two feet of its length at each extension.

Not cut stone, as Finn had imagined as he had strained his eyes through the binoculars. But the actual face of the rock, carefully smoothed and polished. And just visible at the inner point where the right angle turns is another shape – a glimpse of a perfect white limestone block, fitting precisely into the angle.

There can be no mistaking it. A doorway cut into the solid rock. A doorway filled with blocks of carefully carved masonry. *Still in place.*

Finn lays his cheek against the shingle, oblivious of its burning heat.

"Jesus Christ!" he murmurs. "Jesus fucking Christ."

*

It is evening by the time the small boat slides in amongst the reeds and slaps against the mud. Finn jumps out and raises a hand to Ahmed, then starts out across the fields of cattle clover in the direction of the hotel. His whole body aches. Each buttock feels as if it is bleeding. Behind him, the steady popping of the boat's engine can be heard as Ahmed makes his way back towards the West Bank.

Finn turns and stares at the place where he has been. The layers of escarpments are gathered now one above the other in flattened perspective, giving no hint of the numbing kilometres that lie between. The sun is setting and the rock face is shrouded in purple shadow. The very top lip, where he has stood five hours before, is etched out against the sky with a line of white. From the marshes all around comes the shrill repetitive clicking of thousands of frogs. In the twilight, figures in blue *galabiyas* are making their way slowly towards the mud-brick farmhouse to his right.

Finn stretches, trying to ease the pain that has frozen his lower back. The insides of his thighs feel as if they are on fire. The journey down had been even worse than the ascent. The donkey had shortened its stride to cope with the pebble-strewn slope, so that Finn had to brace himself with every step for fear of sliding right down the animal's scrawny neck.

His efforts to clear a space in front of the door had proved futile. The volume of sand was far too great and he needed at least a shovel. But enough had been exposed to reveal the walled entrance disappearing down and down into the bed of shingle. After he scrambled back to the safety of the plateau and dusted the grit from his clothes, he collected stones and laid them at right angles to the edge of the escarpment for a length of some six feet, directly above the opening, by way of a marker. Then he had taken a line of sight to the small specks of the standing donkeys at least a mile to his right on the far lip of the plateau. Every fifty yards he paused to arrange another trail of stones along the line of this imaginary causeway. Once located, each line would lead to the next. At least that was the idea.

As he came closer to the donkeys he had been forced to abandon these markers for fear that the others would notice. Instead he walked directly to the point where the donkey track broke the lip of the plateau. Then he turned to face across the barren rock, keeping the Nile valley behind him. The line of his marked path was at approximately a forty-five degree angle to the line of the escarpment at his back. It was a very rough and ready piece of navigation. But the best he could do. Once he found the first trail of marker stones it would be simple to follow the track. The problem would lie in getting from here to there. He cursed his failure to bring a compass.

Every jarring step of the way down he could feel the eyes of the boy's father branding his back. Could he have guessed the truth? What reason had Hassani given him? There was something about the implacability of the man's stare that was enough to make Finn believe in the ancient curse of the Evil Eye.

And the boy?

The boy had seen everything. Presumably he knew precisely what was going on. Or did he?

Do I even know what thinking is for him? Perhaps it is something entirely different, like a discourse in a strange language. Is it possible that once back in his own house the boy may be transformed into a normal eight-year-old and chatter openly to his father about the day's events, revealing everything?

There is just no way of knowing. Yet something in the blackness of those eyes speaks silence.

Finn shrugs. It's a risk he will have to take. Either that or not return at all.

And suddenly an obscure line of poetry comes into his head:

Shall two know the same in their knowing?

THIRTY-FOUR

Birds are chattering in the thickets of lemon trees that line the front of the Winter Palace Hotel as Finn passes. A few hopeful *caleche* drivers call out to him, but he dismisses them with a smile and a casual wave of his hand. There is a spring in his step this morning. The stiffness in his limbs from the gruelling donkey ride has finally gone and he can feel an electric excitement pumping through his arteries. He shifts the small rucksack, hitching it up higher with a forward sling of his shoulder and holds on tight to the leather strap. It contains the three thousand dollars he owes Captain Naguib, all in hundred dollar bills.

As he reaches the Luxor Balloons office, the tune he has been whistling to himself fades on his lips. The door is shut, the stained khaki blinds still pulled down. He glances at his watch. Ten past ten. He hesitates, then tries the metal handle. It gives. Inside, the place appears deserted. The room looks just as it had two days before, the table behind the grimy glass-topped counter still strewn with papers. He sniffs the air. There's cigarette smoke and something else he can't quite place. Softly he closes the door behind him. Something feels wrong.

He stands for a moment, listening to the faint murmurings from the street, then rounds the counter and pulls aside the striped blanket that hangs over the doorway. The room behind is small, hot, airless.

Suddenly, animal-like, his senses bristle. His observations are coming in slow motion now as, like a man in the dark, he inches his way forward. There's a tall metal filing cabinet in one corner, the drawers wide open. Khaki paint is peeling off its sides in long strips. A poster of Assuan hangs crooked. A fan not working.

In the silence a blue-bottle drones.

A wooden desk askew. No chair behind it. A waste-bin upended. Papers scattered across the concrete floor. Broken glass. A pool of red hibiscus tea. He bends and touches it. Warm.

He rounds the desk, moving carefully.

And then he sees.

Jesus.
Jesus.
Jesus.

He clutches at the thin trunk of a lemon tree and vomits. Someone lays a hand on his shoulder, but he shakes them off. He vomits again, his guts heaving, trying to rid himself of an image he knows will never leave him.

Captain Naguib.

Captain Naguib, lying on his back on the concrete floor, the green plastic chair tipped over behind him.

Captain Naguib, his grey *galabiya* pulled up to his chest, white shorts ripped aside like rags. Brown thighs. Pubic hair caked in blood. And at his centre, a hole. An open gaping wound. Raw meat.

Captain Naguib, his head lolled back. Eyes open, only the

whites showing. A scarlet gash across his throat. And blood. Liters of blood, draining from the neck, hardening black on the concrete floor.

And the mouth. The mouth open. Filled with meat and blood. Raw meat. Like a goat on a butcher's block ...

He vomits again. Feet clatter on the pavement. There's a sudden rush of movement in the street. The boy from Naguib's office comes running past, pulling on the sleeve of a thick-set policeman in black fatigues. They disappear into the shop.

Finn lurches across the street. A taxi swerves wildly, horn blaring. The tyres screech. He staggers to the edge of the corniche, puts his hands on the iron railing and hangs his head over the parapet, staring straight down at the Nile. From behind comes shouting. The crash of the shop door.

He straightens, wipes the back of his hand across his mouth and begins walking unsteadily towards the centre of town. He needs to find Hassani.

*

Mohammed al-Fakhry swelters in his cramped office. At least in Cairo there was air-conditioning. Here there is nothing, not even a breeze from the Nile now that the new museum extension blocks his view. From one side comes the smell of garbage from a waste lot, from the other the constant cries of the caleche drivers. And in front a blank concrete wall. He snorts in disgust and glares down at the typed memorandum on his desk.

To: All Personnel of the Luxor Museum and Antiquities Service.

Subject: Private Possession of State Antiquities.

From today's date no member of the Antiquities Service is permitted to keep ancient artefacts as private possessions. All artefacts are to be handed personally to the Director of the Luxor Museum by 6 pm, August 14th latest.

Omar al-Badri, Director Luxor Museum of Antiquities.

Al-Fakhry crumples the sheet of paper into a tight ball and throws it into the corner. The insolence of the man! Less than six months in the job and already trying to play the pasha. He knows exactly where al-Badri is aiming. He reaches out and picks up the small piece of black stone, a mere fragment, showing a pair of feet resting on a crocodile, two rough lines of inscription on the back. It has sat on his desk as a paperweight for more than fifteen years. He had seen al-Badri eyeing it when he had visited the day before.

Well, al-Badri will soon find out who rules the territory here! He isn't even a local man. He has been plucked from some obscure post in that trash heap at el-Minya just because his fat ox of a sister is married to someone important in the Ministry in Cairo. That's how it goes nowadays – all favouritism and *baksheesh*.

And how he preens himself in public! Two expensive trips to New York in the last four months alone to negotiate an exhibition that will probably never happen. And always coming back with new shoes and smart western suits. You don't get those on a civil servant's salary! And now here he is running around town with distinguished foreign visitors, chatting in English and showing off the museum as if *he* had discovered the famous group of statues in the Luxor temple!

Al-Fakhry takes a sip of coffee and wipes the back of his hand angrily across his moustache.

There is a sharp knock at the door and a boy in a grey *galabiya* enters, holding out a single sheet of paper. He drops it on the metal desk and stands waiting. Al-Fakhry waves him away impatiently with his left hand.

He glances down. The paper is headed: TOP SECRET. As he reads, the furrows in his forehead begin to deepen.

From: The Ministry of the Interior. Strictly Confidential.

To: Mohammed al-Fakhry, Director of Antiquities, Luxor Region.

Preliminary interrogation of suspected terrorists arrested in el-Minya has revealed that other terrorist cells from the region are still at large.

Accordingly the following preventative measures are being enacted:

The entire area north of Luxor, extending through Middle Egypt, will be closed to foreigners until further notice. No coaches or boats will be permitted beyond the northern borders of Karnak Temple. The sites of Denderah, Abydos, el-Amarna will be closed to visitors.

The guards will be reinforced around all existing archaeological monuments in Luxor and throughout Upper Egypt.

Significant new excavations will now be under military protection.

The Minister urges your staff to be especially vigilant at all ancient sites and major tourist centres.

A special watch is to be kept on the Scandinavian

*group led by the Englishman Mountjoy. His rituals are to
continue unhindered in the temples.*

*You will be contacted by undercover agents who are
keeping surveillance in your area.*

*These instructions are at the express direction of the
Minister in conjunction with the Ministry of Tourism
and Chief of Police.*

Husayn al-Shaikh,
Deputy Director, Ministry of the Interior.

Al-Fakhry sits back and puffs out his cheeks. He can feel the
sweat trickling down the back of his neck and soaking through
his shirt. There is a brief knock at the door and Samir, his
deputy, puts his head round. He is frowning, as if wrestling
with a difficult problem.

"There's a visitor to see you."

"Who?"

Samir enters and holds out a small visiting card. Al-Fakhry
takes the card in his stubby fingers. For a long moment he sits
staring at it in silence. Then he straightens in his chair, clears
his throat nervously and nods.

"Oh, and Samir ….."

His deputy stops in the doorway and turns.

"Please stay for this meeting. I shall need you as interpreter.
And as witness." He pauses, wipes his hand across the back of
his neck. "But whatever you hear you must divulge to no one
without my permission. Is that understood? *No-one.*"

Samir nods and disappears through the doorway. Al-
Fakhry listens to the footfalls on the long concrete corridor.

THIRTY-FIVE

Lara takes Edward's arm as they stroll through the winding streets of the bazaar. Closer to the Nile tourism has taken over: the stalls display only King Tut T-shirts, nylon kaftans and gaudy souvenirs. But here, amongst the densely packed houses, are only life's necessities: open sacks strewn with tiny silver Nile fish, misshapen vegetables, scrawny chickens crammed into bamboo cages, bloody carcasses suspended on metal hooks. Lara has insisted on seeing this local end of the market and she moves slowly from stall to stall, gazing in fascination, apparently oblivious of the attention her blonde hair and slim figure are attracting. Suddenly she stops, as if something has distracted her. She holds up her right hand against the sun.

"What is it?"

"Isn't that Finn?"

"Where?"

She points. "There. Christ! But what's wrong with him?"

The tall figure comes through the stalls towards them, stumbling slightly like a drunk. His face is ash white.

"Finn!"

Finn stops and stares.

"Finn, what on earth's happened?"

He looks at them blankly. His face seems to have imploded, as if the muscles holding it together have collapsed inwards.

"Come on," says Edward, taking his arm. "We're going to get you back to the hotel right now."

*

They settle Finn into an armchair in the shade of a tall eucalyptus tree overlooking the Nile. No one has spoken on the taxi ride back. Lara kneels in front of him now. She takes his right hand between her own. It feels ice cold. She begins to chafe it. "Finn, tell us what happened, for God's sake! *Just tell us!*"

For a long while Finn stays silent, staring out across the river as if sightless.

"What happened? You can tell us," she repeats softly.

Finn shakes his head from side to side, like a man trying to rouse himself from sleep. "Haven't been feeling good all day…"

"Come on, Finn," says Edward, putting a hand on his arm. "We're friends, remember? You can tell us the truth. Just say what happened."

For the first time Finn looks at them as if he is slowly becoming conscious of who they are. Then he sits up straighter, pushes both hands back through his hair and clasps them tight behind his neck. He glances at Edward, then down at Lara, as if looking for reassurance.

And slowly he begins to speak.

*

"Christ, Finn, how could you ever get mixed up in something as crazy as that?" Lara's eyes are wide with shock.

Finn sits motionless.

"What are you going to do?" asks Edward.

384

"He's going to take the first plane back to London," says Lara fiercely.

"No!"

Lara's stares at him in surprise. The word has come out with such sudden unexpected force. "Why, Finn?" she asks, keeping her voice soft now. "Don't you see ….."

"No," repeats Finn. His voice has regained its old strength. "If they're making any connection with me at all, that would be the worst thing I could do now, to break off in the middle of a holiday and try to skip the country. They'd stop me at the airport. It would look like ….." He breaks off. Edward and Lara watch him closely. "The thing that's really weird," he goes on, "is that they haven't come looking for me already. It's at least two hours now since they discovered the body."

"But why should they?" asks Edward. "You're just a tourist. You don't go around murdering people and stuffing their genitals into their mouths! I expect the police are trying to keep the whole thing as quiet as possible, so as not to terrify the tour operators. In any case, even if they do know you took the balloon ride, they're probably treating it as pure coincidence."

"Of course they know!" cuts in Lara. "They'll have seen the records. In any case, the boy in the office will have told them." She frowns at Edward as if trying to convey a message.

Edward stares back. "But he only took a balloon flight, for God's sake! That's what Captain Naguib does every day. It's his job."

"In a balloon chartered solo across the mountains into the Western Desert? Nobody does that! And then less than three days later the captain has his throat cut! Don't tell me they wouldn't find that peculiar."

Edmund shrugs. "Just coincidence."

"Oh, for God's sake!" snaps Lara. "And someone in the police …. that smooth character who threatened us after the pyramid collapsed …."

"Al-Shaikh."

"Yes, Al-Shaikh. He knew Finn's name and probably knows he's an antiquities dealer too! If he hears about this – and he certainly will – then they'll quickly start putting things together. *Of course* they'll come looking for him."

There is an uneasy silence, as if no one knows where to go next. A water buffalo that has had been cooling itself in the shallows emerges from the river and lumbers towards the bank, its flanks glistening with mud. Lara rises from her kneeling position and stretches. "At least one thing's clear. You'll have to drop that whole crazy idea about the papyrus and the tomb and everything now," she says.

Finn looks at her as if she has just spoken in a foreign language. "You know I can't do that."

"*What?*" She stares at him, wide-eyed with disbelief. "Why not, for God's sake? You have to! You absolutely *have* to!"

Suddenly Finn shifts forward in his chair. The old vitality seems to be flooding back into his body. He leans towards her and points across the Nile. "Look, just over that ridge there may, *just may*, be the undiscovered tomb of Akhenaten. Do you have any idea what that means? The completely intact burial of a Pharaoh – the rarest thing in all of archaeology! Can you imagine what it would be like to discover it? And right now I'm the only person who knows about it!"

"You don't *know* anything!" snaps Lara. "You don't know a fucking thing. You've just seen one piece of white rock poking out of the sand, for God's sake! And mostly from a fucking balloon! There's probably nothing there at all. But if you start trying to look for it the police are bound to get you. You know that. It's crazy! They might even try to pin Naguib's murder on you, for God's sake! Do you really want to spend ten years in an Egyptian prison for trafficking in antiquities? Or worse!" She turns to Edmund. "*You* tell him. He'll listen to you. Why don't you tell him it's crazy? You know it!" Her voice is shrill.

Edward stays silent. Lara's eyes blaze at him. Finn's life could be in danger and he can't even speak up! She can feel a surge of rage coming up in her.

"Of course it's crazy," says Edward quietly. His voice is so strangely calm that they both stare at him. "But that doesn't mean it isn't possible. I very much doubt I can persuade Finn *not* to do something that he has very obviously decided to do anyway. Whatever we say to him he's going to go ahead anyway. We both know that." He pauses. "But there may be a better way I can help."

"*How?*"

"I'll go with him." There's a quiet certainty in his voice.

"Have you both gone completely insane.....?" explodes Lara.

Finn is staring at Edward with a stunned look on his face. A bizarre sense of recognition has suddenly shot through him, something that has not come from his brain. *This is how it is meant to be*, he thinks. *Our destinies are linked.* And, in that same moment, he feels a terrible, creeping sense of premonition. He rises. His face has gone livid grey again, as if a second wave of shock has just hit him. "I feel exhausted," he mumbles. "I need to lie down ..."

He turns and walks unsteadily across the grass towards his room. Lara stares after him. Then she swings round to face Edward. "For God's sake! Why did you say that? You're the only one he might listen to when he gets into this crazy driven state. Are you suddenly trying to puff yourself up in front of me into some kind of macho hero or something, just because of what happened between us? It was a fuck. That's all it was. I let you fuck me and now it's over!" She stands before him trembling with rage. "Don't you understand? This isn't some kind of Boy's Own adventure that you can just drop into and drop out of! Finn's life is in danger! This is real! *Real! Real!*" A startled group of Japanese tourists turn and stare. She lowers her voice. "Christ! You're so locked into your bloody psychotherapist's head that you just can't believe that anything can actually really *happen* to you, can you? You know what? You're even crazier than Finn. At least he knows why he's doing it. You could both get fucking killed up there!"

She clenches her hands to the sides of her head in desperation. Then she spins round and runs towards the hotel, her legs flying wildly behind her like a child's.

*

When she returns half an hour later Edward is sitting motionless in the armchair, staring out across the Nile. At her approach he looks up. His face has hardened into a mask of indifference.

She spreads her hands, then lets them collapse against her skirt. She shrugs. "Sorry."

"About?"

"You know. What I said. The last part at any rate."

"About it being just a fuck?" His voice is ice cold.

"It wasn't even a very lady-like way of putting it."

He gives a thin smile.

She glances down at the grass, then catches his eyes. "Would you walk with me for a while?"

For a moment he doesn't answer. Then he nods.

At the rear of the hotel, beyond the thick hedge that closes in the cottages, lie fields of vegetables and herbs and, in one corner, a square of vines on a wooden trellis. The cultivation here is criss-crossed by raised paths of banked earth that run down to the channel separating the back of the island from the mainland. They walk in silence until they are staring onto this narrow strip of grey-green water. Lara snaps off a head from a lavender bush and pinches the clustered purple flowers between her fingers. She doesn't know where to start. They begin walking slowly towards the north tip of the island.

Edward watches her from the corner of his eye. Despite her explosion just now, he can sense a new poise and authority in her since that night when they had made love, as if she now fully inhabits herself.

"Well, was it?" he asks at length.

"Was it what?"

"Just a fuck?"

She shakes her head. "You know it wasn't. Not for me at least. For you?"

"No."

She smiles, then touches his hand lightly. She knows they are skirting what really lies between them; but first she needs the gentleness of touch, the ease of talk. And she isn't sure how to be with him now. Are they lovers? Not really. She feels tender towards him, but also confused. The thought that Finn might be in danger has suddenly ripped some protective layer from her, exposing how much, how *very* much, she cares for Finn. As if this is some secret she has kept hidden from herself.

A rowing boat has entered the channel at the north end. A white-robed fisherman pulls in the oars and moves to the stern as the boat glides slowly forwards. The man raises his hand in greeting, then goes back to laying out his nets.

"Why on earth do you want to go with Finn? You know it's mad."

"I was afraid we'd get around to that."

"Is that what you think men are supposed to do? Support each other, stand shoulder to shoulder? That kind of thing …..?"

There is no apparent irony in her voice, yet imperceptibly he draws away. "You think it's just a Boy's Own adventure?"

She shrugs. "I think it's bloody dangerous. What do you think?"

He sighs. "Of course I know what you mean. A sudden rush of blood to my new-found manhood?" He pauses. "All I can say is, that's not how it feels."

She nods. "Okay. Then how does it feel?"

He hesitates and for a moment his face looks puzzled. "There's something about Finn….. It's so hard to describe. You think there's just the Celtic charm and the superficiality – and you think you see through it all. But from the very first moment that I met him, I sensed something else…." His voice thickens with emotion. "I can't explain it. I just felt this incredible warmth for him. Almost as if I had finally found a long-lost brother."

"Or someone you've known before?"

He frowns. "In a sense, yes. I know that sounds like weird David Mountjoy stuff. But it was as if I immediately recognized him, like we were from the same clan. Blood brothers. Or hearth companions or something."

"What's a hearth companion?"

"It's a very ancient expression. It means a devoted friend. Someone you trust absolutely, no matter what happens. Someone who sleeps with you beside the hearth and always watches your back in a fight. And maybe that's why I can't let him go up there alone. It isn't really a choice for me."

For a while she is silent. They are close now to the northern tip of the island, where a group of clipped sycamores grows. Suddenly she stops and turns to him.

"I could come with you."

He shakes his head.

"Why not? Three would be much safer than two."

"It's too dangerous." He hesitates. "In any case, we need someone here who knows where we've gone – just in case we don't come back."

For the first time the full implications of what they are about to undertake hit her. She feels a surge of panic. At the same time, inexplicably, something in the situation feels right. Right that she stays behind. Right even that Edward accompanies Finn. Just simply right in a place beyond her normal logic. Even beyond her normal feelings. She can't explain it. Half an hour earlier she had felt desperate, raging, but now a strange quietness has come over her. They have reached the sycamores. A brilliant green lizard shoots across the path in front of them and disappears under the shade of a rock.

She touches his arm and they stop. She is fighting back tears. "You must do whatever you feel, *at the very bottom of your heart*, is right," she says. "I know that now. But please be very sure of what you're doing. All my senses are telling me that this could be really dangerous. And, for me at least, you don't need to prove that you're a man. You know that."

She comes towards him. He puts his arms around her and holds her.

THIRTY-SIX

The thud of the donkey hooves seems muffled by the darkness. Once clear of the cultivation they have entered a world of stone and silence. The quarter moon gives just enough light to show the edges of the plunging escarpments. At one moment Finn thinks he sees a brief flash far to his right, beyond the horseshoe-shaped blackness of a ravine. He comes abreast of Ahmed and points.

They wait. One minute. Two. Three. Nothing.

"The Bedouins sometimes see strange lights up here," whispers Ahmed. "There are many stories. Some say the place is haunted. We go on?

"Yes."

The slow lurching of the donkeys grows hypnotic.

Finn's mind cuts in and out like a light being fused. And in the dark spaces memories begin to crowd in on him.

Women. They come like spirits. Faces and bodies, gestures, glances. Slithers of underwear, the play of fingers. Christ! Even their perfumes. But not always their names.

And then Nadia. Something frightening in her passion, as if it contains a rage. Her green eyes and lifted chin. Her slim fingers touching her jaw bone. And in the rage a madness.

Lara touching his arm, laughing, 'Be careful!' *Of what?* That look in her grey eyes, part amused, part…? And suddenly, like the ground giving way under his feet, he falls into a place where he can feel her so intensely that here, up on the mountain in the cool night air, he aches to touch her, suddenly aware of how she has taken root in his heart. He shakes himself, trying to get free of the thought....

Other faces drift past. Coming and going. Lascaris's enigmatic eyes and winning smile...

Everywhere he looks a piece is missing.

What piece?

David Mountjoy staring down at the black spider's web of his chart. *Time is running out....* He tries to hold on to his disdain for Mountjoy, like an anchor. But it evaporates in the night air.... The spider's web hangs in the darkness of his mind, holding his past and his future, drawing him towards its dark centre.

Other things are beginning to crawl out from under the eaves of his mind now. The first shock of the Tarot card ..... the tower shattered by lightening. Masonry toppling. Burning figures hurtling from the blaze ..... The lurch of fear in his belly.....

Lara's arm rubbing against his. *I know what you're worth...* The sudden ache of tenderness.

The ache grows worse. The donkey stumbles, snorts. Finn slides forward, bangs his face against the bony neck.

Logic slides further and further into the blackness. Old memories appear like shapes rising through water.

Gold. Gold so bright it blinds his eyes. Fills his brain. Rings big as acorns. Bracelets, breast-plates, swords with inlaid pommels and twisted torques for the royal necks, coiled tight as springs.....

Here was where he belonged. Not in that stinking house. Clutching at her skirt, smell of shit, screams, swinging fists ..... The greyness crowding in. Suffocating.

Never. Never. Never.

Going back.

Ahmed stops. Holds up his hand.

The silhouette of his head, cocked, listening. Edward suddenly alongside them.

They wait. Then Ahmed's legs kick out, dig into the donkey's sides. They move on.

What are they doing here, half-way up a mountain in the middle of the night looking for something that probably doesn't exist? And Edward – safe, sane, mature Edward – what is *he* doing here?

New shapes begin to form in his head. His mind unbuckles. Thoughts without a thinker .....

But you knew all along, that the two of you would go together. It could not be otherwise ....

He trusts Edward. Absolutely. Trusts Hassani .....

But still something is missing.

He struggles to hold on to reality – the click of tiny hooves on the sharp flint, the warm woody smell of the donkey, the cool purity of the night air – for he knows that only in that lies safety. But he can feel himself being pulled further and further away from the present, exposed like a falling man to an onrush of things. The onrush of memory. Memory beyond himself. Memory beyond memory. An ancient knowledge stored in his chromosomes. Somewhere, dimly, he knows that he is no longer the author of his own fate now. Again and again, as his mind struggles to hold on, he is pulled back into the images of el-Amarna – the cry to the rising sun, the elongated, epicene face of Akhenaten.....

A sudden harsh scraping sound. He shakes himself.

Up ahead Ahmed's donkey slithers and scrambles. Then both animal and rider stand clear and still above him against the night sky.

Finn's animal stutters upwards until they are side by side on the plateau under the vast dome of stars. In the darkness he can hear the donkeys' heavy breathing. The white clouds from their nostrils wreathe up in the thin moonlight. The air is chilling rapidly. Finn feels like a man in a waking dream, pulled here as if by magnetite in his brain. And in the place where fear ought to be, there is something else. A kind of disembodied certainty.

Within minutes all five donkeys have appeared. Finn dismounts. Ahmed touches him on the shoulder.

"No torch here. Is seen from the valley."

"Okay. Further in?"

"Maybe after one hundred meters. But then only close to the ground. If you hear an aeroplane or any noise turn off immediately."

"Right."

Finn feels a hand on his shoulder. Edward's voice. "I'll come with you."

Startled, Finn turns and stares at him, obscurely aware of some part of his fate sliding smoothly into place; another footstep on the road to what awaits him. Then he nods. "Yes," he says simply. He turns to Ahmed "You wait here. When we know what's happening, we'll come and get you."

"In'sh Allah."

Finn unstraps the crow-bar and shovels from the donkeys and passes one to Edward. Then he crosses to the lip of the plateau and stands with his back to the edge, at the point where the donkey path emerges. And waits.

He tries to imagine one line going out straight in front of him, another jutting out from his right shoulder. *Forty-five degrees. Give or take.* He makes the half turn, knowing that without that inner compass that had steered him in the dark at el-Amarna he has no hope of finding his first line of stones in the vastness of the plateau.

He turns to Edward. "Just follow close. Keep your eyes on my silhouette. The ground's uneven, so be careful. Count my steps in case I go wrong. Every time we reach a hundred call out."

"Okay."

Finn pauses. If I prayed, he thinks, this would be the moment.

*

Six miles to the north of Finn and Edward, in a deep crevasse at the edge of the Theban escarpment, Yassin Zahawy crouches, cradling his rifle, his heavy rucksack on the rocky ground beside him. Down the valley of the Nile to his left, a hot wind is blowing, like the heat from the mouth of a furnace; but here, exposed to the rock and the desert night, the air is cold. Despite the hollow rumblings in his belly, his mind has an unnatural clarity; his senses bristle with animal intensity.

All his life, it seems, even before the murder of Izat and that terrible, fateful sight in the Cairo morgue, he has waited for this moment. A moment of pure concentration, when he becomes the chosen conduit for a greater force, the willing instrument of a higher fate. He feels a strange calm and a perfect purity, the whole world reduced now just to him and the will of Allah.

The men he has been sent – he does not know their names, each answers only to a number – are tough, battle-hardened, devout: three from Saudi Arabia, two from Yemen, two from Afghanistan. All are hand-picked, silent, brave; not like that babbling fool Amir, whose scrawny throat he has had to slit back in el-Minya.

Zahawy checks his watch. One o'clock. The time is approaching. He shoulders his heavy rucksack, adjusts his hold on the rifle, then pulls his *kafiya* up around his face. He gestures to the waiting shapes behind him.

THIRTY-SEVEN

They begin to clear away the debris.

Following the invisible causeway had been easy. Far easier than Finn had expected. It felt uncannily as if as if his steps had been guided. The line of stones appeared every hundred paces, just as he had placed them. It has taken them less than half an hour to reach the small heap of rocks he had left on the lip of the plateau and lower themselves into the sinking bed of sand.

Starting from the top, buried to their thighs, they shovel the rock and scree away from the mouth of the tomb. At first it is easy, the wind-blown sand slipping freely down the slope into the blackness. Later they come on denser stuff, stones and rubble and smooth flakes of limestone left by the departing ancient workmen to disguise the entrance.

They dig in silence and gradually the shape of the opening comes clear. About four feet wide, carved from the solid rock, a perfect rectangular doorway into the mountain. And in the opening, beautiful limestone blocks laid horizontally, the thin lines of the joints filled with pale yellow mortar.

The two men work side by side, twinned by the swinging motion of their bodies as they drive their shovels into the sand. Edward's whole being is concentrated into this action like a tight beam of light. The constant reasoning of his mind has gone quiet, the antiphonal voices of logic suddenly silenced, as if all his life he has been working blindly towards this point.

He does not know *why* he is here, for that lies outside the beam of where he is. And, at this moment, outside that beam there is nothing.

He knows only the smooth even workings of his body.

And that his presence here is required.

They work down and down, trying to clear the full height of the door, sweating in the darkness. The wooden shafts stick to their hands; their palms blister. Although their eyes are now accustomed to the night like animals, from time to time Finn flashes the torch under the guard of his hand to see their progress.

Down, down, down. The sand swishing away into the blackness, like a mouse scurrying in a roof space.

Then suddenly – Thud! The shock reverberates through Finn's arm and up into his shoulder.

"That's it! We're down! That's the threshold!"

Working faster now, they clear away the last remaining mounds of scree. Finn clicks on the torch.

They are standing on a flattened apron of rock in front of a doorway no more than six feet high. Finn stares in wonder. A humble enough dwelling for a god-king! His torch moves over the limestone blocks, searching for traces of disturbance.

Nothing. Every joint perfectly in place.

"It's intact!" His voice is taut with excitement. "It's never been opened!"

He clicks off the torch.

And suddenly both men are aware of where they are. Standing on the lip of time. Peering into the darkness of thirty-five centuries.

Finn looks up at the stars, listens to the silence. He can hear Edward breathing heavily beside him, sees the pale plume of his breath white in the moonlight. A stone from one of the mounds detaches itself, rolls down the sand, bounces on an outcrop of rock and disappears. They hear it ricocheting into the valley far below.

Edward turns to him. "What now?"

Finn starts, jolted from his reverie. "Hold the torch." His voice is suddenly clipped and matter-of-fact. "Stand close to me and shade the beam with your hands. I'll try to remove one of the stones."

He selects a block at shoulder height, grasps the crowbar and begins to chip at the lower joint with the sharp flattened end. The mortar is rock-hard and comes away unwillingly. He works all around, chipping and levering until his shoulders ache and his arms feel numb.

"Christ, it's hard." He drops the crowbar and slides down, resting his back against the stone wall, drenched in sweat.

"Let me try."

Finn holds the shaded torch while Edward digs the bar into one of the fissures at the lower edge. He levers hard, his spine arching under the pressure.

"It moved!"

"Are you sure?"

"See!"

He levers again, the muscles in his shoulders strain like cords. And this time Finn sees the block shift in its bedding. The mortar all around the edges explodes in puffs of dust.

"It's loose! I can feel it. It's just resting there." He pauses, suddenly aware of the implications. "What do we do?"

For a moment Finn hesitates. Then his voice becomes hard-edged again, as if to brush away any doubt. "We can't pull it out, the joints are too tight. We've no option – we'll just have to push it in."

He reaches up and begins to manoeuvre the stone with his hands. He grunts with the exertion. The block scratches and slides, grates on the loose mortar, sticks. Then slithers. Then sticks again.

And suddenly it is gone. A soft hollow thud as it drops on the other side. A faint whoosh of warm stale air escapes from the chamber. For a moment they stand silent, unable to move, aware that they hold in their hands the power to break the membrane that time has stretched between them and the ancient past. Then Finn takes the torch, puts his face to the opening, clicks it on.

At first nothing, a kindling white light reflected.

Then the scene comes into focus. About three feet from his face is a second wall. *A second wall?* This time covered in rough white lime plaster. He cranes his neck and flicks the torch down. The block is lying on a bedding of sand and rubble. Then sideways – the walls rough-hewn, struck out with a pick, not smooth like the stones of the entrance. Then back to the plastered door. And suddenly the beam picks out something that makes his breath freeze in his chest. Something impressed in the plaster. He squints, and slowly it comes clear. A vertical line of recumbent jackals, ears sharply pricked, forelegs outstretched.

Anubis. The god of the Underworld.

He counts them. Nine. *Nine jackals.* The seal of the royal necropolis. Intact. There is no other possibility. *The undisturbed burial of Akhenaten.*

"What is it?" Edmund's voice is hoarse in the silence.

"A second door."

"A second door? Why?"

"I don't know. Maybe as a double protection to keep robbers out."

Finn's voice is calm. But inside him something is starting to tighten. He knows that the mysterious Tomb Fifty-five in the Valley of the Kings, thought to be the temporary resting place of Akhenaten, also had two doors. *Uniquely*. Until now. And that many believe the barriers were not to keep invaders *out*. But to keep the spirit of the heretic Pharaoh *in*, the ancient belief that to unleash him would bring chaos to the earth.

He brushes this from his mind as superstition, but his hand shakes as he clicks off the torch and turns to face Edmund.

"What now?"

Finn shrugs. "We'll remove enough blocks for me to get into the space and then I'll tackle the second door."

For a moment they face each other in silence.

THIRTY-EIGHT

Finn stands in the narrow space between the two walls. The floor is thick with sand and flakes of rock. The rough roof of the chamber is just above his head.

He has lowered himself down carefully, testing the ground with his feet, stamping hard to detect any sounds of hollowness. He knows the entrance may have been booby-trapped and that he could be descending onto a thin layer of rushes and earth, and beneath it a forty foot shaft carved into the rock, with sharpened staves at the bottom. But all that returns to him is the hard, solid thud of his boots. Edward stands outside, directing the torch over his shoulder.

Carefully Finn scrapes away a section of the fragile plaster with his hands, trying not to disturb the royal seal. Beneath is another wall, the blocks rougher than the first, the joints thicker and less even. Edward passes him through the crow-bar.

Although outside the mountain night is cold now, in this small chamber the air is dense and hot. He begins to chip away with the flattened end of the crowbar, holding it horizontally across his chest. The mortar is soft and peels away in long yellow slithers, disintegrating in puffs of dust under the force of the blows.

He works concentrated, feverish, soaked in sweat, his body a pin-point of attention, trapped in this liminal space between two worlds, dimly aware that, in some way he cannot understand, he has been chosen for this task. He tries not to think, lest thought should betray his actions now. His mind is elsewhere. Lost. And in the darkness of him something is beginning to stir.

He clenches his hands round the crow-bar and digs in deeper, gets the whole flanged edge under the stone block. He levers hard, feeling the strain in his shoulders. And with a sudden crack like the breaking of a stick the mortar explodes all around its edges and cascades down into the small chamber. The air is filled with dust.

He hesitates, only subliminally aware of a choice. He *must* go forward, because not to…. His arms begin to shake.

Carefully he eases the metal flange into the empty space above the block, now fully a finger's breadth wide, room enough to manoeuvre. There is no time for hesitation. He knows he must hold tight to who he has always been or everything will be lost. Slowly he begins to ease the heavy rectangle of stone towards him, not wanting it to fall into the tomb and crush whatever may lie on the other side.

He repeats the process on the left edge, then on the right, gradually angling the block forward, until it rests proud of the wall.

Again he hesitates. He can hear Edward breathing behind him, can feel the thud of his own pulse pumping in his body. He raises his hands and grasps the rectangle of ancient stone.

A slow scraping sound. The sharp edges cut his fingers. His whole body shakes under the weight. A sudden whoosh and an explosion of hot dense air. A warm, musty smell of spices, resin, cedar wood. The torch angles over his shoulder, through the cavity and glows into the darkness. Finn's eyes follow.

At first chaos. A long passageway, unpainted, rough-walled, like a cave. The floor undulates, banked with sand and scree. And strewn over it, a tumble of copper vases sinuously shaped. Painted terracotta pots, red and turquoise, lean haphazardly against the walls. Propped beside them, wooden furniture disassembled, beds, couches, parts of a chair; like an ancient attic, untouched.

Then his eyes focus in. The couch-ends are finished with lions' heads, their manes sheathed in gold, the jaws spread wide, crushing the ebony heads of captives, the long animal fangs are scimitars of gold.

A chair-back, lightly curved, inlaid with gold, silver, glass, lapis lazuli. A scene of ducks exploding out of a thicket of golden reeds. An ivory ibis stalks one corner, watching. Propped beside it a long ebony staff, crowned by the clenched head of a papyrus. Silver, gold and turquoise.

Finn grows aware of his breathing, the weight of the block in his hands. "Shine it further down the shaft!"

Behind him Edward strains his arms. The beam bounces off walls and ceiling. Boxes and caskets.

Until it penetrates directly to the furthest end of the passage. And Finn's breathing stops.

He sees a cavity of darkness where the torch can barely reach, strange shapes hardly visible disappear upwards into a bigger chamber. And before them, at the end of the passage, filling it from floor to ceiling, one leg thrust forward, blocking the open space, a figure. One hand juts out holding a staff, barring the way.

Silver sandals, ivory calves, the pleated kilt glimmers gold. And above, the full arc of the belly, the prominent ivory white ridge of the collar bones, the long protruding jaw and fleshy nose. In solid gold. The unmistakable features of the Pharaoh. Akhenaten. Standing guard.

Finn shudders. Somewhere in himself he is aware of a choice. It is only a split second. A moment on the wing. But it will decide his life.

The flash of gold. The spear of longing. Something breaks free in him like a bird into the night.

And he is left with just this:

A massive sense of impiety before the gods.

THIRTY-NINE

Lara turns over and picks up her watch. The luminous dial shows almost two o'clock. Sleep is impossible. Her whole body feels charged with electricity, as if at any moment it might crackle and fuse. She sits up, peels off her T-shirt and throws it on the floor, then pulls her knees up under her chin and wraps her arms around them.

She tries to picture them now up on that mountain. Finn she couldn't have stopped. She knows that. There's a wildness and a drivenness in him that is beyond her. But with Edward at least she could have reasoned or pleaded. She pushes her fingers back through her hair. It is lank with sweat. She can feel the energy inside her burning her up. She jumps out of bed, pulls on a pair of shorts and a loose shirt and opens the door of her cottage. Above her the sky is paved with stars. A water-melon slice of moon hangs over the faint outline of the western mountains. The night around it is a circle of deep indigo. In the distance she can see a few scattered pin-pricks of light on the West Bank.

She feels the coarse, damp grass under her bare feet, just as she had that morning after she had made love to Edward. But now it isn't Edward who is penetrating deeper and deeper into her heart, but Finn. Her brain spins with confusion. It's as if by making love to Edward she has somehow betrayed Finn. And yet, with these feelings welling up for Finn, she is somehow betraying Edward. And now both men are up on that mountain risking their lives. What if they miss their way on those huge cliffs in the dark? Or are being trailed by al-Shaikh's men? Or .....?

She starts forward until she reaches the edge of the embankment. In spite of the warm night she is shivering. She hugs her arms around her. On the flat ground below an animal shifts heavily in the long grass. The chattering of frogs dins in her ears. She feels helpless and frightened. But as she stands there, alone in the darkness, something else is welling up inside her, a huge primal wave of panic that threatens to engulf her completely. Terrified, she spins round, stumbles and falls hard on the grass. And then she is running as fast as she can back towards the hotel. Towards the only person she knows might help her.

David Mountjoy blinks as he peers into the darkness. In the light thrown from behind, his silhouetted hair stands up in tight spirals all around his head, making him look like a rag doll. He is wearing an ankle-length nightshirt. He pulls on his thick glasses, hooks the wire ends into the mass of curls around his ears and stares at her. She is breathing heavily. Her eyes are wild. There's a broad grass stain across the front of her t-shirt.

He steps aside and beckons her into the room. He seems unperturbed, almost as if he has been expecting her.

"They've gone, haven't they?"

"They? Who?... You ... You *know*...?"

He gives a small shrug. "I don't know what they're doing. Though I could have a good guess. But I could certainly tell from their charts that something important was going to happen to them this week here in Luxor."

She stares at him in confusion. "Then why didn't you ....."

"Stop them?" He raises his eyebrows enquiringly. "There was absolutely nothing I could do." Calmly he closes the door, turns and goes back to the rumpled bed. He props up two pillows and leans against one of them, then pats the space beside him. "Come and sit if you wish. I think we may have a long night ahead of us."

She hesitates. Then crosses the room and sits awkwardly on the edge of the bed.

"Well...?" He says at length. "What *are* they doing?"

"Searching for a tomb."

"Any particular tomb?"

"Akhenaten's."

"*Akhenaten's?*" He catches a whorl of beard and curls it around his fingers, thinking. "Akhenaten's indeed...."

She stares at him blankly, trying to read his thoughts. But then he veers off on his own track. "I remember the morning all your replies arrive – all three by the same post! And then when I looked at your charts...." He spreads his hands in disbelief. "You were all so obviously connected astrologically that I automatically assumed you must be friends. And, in a way, you were. But only karmically. Your physical meeting was fated to happen here in Egypt – and at this particular time. There was a kind of inevitability to it."

She doesn't understand what he means by *karmically*. But she recalls vividly that strange feeling of half-recognition that had shot through her the first time she met both Finn and Edward. "You could tell that from our charts?"

"Of course."

"So could you also see that the three of us would get trapped in that pyramid and nearly die?"

"No. Specific incidents like that I cannot see. All the same, it wasn't just a random event. It was clearly Plutonian. Pluto is the god of the Underworld, of confined spaces. He's the one who can really shake our foundations and open us up to change. That's a frightening experience for most people, of course. But it can also be a very positive one. It's what I would call a fertilising shock, an opportunity for something new to come into your life. The crucial issue, of course, is not the shock itself but how you react to that shock. Do you try to go back to your old ways and pretend that nothing has happened? Or do you move forward into the new life that is there waiting for you?"

She sits for a while, puzzling over this, remembering that terrifying night. Then she says slowly, "We certainly all reacted in very different ways, if that's what you mean. Edward was ..... well, ... frankly he puzzled me. He was perfectly calm, almost as if he was ....." Her voice trails off.

"At home there?"

She nods. "Yes. Something like that."

"Well, he would be. Pluto is very prominent in his chart. It's what gives him his depth. So to him it would feel quite familiar, a kind of monk's cell, if you like. That's the world he instinctively inhabits. For him the crucial issue is not whether he can *endure* the isolation. That's relatively easy for him – perhaps too easy – but whether he can finally break free of it and step out into the daylight of his life."

"So what would help him to do that?"

Mountjoy smiles. "I should have thought that *you*, above all people, would know the answer to that." She looks down and can feel herself begin to blush. "You've heard the story and seen the paintings of Isis and Osiris," goes on Mountjoy. "I rather imagined you might have already helped to bring him back to life. At least in the physical sense."

She nods shyly, wondering how he knows, remembering too the overwhelming intensity of Edmund's passion as they had made love that night. She turns to him. "And if he doesn't break free of his monk's cell, as you call it? What then?"

Mountjoy shrugs. "Then I imagine he'll stay pretty much where he is – in his own Underworld, alive but emotionally inert. A bit like Osiris. He will remain the Wounded Healer, wonderfully capable of helping others, but unable to fully come back to life himself. It's clear from both your charts that you've come into his life at this moment to offer him that vital chance." He smiles. "Perhaps like Isis, to fan life back into him with your beautiful rainbow-coloured wings."

She smiles at the image. "But can he really respond?"

Mountjoy spreads his hands. "The constellations only tell me that this is a crucial time of choice for him. It won't come again. But which path he will ultimately take – *that* choice is not fated. It's up to him."

She nods, aware that his words have brought a weight of sadness down on her. Then she turns to him. Her face is suddenly intense. "And Finn?"

Mountjoy lets out a puff of breath. "Well, Finn, of course, as you know, is the exact opposite. He has his Moon in Aquarius. So for him being trapped is the worst thing of all. That's why he's constantly moving on in life, never fully committing, charming people, skilfully wriggling his way out of difficult situations. That's also why he does what he does – digs up antiquities *literally* and then makes huge amounts of money out of them, instead of digging deep into his own soul and trying to find the riches there. But, of course, he doesn't like to do that."

She looks at him in astonishment. "*You knew?*"

He laughs. "About the antiquities? Of course. Even if I hadn't studied his chart that wouldn't be difficult. After all, does he *behave* like a banker?"

Lara can't help smiling.

"You see, I think it's no coincidence that it's Akhenaten's tomb he's so obsessed by. There's a kind of karmic symmetry to it."

She frowns. "I don't understand."

"Well, Akhenaten banished all the gods except the Aten, the sun god. When you do that you deliberately exclude all the darkness, all the shadow, all the inconvenient bits from your life. But, of course, then you also exclude the riches and the potential that can be hidden in those dark, interesting place. So then you may be charming and successful, but you also become superficial and two-dimensional, lacking depth and out of touch with your potential. And that's what has happened to Finn. He isn't prepared to go down into the dark places of his soul and learn from them. But charm and resource alone won't get him through this particular phase of his life. He didn't get that Tarot card with the shattered tower for nothing, you know. He will have to find the courage to accept and embrace the darkness of his past, all his hidden grief and pain, and allow his old, superficial way of life to disintegrate. He can't run away from that choice for ever. Pluto is a harsh god and he won't allow Finn to squander his talents in that way." He fixes his eyes on hers. Then he says slowly, "There's great urgency in Finn's chart at this moment."

Lara feels a numb fear take hold of her as she thinks of Finn up on the mountain in the darkness. And with it comes a terrible feeling of regret. If only she had acted differently! If only she had opened her heart to him! Then he might not have been so reckless. She spins round so that she is kneeling in front of him. She searches his face, pleading. "But can't you see …?" Her voice trails away.

There is a long silence between them.

"Whether he will die up there?"

She nods silently. Her face has gone white.

Mountjoy holds her gaze. "There are no constellations in a horoscope for death."

"But why not? What's the use .....?"

"There's an old Irish saying," cuts in Mountjoy gently, "that says, 'Death is the middle of a long life'. That's exactly how astrology views it. All I can say is that right now there's a conjunction in Finn's chart that signifies an ending. But whether that simply means the dying away of his old way of life – all the superficiality and dissembling – or whether it's *literal*, physical death, that I cannot see. But right now, here in Egypt, just like Edward, he is facing some kind of crucial life choice." He hesitates, pushes both hands back through the thick tangle of his hair. "There's also something very curious in his chart, very curious indeed, which may help him. It's something I've never seen before – Chiron and Pisces trined Neptune in the Fifth House, which is the House of children."

"But Finn doesn't have any children, does he?"

Mountjoy gives a small smile. "Not that I know of. Probably not that he knows of either. But the constellation is odd. It seems to be about a meeting with a child who will help him. Perhaps a kind of guardian angel? But whether that's a real child, or a young, innocent part of himself that he's long ago abandoned, I don't know." He shrugs. "Perhaps both."

Lara feels a terrible tightness in her chest. Her hands have gone numb. To her surprise Mountjoy reaches out and takes them. He begins to chafe them between his own, slowly bringing back the blood. Tears gather in her eyes. Through her tears she says, "I'm just so terribly frightened for him! He can be so reckless. Nothing was going to stop him going after that tomb, even though he knows it's completely crazy.

413

And dangerous. *Nothing*! He's like a man in the grip of an obsession."

There is a long silence. Mountjoy seems to have retreated to some world of his own. At length he says, "Finn's is not a trivial chart. It's a very demanding one. The problem is that he has very skilfully learnt to live his life trivially, and has kept Saturn and Pluto at the edges of his existence. But that can only last so long. Eventually the planets will come back to take their rightful places in his life, one way or another."

She looks at him pleadingly. "*But what's going to happen to him?*"

Mountjoy lets go of her and folds his hands in his lap. He closes his eyes. She can sense him sifting down through layers and layers of thought, trying to descend into a place that will help her. When at last he speaks his voice has become neutral, almost like a mantra, as if coming from another place. "If Pluto, the god of the Underworld, seizes you, it is always for a reason. In your fate something is required of you. There is something you need to learn. Finn's chart is crystal clear in that respect. He has skipped out of Pluto's clutches more than once, turned his back and gone on with his old way of life. But Pluto will come for him again now. And this time he will pull Finn down into the Underworld, whether he tries to resist or not. But how that will happen exactly, I cannot see."

Lara gasps. "But what if he tries to escape again, as he always does?" She remembers Finn's jokes and the glasses of champagne after they had escaped from the pyramid.

"That will be Finn's choice. But I fear that Pluto will then hold him fast. And he may disappear from our view altogether."

Lara shakes her head. The tears well up again. "But Finn's *always* skipped out of everything! You know that! That's how he's built his whole life. What would make him change now?" She clenches her fists in desperation. "*What?*"

David Mountjoy removes his glasses and looks at her. She holds his eyes.

And then he says quietly,

"Love".

FORTY

Slowly, as if his body is coming back to life, Finn becomes aware of the weight of the stone in his hands, the dull ache in his arms. The sound of his breathing. With a final gasp he braces his shoulders. His whole body trembles with the effort as he forces the block back into place, sealing in the tomb again. Then he turns, grips the edge of the outer opening and pulls himself up. He slides through the narrow space into the night air.

The two men stand on the ledge of flattened rock. For a long while they are silent. In the west the quarter moon is setting. The sky darkens and the dome of stars is vast above them. Their white breath wreathes upwards in the cold air and vanishes into the night. Subliminally Finn is aware that inside him something has been released, like a rock coming loose.

He says, "We're not going in."

"I never thought we would."

And suddenly they are both laughing hysterically, crazy in their recognition of the truth.

Then Finn crouches down, and with all the force he can summon, he lifts the final block and raises it to the gaping hole in the outer doorway. His shoulders are numb and his strength is ebbing. There is a hot, sharp pain in his arms. He forces one corner into the flat space of the opening, manoeuvres the other edge up into it. And slowly slides the stone into place. He slumps back against the rock-face, watches the white cloud of his breath in the moonlight. For a moment they are still, listening to the vastness of the silence.

Then Edward stoops to pick up the shovel. Suddenly his voice is hoarse with anxiety. "Let's get out of here."

"No, wait!" Finn puts a hand on his shoulder.

Edward straightens up and stares at him. "What is it?"

"I don't know ….." Finn's senses are razor-sharp, bristling as if he might hear a rat scuttle on the valley floor a thousand feet below.

"*What is it?*" repeats Edward.

But Finn isn't listening. His senses are elsewhere. Pieces of the jigsaw that have been scattered in his mind begin to implode, hurtling together. The elongated face of the stranger in the public garden at Luxor; the great plain of el-Amarna; Captain Naguib sprawled in a pool of blood. And then, filling the whole picture, the blank, wide-eyed, crazed look in Nadia's eyes…

A small stone detaches itself from the top of the slope and slithers slowly down, taking a clutch of sand with it. The soft grating sound roars in Finn's ears, fills his head.

And suddenly he knows.

He spins round to Edward. "Watch out …!"

In the same moment the air is filled with white. It burns across the night sky like a thunderbolt, blinding them. Edward crashes towards Finn, knocking him sideways. There is a crack like a stick breaking. The torch goes out as something hits Finn hard in the chest and a flame passes through his shoulder. Then the ground gives way.

And everything is swallowed up in the roar of the sand.

*

Edward's legs are pumping. Pumping hard. He runs doubled up, close to the ground, sensing his way with animal instinct. Behind him the gun shots crackle. A terrible scream, like a wounded animal, spirals up then dies away. Then the fast clicking of automatic fire.

His shoulder burns as if he has been branded. His lungs ache, his mouth feels full of blood. He falls hard, cutting his hands and face, runs right on, his head too numb for either hope or prayers.

When he reaches the far edge of the plateau he stops, gasping for air. Far below him in the distance lies the steel glint of the Nile and the vast expanse of shadow and white ridges between like a moonscape.

But how to cross this wasteland alone? And when he reaches the river, what then? Behind him the gunfire is distant now, muffled, more sporadic. He doubles up, holding his ribs as he sucks in air.

Something moves to his left. He spins round.

"Mister! *Come quick! Come quick!*"

A figure emerges from the shadows of the lip of the plateau, leading the donkeys.

"Ahmed!"

"For the love of Allah, come quick!"

*

The long descent seems endless. Fragments of what has happened begin to disjoint themselves in his mind.

Finn is gone. It felt as if the whole mountain had moved in a landslide, the entire sandbank avalanching down into the valley. He knows there was nothing he could do to save him. Only his own desperate hold on that hard pinnacle of rock has kept him from being swept away himself as the ground disappeared from under his feet. That and the wild scramble back up to the plateau as the gunfire snapped around him and bullets whined off the rock-face in the dark.

Who were these people?

Who has attacked them? And who were the others? Could it have been a mistake, a confusion in the darkness? Two groups of soldiers on patrol, unaware of each other? Who else would be up on that barren plateau with automatic weapons in the middle of the night? *Christ, what people has Finn been messing with?*

His memory tracks back over every detail of the last ten days, trying to make sense, but always his circling thoughts keep returning to Finn. Could he have survived the fall? Finn had said it was over a thousand feet to the valley floor. His heart contracts to a tight, hard ball, as if trying to shrink from the grief that is welling inside him. The pain in his shoulder has turned into a terrible dull ache. He knows he is losing blood.

Ahmed drives the donkeys furiously, whacking them with a stick, dragging Edward behind on a rope. Often they slither in the dark. Once Edward's mount stumbles and falls to its forelegs, pitching him forward onto its neck. He stares down into the blackness of a ravine. But the capacity for fear seems to have deserted him.

It is shortly after four when they reach the Nile. Ahmed ties the donkeys to a tree and pushes the narrow boat out from a clutch of reeds. The broad stretch of river glimmers in the dark.

Edmund sits in the bow staring back at the outline of the mountains above the West Bank. Half-way across a flash of light splits the sky above the topmost ridge. For a moment his mind grapples to understand. *Lightning? Sunrise?* Then a huge ball of scarlet flame rises slowly into the sky, expanding like a balloon. And a low bass thud echoes across the Nile.

"Jesus!"

Ahmed whips round, gasps something in Arabic, opens the throttle wide.

Half a minute later they slap into the mud amongst the reeds.

"*Go! Go! Go!*" shouts Ahmed. "No speak! No speak!"

And Edward is out of the boat, running fast across the farmland, the chorus of frogs dinning in his ears.

In the distance he can hear the rhythmic hum of Ahmed making his way back towards the West Bank.

FORTY-ONE

Lara stands in the open doorway framed by the light. Her face is white, her eyes red-rimmed and hollow. She stares in shock at his cut and bruised face. Then she steps back to let him in. Edward passes her and immediately closes the door behind him. At the sound of its click she looks wildly around.

"*Where's Finn?*"

"Still up there."

"Can't we go and help him?"

Edward shakes his head. "There's nothing to be done."

She looks into his face, imploring him to give another answer. Then, as he stands there silent, her eyes widen and her open hand flies to her mouth. "*Oh no! Oh Christ! Oh Christ!*"

She throws herself against him, pummelling his chest with her fists. "*He can't be! He can't be!*" He holds her hard until the strength goes out of her and she clings to him, her body shuddering. At length her sobs subside. She draws away, gazes blankly at her left hand. The palm and fingers are smeared with blood.

"*You're wounded!* What's happened? Come over here. Let me look."

Like someone in a dream, she leads him to the bed, opens his shirt, her fingers deft, moving fast, as if the activity will calm her. Edward groans as she pulls away the linen.

"You've been shot!"

"I think so."

She wipes away some of the blood with the edge of the sheet.

"Christ!"

Running across the top of his upper arm is a shallow groove, as neat as if it has been carved by a chisel. The blood begins to flow again. She runs into the bathroom, comes back with a bottle and some dressings.

"It must have just grazed you. You're lucky to be alive."

She begins to clean and dress the wound.

And as she does so Edward tells the story.

Gradually his words begin to slur and within minutes he is in a dead sleep, his head slumped against her shoulder. She stays for a while, listening to his breathing, then slowly eases herself out, settles a pillow behind him and crosses to the armchair.

She sits, her hands folded in her lap, staring at the tiled floor, feeling the numbness seep through her, crushed by Finn's disappearance – and by the knowledge that there is nothing, *nothing in the whole world,* anyone can now do to help him.... *Please God ..... Please God ..... Please..... Please...*

*

Rap! Rap! Rap!

Edward groans, turns in his sleep, then clutches at his shoulder.

Lara opens the door. David Mountjoy stands there, his hair dishevelled. "We've got to pack and leave at once!" He looks past her at Edward. "Are they alright?"

"Finn's not back. He's disappeared."

Mountjoy lets out a low puff of breath and shakes his head.

She looks at him imploringly, but he says nothing. Then: "You've got to get ready immediately."

"Why? What's happened?"

"*You* should know what's happened! There's been an explosion on the West Bank. The whole place is in uproar. They think it's a terrorist attack. The hotel's crawling with soldiers. They're evacuating all tourists from Luxor immediately. Our group is on the first flight out. They want us all in the hall inside half an hour."

"But we can't go without Finn! We have to know what's happened to him!"

"You haven't got much choice," snaps Mountjoy.

"*I can't!* Not without Finn! I ..." Her eyes are wild.

Mountjoy lays a hand on her arm. "Look," he says more gently. "The only thing you can do is speak to the man at the reception. Take Edward with you. But I wouldn't hold out much hope. These people are in a hurry and they mean business. They're not being very gentle." He glances over her shoulder at Edward, who is pulling himself unsteadily upright on the bed. He sees his swollen face. "And it would be wise to get him out of the country fast, before they start asking too many questions."

The hotel lobby is in chaos. Tour guides are standing on chairs, waving their arms and shouting. In one corner, two elderly women are fighting over a suitcase. From the surge of bodies a hand brandishes a wad of hundred dollar bills. Soldiers in battle dress patrol the perimeter, holding sub-machine guns in the crooks of their arms.

Edward and Lara push their way through the heaving mass. "We're not leaving," shouts Edward to the man behind the reception. "We're supposed to be on the first 'plane, but we're not going without our friend. He's ....."

The man's dark eyes shift from one to the other. Then he looks to his left and gives a brief nod. They followed his glance.

Unperturbed by the chaos, a figure with close-cropped hair, dressed in black trousers and a short-sleeved white shirt, is sitting casually in a leather armchair at the end of the reception desk. Lara instantly recognises the bodyguard who had driven them after the pyramid collapsed at Maidum. Her heart clenches with fear. As he rises and comes towards them, she notices the bulging black pistol holster strapped to his hip.

"Mrs Raven? Mr Cavanagh?" he enquires in perfect English, as if they are just checking into the hotel.

"We're not leaving until our ..."

He raises his hand to cut her off. "I have specific instructions to escort you both to the airport." He pauses. "Under armed guard if necessary." He cocks his head slightly to the left and two soldiers start towards them. "Please pack at once. The bus will leave in twenty minutes."

"But we can't ...."

"Please," says the man. His hand tightens on Lara's arm. "We do not wish to do anything that would prove regrettable for you."

*

Luxor airport is overflowing as tourists pour in from all over the area. The automatic doors have jammed open, the air-conditioning has broken down and the temperature is spiralling. Porters with baggage carts piled high slam their metal trolleys into the terrified figures in front. Suitcases and cardboard boxes crash down, exploding their contents across the concrete floor. The loudspeakers call vainly for calm, and all around the air is dense with the claustrophobia of panic.

Edward and Lara follow the white shirt and cropped bullet head straight to the front of the bulging passport line. The man spreads the two passports in his raised right hand like a fan and the official waves him through with a nod. Once past, he speaks briefly to a soldier standing guard behind the kiosk.

On a sudden instinct Lara glances round. To their right, at the head of another surging queue, she can see the tall figure of Bernard Dortmann. He is standing erect, staring straight ahead. His face is set in a cold, tight mask. He looks old and lined. All the energy she has seen in him the previous week seems suddenly to have drained. In front of him, Nadia is holding out her passport for inspection. The guard glances at it swiftly, then hands it back.

As if sensing Lara's attention, Nadia turns. Her face is ash-white, expressionless, as if it has imploded. When she sees Lara she gasps. There is a look in her eyes that Lara will never forget; something that feels like a terrible premonition. Then Nadia turns quickly and follows Dortmann, who strides away, ignoring her. And the two of them are instantly swallowed up by the crowd.

Their escort stops. "You will go with this soldier," he says. "You are now under his guard." And with a brief nod, he is gone. The soldier salutes, then turns and starts off, leading the way, machine-gun crooked in his right arm. Occasionally he turns to check. They pass through a set of glass doors, down concrete steps to a long marble-tiled corridor lit by neon tubes.

Lara's throat goes dry. *Why down here? Why not to the 'plane?*

Towards the end of the passage the guard halts.

Edward's mind is fracturing. A shuffle of images. Something strange about the smell…..Trapped in the pyramid… But not that ….. Later. *Where?*

Even before the door opens he knows who will be there.

FORTY-TWO

Husayn al-Shaikh, dressed as they had last seen him in a grey suit and light grey tie, is sitting behind a metal desk. In front of him lies a flat gold cigarette case, a gold lighter and an ashtray. The air is dense with the aroma of Turkish tobacco. Apart from the desk and the three chairs, the room is bare and windowless, hardened by the glare of neon light. He rises as they enter and gestures to the two empty chairs. The door closes behind them. There is a shuffle of feet as the guard takes up position outside.

"I had hoped," says al-Shaikh quietly, "that after the regrettable incident at Maidum we would not have to meet again." He looks fastidiously shaved and groomed, but the black rings under his eyes show that he hasn't slept. "Your group has been closely followed all the way. But, it would appear, not quite closely enough." He clicks open the gold case and extracts an oval cigarette. "I wanted," he goes on slowly, "to see you before you left, so that you do not do anything foolish, or embarrassing, on your return to England. Embarrassing either for my government. Or for yours." He raises his eyes and looks from one to the other with a strange lidless stare. "*Or for yourselves.*" He taps the cigarette on the metal desk and lights it.

"What the hell has happened?" asks Edward, suddenly angry with the Egyptian's threatening tone. "Where's Finn Connors? What's happened to him?"

Al-Shaikh's eyes pass ostentatiously over Edward's cut and bruised face before he replies. "My information is that *you*, Mr Cavanagh, should know that as well as anyone. We could, of course, detain you – antiquities smuggling, terrorism, sedition, murder …The list of possible charges is almost endless." He leans forward, folds his arms on the desk and stares at Edward. "Men are dead, Mr Cavanagh. *Egyptian soldiers are dead.* This is not some academic game we are playing here."

He allows a long silence for the implications to penetrate.

"But you are a psychoanalyst. You are not what we were after. You would be ….." he shrugs, "a diplomatic encumbrance. That was not what our governments had agreed."

Edward stares at him in bafflement. "*Our* governments?"

"Certainly. Stopping the trade in antiquities is very important to the Egyptian government. Selling arms is important to yours. Such large agreements are usually brokered by smaller ones. It oils the diplomatic wheels." He flicks the sag of ash from the end of the cigarette. "The understanding was that if we caught our two criminals in the act of plundering a tomb and were allowed a public show trial, together with full Egyptian justice and the harshest penalties – but without the usual troublesome diplomatic protest from your Foreign Office, indeed with their wholehearted backing for once – then our minister would sign the contract to buy your British missiles. Two insignificant British civilians against a hundred million dollars of arms – it wasn't much to ask. Your Foreign Office probably thought we were stupid. But they underestimated our need to preserve the antiquities. Without them we would have no tourist trade – and no income. And without that, as you are doubtless aware, our country would descend into anarchy. And *that* we are not prepared to allow."

Lara sits frozen. Something in the steel behind the words, 'the harshest penalties' has squeezed her heart.

"As you already know," al-Shaikh is saying to Edward, "the plan did not quite work. At first everything went perfectly. Mr Lascaris did his research with great care, infiltrating himself into the antiquities market, holding out the lure of the little cosmetic box we had lent him from the Cairo Museum. It was, of course, Mr Connors who took the bait – just as we guessed he would – and followed the trail precisely. Our research into the art world indicated that he was arrogant, greedy and, above all, ambitious to the point of recklessness. And, just as we guessed, he swallowed the Mountjoy story, even if he found the logic ridiculous. Men like him will grasp at the thinnest straws if the prospect of money is offered. He was just too ambitious not to." Al-Shaikh pauses. "Also, of course, he was in financial difficulties. In short, he was the perfect target for our purposes."

Edward's mind is racing to make sense of all this. The Egyptians had somehow persuaded Lascaris to set Finn up. And then?

"So you bribed Lascaris to betray him to you?"

Al-Shaikh gives him a dismissive stare. "Neither *bribed* nor *betray* are the appropriate words. We did not pay Mr Lascaris. We merely promised him what he had been begging our Ministry of Tourism for years – to be allowed to film the tombs in our closed military areas. Egypt has hundreds of thousands of hectares under military control. Mr Lascaris seemed obsessed with gaining access. For us the deal was well worth it, because finally we would be able to produce the kind of scandal your western newspapers love. We would suddenly have an international expose of 'respectable' British citizens caught in the very act of tomb-robbing. Eyewitness accounts, interviews, photographs at the door of the tomb… What a story! There would be a journalistic feeding frenzy. And finally a public outcry. And the whole dirty, destructive world of tomb robbing and antiquities smuggling would be spectacularly exposed. This time your western governments would have no option but to support us, instead of trying – as they usually do – to turn a blind eye to people like Mr Connors and his trafficking. Even the Americans with their billionaire 'philanthropist collectors'" – he etches the words ironically in the air – "and their corrupt museums would have to fall into line. It was only at the very end that we had, shall we say, some unexpected interference." He gives a small shrug. "But we are an old culture. We can wait. There will be other plans, other people. In the end men like Mr Connors are dispensable. There will be many more just as hungry. There always are."

"*Dispensable?*" Lara's voice is choked with disbelief.

Edward eyes the man opposite carefully. Al-Shaikh has clearly hatched some intricate plot and, for so ambitious a man, its collapse must be a huge set-back. *So why is he telling us all this?* Is it just the compensation of the narcissist? Denied his great public triumph of a spectacular exposé, does he need to display his grand plan at least to *someone*? And if so, what else might he reveal? "So does Lascaris get to film in your great tracts of military zones? Or is he dead too?"

"Mr Lascaris apparently is not dead – but he has disappeared. Temporarily. We shall find him in due course. He too, of course, is dispensable." Al-Shaikh gives a sardonic smile. "And no, he does not get to film. The agreement was for two fish together in the net – one high-profile dealer and one internationally recognised museum curator. In the end, of course, he produced neither."

"*A museum curator?*"

"Come now, Mr Cavanagh. Surely you know that Mr Connors and Doctor Rusedska were in league in this illegal exploit. Doctor Rusedska provided the Egyptological knowledge, Mr Connors the criminal skills. A sort of unholy alliance." He pauses, a look of disdain in his face. "At least until, rather unexpectedly, Dr Rusedska turned, as you would say, Queen's evidence."

"*Nadia?*" Lara stares at him in disbelief. "*Nadia betrayed Finn?*"

Al-Shaikh nods. "But unfortunately to the wrong people. Our director of the Luxor Museum, Doctor al-Jawad, was a new appointment. I voted against it. A distinguished archaeologist, certainly, but my contacts had indicated to me that he had developed ….." He pauses, for once apparently searching for the right words, "….. unsafe political tendencies. It seems I have been proved right by last night's events. He will pay the full price."

Edward stares incredulously. "Unsafe political tendencies? *You mean your museum director turned out to be an Islamic fundamentalist?*"

Al-Shaikh gives Edmund a look of distaste, as if he has just uttered an unpardonable obscenity. Then he leans forward and places his hands flat on the desk in front of him. Suddenly there is a tigerish intensity to him. "It is not possible, Mr Cavanagh, for a westerner like yourself to understand the complexities of a country such as Egypt. Our issues here cannot be resolved by committees, parliamentary debates", the words are heavy with sarcasm, "….. democracy, late night chat shows. Here the divisions are clearer and harsher – and require clearer and harsher solutions."

"So that was where the attack and the explosion came from?" persists Edward, trying to piece together the chaotic fragments of that night on the mountain. "From Fundamentalists?"

Al-Shaikh stares impassively back. Then he says, "Let us say there are some undesirable elements in our country who do not want us to make spectacular new archaeological discoveries, such as the lost tomb of Akhenaten, because they bring in too many tourists. These people do not want tourists at all in our country, bringing in their western ways. Nor do they want us to enjoy the prosperity they bring. And they will stop at nothing to destroy it all."

"And Mountjoy? Was Mountjoy, the rituals and everything, just a total set-up?"

"Ah, Mr Mountjoy." Al-Shaikh sniffs and nods his head slightly, as if savouring a memory. "No, he was not exactly a set-up. But everywhere he went he laid a beautiful clear trail – without even knowing it. He was like some dumb animal totally unaware it is being hunted." He takes a long draw on his cigarette and exhales deeply towards the ceiling. "We have had our eyes on Mr Mountjoy for a long time. That is why we permit his eccentricities in the temples. Do you really think that just anyone can dress up like the Arabian Nights and do their dances in our most famous archaeological sites?" He raises his thick eyebrows in mock surprise.

For a moment Edward and Lara glance at each other. Then Lara says, "You mean you actually *believed* in Mountjoy's rituals?"

Al-Shaikh shrugs. "Your Secret Service would doubtless have classified Mr Mountjoy as harmlessly deranged and discarded him as useless, a crank. But we are a far older culture. Even politicians and police here know that there are more realities than can conveniently be fed through a computer. Egypt remains a country of mysteries. We all recognise that.

And what Mr Mountjoy did was just such a mystery. But a potentially very useful one."

Edmund stays silent, waiting for al-Shaikh to continue, hoping that, in his egotistical need to talk, the Egyptian may reveal some clue to Finn's fate.

"Yes, it *had* come to our notice that every time Mr Mountjoy performs one of his extra-elaborate rituals, the ground seems miraculously to yield treasure. The confirmation – if we needed it – was the sensational discovery in the court of the Luxor Temple some years ago. After that he was trailed everywhere." He pauses. "In recent years it has not been easy to attract visitors to our country in the disruption caused by extremists. Unfortunately your newspapers trumpet every minor incident as if it is a catastrophe. And you see the results all around you – half-empty hotels, idle cruise ships on the Nile, unemployment, falling revenues. But ....." He leans forward and folds his hands on the desk, "can you imagine what it would do to our tourism if we made another discovery as important as Tutankhamun's tomb? Or even more spectacular?" He spreads his arms in an uncharacteristically expansive gesture. "Mr Mountjoy was our great hope for that. He was like a wondrous new piece of technology. That is why your eccentric little group was followed everywhere, so that we could see exactly where he performed his rituals. And, at the same time, he would unwittingly help us to unmask a band of tomb-robbers, because Mr Connors was also aware of his strange powers and could not resist the temptation. The idea was perfect. That is why we also took good care to follow Mr Connors' exploits on the mountain." He allows himself a thin smile, barely able to

Edward leans forward and stares at al-Shaikh. "So you mean the tomb *was* real after all! And now, between them, your soldiers and the fundamentalists have blown it to pieces. *You've destroyed the tomb of Akhenaten….!*"

"Tomb?" Al-Shaikh raises his eyebrows ironically. Then he gives Edward a cold, frightening stare. "There was an explosion, certainly. But tomb? There was no tomb, Mr Cavanagh. *There was no tomb.*" Each word comes out as if cut by a chisel.

"But I saw it! I saw ….."

"You saw nothing!" cuts in al-Shaikh, suddenly raising his voice. "If you had been at the illicit opening of a tomb, I would be forced to arrest you for trafficking in antiquities. The penalty would be a minimum of ten years hard labour."

"But ….."

Lara puts her hand on Edward's arm.

"What happened was just a rather minor terrorist incident. Yes, certainly an explosion, but ….." Al-Shaikh gazes up at the ceiling as if searching for inspiration. "Shall we say ….. some suicide bombers, packed with explosives, were apprehended in the night on the edge of a cliff above the Western Desert by the efficient and heroic Egyptian army. After a brief gun battle, the terrorists blew themselves up. The tourists were evacuated merely as a precaution. In ten days they will be able to return without risk. No foreigners were harmed. No tomb was involved. Everything is in order." He eyes them sardonically. "That is what you will read in your polite English papers tomorrow morning. That is all."

"*All?*" Lara sits forward and stretches her hands out on the desk so that they were almost touching al-Shaikh's, challenging him. Her eyes are blazing. "*And what about Finn Connors?*"

Al-Shaikh doesn't move. He stares back. "Mr Connors will not be bothering us any further," he says brutally. Lara gasps, but al-Shaikh ignores her and waves his hand as if conjuring a story out of the air. "He was known to be an erratic character with criminal tendencies, wasn't he? A womaniser and a hard drinker. It seems he had an unrequited love affair with a young British Egyptologist in Luxor. Over the last few days certain reliable members of the hotel staff have observed him drunk on several occasions. It is not unknown for such people to stagger into the Nile and drown. Sometimes their bodies are found." He shrugs. "Sometimes, unfortunately, they simply get washed down into the Mediterranean and disappear." He pauses. "*That* is also what you will read in your English newspapers next week."

Lara slumps back in her chair as if she has been hit. Apparently oblivious of her pain, al-Shaikh sits back. His voice carries the sombre finality of someone who has come to the end of a long speech. "And the far edge of the plateau above the Western Desert will remain for the next three thousand years exactly what it has been for the last three thousand years – an empty barren waste of rock and landslides. And the undiscovered tomb of the Pharaoh Akhenaten will remain a tantalising mystery. *For ever.*"

He snaps the gold cigarette case shut, rises and slides it into the inside pocket of his suit.

"You will now be escorted to your aircraft. I wish you a safe journey." He moves towards the door, then pauses, his hand on the metal lever, as if he has just remembered something. "Of course, I cannot stop you talking when you are back in England. But I do assure you that no one will believe you or any of your wild stories about a lost tomb. It would be your word against that of the Egyptian government. You would merely be considered part of the lunatic fringe of amateur archaeologists. Or worse." The eyelids hood a little as he gives Edmund a sardonic smile. "I imagine that would not be very favourable for the practice of a respected psychoanalyst. Or even for his professional status."

He opens the door. The soldier clicks to attention and salutes.

FORTY-THREE

All is darkness. All is silence. He tries to move a foot, a hand, a finger. Nothing responds. Is this how it is to be dead? No sense, no feeling, no movement. Then something slides in his mouth. His tongue! He can move his tongue! It feels rough and solid, but the sensation sends a rush of hope. He tries to open his eyes, but they seem stuck, as if someone has carefully stitched the lids together. But slowly, gradually he sees pinpricks of light. Then flashes. And suddenly he is staring into a pair of black eyes less than a foot away from him, staring back.

It takes only a moment for him to understand where he is. The dawn desert light is grey around him. He is buried to the neck in sand and grit, totally unable to move, barely able to breathe. It's as if he has been encased in concrete. Even in his dazed state, all this he can understand. *But the boy?* This is the boy from the mountain, the one who had shown him the way to the tomb. *But what is he doing here?*

For a long moment they gaze at each other. Then the boy begins to dig, feverishly scraping the sand away with his hands, starting from the top. Slowly Finn's arms and torso begin to come free. And only with this partial liberation does the pain kick in. His left shoulder feels as if it is on fire. And lower down, in his ribs, every breath brings a flash of agony. Distantly, from high above, over the lip of the rock-face, he can hear shouting.

Gradually he emerges from the sand, like some mummified figure coaxed back into life. The boy holds out his hands and pulls him free. But with the first step his knees buckle and he falls. Then, staggering to his feet, he takes the boy's outstretched hand. Stumbling behind him, his brain is veering wildly. He thinks of other men led blindly by the hand, Lear..... King Oedipus...

After less than a hundred yards the boy slides through a fissure in the rock-face. He beckons Finn to follow. Finn squeezes through and emerges into a narrow ravine. The sides rear up, scarcely six feet apart. High above them the dawn light is a narrow slit of bleached grey. At the end of this passage the black mouth of a cave gapes. He follows the boy inside, stumbles and collapses onto the rocky floor as the darkness reels around him. Still conscious, he can just make out the narrow opening of the ravine as it reveals itself in the growing light.

*

And so Finn's long vigil begins. Occasionally he sees soldiers carrying sub-machine guns pass the mouth of the ravine less than a hundred yards away. Otherwise he is alone, except for the boy who comes daily, just before dawn, carrying a bottle of water, bread, sometimes a little dried meat. On the third day he also brings bandages and iodine and a packet of white powder. Finn points to the iodine and spreads his hands in question. The boy stares at him. Then he says, "Hassani". It is the first and only word Finn hears him speak.

The pain in his shoulder is becoming unbearable. The bullet seems to have entered through the front and then exited out of the side of his upper arm, leaving a gaping, bloody hole.

It aches like some slow drill boring into his body. He knows that even with the iodine and the powder the risk of infection is enormous. His right knee is badly twisted and both wrists sprained. His breathing is excruciatingly painful; probably he has broken several ribs. But he knows he is lucky to be alive. Without Edward's sudden lunge across him the bullet would surely have gone through his chest. And what act of providence has kept him from being drowned in sand as the landslip swept him to the valley floor?

Often he wonders about Edward. Has he escaped? And Lara? But there is no way to gain information from the boy. He is a man alone, as isolated as if he is trapped on the moon. Waiting.

In the nights, when the shaft of light has been obliterated from the mouth of the cave, and he is entombed in darkness, left only with the sense of touch, he falls into a space between sleep and waking, a deep gap between dream states, where memories return, things long exiled beyond the walls he has built around himself.

Edward and Lara come then too. Lara, laughing, her grace and gravity. The thin rim of dark blue that encircles her eye
.....

..... *I know who you are. And I know what you're worth ...*

The three of them together crouched on the ledge at el-Amarna ..... trapped in the dark of the pyramid..... David Mountjoy..... *Pluto, the god of the Underworld, will drag you down.....*

He sinks deeper, feels himself grow backwards in time. And slowly, through the fog of memory, he returns like a foot-soldier out of no-man's-land, carrying with him all that he has forgotten. All that he has not wanted to see, plunging him back into the pain he had thought obliterated forever. He is back in the tomb and he knows he is being given a second chance.

He grows weaker. His wound is not healing. There is nothing he can do but wait.

The boy continues to come daily, bringing his small sack of provisions and the plastic bottle. The water may be from the Nile. Finn doesn't care. He only knows that he must survive, must talk now, must vomit up his life. He doesn't know why. It's a sensation that comes from elsewhere. In the hours while the boy is there, he talks endlessly. And the boy stands motionless, silent, or squats on an outcrop of rock, hour after hour, listening to a language he cannot understand, washed only by the sound. But *listening*, witnessing, penetrating behind the words. And Finn knows that something binds them, something more ancient than themselves.

He talks on and on, his voice hushed in the silence of the cave, a long Homeric telling of his life, a recapturing of his story, of parts of himself long exiled. All the shame, all the fear, all the sorrow. The words stripping him back to a place before fear. And in the telling the well of his soul fills.

On the eighth morning the boy does not come. Like a prisoner, Finn has scratched the days on the rough wall with a piece of flint, afraid only that he may lose his sanity, lost in the memories. His fingers explore each groove now, searching out hope, holding on.

But as night draws on, parched with thirst, his belly grinding with hunger, he knows he is starting to hallucinate. Visions come and go. He is outside of time's geometry now, floating free. He sees himself a living deadman, too weak to move, hanging by the single thread that is a young boy.

Is this how it is to end? That having reclaimed himself he will die alone in this rocky defile on the edge of the Libyan desert? He dreams of jackals, picking the bones of his exposed body clean. Then this too fades, and there is only one image, like a spark in the darkness – Lara's face, coming and going ..... dissolving ... reforming. Only this. He strains with the last fragments of his will to hold her face clear against the blackness that threatens to invade it. For without this he knows he will perish. But gradually, too weak to resist, he feels his strength drain from him and, helpless, he slips into darkness and is gone.

PART FOUR

How can people come back from Egypt
and live lives the way they lived them before?

Florence Nightingale
Letters from Egypt, 1849-1850

FORTY-FOUR

Lara sits alone in her flat. Her legs are drawn up under her blue cotton dress. Her blonde hair has grown and brushes against her collar as she cocks her head to one side and inspects the drawing on the sketch-pad crooked in her left arm. The evening sun slants over the rooftops opposite and through the long windows into the sitting-room. There is the first hint of autumn in the air. Finn has been dead for eight weeks.

She lays aside the pad, rises and goes into the kitchen to check the pot simmering on the hob. She lifts the lid and sniffs: coriander and cumin – the scents of Egypt. She smiles sadly to herself. Already she knows that those sixteen days have changed her forever. Perhaps not so much changed, as simply left her more revealed; as if all the awkward bending and twisting she has had to do to accommodate to life's demands are no longer needed now and she can grow straight.

She returns to the sitting room, picks up the newspaper cutting from the table and stares at Finn's photograph. The face smiles back at her with all the ease and confidence that she has come to love. The article reports his disappearance exactly as al-Shaikh had cynically predicted. She sets the paper down and sits on the edge of the sofa with her hands folded in her lap, gazing out into the sunlight. This is not how she has expected grief to be. It is exactly like being in love – the colours are brighter, the sounds are clearer, the morning air fresher – only there is no-one to love and nothing to look forward to. And within this grief, she knows, are many earlier griefs that are now unrolling into her life.

She has been stunned by the force of her loss for this stranger who has blazed through her life like a comet. Yet, despite the pain – *perhaps because of the pain* – she senses that everything that has happened in these past weeks has laid bare a part of her that she has never known. A quiet, female part. An Egyptian part. Slow, patient, trusting in tomorrow. A trust that *whatever* happens, whatever grief she may have to endure, the Nile will still flow and the sun will still rise over the broad plane of Luxor. And for now, despite the pain, that sustains her.

She yawns and stretches, feeling the sinews lengthen and the muscles curl. How odd that in her celibate, grieving state she feels more a woman than she ever has. She sighs and checks her watch. Ten to seven. Edward will be here by half-past. She should tidy herself up. But she stays sitting, staring out over the rooftops. A pigeon settles down on the central window ledge, preens itself and ruffles its pearly feathers in the evening light.

From that first moment when the plane landed in London she knew that an unbridgeable gap now separated her from the person she had always been. Even the memory of that person seemed unreal. Tim looked at her and saw it immediately. He raged then with the fury of a man whose wife has moved into another orbit, leaving him only his anger and his impotence. For a moment, as they stood facing each other, she thought he might hit her. She stood quite still and stared him in the eye. And then suddenly he had doubled up and gone down on his knees on the grey tiles, weeping. Only for an instant that old tug gripped her heart, urging her to sink down and comfort him. Then it was gone and she was out in the cobbled mews closing the front door behind her.

On the second day she called Colin, who owned the graphic design studio she had abandoned six years earlier when she married Tim. He studied her gaunt face and blackened eyes over the cappuccino and offered her some free-lance work she could do at home – if she wanted. She knew it was charity, but she accepted anyway. She had expected her drawing to be rusty, her ideas out of fashion. Instead the pen flowed as if it had a life of its own. Now Colin was pressing her to work full-time. And, after years of emptiness, her painting has begun again, grief unblocking something in her that had become frozen in the quiet dishonesty of her life.

Her eyes wander, taking in her surroundings. She likes her small flat with its single white-washed bedroom, its airy living space, the wooden floors, the stripped pine table and wicker chairs, the easel and canvases stacked in one corner to catch the light. She has piled up her books on the floor and feels like a student again. She knows that these things, this time, will travel with her all her life.

Edward comes most evenings, though usually he is late, giving his energy now to a new project to set up a hospice for children. Often she thinks of Mountjoy and their talk beside the Nile – the myth of Osiris, unable to rise, healing others from his place in the Underworld – and that saddens her. Yet, despite this, Edward is like a man who has finally found his true purpose. It's as if for him too a way has opened, though it is not *their* way. Gradually a kind of meta-language has grown up between them. With so much silently understood, less and less needs to be spoken.

And something in his dedication and seriousness is an inspiration to her, calling to her own depth and courage. She knows he will always be there, like a steadying hand in her back. Of course, there have been times when she aches for something more, for the sheer physical comfort of him again. But they are like brother and sister now, bound together by a common loss. She knows that that night in Luxor she has used him. There had been something ruthlessly biological in that urge, like the blind need of the chrysalis to break free of its bondage and fulfil itself. And perhaps what had happened then wasn't meant to be a *solution*. Perhaps each of them had been just a gateway through which the other could pass. Somehow it seems more honest this way, even more loving.

And Finn? She feels as if she has taken part in the prelude to a play that will now never be performed; something violently chopped off before its prime. Often these days she remembers her father, the aching disappointment he could engender in her – and all the ways she has learnt to hold herself back from her feelings. And with these thoughts comes a searing sense of regret. She knows it will take time – perhaps a whole lifetime – to come to terms with what has happened. How blindly she and Finn had circled around each other, so warily protecting themselves!

Tears begin to prickle her eyes. She rises, brushes a loose strand of hair back from her cheek and starts towards the bedroom. The telephone rings. She checks her watch – probably Edward to say he is late. She picks up the receiver.

"Lara?"

The hands of the clock stand at two minutes past seven. The vase of speckled lilies is etched against the white wall. Specks of dust dance in the fading sunlight. Her body goes cold.

"Who is that?"

"It's me."

Silence.

"Finn? …. *Finn!*"

"Yes. It's me."

Her hand shakes so violently that the receiver crashes to the floor. Her legs falter. She slides down and rests her back against the wall.

Blindly she fumbles for the telephone. "Is it really you?"

"Large as life!"

"*Where are you? How are you?* Tell me! *Tell me!*"

"I'm just round the corner. I finally got your whereabouts from your unfriendly husband. He didn't seem too thrilled. Can I come up?"

He stands in the open doorway. He has lost weight and his face looks haggard. There is a gash down his right cheek just in front of his temple and his left arm is heavily bandaged. He stares at her with a sense of wonder, as if seeing her for the first time.

Tentatively she reaches out and touches the back of his hand as if to reassure herself, then runs her fingers down his face. And suddenly with a cry she presses herself against him, clinging to him desperately with both hands. He holds her gently, cradling her head against his chest. And slowly she begins to sob. Sobs uncontrollably with the force of life coming back into her.

It takes Finn just twenty minutes to tell his story. He tells it laconically, like an event that has happened to another man. How the boy rescued him and led him to the cave buried in the mountains, where he had babbled crazily day after day,

447

talking to a young boy who didn't even understand the words; but finally telling the truth about his life, seeing all the things he had never wanted to see. And how, after he slipped into unconsciousness, he had woken in darkness to feel water being dribbled into his mouth.

With the very last vestiges of strength that he could muster, he managed to stand. The boy beckoned him to follow. He was so weak now that he could barely walk and had to lean on the boy's shoulder for support. Each step was agony, the recurring pain in his side like a vivid flash of colour. They skirted the northern tip of the escarpment. Even in the dark the boy seemed to know the way with the ease of a nocturnal animal.

Wedged deep in the rushes, a rowing boat was waiting. Half an hour later Finn was stretched on a hard wooden bed in a mud-brick house close to the Nile, well north of Karnak village. Dawn was just coming up.

That night two men heavily swathed in *galabiyas* visited him. Hassani's face was creased with worry, but he embraced Finn warmly, making him wince from the pain in his shoulder. The other man was a doctor. He examined him for almost an hour, cleaned and dressed the wound, muttered to Hassani in Arabic. Afterwards Hassani settled down on the side of the wooden bed.

"You are a lucky man, my friend. Crazy, but lucky. The doctor says, 'Five centimetres this way,'" he gestured towards the centre of his body, "No lungs. Five centimetres this way ….." The fingers moved down "….. No heart. It seems the gods must love you." He paused and looked grave. "I cannot come again. It is too dangerous. No one is sure if you are dead. They find no part of you. The police are watching everyone. The Secret Police look for you. The Fundamentalists look for you.

Everyone is looking for you. You are a popular man. Also the old Professor came to me. He guessed that you may still be alive. He has offered help. He has many influential friends. But we must wait until your wound heals more and they stop looking. Then I have men who can help you to safety. But it will take time. The doctor will come again if he can."

Finn struggled upright. "What happened up on the mountain?"

Hassani shrugged. "Many rumours. But no one knows the truth. All is top security."

"My English friends? The one who was with me?"

"All tourists have left Luxor," said Hassani. "That is all I know."

"And the cinema man?"

"He is dead. The newspapers say he was caught in the crossfire. But people on the West Bank saw his body – shot in the back of the head at close range." He shrugged slightly. "Perhaps he knew too much. Such things happen."

"And Nadia? The English Egyptologist?"

Hassani looked down and laced his fingers. Finn sensed there was something he didn't want to reveal. "She has disappeared," he said at length. "The Professor told me." He paused. "It seems they are no longer friends."

There was a long silence.

"There is no way I can ever repay you," said Finn. His voice cracked. "You must know how much I ....."

But Hassani held up his hand. "You are my friend," he said simply. "That is enough."

Then he embraced Finn and rose. At the door he stopped and smiled. "Go well .... And go safely. *In'sh Allah.*"

And he was gone into the night.

The house was infested with flies and cockroaches. He

449

ached for sunlight and air, but Hassani had told him never, ever to go outside. The doctor came twice more but the wound refused to heal. He had dysentery and was getting weaker. In the shuttered twilight of the house the days began to blur. Time was losing its usual markers. He knew he was hallucinating, but something in him refused to yield.

It was after five weeks, in the grey hour just before dawn, that he heard a truck stop outside the house. He listened to it shudder, then thud to a halt. In the silence two men entered. Within a minute he was hunched in the back of the truck surrounded by vegetables. A tarpaulin was thrown over him.

In the darkness the journey seemed endless. Twice they stopped. He heard voices in Arabic, then the truck moved on. Seven hours later the tarpaulin was pulled back and he emerged blinking into the sunlight, beside a long featureless beach. He ached in every joint from the bone-shuddering journey across the Eastern Desert down to the Red Sea.

A fishing boat captained by a giant of a man with a black beard and a laugh like thunder took him round the barren southern tip of Sinai, up the mirror-smooth gulf and landed him on a beach east of Aquaba, where another truck was waiting to take him to Amman. Hassani's arrangements never faltered and none of his helpers along the way would accept his proffered baksheesh.

With the help of Bernard Dortmann's contacts he spent ten days in a private hospital in Amman recovering. He shrugs. The most unpleasant part had been dealing with the disapproving British consul, who had finally, reluctantly, issued him with a temporary passport.

The light has faded. He has lapsed into silence. He turns to Lara. She sits ashen-faced, her eyes glistening. He smiles and holds out his hands.

She takes them and studies him closely. He looks older. His whole face, even his smile, is marked by suffering. But there is a tenderness about him now that she has always sensed but never truly seen, something gentle and vulnerable around his eyes and mouth. And a kind of gravitas. Deep down she knows that only his willingness to suffer, to be pulled down by the god, has allowed him to survive. In resistance he would have been snapped like a stick. And in that willingness has come a wisdom. She stares at him, remembering her desperate question to David Mountjoy that long night in Luxor.

But what would change Finn now?

And Mountjoy's quiet reply:

Love.

As she stares at him she can sense the truth of that word. Nothing else could have given him the strength to endure. She holds his hands tight, running her thumbs over the backs of his fingers.

"How are *you?*" he asks gently.

Her eyes fill with tears. She shakes her head. "Oh, Finn ..... I don't know .... I'm not sure I've understood yet ....."

"Understood?"

"That you're here. That you're alive. That ....."

In the distance a church clock strikes a single deep note. It is dark now.

She stops, holds her arm up to the rectangles of light on the wall, checking her watch. "Oh God!" She jumps up. "I'd almost forgotten. Edward's coming over. He could be here any minute."

"He saved my life," says Finn quietly. "And could have got himself killed in the process. He threw himself right in front of me."

She nods. "I know. He hasn't told me exactly, but somehow I guessed."

"How is he?"

"He's fine. A bullet grazed his shoulder, but otherwise he's fine, except ….." Her voice falters.

Finn rises, and for a moment they face each other uncertainly, like two dancers waiting for the music to start.

"Lara …"

The entryphone buzzes. Without a word she crosses to the hall, lifts the receiver, flicks on the light and presses the red button without speaking.

"Just tell me before he's here….. *I have to know.*"

There is a soft knock.

She turns to face him. Her face is radiant. "I learnt to trust a phrase in Egypt," she says simply. "*In'sh Allah* – If it is the will of God."